## PRAISE FOR JODIE LARSEN

# "A MASTER STORYTELLER!"*

## *Deadly Company*

"Exciting . . . smart."                    —*Publishers Weekly*

"*Deadly Company* takes readers into the mind of
evil. . . . Jodie Larsen writes with flair and passion.
Her characters are vivid."          —*Affaire de Coeur*

"A white-hot medical thriller . . . pulse-raising . . .
the writer spins a compelling tale . . . terrifying . . .
exciting. . . . This book will please fans of Patricia
Cornwell and Robin Cook."
                    —*Ponca City* (Oklahoma) *News*

"Harrowing twists and turns."
                    —*Jenks* (Oklahoma) *Journal*

## *Deadly Silence*

"Fast, furious and riveting! Larsen presents a
thoroughly researched, complex plot with innovative
twists, turns, and resolutions. You won't second-guess
her. But she will, I guarantee, scare you to death with
her no-holds-barred suspense."          —*\*Tulsa World*

"Exciting . . . intriguing . . . sure to keep readers on the
edge of their seats from the first to last page."
                    —*Jenks* (Oklahoma) *Journal*

"Jodie Larsen keeps the pace up and the heat on,
leading readers racing through the twists and turns. . . .
Hold on tight and remember to breathe."
                    —*Tulsa Woman*

# Jodie Larsen

# DEADLY RESCUE

A SIGNET BOOK

SIGNET
Published by the Penguin Group
Penguin Putnam Inc., 375 Hudson Street,
New York, New York 10014, U.S.A.
Penguin Books Ltd, 27 Wrights Lane,
London W8 5TZ, England
Penguin Books Australia Ltd, Ringwood,
Victoria, Australia
Penguin Books Canada Ltd, 10 Alcorn Avenue,
Toronto, Ontario, Canada M4V 3B2
Penguin Books (N.Z.) Ltd, 182–190 Wairau Road,
Auckland 10, New Zealand

Penguin Books Ltd, Registered Offices:
Harmondsworth, Middlesex, England

First published by Signet, an imprint of Dutton NAL,
a member of Penguin Putnam Inc.

First Printing, October, 1998
10  9  8  7  6  5  4  3  2  1

PUBLISHER'S NOTE
This is a work of fiction. Names, characters, places, and incidents either are the
product of the author's imagination or are used fictitiously, and any resemblance to
actual persons, living or dead, events, or locales is entirely coincidental.

*For the best relatives in the world:*
*John & Vivian*
*Gary, Vivian, Brooke & Hunter*
*Dale, Nancy (the computer wizard!), Jessica & Natalie*

*and my loving family,*
*Mark, Amanda & Jon*

# ACKNOWLEDGMENTS

Special thanks to John Heinsius, aka the Rock Doctor, for his patience, expertise, ideas, and wealth of geological information. This book came to life because of his professional advice and guidance, and I'm truly grateful.

Friends and family are an essential ingredient in writing a novel. These are only a few of the special people who inspire me while offering unconditional support and encouragement:

Joan, Randy & Courtney Rhine

Dennis, Karen, Garrett, Erin & Micah Larsen

Pat & Larry Larsen

Joy & Fred Ondracek

Julie & Ken Smith

Chester & Debbie Cadieux

Ben & Kathy Gorrell

Pat "Weird" Ward

&

Sherrie Dixon of Esq. Literary Productions

# Prologue

From the corner of his eye the killer glanced at the specially modified briefcase, confident his unique weapon was secure. *Lightning bolts,* he thought. *Silent, powerful, and visible only for a few deadly seconds.* If they worked half as well on human flesh as he expected, the painstakingly carved molds would almost certainly be used again.

Observing the pathetic tennis match on the court below, he played a different game of his own for several minutes. As he gripped the sleek, quiet weapon, his inner confidence grew. Recent advances in technology had greatly changed the odds of success—in his favor, of course.

With starlight binoculars he could see in the dark as well as any raccoon. The pocket-sized satellite-guidance system allowed him to maneuver through the thickest forest on the blackest night of the year. Plus, the laser scope precisely pinpointed any target, virtually assuring his aim was not only accurate but lethal.

Floodlights bathed the tennis courts in a soft amber glow. For a few moments he switched his sights to the other player, an equally impressive and influential senator who chose to co-sponsor the wrong bill at the wrong time. The killer scoffed as he watched the second target double-fault. *Maybe you can practice in hell,* he thought.

The longer he stayed, the more chance he had of being exposed in the dense foliage, although he was certain the risk was minimal in the dark. The hillside behind the exclusive tennis club had been almost impossible to access, but the extra effort was paying off. Pulling back his camouflage sleeve, he glanced at his watch. Sixteen hours. Although he had waited patiently first for the sun to set, and then for the targets to arrive, he was starting to get restless.

Cautiously shifting his weight, he bent stiff knees until they were near his chest. Balancing the lightweight weapon atop them, he slowly, gracefully reached for the starlight binoculars to scan the surrounding area. When he was certain he was still alone, he slid the oversize briefcase out from under a nearby shrub. It was heavy, leaving an impression in the thick, lush grass that would spring back to normal long before any FBI evidence team thought to look for clues there.

Being careful not to make a sound, he unlatched each side of the specially designed case and lifted the top. The change of clothes was still sealed inside, along with a bag to be used to incinerate the things he was currently wearing. As a last precaution he checked each gloved hand, making certain the cabretta leather fit perfectly over his slender fingers.

His right hand rested on the latch that would open the lower section of the briefcase while he picked up the crossbow with his left hand. Once again steadying the weapon on his knee, he flicked the red dot on the first target's muscular neck for a millisecond. Waiting, he knew both the tennis game and his own game would soon be over. In a streak of fluorescent yellow, the tennis ball whizzed past the first target. As the senator bent to catch his breath, the killer eased open the lower section of the briefcase.

White vapor curled sensuously around his gloved hand, the slight evening breeze swirling it toward him. Even through his clothes the frigid fog wrapped around his legs, sending shivers of excitement to his bones. With one eye still trailing the target through the scope, his fingers closed around the first bolt. Slowly he lifted it, then slid it effortlessly into the crossbow.

Squeezing the button on the grip, he watched the red dot

appear on the senator's sweaty neck muscle. Putting steady pressure on the trigger, he felt the weapon flinch. Every nerve in his body sang as the bolt struck home. There was no time to enjoy the spectacular sight, although he inwardly smiled when he realized the slick bolt had pierced both the man's jugular and windpipe before it shattered into a million pieces on the court.

With the same calm movement he trained the red dot on the other senator, who was now running to help his friend. After sliding a second bolt into the crossbow, he squeezed the trigger again. The bolt flew as straight as the first, cutting through layers of flesh and muscle before it, too, shattered. The second man slumped lifelessly on top of the first, his racket clattering as it hit the ground.

Bloodstained fragments of the icy bolt melted on the warm court, leaving behind only harmless, untraceable drops of water. The killer could barely hear the last gurgling gasps of his two victims as he packed his gear into his backpack and began the hike to freedom. Resisting the urge to study the scene below, he pulled the small guidance system from his pocket. With the help of his starlight binoculars and years of training, he navigated easily through the darkness.

By the time sirens wailed in the distance, he had already changed clothes. He slid the briefcase and backpack under the false floor in the trunk of his car, then eased into the driver's seat. First one ambulance, then another passed him as he casually drove away. *Hearses would be much more appropriate,* he thought as the beginning of a smile creased his weary face.

Thirty minutes later, after his clothes had been incinerated, he found a pay phone. "Is the line secure?" he asked.

"Yes."

"The job went perfectly. Fluidly, you might say."

"Congratulations."

"We make a good team. Our goal is getting closer."

"I'm sure we'll be there soon."

He smiled, rubbing burning eyes. "I'm counting on it."

"I still want to participate . . . someday."

"Too dangerous. You're needed where you are." He hung up and sighed, his shoulders, arms, and legs aching from extreme fatigue.

As he headed to the airport, he knew he was breaking one of his own stringent rules on this job, but he had too much time and energy devoted to the crossbow to destroy it like every other weapon he had used to further his cause. Unlike a simple gun, or knife, the crossbow was sheer brilliance. Thinking of its clean, sharp power made him smile, a smile that widened as he imagined using it over and over again.

# Chapter 1

Rae Majors slid the keys out of the rental car's ignition and took a long, deep breath. Glancing at her watch, she knew she had arrived for the most important interview of her life right on time. At least she would be, if she could find the courage to go inside.

RESCUE, Inc.'s impressive glass building loomed before her, sparkling in the morning sun. *What am I doing here?* she wondered. *I'm over a thousand miles from home, a thousand miles from my family, from him. What was I thinking?*

"Moving on," she said to the troubled brown eyes staring back at her in the rearview mirror. "Ken is gone. It's time to make another life, find new friends, in a new place." Closing her fingers around the handle of the leather briefcase her grandparents had given her for graduation, she felt her confidence climb. Her family believed in her. Her professors believed in her. It was time to believe in herself.

Her steps came slowly at first, then a little more quickly. Within a few seconds she found herself striding eagerly inside, only to stop as soon as she entered the building's striking foyer. For a moment she couldn't believe her eyes or ears. The cloak of self-doubt instantly fell away as her nervous energy was replaced by pure fascination.

Rae was sure she'd somehow stumbled into Eden, or at least a man-made version of it. Easing the sunglasses slowly from her eyes, she stared at the huge open area. Tropical plants, some of them several stories high, swayed in a slight breeze. A waterfall fell from the third floor, crashing into a pool that covered half the floor. The pool had no sides; the marble floor merely sloped gradually down to where small waves lapped gently at its edge.

Fish moved steadily under the shimmering surface of the water, dodging lily pads as they zigzagged along. Rae began to stir, her attention drawn to the walls. She was about to reach out and touch the rough surface when she heard her name called from nearby.

"Rae Majors?"

Whirling around, she almost lost her balance as she nervously snapped, "Yes. I'm Rae Majors." Bounding toward her was a tall, lanky man wearing a SAVE THE EARTH T-shirt, khaki slacks, and tennis shoes. His sun-streaked brown hair was shoulder length in back and feathered neatly away from his ruggedly handsome face. Slightly dazed by the intensity of his green eyes, she simply stood, awkwardly waiting.

Extending a muscular arm, he smiled. "Good morning and welcome to RESCUE. I'm Ashe Freeman. Nathan Greenwall asked me to meet with you first. He'll be ready for your interview in about an hour. I see you're admiring our NatureAir system. It's one of RESCUE's many promising products."

"This is one of your products?" she asked, all the while hoping she hadn't shaken his hand too firmly or, even worse, not firmly enough.

Flashing an even brighter smile, he replied, "It's one of my favorites. A little expensive, though, but we're working on cutting the cost of the materials without losing any of the system's integrity." Crossing behind her, he laid his hand against the wall. "For instance, this surface you were studying. It's a man-made, extremely porous, lightweight rock. The air from the entire building is sucked through this room via the holes in this material."

Pushing her shoulder-length brown hair way from her face, Rae touched the uncommon surface. "Is that what creates the breeze?"

He nodded. "You may have noticed solar panels running up all four sides of our building. They power this system, as well as a few other key maintenance needs. This is actually a self-sustaining ecosystem."

"Maintenance free?"

"Well, almost. The plants have to be trimmed every once and a while, but the moss, fish, algae, and constant circulation keep the water clean and oxygenated. The insects handle pollination and serve as food for the other inhabitants, just as they do in the wild. Nature is very good at cleansing itself if people don't interfere."

"It's beautiful," she said.

"Thanks. But I'll bet what you're really wondering is, Why would any company spend so much money just to have fresh air? Why not open a few windows or install a couple of electrostatic filters?"

Rae tensed, certain she was being tested. Since she desperately wanted to make a good impression, she thought for a couple of seconds, then timidly replied, "I'm sure a corporation would have fewer employee absences from allergies and illnesses if the air supply was pure. Stress reduction alone would probably result in greater productivity. Fewer headaches, happier people. It's an intriguing concept."

"My thoughts exactly. Why don't we go up to my office and I can fill you in on the requirements of the job?" He gestured to his own casual clothing and added, "As you can see, we're not a very formal organization. Nathan believes comfortable employees will focus more energy on creativity than their stiff-necked, high-heeled counterparts." With an open glance down her slender legs to her three-inch heels, he grinned. "No offense."

"None taken."

"Stairs okay with you?"

Rae nodded as she rushed to keep up with him. "I can't wait to meet Mr. Greenwall. He sounds wonderful, and he was very encouraging when he called to ask me to come interview. To tell you the truth, this is the first time I've had on high heels since . . ."

Ashe seemed like he was ready to break into a run but was holding back for Rae's sake. He lightheartedly encouraged her by saying, "Since . . . ?"

"A funeral. Since my husband's funeral."

His pace slowed, and his expression darkened. "Oh, I didn't know. I'm sorry. I . . ."

"It's all right." She smiled warmly. "Really. It's been years." She took a deep breath, adding, "Since then I've lived and breathed geology. Did Mr. Greenwall give you a copy of my résumé?"

"No. He just told me you recently graduated and that your background was perfect for RESCUE. Care to fill me in on the details?"

They were mounting the third flight of stairs as she answered, "I'll be honest with you. Other than the college requirements, my field experience is nonexistent at this point. I worked for ten years as an accountant. My husband ran a small printing and copying store. I always dreamed of being a geologist, and we lived near the Sarkeys Energy Center at the University of Oklahoma. I started going to night school about six years ago. My husband always supported my decision to change professions, so when I suddenly found myself alone, I sold his business and made school my only priority."

Ashe quietly asked, "Was it an accident?"

Rae's brown eyes hazed with emotion. "No." Her breath caught as she started to add an explanation, then abruptly stopped.

Filling the awkward silence, Ashe quickly said, "It sounds as though keeping busy in school was a healthy thing to do after his death."

She nodded, composure already returning to her voice. "Studying helped me survive."

"I'm sure it did."

With a smile and an upward glance, Rae added, "Since

the day I lost him, I've always felt he was up there watching me, pushing me to build a new life. He would have wanted me to go on, to make the world a little better."

"Then you're in the right place. How long have you been in the job market?"

"I graduated last month, and have been looking ever since. I want to be busy. I need to work. I'm sure you know how tight the field of geology is right now—especially for thirty-eight-year-old women."

If her age or background shocked Ashe, it didn't show. Instead he said, "Your grades must have been impressive to get Nathan's attention. He's known for being very selective."

"I don't think my grades had anything to do with Mr. Greenwall contacting me."

"Really? You didn't send in a response to one of our newspaper ads?"

"No. Apparently, he read an article I wrote for *Transforming Today for Tomorrow*. He called to tell me how much he enjoyed it, and the next day a round-trip ticket plus an invitation to interview for a position with RESCUE came by FedEx. To tell you the truth, I'm still rather stunned by the whole thing."

They reached the fifth floor and headed down a hall. "Must have been a hell of an article. What was it about?"

"Underutilization of Hot Dry Rock energy due to lack of technological drilling advancements in the last two decades. Everyone else is certain that a combination of solar and wind energy is the path for the future. I'm afraid I'm one of the only people in the world who believes geothermal energy can be economically mass produced."

"You mean it isn't already?" Ashe sarcastically asked.

She smiled. "Only a few of us are crazy enough to chase dreams. That's why I chose geology. I thought it was a field where I could find ways to make positive changes. If there's one thing I've learned from the last few years, it's that I want my life to make a difference."

They turned into a striking hallway. Its blue-grey walls

were lined with exquisite portraits of nature—luscious green fields and crystal-clear mountain lakes. Rae was admiring their beauty until she turned her head to the other side of the hall. Along that wall were equally large portraits, but these were of mankind's worst ecological blunders—oil-soaked birds, a river where bloated fish drifted atop thick brown scum, a beach covered with medical waste.

Ashe gently touched her shoulder. "I'm sorry. Those are to remind us why we're here." Moving to the other side of her, he effectively blocked her view as they walked along.

Turning away from the wall of horror, she quietly asked, "So, what does RESCUE stand for? I went to the library, but couldn't managed to dig up much on the company. I found a picture of Mr. Greenwall. He's relatively young to be head of such a large company, isn't he?"

"Late thirties. We old guys kid him all the time."

"You don't look like you're exactly ancient yourself."

He smiled. "Depends on your definition of ancient. I just passed forty-two. I'm a dinosaur compared to most of our employees."

Her hand automatically went to her temple, where the first few strands of gray were rapidly taking hold. "I guess that would make me prehistoric, too."

"Ah, yes, but you're a very well-preserved specimen."

It had been years since anyone had complimented Rae on her appearance, and she was surprised to feel color rush to her cheeks. "I noticed that RESCUE was mentioned in several transcripts of congressional hearings."

"We do tend to voice our opinions, but at the same time we maintain a relatively low profile. We're actually a conservative organization with progressive goals. You probably didn't find much on RESCUE because it's a privately held corporation. Nathan founded it eight years ago and still owns controlling stock. Loyal employees hold the rest of the stock, so what we do here is kept relatively confidential.

"RESCUE stands for Renewable Energy Sources for the Conservation and Unity of Earth." Ashe instantly held up his hands. "I know, I know. It's a little pretentious, but everything Nathan is involved with shows his passion for the environment." They had reached the far end of the hall. Motioning for her to enter his office, he asked, "Would you like something to drink?"

"Let me guess. Bottled water?"

"Better. We purify our own. Plus, we use it to make natural lemonade and a variety of organically grown herbal teas. I should warn you, though, our Pure Nourishment division uses the rest of the company as guinea pigs. If your have a weak stomach, you'd better ask what something is before you eat it."

"Thanks for the advice. How many divisions are there?"

"Let's see. Pure Nourishment develops organic foods. Research & Development scopes out the scientific community, trying to catch ideas before they can be buried. We call them the ZT's."

Rae almost laughed as she pictured a bunch of nerdy scientists. "ZT's?" she asked.

"Zero tolerance. They've got a reputation for being a little on the radical side. The head of the department, Brada Stevens, grew up with Nathan. She's brilliant. Brutal, too."

With raised eyebrows Rae asked, "Brutal and radical, as in Greenpeace-style chain-yourself-to-a-tree tactics?"

"No. Radical as in fanatically zealous at times. Once she gets on an idea, she holds on like a mad pit bull. About a week ago she discovered some payments were made by certain individuals in the petroleum industry to buy a graduate student's silence on a revolutionary type of drilling technology. It supposedly would've greatly increased the depth of conventional technology while actually reducing costs. Brada and her crew have been ranting and raving for days about that one."

"Why would the oil companies want to keep new technology quiet? It sounds like something they'd love to exploit."

"In this case the new technology would make their fleet

of drilling rigs obsolete practically overnight. But mainly they handle things quietly for publicity reasons. For instance, if the public knew the technology existed to build inexpensive, solar-powered cars right now, what do you think they'd do?"

Rae was wide-eyed. "Does it exist?"

"Probably, but you didn't answer my question."

"They'd be outraged. If there's an economical way to provide transportation that doesn't pollute, political pressure would force Congress to enact laws requiring conversion, especially in cities on the EPA's dirty-air list."

"So, if you were the head of an oil and gas firm, and you happened to own a substantial amount of stock in a major automobile manufacturer, would you want to run out and buy the patent on an invention that could cost your industry billions?"

Rae nodded. "I suppose I would if it gave me control of the product."

"But there would be public record of your purchase. Conservationists would spread the word that you're hindering progress so you can exploit every drop of oil the world has."

"So I'd find a way to accomplish the same thing without public records. Very clever. But what can RESCUE do about it? The invention belongs to the inventor. They can legally sell the information any way they like. Right?"

"Yes. All we can do is watch. If we get a chance, we try to convince them to do what's right, instead of what's profitable, but it rarely works. That's one of the facts of life in this business. We're just little fishes trying to mind our own business in an ocean filled with piranha. None of us can change the world's dependence on oil overnight, and we're not trying to. Changes take time. We mainly want to make sure that when the time is right, there are viable options. Of course, the sooner the better."

Rae slid into a chair Ashe extended for her. "The petroleum industry isn't that bad, is it?"

Ashe grimaced. "It's nice to be interviewing someone who isn't twenty-one years old and ready to conquer the world. We've both been around long enough to know we're surrounded by good and bad in every part of our lives. Unfortunately, a handful of major oil companies carry substantial weight in D.C.—and worldwide, for that matter. Think of all the countries whose economies would collapse if suddenly petroleum products were even significantly reduced, much less eliminated. As a matter of fact, that's why Nathan is running late today. He's in a meeting with two oilmen who flew in yesterday from Midland, Texas."

"Would it be too inquisitive to ask what they're meeting about?"

Ashe shook his head and shrugged. "To tell you the truth, I'm not sure. I've been out of the office for weeks. It may have to do with the drilling-equipment problems we've been having."

"Problems?"

"The equipment keeps mysteriously breaking down. I just came back from a month in the field, and I have to admit, it's absolutely maddening." Ashe took a deep breath and raised his eyebrows. "Sorry, I digress. I never told you about the last division at RESCUE, Solar and Wind Energy. It's a good thing they're lumped together. Each group thinks it has the only viable long-term energy solution for the planet. Teaming them up was one of Nathan's smartest moves."

"And which division is the job I'm interviewing for in?"

Ashe spread his arms. "Mine, of course. RESCUE's red-headed stepchild—Geothermal Exploitation. Luckily, Nathan believes the world is overlooking the potential of Hot Dry Rock, which we call HDR. We think it has the long-term potential to supplant almost every other kind of energy. The biggest problem is all too obvious. In most parts of the world, drilling costs today make it uneconomical. But the Earth's heat is, practically speaking, unlimited. Our job is simply to tap it in a way that's less expensive."

Rae smiled. "You make it sound easy enough."

"How did you develop an interest in HDR technology?"

Her eyes sparkled in anticipation. "When I was a kid, my parents took me to Yellowstone. I sat and watched the bubbling mud pits for hours, wondering why the heat never ended, even in the dead of winter. My husband and I spent our honeymoon there. I guess that's why I've always wanted to be a geologist. It's something I love, and it makes me feel close to him."

"Geology does get in your blood."

With a broad smile Rae nodded excitedly. "When I was a junior in college, I read a report by the Geothermal Resources Commission. I was intrigued that there was such a readily available, inexhaustible source of energy that was being ignored by both the government and industry."

Ashe nodded. "The tough part is getting at it. I'm sure you know that, in principle, it's as simple as drilling deep holes and installing the necessary plumbing to pump water through the hot bedrock and return it, heated, to the surface, where the steam generates energy."

Rae was eager, brimming with enthusiasm. "I studied the results of the New Mexico test site, as well as the plants run by steam-filled reservoirs north of San Francisco. It was fascinating. Imagine, power plants with the capability to produce electricity at competitive prices, around the clock, with no harmful emissions or pollution whatsoever."

Ashe leaned back in his chair and smiled as he listened to Rae, excited in more ways than one. As she spoke, he studied her delicate, high cheekbones and watched her brown eyes glow with anticipation. He couldn't remember ever meeting a woman who made him feel so unsettled, so quickly.

There was something about her, something that made him hunger for things he had long ago decided weren't meant to be. Maybe it was because she seemed so perfect for RESCUE, or maybe it was some crazy instinct making him want to protect her, to keep her from getting hurt again.

But one thing he knew for certain—the chemistry between them was making it practically impossible for him to concentrate. Looking away, he mentally scolded himself. *Stop it! I'll end up getting sued for sexual harassment if I'm not careful! This is work. She's here to find a job, and she deserves my respect.*

Brada Stevens suddenly stuck her head in Ashe's office. When she saw he wasn't alone, she quickly remarked. "Excuse me, I didn't realize you were in a meeting."

Welcoming the distraction, Ashe replied, "It's all right. Rae Majors, this is Brada Stevens. She's head of R and D."

"Nice to meet you," Rae said, quickly noting the woman's unmistakable air of authority in spite of her lack of makeup and her very casual clothing.

Ashe asked, "What brings you way over to Geothermal?"

Brada practically ran to the far corner of Ashe's office to turn on a small television to CNN. "This is why I came. You aren't going to believe it."

The screen flickered to life, showing a brunette holding one hand to her ear as her other hand tightly gripped a microphone. A fierce wind whipped the reporter's bobbed hair around her face as she stoically said, "This is Cindy Bear reporting live for CNN from Washington, D.C. I'm here at the scene of last night's double murder of Senator Ross Evans and Senator Peter Giles. The two were brutally struck down by a sniper, whom the FBI now believe was hiding on this hill, which is directly behind the main bank of tennis courts." The camera zoomed in on a hillside covered with men in a variety of law enforcement uniforms.

"Senators Evans and Giles recently gained national attention as the Republican co-sponsors of the controversial Evans-Giles budget-reduction bill, which pertains to government support of alternative-energy sources. If passed in its present form, the bill would result in significant reduction of government funding and tax credits for research and development of both solar and wind energy, as well as total elimination of all government-supported geothermal energy-source programs." She hesitated for a second, nodding slightly as she said, "I've just been informed that we have footage of a statement made only yesterday by Senator Giles regarding the bill."

As the tape rolled, Senator Giles was seated in his office. His weathered face and lack of hair made him look older than his fifty-two years. In a deep, husky voice he declared, "Our current economic crisis is exactly that—a crisis. Funding any program that's not absolutely necessary at this point is not prudent. I truly believe that in our free-enterprise system, alternative-energy sources will be explored by the private sector with or without government backing. Demand for a product will bring about its production, as it has done for centuries, and I am confident American ingenuity will rise to the occasion."

The tape ended, and the reporter's grim face appeared once again. Ashe walked over to switch off the television. As the screen faded to black, he slumped into his chair and muttered, "What is this world coming to?"

# Chapter 2

"Damn it! Don't you ever listen?" Although Chuck Kelmar had barely raised his voice, growing red blotches on his cheeks betrayed his underlying frustration. "We didn't come here to rehash who's right. We came here to negotiate the sale of a drilling rig."

"Why would we want to buy something that's constantly broken?" Nathan Greenwall turned away from the window to glare at Kelmar. "I've been sitting here, patiently listening for almost two hours. So far all I've heard from the two of you is more of the same old crap about conventional drilling rigs being inadequate for our needs. That the geothermal gradients we're trying to reach require deeper penetration depths than the equipment can handle. The old technology is exactly that—old. We know you have the TriPlate designs. Why do you keep denying it?"

"TriPlate technology is fiction, Greenwall. Your R and D boys bought into some crazy college kid's story."

"That *kid* was a twenty-four-year-old graduate student named Marilyn Prosser, who had an unfortunate car accident the day she secretly met with one of my 'boys,' as you call them. She's still in a coma. Quite a coincidence, don't you think? And by the way, the head of RESCUE R and D is Brada Stevens. And *she's* not the type to jump to conclusions without all the facts."

"Then she should stop pointing fingers at innocent people," Karl Ross snapped. He and his colleague, Chuck Kelmar, shared many traits. Even though both men were barely forty years old, they had already scaled one of the tallest corporate ladders in the United States. As senior vice president of PetroCo, a huge conglomerate with offices worldwide, Kelmar was well-known for his cutthroat tactics. Ross was a vice president, the man personally responsible for handling the millions of dollars PetroCo spent lobbying on behalf of the petroleum industry every year.

Nathan glared at Kelmar for a few seconds, sensing that he was toying with him, blatantly playing the game for all it was worth. Finally, he held up his hands, unwilling to stoop to their level any longer. With a steady voice he stated, "Let's get back to the reason I asked for this meeting. The rig we're leasing from you for our geothermal test site in western Oklahoma is still not functioning adequately. Out of the last twenty drilling days, the equipment has failed thirteen times. That's why we haven't forwarded our latest lease payment. Your own service people don't have either a reason for the repeated failures, or a way to fix the equipment once and for all."

Kelmar jumped up. "We're doing the best we can to help your site technicians. Our field people say the most likely cause is, well, to be blunt, a lack of experience on the part of your employees. That's what's generating the equipment problems. Nothing else."

Nathan turned slowly, then suddenly slammed his fist onto his desk. "Bullshit!" he roared. "At least half the RESCUE team was hired from the petroleum industry specifically to prevent such accusations. They've drilled countless oil and gas wells. It's the same equipment, the same hole being punched in the ground. The only difference is that our goal isn't to exploit a rapidly disappearing natural resource."

Kelmar rolled his eyes. "You just intend to exploit the world in a different way. Have you ever thought about that? Who are you to say that pumping huge amounts of water into a deep hole won't cause changes in the earth's crust that can't be predicted? Some of our corporate scientists think the lack of studies on potentially harmful seismic activity should be enough to keep you from testing your theories, much less marketing them. What are you going to do when your precious HDR plant ends up demolishing a major city by triggering a quake that'll go off the Richter scale?"

"That's absurd. There have been plenty of studies, and none of them show anything harmful. Besides, the need to eliminate the problems caused by burning fossil fuels far outweighs the slight risks involved. Let's get back to the point. What is PetroCo going to do about the problems with the drilling rig?"

The two men exchanged a knowing glance as Kelmar apathetically replied, "We're doing all we can."

Nathan's eyes narrowed. "Our crew thinks there's some kind of sabotage going on. They feel damned lucky no one has been hurt . . . yet."

Ross impatiently shook his head. "It's PetroCo equipment, Greenwall. Why would we do anything to hurt our own assets?"

"To drag out the lease time. To make sure our geothermal test well is a financial disaster." *But mostly because you're a bunch of goddamned pricks who care only about lining your pockets with money!* he wanted to scream.

Kelmar paced as he launched into the same speech Nathan had heard countless times before. "You environmentalists are all alike. You make the oil industry into some horrible monster that's solely responsible for all the world's problems. It's our fault there's a hole in the ozone layer, you claim. You conveniently forget that PetroCo is also a leader in medical-product research. Our subsidiary is responsible for developing the synthetic material that surgeons use to reattach severed limbs, the artificial arteries used in transplants—"

"Save your breath, I've seen the commercials," Nathan interrupted.

Ross fervently joined in. "What about all the other petroleum products that make people's lives better every day?

People like you were probably behind the assassinations of Senators Evans and Giles last night," he sneered. "Wouldn't want to lose your federal funding, now would you?"

The color drained from Nathan's face. "Evans and Giles are dead?" he asked.

"As a hammer. Drowned in their own blood. A sniper took them out during their weekly tennis game. Probably some environmental nut at work again."

Nathan slumped into his chair. "I—I hadn't heard."

Ross still didn't let up. "Oh, come on. You don't expect us to believe you give a crap about either of those two. They were like a boil on your ass. Besides, liberals everywhere are overjoyed. Without its sponsors the Evans-Giles budget-reduction bill doesn't have a prayer."

Nathan never raised his eyes as he shook his head and muttered, "On the contrary, now it will almost certainly pass."

In the executive reception area, the person listening smiled. So far everything was going exactly as planned. It wouldn't be long before Nathan's world started to fall apart, not long at all.

Even though Ashe acted as if he had nothing better to do than escort Rae on a tour of RESCUE, she felt guilty for monopolizing so much of his day. Rae was certain she'd never be able to remember all the people he'd introduced her to, but she wouldn't forget the genuine spirit of purpose they all seemed to share. She'd seen that type of unity only once before, among the rescue workers who finally recovered her husband's body.

Ashe walked her through the entire building, stopping in each division to show off their latest technological advances. Along the way, he expertly covered RESCUE's short- and long-term goals, then treated her to an early lunch. Although she should have felt at ease when he dropped her off at the door to Nathan Greenwall's office, her nervous sense of urgency crept back. The nagging voice inside her head reminded her how many years of unending work had led her to this point, years that would be wasted if she missed this opportunity.

Nathan's secretary, Dinell Blanchard, was a pretty woman in her fifties with chin-length chestnut hair and penetrating dark eyes. She politely welcomed Rae, then ushered her into the executive suite, after Nathan and Ashe quickly exchanged a few words.

After all the impressive things she'd seen that morning, Nathan's office shouldn't have been a shock, yet it was. It was glass. The walls were glass, the huge desk was glass, even the base of the sofa and chairs were glass, with fluffy cushions scattered on top. She wondered how he ever had any privacy until he casually pushed a button on the corner of his desk. The previously clear walls magically became opaque, making the office quite private.

"I love to watch people's faces when I do that," he said, waving his hand toward the now creamy gray glass walls surrounding them. "It's done with liquid crystals. I apologize again for not being able to meet you sooner. Please have a seat and tell me how your day has been."

Rae took a deep breath to settle her nerves, then spent the next fifty minutes discussing business with Nathan. He was a tall, muscular man whose sharp blue-green eyes revealed his passion for RESCUE as he described its goals. Although he seemed relaxed, she sensed he was troubled as he spoke. Watching his index finger continually circling the equator of a crystal paperweight of the Earth, she couldn't help but wonder if he was even listening to her. Instead she had the feeling he was contemplating something much more serious.

By the time he stood to extend his hand, Rae was certain he would rather hire a trained monkey than her. Gripping his hand firmly, she pushed down the urge to flee from another certain rejection. With a steady voice she said, "I'm so glad you contacted me. You should be very proud of the wonderful organization you've built."

"Thank you. I'm confident that Hot Dry Rock technology will change the way we live. HDR is efficient all day and all night, whether the wind is blowing fiercely or the day is calm. Whether it's rained for a week or the skies are clear."

"From what I've seen, your company can make it happen."

"Did you know that the economic feasibility of any project comes down to three things?"

She shook her head.

"RESCUE has plenty of the first—willpower. The second, political cooperation, can be influenced by the last thing it takes—cold, hard cash. We *will* develop the world's first commercial 'heat mine,' and I hope you'll be on our team when it happens."

Rae drew in a ragged breath, totally shocked. Feeling like she was about to jump off a cliff without looking first, she quietly said, "I think I'd like to be."

At the door she stopped. Shaking his hand again, she determinedly said, "No, Mr. Greenwall, I *know* I want to be."

"Fantastic!"

After spending a few minutes going over details, they said good-bye. Walking down the hall, Rae appeared to be calm and collected. There was no one around as she bounded cheerfully downstairs with a broad smile lighting her face. Every detail came alive as she zealously viewed her new world.

Anticipation fueled a strength deep within, filling her with something she hadn't had in years—hope for tomorrow.


"Sorry I didn't get back to you sooner, I've been tied up in meetings all morning. The murders of Evans and Giles have really thrown our whole office into a spin. They were both clients."

Nathan recognized Sherrie Rosen's energetic voice immediately. She was not only his lawyer, but one of his best friends from the East Coast. In fact, he had hoped they would become more than just friends for years. Leaning back, he relaxed and said, "Believe me, Sherrie, I understand. It was quite a shock to us, too."

"I'm sure it was."

"Is it your case?" he asked.

"I did the estate planning for both of them, so, yes, my caseload has just mushroomed. I suppose working sixty hours a week will seem like a vacation after this is all cleaned up."

"I guess that means if I'm in town anytime soon, you won't even let me buy you dinner."

Sherrie laughed. "You can buy me dinner anytime, as long as it isn't anything made with tofu. One tofu soufflé was enough to last me a lifetime."

"I promise. It can moo when you stick your fork in it for all I care." Nathan hesitated, then added, "Listen, I called as soon as I found out about the murders. I need some advice."

"I thought that was probably why you called. You haven't telephoned about your mother's estate—or anything else, for that matter—in ages."

He laughed. "Maybe you've rejected my proposals so often, I finally gave up. Seriously, Sherrie, we both know my mother's money will only go so far. Pretty soon RESCUE will have to stand on its own. So give me your best, New York City lawyer opinion on what the senators' deaths will mean for the future of the Evans-Giles bill."

"Remember, I'm an estate expert, not a political specialist. But when I got your message, I ran a few what-if's by a couple of our partners who keep, let's call it 'active,' in those circles. They were initially surprised by your take of the situation, that the senators' untimely deaths might actually improve the bill's chance of passing."

"We're sunk, aren't we?"

"Not necessarily. They both seem to think the sympathy vote will carry only so far. Time may be on your side as well. The Senate adjourned until after the funerals, which have been scheduled for Friday. That means by the time the issue comes up again, almost a week will have passed. We all know how short a memory politicians have. I know, tacky. Very tacky. But what do you expect from a New York attorney?"

Nathan laughed. "Do you think I should send some people to D.C. to sway as many votes as we can?"

"Couldn't hurt, but there probably won't be a vote for a while. By the way, how is your latest project going? It's called HDR, isn't it?"

"Yes, and it isn't going very well. The bastards at Petro-Co are making sure we run into every problem in the book with the rig we're leasing from them."

"Then why don't you lease a rig from a company you trust?"

"PetroCo is the only one in this part of the world who has the type rig we need. Otherwise, I'd never even consider doing business with them."

"You don't think they're actually undermining RES-CUE's drilling, do you?"

"Unfortunately, I do. I just don't know how to prove it." Nathan hesitated, worrying again that his grand plans for RESCUE might not work after all. Finally he said, "Listen, Sherrie, I think I'll come to D.C. myself, so you're on the hook for that dinner. Stopping the Evans-Giles bill is too important to risk failure; plus I'd really like to have a chance to discuss some of our problems with you. You've always been my favorite sounding board."

"I can't wait. See you soon."

Softly cradling the phone, Nathan stared blankly ahead. *One way or another, RESCUE will survive! If it takes stooping to PetroCo's level, then fine. Two can play at that game, and I'll be damned if I'm going to lose!*

\* \* \*

Aboard the PetroCo private jet en route to Midland, Kelmar and Ross were thoroughly enjoying themselves as they discussed their brief trip.

Both men stood and stretched as Ross asked, "Is our man on top of that college girl?"

Kelmar grinned at the sexual innuendo. "You know he's a perfectionist. The first attempt to take her out may have failed, but he never gives up. Never."

"What about the professor?"

Kelmar answered, "Not a problem. He's been loyal for years."

"Are you sure? I still think he seemed pretty shaken by the car wreck."

"He can only suspect. If anything, this would make him even more loyal by pointing out how expendable any one person really is. Besides, we need him. He's come up with several brilliant students in the last few years. This just happens to be the first one who couldn't keep her mouth shut." Sitting back down, he sighed. "RESCUE's really beginning to be a major pain in the ass, isn't it?"

Kelmar laughed, his deep voice filling the small plane's cabin. "But not for long. The wheels are already in motion to end our problems with RESCUE once and for all."

"How'd it go with the PetroCo gentlemen?" Ashe asked lightly.

Nathan scoffed. "As well as can be expected. I'm always amazed at how well Kelmar and Ross can slither around obligations, and I'm not talking about just the legal variety."

"Moral, ethical, environmental—they seem to be immune to them all."

Nathan turned toward the window and sighed. His voice was harsh as he said, "Someday soon they'll get what they deserve."

"Wishful thinking?" Ashe joked.

Nathan shrugged, but his face was dead serious as he replied, "Maybe not. By the way, I'll be going to D.C. to see if I can influence a few people on the Evans-Giles vote."

"How soon?"

"Depends on when it gets back on the calendar. Sherrie Rosen seemed to think it might be awhile."

"I'd still like to meet her someday. She must be quite a woman to keep you off the market from a couple thousand miles away."

"Maybe you should go to New York with me. What are your plans for the next few weeks?"

"That depends on how your interview with Rae Majors turned out."

"I took your advice. Hired her on the spot. She's officially starting on Monday, but she said if you need her any sooner to call."

Ashe paced back and forth, his nervous energy apparent as he replied, "I may have her meet me at the HDR site in Oklahoma day after tomorrow. I'll have Dinell rent her a furnished place here, so when we get finished at the site she won't have to worry about moving her things to California for a few weeks. We might as well break her in right."

"Sounds good. Send her an advance, Ashe. Her background check showed she's running on a pretty tight budget. We'll cover her moving expenses, but she still might need some cash up front."

"Did you know she's a widow?" Ashe asked, realizing for the first time that *widow* was actually a rather disgusting word.

Nathan nodded. "She keeps it quiet, but it turned up in the background check. Rae seems pretty tough, though. Her professors said she was quiet but extremely diligent. How do you think she'll handle the field problems we've been having?"

"I don't think you could've found a better fit. Since she

doesn't have much field experience, maybe she won't be as frustrated as the rest of the crew. Besides, she'll just be observing for a little while. Maybe by the time we get back down to serious business, our streak of bad luck will be over."

Nathan laughed. "Getting tired of baby-sitting?"

Ashe walked over and grabbed a handful of carob-coated macadamia nuts from the corner of Nathan's desk. "Don't get me wrong. Our crew is the best. It's just I'm sick of the mood swings. One minute they're so enthusiastic you can't hold them back, and the next minute they act like the world is going to end because of some minor setback. Plus lately their imaginations are getting the best of them with all this talk about sabotage. A little levelheaded maturity would be a welcome change."

"Let's hope so. Are you still taking Brada with you to the HDR site?"

Ashe nodded and laughed. "Like I could get out of it even if I wanted to? We're leaving tomorrow. Maybe she can help put this project back on schedule."

Nathan ran his fingers through his hair, kicked his shoes off, and slumped onto the sofa. "Just remember, Brada thinks she can solve the world's problems all by herself. I'm not so sure it's a good idea to get her in the middle of this mess. But if there's something shady going on at the well site, she's certainly got the nose for trouble to find it. Has she seemed all right to you lately?"

Ashe hesitated. "Distant, even distracted, but that's pretty typical." After years of working with both Nathan and Brada, he never knew exactly where to draw the line when it came to handling their personalities. He quickly decided to tell Nathan the truth. "Honestly, Nathan, taking Brada to the HDR site worries me. Even though she's attended every meeting we've had here at headquarters, I just don't see why she's so certain she can help. Her background is in solar and wind, not geothermal."

Nathan nodded. "Which is exactly why she begged for a chance to get involved. She's tired of warming the bench. Everyone needs to feel like they're contributing. Going with you will bring her back to earth, so to speak. Come on, Ashe, we both know Brada. If she could, she'd do every job in the building by herself. She'd work twenty-four hours a day and then some. I'm worried about her. She's been under a lot of stress lately."

"Haven't we all?"

"Of course, but Brada's got more emotional baggage than anyone I know. Her mother's an alcoholic, you know. It really eats away at her, and sometimes I think she takes it too personally. She never seems to have fun anymore." Nathan turned to look Ashe in the eye. "Hell, when we were kids, Brada invented our fun. What an imagination!" He shook his head and added, "Now she's so driven, she's all business, all the time."

Ashe stood and headed for the door. "I'll see if we can round up the crew for a night on the town, even though painting a little town in western Oklahoma red may not qualify as Brada's idea of fun."

Nathan smiled. "Or anyone else's—" The intercom beside him buzzed. Pressing the speaker button, he answered, "Yes."

His secretary, Dinell, quietly said, "I'm sorry to interrupt you while you're in a meeting, Mr. Greenwall, but I thought you'd like to know." She hesitated, then continued, "The hospital just called. That student who was in the car wreck, Marilyn Prosser, she uh, well . . . I'm afraid she just died."

Brada was already pacing Ashe's office when he arrived the next morning at seven. Her short black hair was uncombed, and she wore the same ragged jeans and midriff-length black sweater he'd seen her in yesterday. Even though she was in her late thirties and was a highly paid professional, she still dressed like she was barely scraping by, partly because she didn't want to be bothered, but mostly because she just didn't care.

*Bitch Brada's haunting my office. What a way to start the day,* Ashe tiredly thought, realizing how appropriate her nickname usually was. "Rough night?" he asked.

"Damn straight," she mumbled.

She stopped in front of him and stared. Deep blue eyes hinted at something more than just a mixture of exhaustion and anger. Ashe fleetingly wondered if she was going to hug him or belt him. He was relieved when she chose the first, even though it made him slightly uncomfortable. Brada was a pretty woman, about five-eleven with big, bright eyes. Some might even consider her beautiful, but Ashe knew her too well to harbor any physical attraction.

Ashe had heard the office complaints about Brada. Depending on whose viewpoint you heard, she was either an aloof snob or an obsessed workaholic—either way she was a bitch. The people who worked with her on a daily basis had learned to deal with her personality quirks. They were used to her abruptly walking off when they were in the middle of a sentence. She wasn't rude, she was just on a different level. *A higher level than most of us?* Ashe wondered.

Brada had grown up with Nathan. Although they attended the same school back East, their backgrounds couldn't be more diverse. While Nathan's family had wealth and power, Brada's family struggled by. They'd kept in contact during college, and after they graduated, she accepted a job with PetroCo, even worked with Chuck Kelmar. It was a choice she apparently regretted from her first day on the job. When Nathan founded RESCUE, she begged him to let him join, even offering her services for far less than she had been making at PetroCo just to get away.

In a short time she more than earned her position at RESCUE. Her brilliance was proven over and over again in the first few years after the company was founded. She had a knack for looking at designs and making them better. It was as if she could not only see all the trees in the forest clearly, she could mentally rearrange them to improve the overall picture.

Ashe finally drew back from her. "What was that for?"

"I needed a hug." She sighed and added, "Loosen up, Ashe, how could anyone have a problem with a friendly hug?"

"In the eight years I've known you, Brada, I've never once seen you need anything. Are you ready to go to the HDR site, or is something wrong?"

She scowled, "I'm ready. I'm just exhausted." Resuming her pacing, she shoved her fists into the pockets of her jeans. "Marilyn Prosser was brilliant. She was full of life and ingenious ideas that could actually make a difference in the world. And what did she get for it?" Brada angrily answered her own question. "A few thousand dollars and a coffin!"

Ashe extended his arms, but she stomped away from him. He calmly said, "People have car wrecks every day. When it's a young person's life, it's particularly hard to accept. It really could have been an accident."

"Bullshit!"

"You're wasting valuable energy, Brada. Do you have any actual proof that PetroCo was involved?"

"Only what she told me."

He walked over, sat in his chair, and propped his feet on his desk. "Nothing concrete?"

"She was going to bring the information when we met the next day. The rest is pretty obvious."

"Isn't there anything else she told you?"

She dejectedly shook her head. "I should have asked more questions, pulled the details out of her. Marilyn was young and gullible. All I know is that one of her professors talked her into selling the idea. She said he handled everything. The night I met her she was terrified." Slumping into a chair, Brada dropped her head. Her voice caught as she added, "I told her not to worry. I convinced her to meet with me again and to bring what little information she had. Ashe, I might as well have put a gun to her head and killed her myself!"

# Chapter 3

A few miles ahead and a thousand feet below, bright after-noon sunlight reflected off a sleek oil derrick that Rae hoped marked their destination. While one of her white-knuckled hands held onto a safety strap for dear life, she tapped Ashe's shoulder with the other. Shouting over the drone of the helicopter, she asked, "Why was this particular location chosen?"

Leaning so close his face touched her hair, he answered, "In the thirties and forties the Anadarko Basin proved to have huge reserves of deep natural gas. Over the next forty years the oil and gas industry exploited the area, penetrating these plains with hundreds of wells, some almost six miles deep.

"RESCUE bought this well two years ago. It was one of the few wells that never hit and holds the record for the deepest dry hole ever drilled in the area. According to the geological reports on the initial drilling logs, it was a 'sure thing.' We all know how 'sure things' go in the oil business!

"At any rate, their loss is our gain. We have a perfectly good, deep well to start our test work. It's even close enough to Elk City to become a viable energy alternative for the area someday."

Rae asked, "What stage am I coming in at?"

"Actually, pretty early. We've been trying to rework the old well for the last month."

"How deep was it?" she yelled.

"They gave up around 21,000 feet."

"How deep till we reach a viable HDR core?"

"Best estimate is between 28,000 and 32,000 feet. Obviously, the deeper the well, the longer it will take to drill."

Rae nodded, eager to absorb every bit of information.

Ashe was still shouting, "We've had more than our share of slow-downs—equipment failures, unexpected high-pressure gas flows, even the flu knocked out the whole crew for a week. Like I told you on the phone, all I want you to do on this trip is get a feel for how the site works. You'll have plenty of time to study the reports, logs, et cetera, when we get back to headquarters. Right?"

"Right," Rae called back. The drilling site seemed to grow larger and larger. In the center a 180-foot-tall rig marked PetroCo #114 in glistening gold letters towered above the other meager structures. To the north Rae saw a line of tents fluttering in the wind. On the southeast side was another familiar oil patch fixture, a shabby white mobile home. And to the southwest was a rough dirt road with several old trucks parked haphazardly on the grassy shoulder.

The helicopter began its descent, sending clouds of dust whipping around the derrick. Members of the six-person crew fled for cover, burying their faces in the sleeves of well-worn coveralls. It was a futile attempt. The pelting, stinging dirt was impossible to avoid. Within seconds after the helicopter touched down, Ashe, Brada, and Rae jumped out. Each grabbed a large duffel bag and ran toward the campsite, ducking away from the whirling blades.

In the wake of the helicopter's departure, a peculiar hush descended on the camp. The diesel-powered rotary rig was obviously not drilling, since the only sound was that of the never ending Oklahoma wind.

Feeling as if she'd just stepped off a roller coaster, Rae gazed around the site, still unable to believe she not only had a job, but she was actually starting work. Today. She was finally getting used to the fact that abrupt, inconceivable life changes were part of her destiny. The knot in her stomach began to loosen, partly from Ashe's sincere welcome, but mostly because her growing excitement left little room for worry.

She followed Ashe and Brada to a spot near the mobile home that was obviously being used as the site's drilling headquarters. A tall, lanky young man smiled and ran toward them from the other side of the field. When he reached them, he breathlessly greeted everyone as he shook Ashe's hand and slapped him on the back.

Ashe said, "This is Andy Phillips. He's our drilling supervisor for this project. Andy, meet Rae Majors, RESCUE's newest employee." Ashe nodded toward Brada, who had already left the group to head toward the rig. Ashe explained Brada's rude behavior by adding, "I guess Brada's anxious to get started, as usual."

Andy held out his hand and shook Rae's vigorously. "Pleased to meet you, ma'am. Anything you need while you're here, you just ask. I'll personally make sure you get it."

Rae smiled shyly. "Thanks."

Ashe said, "I tried to call and let you know when we'd be here, but apparently the cellular phone isn't working."

"It's probably ringing somewhere, along with the other equipment that was stolen last night." Andy reached up and opened the door to the mobile home, motioning inside. "Someone trashed the place while we were in town getting supplies."

Ashe glanced into the vandalized trailer, then quickly asked, "Who stayed here at the site? Were they hurt?"

"Collins and Joyce were on duty, but the rig wasn't running. It was quiet, yet they didn't see or hear a thing." Andy pointed at the far north end of the rig as he added, "They were both working on the other side until about nine o'clock, then they went straight to bed. We got back from Elk City a little after midnight. I suppose it could've happened even after we were back, since we didn't check inside the trailer until this morning."

Rae and Ashe exchanged a troubled look. "Why aren't we up and running?"

Andy shifted nervously. "We were all pretty spooked. Whoever trashed the trailer could've done something to the equipment. Again. We've spent all morning checking everything. We want to be damn sure it's safe before we crank her back up." He hesitated, throwing a questioning glance at Rae. "There's something else you need to know."

"RESCUE doesn't have any secrets. If you can tell me, you can tell Rae."

Andy shrugged, looking especially young and sheepish as he said, "Joyce gave her notice this morning. She's had it with this job, wants to leave as soon as she can. Collins is thinking about going with her."

Ashe ran his fingers through his hair. "They understand they're being paid by the hour, whether we're drilling or not. Right?"

"It's not just the money. I know it sounds crazy, but they're convinced this job is jinxed, and that it's just a matter of time until someone gets hurt, or worse."

Ashe shook his head. "Fine. We'll replace them. Do they have their own transportation?"

Andy nodded.

"Then tell them to hit the road. Right now is fine." He pulled a palm-sized cellular phone out his pocket and tossed it to Andy. "Use my phone to call headquarters and have them mail their final checks." Ashe turned to Rae and added, "Ready for a tour?"

As they walked slowly toward the derrick, Rae said, "Sounds like things aren't going very smoothly."

Ashe laughed. "You could say that. But then again, how much in life goes smoothly? We'll come through this, one way or another. I hope it doesn't worry you."

"I have to admit, this isn't the most secure feeling I've ever had. A few years ago it probably would've sent me packing, but I suppose I've learned to adapt."

Ashe stopped and looked into her eyes. He seemed as

though he were about to tell her some deep, dark secret, but after a few awkward seconds he said, "I'm really glad you came to work for RESCUE. I promised Nathan I'd take the crew out for a night on the town. You're one of the crew now, so that means you've got to go."

"Doesn't someone have to stay here and hold down the fort? Being the newest, I'd think that job would naturally fall in my lap."

"I've got buddies around here who owe me some big favors, so you let me worry about guarding the fort. Besides, it looks like we won't be up and running again until tomorrow, maybe longer if we can't find replacements for Collins and Joyce. Just promise you'll try to have fun tonight. We've got a lot of work ahead of us."

The idea of going out with Ashe intrigued Rae more than she cared to admit. Shyly she said, "I'm looking forward to it. The work, that is."

Ashe genuinely smiled, his gaze holding hers a breath longer than necessary. "Me, too."

The phone rang twice. Glancing at the Caller ID screen, the man smiled. As expected, the originator of the call had blocked the number. After five more rings, he finally answered but didn't say a word. All he did was listen.

"I think it's time."

A different device monitoring the phone line glowed a green light. The line was clear of listening devices. "I agree," he said.

"We'll have to move fast. They'll start drilling again sometime tomorrow. Did you get it?"

"Yes, but not much. It's hard to come by, you know."

"It won't take much. A little will work just fine. Were the international connections we discussed reliable?"

"As reliable as any such sleazy sources could be." He ran his hand over the briefcase beside him. In some ways it was identical to the one he'd designed to hold the frozen crossbow bolts. But in others it was entirely different. The refrigeration chamber had been replaced with lead. Inside that were layers of waffled, shock-absorbing gray foam. The case could probably be thrown from the top of a twenty-story building, and the cylinder nestled inside wouldn't have a mark on it.

"Can you handle it tonight?"

"I'll be there."

"Start thinking about Greenwall, too. I have a feeling it's almost time. But it can't be anything permanent, right?"

"Just creative."

"That's your trademark. By the way, the senators' untimely deaths were fluidly handled."

"I take pride in my work."

"Which is why we make such a good team."

"How true." As he hung up, the rush began to build deep inside. Glancing at his watch, he knew there wasn't enough time to prepare properly. *Not enough time to scout the location, or to set up an alternate escape route,* he thought. *Another precious rule shot to hell.*

Years ago he couldn't have done it, couldn't have risked everything without batting an eye. But after a lifetime of caution, he smiled at the danger he was creating, certain the years of experience had finally made him invincible— a true killing machine.

Dinell flipped on the lights to the executive suite and dropped her purse in a desk drawer. After glancing nervously down the dark hallway one last time, she rushed into Nathan's office and riffled through the papers stacked on the corner of his desk. Finding the ones she was looking for, she scurried back to her desk and slipped them into an unlabeled file.

Her heart almost stopped when Nathan appeared in the doorway and asked, "What are you doing here at this hour of the morning?"

"You scared me half to death!"

"Sorry. I'm usually the first one here."

Taking a deep breath, she nervously explained, "I had to finish up the progress reports for the staff meeting this afternoon. Besides, I couldn't sleep."

"Anything I can do to help?"

Shaking her head, she replied, "No. But it's nice of you to offer. I'll bring you some coffee as soon as it's ready."

Nathan nodded and slipped into his office. Dinell's heart was pounding so hard she could feel it in her fingertips as she shakily measured the coffee grounds. *What if he noticed the latest financial reports were gone? With all that's going on right now, the last thing I need is for him to be suspicious!*

The starlight binoculars were necessary only for a small part of the approach, even though no moon lit the night. Huge floodlights mounted on the sides of the drilling rig illuminated the area almost as well as daylight. But there were still random shadows, a few places to blend into nature.

The entire site covered less than twenty acres, and was quite literally in the middle of nowhere. Under different circumstances, the structure would have been a sight to behold. The derrick was a magnificent work of brightly lit angles with a clear, star-filled sky as its backdrop. Wind whipped through the rig, making some stray piece of metal scrape softly in the night.

He crawled from trees to bushes, avoiding the south road, where several trucks were parked. Moving closer and closer wasn't an easy task, as the heavy briefcase had to be pushed in front of him, inch by inch. Even though he'd never been to this site before, it was exactly as expected. Drilling sites hadn't changed much in the last twenty years. Rigs hadn't either, no thanks to people like that college kid who sold out for a few lousy bucks. A chill of satisfaction ran through him as his mind replayed the last, ragged breath of her life. PetroCo had paid him nicely to take out the traitorous slut. Little did they know he would have done it for free. Destroying a PetroCo rig was going to be a pleasure!

Gazing up at the sign that declared this particular rig to be PETROCO #114, he felt his stomach turn. For him the journey to this night had begun on a rig exactly like this one. PetroCo #46, to be exact. In twenty years his memory of that day hadn't faded. Instead, it was nourished by his hatred. His father had died on rig #46. Just another roughneck in the wrong place at the wrong time. Back then accidents on drilling rigs were frequent. Families didn't sue, they just limped along without any help from anyone. Kids still grew up. But the lesson was learned.

Pushing the lead-lined briefcase past the mound of dirt surrounding the mud pit was out of the question. It was too heavy to run with, and would be too noisy if it accidentally bumped against any of the equipment or was dropped. He knew he was risking fatal exposure if he handled the cylinder directly, but he didn't give a damn. He seemed to be taking more and more chances these days. Deadly chances.

For five minutes, he stared at the path he would take, mentally picturing each step, each movement, until he was certain he was ready. Out of habit he glanced at his watch. It was exactly 2:16.

Silently, carefully, he eased open the case and wrapped his gloved fingers around the cylinder. Moving like a cat, he wove in and out of shadows quickly, efficiently. Covered from head to toe in camouflage, he was almost invisible each time he froze to listen and scan the area.

In seconds he mounted the rig floor. Keeping low against the black surface, he blended easily into the stark merger of machinery and night.

He moved quickly, stealthily crossing to the center of the derrick where the rotary table, which turned the drill pipe, sat motionless. From a hole in the center of the rotary table rose the threaded end of the six-inch diameter drill pipe, the other end of which lay almost four miles beneath his feet. He stood before it to peer down the black hole. *Metal violating the precious soil. A pathway straight to hell! Now it will be useless. . . .*

One by one his fingers opened until the cylinder fell. Gravity pulled it end over end down the twenty thousand-foot shaft, where its mere presence would result in irreparable damage when the first few turns of the drill bit pierced the thin encasement, shredding it into a million pieces.

A smile creased his face. Turning away, he was thankful it was done, more than ready to slink back into the night as he stepped away from the godforsaken hole. But he wasn't alone. From out of the shadows, a tall, lanky man appeared with a crowbar poised ominously over his head. In a surprisingly calm voice he said, "Move an inch and I'll beat the living shit out of you. We've had enough of your little games. Exactly what the hell did you just drop in there?"

Although it seemed like minutes passed, the killer made up his mind in less than a second. The human body, when expertly used, is just as lethal as most weapons, and usually caught untrained adversaries off guard. He instantly judged this crowbar-wielding adversary to be as untrained as they came.

In a blur he whirled toward the man, his right foot landing a lethal blow directly to the front of the man's neck, instantly crushing his windpipe. Even as he was falling, another kick snapped his neck again, this time breaking the vertebrae. The crowbar clanked loudly as it flew against the metal flooring, its hollow sound reverberating in the wind as it slowly came to rest.

As the killer ran into the brush, the camp came suddenly to life behind him. He didn't care, didn't even look back. He merely grabbed the briefcase and continued carefully on his way.

The only evidence he had left behind was the cylinder itself, and it would soon be crushed beyond recognition thousands of feet inside the earth's crust.

Ashe heard the unmistakable sound of metal falling against metal, and bolted upright on his cot. He pulled a pair of sweatpants over his underwear and snatched a battery-powered lantern that was on the floor beside him. Glancing quickly around, he searched for anything he could use as a weapon, grabbing the only thing he saw that looked even slightly menacing—a large golf umbrella that ended in a nasty metallic point.

At a full run he headed for the rig, but stopped halfway when he heard someone call his name. Rae was twenty feet to his left, waving frantically. He ran to her, shouting, "What are you doing out here?"

Rae was barefoot, wearing a gray sweatsuit and holding the tiniest flashlight he'd ever seen. "I couldn't sleep," she said as she waved the little light. "I was reading when I heard the noise. I looked out and spotted someone running that way." She pointed at the far side of the rig, where there was a narrow opening between the field and the mud pit.

Ashe ordered, "You stay here!"

Grabbing his arm, she stopped him. "What are you going to do, skewer him with an umbrella?" Reaching under the side of her sweatshirt she pulled out a small revolver, which she quickly traded for the umbrella. Ashe was shocked. "We can discuss the morality of the gun issue later! Just be careful. It's ready to fire when you pull back the hammer."

Ashe didn't know what to say, but he knew every second counted. As he rushed past the rig and into the brush, he wondered what kind of damage the bastards had done this time.

Rae stood for a few seconds, watching Ashe disappear into the night. She wondered what she could do to help. A noise by the tents caught her attention. Brada was zipping up a pair of faded blue jeans as she came rushing out. When she spotted Rae, she yelled, "What the hell's going on out here?"

Rae answered, "We heard a noise. I saw someone running away from the rig. Ashe went after him."

"Shit. I hope he's careful. We don't know what kind of crazy people we're dealing with."

"Shouldn't we check the rig?" Rae asked.

Brada shook her head. "I'll go wake up the rest of the crew. You stay here. It could be dangerous."

Rae shrugged as she said, "I doubt it. The guy I saw was in a big hurry to get out of here."

Brada was heading quickly away from her. Over her shoulder she raised her voice and said, "My point exactly. What if the asshole planted a bomb?"

Rae's knees almost buckled as a chill temporarily paralyzed her. Ashe's umbrella fell to the ground with a soft thud. She tried to breathe, but she felt as though she'd been slammed by a staggering blow to the chest. A bomb! Tears jumped into her eyes, but they couldn't blur the mental pictures her mind was unwrapping. Like horrible souvenirs from a visit to hell, she relived the destruction, felt the strange crunch of fertilizer beneath each carefully placed step, saw the blood run in the streets.

Slowly at first, then faster and faster she ran into the darkness, away from the rig. More agonizing memories tormented her: the news flash she'd heard on the radio just minutes after the explosion; the frantic trip back to the print shop, only to find it empty; hours that turned into days of hoping and praying; the funeral for what was left of her husband's body.

Rae's stomach clenched again, and she realized she must have been running for quite some time. A violent wave of nausea dropped her to her knees, and she lost what little was left of their celebration dinner in Elk City. She wandered slightly farther, then slumped against a nearby tree. Pulling her knees to her chin, she closed her eyes, leaned back, and let the memories rip out her heart one more time.

Ashe knew his search was hopeless after only a few minutes. The brush was thick, and the ground was hard. There were no footprints to follow, no sound of anyone moving ahead. At first the light from his lantern had shown a few broken twigs, but even that trail quickly disappeared. He turned to walk back toward the rig, then broke into a run when he heard one of the men shouting.

As fast as he could, he climbed the stairs. On the rig floor, one of the crew members stopped him by grabbing his shoulders and quietly saying, "It's Andy."

"What about him?" Ashe asked breathlessly.

"He's dead."

Ashe pushed the man out of his way, storming past him. "Come on, this isn't funny." A few steps later, his eyes fell on his friend and co-worker. The horrifying realization that it was true struck home. He knelt bedside Andy's body to check for a pulse.

An overwhelming sense of loss rushed through him, followed by an anger that seemed to rip holes in his soul. Rushing off the platform, he shouted, "Has anyone called the police?"

Someone's voice echoed in the still night. "They're on the way. Brada is waiting on the edge of camp to flag 'em down."

Ashe's eyes darted about the campsite. For several moments he just stood there, fighting his own demons. *Why does RESCUE even try? Is anything worth losing a good man like Andy? What about Rae? What the hell have I dragged her into?* The last thought hit him with the force of a brutal kick. Searching the site, he stumbled across the umbrella she had taken from him. "God, no," he cried, pushing down another surge of anxiety.

Rushing across the site, he found Brada pacing at the edge of the dirt road. "Have you seen Rae?" he breathlessly asked.

Brada thought for a second. "Not since all this started, maybe ten or fifteen minutes ago. She was standing in the middle of camp when I went to wake up everyone."

"Did she say anything?"

"She wanted to check the rig, but I told her to wait, that it might not be safe."

Ashe was pacing back and forth. "When I left, she was holding this umbrella. I found it lying in the dirt. You don't suppose something happened to her, too, do you?"

"Let's hope not." Brada laughed nervously. "I'm still half worried that man might have dropped a bomb down the hole before he killed Andy. I hope the sheriff gets here soon."

"Shit," Ashe said, knowing she might be right. Jogging back to camp, he studied the area again. Rae's tent was still empty, she wasn't in the mobile home, and no one had seen her. Checking his watch, he realized it was still more than three hours until sunrise. Marching back to the spot where he'd found the umbrella, Ashe looked around. If she had left the way the killer had, he would've spotted her during his initial search. There was only one other clear way out of camp, in the opposite direction from the derrick. Turning his lantern back on, he headed into the darkness.

A thousand things crossed his mind as he walked. *Were there several people here tonight? Was the man Rae spotted a decoy, leading us away while someone else still lurked in the camp to do more damage? What was Andy doing on the rig floor in the middle of the night? Who would want to kill him? What if they kidnapped Rae, or hurt her?*

The moment the thought of Rae being hurt crossed his mind, he felt the oddest sensation pulse through him. It made him sweat, made his muscles tense as if he should ready himself to fight some invisible demon. Ashe started walking faster, practically running with his flashlight, scanning the horizon as he shouted her name. Even though they'd only met a few days ago, he already knew he didn't want to lose her.

Rae opened her eyes, realizing her heart was no longer threatening to leap out of her chest. Dragging a deep, ragged breath, she was suddenly embarrassed. *God, my chance to prove I can make it alone, and I run away at the first sign of trouble. What will Ashe think? He'll think I'm a coward, a pathetic, frail woman. Shit!*

Drying tear-streaked cheeks with the back of her sleeve, she quickly stood and brushed the leaves and dirt away. It was dark, and she had no idea where she was or which way led back to the drilling site, but she had no intention of staying put until someone stumbled upon her. To the trees she proclaimed, "I don't want their sympathy, and I'll be damned if anyone from RESCUE is going to have to rescue me!"

Moving to a clearing, Rae searched the night sky. Closing her eyes, she pictured the place on the south end of camp where she had been standing before she panicked. With rising confidence she pinpointed the north star and began hiking in that direction. It wasn't long before she heard Ashe calling her name.

"I'm over here," she shouted, pushing through a wave of fear. Seeing the worried look on his face made her even more ashamed. Trying to sound normal, but not quite succeeding, she asked, "What in the world are you doing out here?"

"Looking for you! Are you all right?"

Without meeting his curious gaze, she tramped past him. "I'm fine. I was just heading back to camp. Sorry if I caused any concern."

At the instant she felt his hand on her shoulder, she whirled around. "I said I was sorry!"

Taken aback by her sharp retort, he snapped, "Sorry for what? What the hell are you doing out here, anyway?"

*Lie!* her mind screamed, but the pain and concern in his eyes made it impossible. Staring at the wet leaves beneath her feet, she sighed. "I needed some fresh air. I just had to get away for a little while. I really didn't think anyone would even notice I was gone."

Ashe's slender fingers grazed the line of her chin, lifting her face to meet his questioning gaze. "I'm not mad, Rae. I'm just worried. Why'd you run off?"

Rae hated to lie to him, but she despised the sympathetic look in his eyes even more. "Okay, so I got scared. With all the problems at the site, I didn't know what to expect, who to trust. I thought it would be safer to kill some time out here until things settled down." Seeing him wince at the word *kill,* she asked, "Exactly what happened?"

"Someone killed Andy on the platform."

A fresh wave of tears rushed to her eyes. "Oh, my God, Ashe! He was such a sweet man, and I know he was your friend. I'm so, so sorry."

"Me, too." This time it was Ashe who looked away, fighting to rein in his emotions. After taking a deep breath, he said, "Listen, the police are probably at the site by now, so I really need to get back. I have a lot to worry about right now, and I'd rather not have to add you to the list."

Mortified, Rae trudged back to camp, certain that one way or another she would earn his respect again. She had to.

"You look exhausted," Nathan said the next day as he watched Brada slump onto the sofa in his office. "I just talked to Ashe. He said the site is still crawling with people from the sheriff's department and every other law enforcement agency in the area. Everyone is in shock."

"I'm glad I left. A few hours of endless questions were more than enough for me, and seeing the look on the face of Andy's wife was the worst experience of my life."

Nathan shook his head. "Ashe feels horrible, like it was somehow his fault."

"It wasn't."

"I just wish there was something I could do. I feel so damned helpless here. It just doesn't seem real that Andy is dead. He was only twenty-eight years old. Ashe said they think he was hiding on the rig, waiting to see if someone was really sabotaging our work."

Brada sighed. "Unfortunately, he found the answer to his question. It's too bad he didn't have someone with him. Any of us would've helped stand guard. Maybe—"

Nathan spun around. "Maybe you'd be dead, too!"

She walked over and hugged him. "It's too late to change things now."

He nodded. Pulling away, he quickly changed the subject. "When are you scheduled to testify before the grand jury about your meeting with Marilyn Prosser?"

"Tomorrow afternoon."

"You don't sound very thrilled about it."

"We both know how it will go. I'll waste an entire afternoon telling them everything she told me, which is pretty incriminating except she never mentioned the name of the company that paid her off or which professor gave her the contact."

"You can never tell. Maybe she talked to someone else we don't know about, or the police found something to implicate one of her professors. After all, they don't convene a grand jury for no reason." Brada tiredly rubbed her temples. "I don't envy the police on either case—first Marilyn, and now Andy."

"Do they have any leads in Andy's murder?"

"They wouldn't tell us anything. I did overhear a couple of them talking, though. They said the coroner's initial impression was that whoever killed him was probably into martial arts and in extremely good physical condition. A lot of help that is. It might narrow the list of suspects down to a few hundred thousand people."

Nathan walked over and sat on the couch beside Brada. "At least Andy stopped them before they damaged any of the equipment again."

"He'd have been proud of that."

He shook his head, then slumped farther into the soft cushion. "Sometimes it just makes me want to give up. With these kinds of people running around, maybe the world isn't worth saving. Maybe extinction is the right idea."

Brada shifted, moving closer to Nathan, so her shoulder touched his. She gently stroked the back of his hand as she said, "You sound like you could use a rest, too. What happened to those high and mighty dreams of yours?"

He scoffed. "I'm beginning to think that's all they are. No one else knows this, Brada, but I know I can trust you. Even with all the money I've invested, if we can't present a realistic three-year profit plan, we may lose everything."

"But how? I thought the money you inherited from your mother was more than enough to keep RESCUE going."

"So did I. Thirty-five million sounded like it would last forever. Right off the bat, five million went to build RESCUE's headquarters. Payroll expense and benefits run almost a quarter million a month. Believe me, it adds up fast."

"Isn't the Solar division holding its own?"

"Both Solar and Wind are marginally profitable since we stepped up our advertising and started mass marketing. Pure Nourishment is profitable on the West Coast and a few trendy markets on the Eastern seaboard. Everywhere else, we're losing our shirts. And, of course, Geothermal is sucking a lot of research money. The last thing we needed were more problems at the site."

Brada sighed. "Maybe we should give up on HDR. For now, at least. Put more money into solar instead."

"We're too close. Besides, it has the potential to beat everything else combined." He drew a ragged breath. "I can handle the financial end of things. Sherrie Rosen has a lot of connections in New York. She's already quietly watching for potential investors for us. I didn't mean to dump more problems in your lap. I know you've had a rough time lately with your mother. How is she since I last saw her?"

Brada shrugged, glancing away. "She should graduate from the rehab clinic again any day now. Too bad they don't guarantee their work."

"I know how hard it's been. If there's anything I can do

to help, just say so. She doesn't have to know where the money came from. I'm sure she wouldn't accept any help from me."

Brada stared at him, her expression fiery. "Thanks," she managed, trying to keep her emotions in control.

Nathan picked up a picture of the Oklahoma drilling site and stared at it. "How are the other employees handling Andy's death?"

"No one was talking much when I left. By the way, what's the deal with Rae Majors?"

"What do you mean?"

"Just after the murder, Ashe was looking all over the place for her. He finally found her out in the middle of a nearby field. He says she's fine. I think that's a pretty strange reaction, no matter how stressful the situation."

Nathan was tired and didn't care to invade Rae's privacy by elaborating. "Let's just say Rae has had a tough life. We all need to help her whenever we can."

Brada yawned. "Whatever you say. I hope I get a chance to get back to the site if they ever start drilling again."

Nathan stood, pulled her off the sofa, and pushed her toward the door. "That's when, not if, they start drilling. You'll be the first to know. Right now, get the hell out of here. You need to be alert for the grand jury. Go home. Take a nap. Relax for once."

Brada smiled and left. As she walked down the hall she mumbled to herself, "I'll relax when you do, Nathan. At the rate we're going, that'll be the precise moment we can snowboard together in hell."

Four days after the murder, the yellow crime-scene tape was removed. The steady stream of law enforcement officers who had invaded the drilling site finally dwindled. Occasionally one would appear, wander around as though just being there might help solve the murder, then slip away. A few local reporters would still stop by, but once they realized no one was going to tell them anything, they quickly hopped back in their fancy satellite trucks and vanished in a cloud of dust.

Ashe studied Rae from a distance as the crew gathered for a meeting. She sat alone, off to one side with her shoulder-length brown hair gleaming in the sunlight. It tumbled freely around her face, perfectly framing big chocolate eyes above a nose and cheeks sprinkled with freckles. He sighed. Every day he noticed something else that attracted him, pulled at the very center of his being. He wanted her near, yet at the same time he hoped he wouldn't regret it later. The way she had acted the night Andy was killed still haunted him. Why had she run off? What was she hiding?

In a few steps he was at her side. "You look awfully serious."

"I was thinking the same thing about you."

"I wish you'd gone back to headquarters with Brada."

She glanced at the grim faces surrounding them. "And miss all this? You've got to be kidding!"

The last of the fourteen crew members arrived, and Ashe walked to where everyone could see him. After taking a deep breath, he said, "I know we're all still a little shaken by what happened to Andy. What we're here to decide is whether we can get back to drilling. It appears that who-ever killed Andy wasn't successful in his attempt to sabotage the rig, so it should be ready to go.

"You all know we've hired four armed security guards who'll be positioned both on the derrick and in the sur-rounding woods from now on. They've rigged booby traps that will set off alarms if anyone is messing around the pe-rimeter of the site. There isn't much more we can do ex-cept stay alert. The question is, are you willing to try one more time?"

The sun was beating down on Ashe, and even though there was a chill in the air, he felt a bead of sweat trickle down his forehead. Hiring a whole new crew would add even more time and money to a budget that was already stretched too far. He honestly didn't think the project had a chance if they didn't get started again. Right away.

Finally, one of the men said, "I'll keep going. Andy was a great guy. He died trying to stop these bastards. He wouldn't have thrown in the towel, and I don't think he'd want us to now."

Another man agreed. Then another. Pretty soon everyone was nodding in agreement. Ashe glanced at Rae, who smiled back at him.

Ashe was relieved, yet in some ways even more worried—the safety of these people rested in his hands. Standing, he dusted the dirt off the seat of his pants. "Then it's settled. Let's get this sucker up and running."

The men patted each other on the back and headed for the rig. Pulling on grimy overalls and gloves, each began to do what he did best—work.

The air was heavy with nervous apprehension. Everyone was thinking the same thing, but no one uttered a word. *Could the killer have sabotaged the well without leaving even a trace of evidence behind? Was there something down the hole?*

Ashe and Rae walked slowly toward the rig. They stood back, watching the crew as they brought the huge network of machinery to life. It cranked slowly at first, then began to hum rhythmically. Minutes passed, each person anxiously waiting to see if they'd finally be back in business.

Ashe led Rae to a spot on the side of the rig where they could watch, but still be out of the roughnecks' way. "We can wait here. At this depth the trip out could take awhile."

Rae knew the *trip out* was the field term for how long it would take the cuttings from the bottom of the hole to travel up the pipe to the surface. A chill of excitement pulsed through her as she realized she was finally a professional geologist.

As they waited, Ashe reached into his pocket and pulled out the gun she'd given him the night of the murder. "Almost forgot. I've been meaning to give this back to you."

Rae casually took it from him, made sure it wasn't loaded, and smiled. "Thanks," she said as she slid it into the pocket of her jacket. "Aren't you going to ask why I have a gun with me?"

Ashe tried to act nonchalant, even though it was killing him. "I just assumed you feel safer having it around."

She shook her head. "Not really. It was part of my college graduation present. The gun, plus lessons at a firing range."

He raised his eyebrows. "Interesting choice for a gift."

She ran her fingers over the cold metal in her pocket. "My father grew up hearing stories about how rough the oil patch is. He was sure I was going to be raped and killed on my first job as a geologist. I promised him I'd bring it with me."

"Maybe you shouldn't tell him about Andy's murder."

Rae nodded. "Good idea, as long as he doesn't read about it in the paper."

"We're pretty far from Oklahoma City, so I doubt if it will make the news. It is a nice little gun."

Rae shivered in the wind. She rubbed her hands up and down her arms to try to stay warm. " 'Light but lethal,' I believe the guy said. It's a .38 Smith and Wesson Airweight Bodyguard. I think my father cared more about the name of it than anything else. Since Ken, my husband, was killed, he worries about me too much. He liked the idea of me having a 'bodyguard.' "

*So do I,* Ashe thought. He moved closer to her, blocking as much of the biting wind as he could. "I'm just glad I didn't have to use it."

"Me, too. I hope I never have to use it, but it does sort of make me feel more secure. Especially at night. I never knew hours could drag by like they have in the last few years."

Ashe put his arm around her shoulder, then abruptly pulled away.

Rae looked at him, then grinned as she read the worried

look on his face. "It's all right. I'm not the type of woman who's going to scream sexual harassment over a friendly gesture."

"Things have certainly changed in the last few years," Ashe said, moving close again. "It makes it damned hard to know what's allowed and what's not." He was several inches taller, and she seemed to fit perfectly beside him.

"I came here hoping to find new friends, build another life. Being around people like you, people who really care about what they do, makes it easy."

"I know you've had a hard time. If you ever want to talk about it . . ."

Rae simply nodded. "Maybe later, as long as you promise not to tell me that time heals all wounds. It doesn't. All the time in the world isn't going to help what happened make sense. Ask Andy's wife and kids in a few months, even a few years. We accept our fate, but for the rest of our lives we have to make a choice. We can either exist from day to day, or we can fight to really live our lives. All because some senseless bastards killed our innocence along with the people we loved!"

Ashe squeezed her closer to him, sighing. "I know I'm not much help, but I'll be happy to listen anytime."

Rae nodded, slightly worried that she'd expressed too much of the anger she fought every day.

They stood there quietly for a long time. Finally, the trip out was finished. Shouts of excitement came from the crew as they realized they were up and running smoothly. Rae motioned for Ashe to follow her across the rig floor, then into the small enclosed area known as the doghouse. Its walls provided protection from the weather, and it was where most of the drilling gauges and geological test equipment was located. They were both thankful to be out of the cutting wind.

Rae shyly said, "Sorry about my tirade."

"No apology necessary. I'm just glad you felt comfortable enough to confide in me."

She nodded and smiled. "You're a good listener." Moving closer to the shelf, she said, "I know I'm just supposed to watch while I'm here, but I'd prefer to be productive. I noticed this the other day when Andy showed me around." She dragged a large, dusty black case out from under the narrow shelf. "Everything I need to test rock cuttings and fluid samples is right here. Would you mind?"

"Of course not. In fact, if it won't bother you, I'd like to watch. Contrary to popular belief, old dogs love to learn new tricks."

She grabbed a sample bottle, and they headed back outside. Fluids and sludge brought up from the bottom of the hole flowed from a pipe into the mud pit. Holding the bottle near the pipe, she filled it with the brownish-red substance. Before Rae pulled the bottle away, the wind suddenly shifted violently to the north, blowing globs of the viscous, oily material onto her blue jeans and windbreaker. "Shit!" she exclaimed.

Ashe was staring at the ominous clouds rolling in. "We'd better get this finished. It looks like we're in for a storm."

Jogging back to the doghouse, she said, "It won't take long."

Once inside, Rae hurriedly set up some of the equipment. "Do you know how this works?" she asked, pointing at the apparatus in front of her.

"Nope. But if you don't mind, I'd like to watch." Ashe could tell by the smile that lit her face she was finally in her element. "One of the things I love about my job is learning new things. Since my background isn't in geology, I find all this fascinating."

"What did you major in?"

"I've got an MBA in business administration."

"Then we'll start with the basics. This is called a light box. It's simply a microscope attached to a box that can be flooded with ultraviolet light. If we were drilling an oil well, this would tell us if we've hit pay dirt. Oil fluoresces under ultraviolet light, making it easy to spot."

"What will it tell us about an HDR well?"

"If there is any oil in this well, we need to know. Almost all of the water injected into an HDR well will be recycled. Oil in the water could complicate things tremendously."

Ashe listened and learned as she walked him step by step through each test she ran on the sample. Finally, she smiled and asked, "That's it, everything turned out perfect for our purposes. Do you feel enlightened? Or maybe I should say relieved?"

"All of the above." He pulled a small, hand-held piece of equipment out of the very back of the black case and asked, "You used everything else in here. Why didn't you run a test with this contraption?"

Rae took it from him and said, "I'm not sure why that's even in there. Geiger counters aren't exactly standard equipment on the well sites I've seen, although I suppose it could have something to do with NORM."

"Who's Norm?" Ashe asked.

She laughed. "Not Norm, like the guy in *Cheers*. NORM, as in Naturally Occurring Radioactive Materials. I had to answer an essay question about NORM on one of my finals last month, so I'm pretty well versed about it. Basically, NORM constitutes a large group of low-level natural radioactive materials such as shales which are extracted from mining or drilling operations.

"Not too long ago, the materials in the sludge were just buried and forgotten. But in the past few years ecologists have convinced enough bureaucrats that they constitute an environmental hazard and must be disposed of in a safer way if they measure over a certain specified radioactive level. So NORM laws were passed making it illegal to ignore the problem. That doesn't mean something is always done about it. It just means that if someone pushes for a site clean-up, they can use the law to force the companies to take responsibility."

"I can see why your grades are so high. You sound like you memorized the textbook."

"I had to," she laughed, "My professor wrote it."

Ashe playfully grabbed the Geiger counter. "I don't know about old Norm, but let's see if you're radioactive."

She moved away as she threw back her hair and provocatively joked, "I've been told I have a radiant personality, but I don't think that means I glow in the dark!"

Ashe flipped a switch to the On position and waved the wand close to Rae. The doghouse was immediately filled with the sound of intense clicking, and the needle on the face of the gauge almost touched the red zone. He stepped back and the clicking decreased, but never totally stopped.

Rae smiled, playfully asking, "How'd you make it do that?"

Ashe shrugged. "I just turned it on." He tapped it on the shelf. "It must be broken."

"Let me see. We had the same model at school." She took it from him and waved it over him. Nothing happened, just the same low background noise. After adjusting a knob on the side, she held it close to her body again. It clicked frantically.

Rae's smile faded as she noticed the clumps of dirt splattered across her clothes made the Geiger counter practically sing. She moved cautiously toward the shelf, until the wand was directly over the fluid sample.

Outside, the first threatening clap of thunder rolled over the rig, but inside the doghouse the Geiger counter's clicks were so fast and furious neither Ashe nor Rae noticed.

# Chapter 4

For a few moments Rae stood paralyzed, staring wide-eyed at the Geiger counter. Logically, she knew the sample might actually be radioactive, but the sickening image her mind immediately linked with radiation poisoning was something she couldn't quite confront. Another clap of thunder, this one close enough to rattle the very structure of the derrick, brought both Ashe and Rae back to reality.

Ashe snapped, "Leave everything here. Your jackets and jeans, too." Rae threw him a nasty look. Swiftly peeling off his overalls, he stood in jeans and a T-shirt. "Here, put these on. I'll pull the crew off the rig until we figure out what the hell is going on." Running out of the doghouse, he shouted, "Meet me in the mobile home."

Rae kicked off her boots, then peeled down her jeans, being careful not to touch the splattered mud stains. After slipping the gun out of her jacket, she wiggled free of it, too. Ashe's overalls were several inches too long, so she quickly cuffed them, then started to put her boots back on. Seeing they were caked with mud as well, she tossed them aside and grabbed the Geiger counter. Passing the wand over her boots, then her socks, she knew they were contaminated, too.

Barefoot and shivering from a chill that came from deep inside, Rae stepped into the pouring rain, slamming the door to the doghouse behind her. She crouched as she carefully ran, shielding the gun and Geiger counter she'd tucked inside the overalls away from the pouring rain. Mud oozed between her toes and cold trickles of water snaked down her back as she scrambled to the mobile home on the far side of the camp.

By the time she climbed inside, she was soaking wet. Finding a roll of paper towels, she wiped her feet, then dropped to her knees to try to clean up the tracks she'd left across the floor. She was still mopping up mud when Ashe rushed in, scattering a fresh layer on the floor.

Pulling Rae to his side, he said, "Leave it. We've got much bigger problems to worry about."

From the look on his face, she already knew the answer to her question, but she still asked it. "How did the crew take getting kicked off the rig again?"

"I told them we were shutting down because of the storm. They looked at me like I was some sort of maniac, but I was pretty insistent. I didn't think we should scare the hell out of everyone by mentioning radiation until we know for certain what we're dealing with."

"Good. Besides, it would be smart to do some damage control on the front end of this problem. Maybe come up with some sort of long-term medical package to keep them from panicking and running to the nearest lawyer."

His face fell. "Do you always have to be so logical?"

"Sorry. It's the accountant left in me. Maybe it'll wear off in a few years." Taking the Geiger counter, she tested the mud clinging to Ashe's boots. Nothing happened. "That's encouraging," she said.

"What?"

"Apparently, the contamination isn't everywhere. Maybe we just drilled through some of the very materials NORM was designed to protect people from." She shrugged and added, "Then again, NORM specifically targets low-level radiation, and I certainly wouldn't classify this as low-level. Maybe someone illegally dumped some nuclear waste near here. It could travel through the groundwater and come up in the mud, even if it was dumped miles away."

He doubted that was the case, but his eyes softened as he replied, "We can always hope."

Rae walked around the mobile home, waving the wand everywhere. It was virtually silent, only an occasional background click. Finally she sighed and said, "You know, the Geiger counter could be broken. We may be blowing this way out of proportion."

"Just for argument's sake, let's assume we aren't. How the hell could something like this happen?"

She shrugged. "Could be a freak of nature and we're just the first ones to stumble across it."

"Wouldn't the workers on the original well have gotten sick if radioactive material was being circulated out of the well bore?"

"I'd assume so, eventually. I think most exposure-related illnesses happen years after the fact, like thyroid cancer and birth defects."

"Great." Ashe was amazed at how unemotionally Rae was handling all this. For someone who had just made a Geiger counter hit the red line, she seemed totally unalarmed. He wished he felt the same way. Right now his heart was beating at twice its normal rate, and he was sweating in spite of the fact the room temperature was probably fifty degrees.

Rae turned and asked, "Wasn't this site abandoned for several years?"

He nodded.

"It's a pretty obscure area, a great place to dump some toxic waste without anyone ever suspecting a thing. A four-mile deep hole would hold quite a bit."

"I suppose so. It would have had to have been dumped above ground, though. The hole still had its original plug when we got here."

Rae frowned. "Then it happened another way. The sample I took was from twenty-one thousand feet down, yet the surface dirt on your shoes seems fine. At this point it's just a guess, but it sounds like the radiation is from deep inside the well bore."

"How in the world could that happen? Mark Olender, the geologist you replaced, read every log on this site, every report ever filed. There was no mention of any problem with radiation."

"Ashe, he may not have tested for it. Maybe this place glowed in the dark all along."

"Not according to Mark, and he's one of the best."

Suddenly suspicious, Rae cocked her head to ask, "So why'd he leave?"

"Relax. Nothing sinister. He and his wife decided to retire to New Zealand."

Shivering, Rae smiled. "Smart man. It's probably warm there."

The return of her nonchalant attitude had a calming effect on Ashe. Rubbing his stiff neck muscles, he replied, "I'm beginning to think we should all move to New Zealand. But seriously, have you ever heard of anything like this happening?"

"We studied several wells in the Anadarko Basin in college. I remember they ran into some problems with poisonous sulfides, and extreme temperatures, but I never read anything about the kind of radioactivity we're up against. NORM is pretty recent, and most of these wells were drilled before testing for radioactivity was a standard procedure. Any test would've shown this was a problem."

"What's that supposed to mean?"

"If the Geiger counter is working right, we're . . ."

"In deep shit?"

She nodded, then began pacing back and forth. She was trying to ignore how cold her bare feet were, but it wasn't easy. "Are there any nuclear reactors in this area?" she asked.

"Not that I know of."

Suddenly, Rae threw back her head and laughed. "I know! They must have done a thermonuclear frac job!"

Ashe's face was drawn, his eyes wide. "What the hell is that?"

She walked over and put her hands on his face. "Lighten up, Ashe. It's just an old joke from college. You know what a frac job is, right?"

"Of course. It's where fluid is pumped into a well at extremely high pressure to fracture the reservoir rock so the oil or gas, or water, for that matter, will flow to the surface more freely."

"Exactly. In the early nineteen hundreds, guys called 'shooters' used to frac wells by dropping nitroglycerin in the hole and running like hell. A guy in one of my classes joked that a thermonuclear frac job would penetrate so well they could suck out every drop of oil there was in a five-mile radius. The professor embarrassed the hell out of the poor soul. He demanded to know why, other than the obvious reason, even a tiny nuclear device couldn't be used to frac a well."

Ashe was listening intently. "So . . . why couldn't it?"

"Because any nuclear device would contaminate the hole and make it totally useless. If I remember right, the half-life of plutonium is around 24,000 years, so anything that came out of that hole would be radioactive for a long, long time."

"Anything?"

"Anything. Dirt, water, oil, gas . . . every single thing."

"Are you sitting down?" Ashe asked.

The storm was interfering with the reception, making Nathan's voice scratchy over the cellular phone. "I am now."

"Is Brada around? I think we're going to need some of R and D's help on this problem."

"She's testifying before the grand jury today, but knowing her, she'll still come by the office tonight."

"Do you happen to know what kind of insurance we're carrying on the HDR site?"

"Minimal. Workman's comp and blowout liability. Cut to the chase, Ashe. Exactly what the hell is going on out there?"

"It's too soon to know, but we may have a major problem. There's a thunderstorm on top of us right now, so it'll be a few hours before we can get out of here. We'll have to go to Oklahoma City or Amarillo, since I doubt if any of the small towns around here would have Geiger counters."

"I know better than to ask this, but I'll take the bait. What do you need more Geiger counters for?" Nathan asked, his patience growing thin.

"There was one in the geological test case in the doghouse. We're hoping it isn't working right, since we got some very high radioactive readings on a deep fluid sample." There was a long moment of static before Ashe asked, "Nathan, are you still there? Nathan?"

"Yeah, I'm still here. I'm thinking."

"Same here."

"Is the crew in any danger?"

"I don't know. Rae and I were the only ones working around the mud pit. Some fluid splashed on her clothes, and we did tests on the sample for about fifteen minutes before we discovered it might be radioactive."

"Didn't Mark Olender run some preliminary tests when we first opened the hole?"

"Yes, he did."

"I'll get in touch with him. Maybe he'll have an idea."

"Ask if he kept any of the original samples. That way we could compare them, see if this is something new."

"I will," Nathan said. "Shouldn't the two of you be heading for a hospital right now?"

"We talked about it, but we don't think it would do any good. Rae and I both know that people working in potentially dangerous areas wear tags that show how much radiation they've absorbed. That way they know when to run like hell. If it turns out there really is a problem here, we'll just have to live with not knowing how big a dose we got.

I don't suppose you know how much exposure is considered too much?"

"I haven't got a clue, but I'll get our people on it right away."

"We'd appreciate it. Meanwhile, I pulled everyone off the rig again. Rae and I are going to sweep the area with the new Geiger counters as soon as this blasted storm lets up. I'll probably send the rest of the crew into town just to minimize questions. When we have a better idea of what we're up against, I'll talk to them."

"I don't like the idea of the two of you sweeping the area. Be careful, Ashe. Understand?"

"Whatever you say," he promised. "Rae and I also discussed the possibility that this could be a result of deep-well injection of hazardous waste. Rae tells me contaminated groundwater from nearby wells could easily have seeped here."

"I'll have someone check the Corporation Commission records on the entire area; then I'll run down to R and D and see if anyone can reach one of our connections at the EPA. Maybe we can get some kind of useful information on allowable radiation levels and exposure hazards."

"The EPA will shut us down so fast it'll make your head spin, and I can't blame them." Ashe looked at Rae, who was sitting on a stool watching him as though none of this were even slightly out of the ordinary.

After a few seconds Nathan softly said, "So that's what Andy interrupted."

"What?" Ashe covered his other ear with his hand, trying to hear Nathan's voice over the sound of the pounding rain on the metal roof.

"The bastards contaminated our well, and they did it in a way it can never be used again. Son of a bitch!"

"Get real, Nathan. In order to do that, someone would've had to drop some uranium or plutonium down the hole. Last time I checked, you couldn't just stroll into Wal-Mart and pick up a six-pack of the stuff."

"And last time I checked, PetroCo had offices in every third world country you could think of—Iraq, Tunisia, you name it. Besides, enough money can buy anything."

"But we discovered this purely by accident. Our workers would have been exposed for years before anyone thought to test for radiation poisoning. Personally, I seriously doubt that anyone would have figured it out for a long, long time."

Nathan sounded as though he was talking more to himself than to Ashe as he said, "Haven't you learned by now that they always have something up their sleeve? Some inspector on their payroll would've stumbled onto the radiation after they tipped him off. The press would've been notified, and in a flurry of hot news stories they'd have smeared our name and made sure we never drilled another well. In fact, this will probably really piss them off."

Ashe was both stunned and amazed by Nathan's slant on the problem. "How's that?" he asked.

"Think about it. We'd have sunk millions more of RESCUE's dollars into that site. First completing the original well, drilling the return well, then installing the HDR equipment. We would have spent—hell, you know the budget for this project better than I do. I'm sure their idea was for us to be shut down just about the time we were finally ready to make a profit. Your discovery probably saved our asses."

Ashe didn't know what to believe at this point. Almost to himself he said, "If you say so, Nathan. If you say so. I'll call you back as soon as we have better information."

"I'll be waiting."

Ashe punched the button on the cell phone and shook his head.

Rae stood and walked over to him. "Well, what did he have to say?" she asked.

She was standing so close Ashe caught the citrus fragrance of shampoo in her wet hair. "He thinks someone dropped radioactive material into the well on purpose the night Andy was murdered."

Rae raised her eyebrows but didn't say anything while she contemplated the idea. A flash of light came through the windows, followed closely by a clap of thunder. Just as she was about to answer, the lights flickered, then died. "Maybe my father was right. This is pretty rough country, isn't it?"

Ashe sighed. "I never thought so before, but I do now."

Standing so close her breath was hot on his skin, she looked him straight in the eye. "It would be a perfect way to do it."

For a second Ashe was confused, more by his urge to take her in his arms than by her statement. Those sexy brown eyes seemed to be toying with him in the dim afternoon light. Clearing his suddenly dry throat, he softly asked, "It would be a perfect way to do what?"

"To sabotage a well. Isn't that what we're talking about?"

*I wish it wasn't,* he thought. Ashe lightly shook his head to clear his erotic thoughts before he answered, "Yes. Why do you think so?"

"It's quite ingenious, actually. You drop a small amount of uranium or plutonium, or maybe even some nuclear waste, down the hole and wait. Days, months, or even years down the line, basically whenever you decide the time is right, you make sure the EPA finds out there's a radiation problem. Meanwhile, depending on the dosage, your enemy's employees will be slowly exposed while they work. Most doctors never treat radiation poisoning, so when the workers finally do get sick, the chances of their problems being traced back here would be minimal. Even if there were some physical evidence to begin with, it'd be long gone by the time anyone caught on."

"How true."

"Sorry for eavesdropping, but what did Mr. Greenwall say about insurance? If this site is ruined, will the loss be covered?"

Ashe shook his head. "Nope. It'd be a total loss."

Rae hesitated. "Sorry, but ten years of being an accountant makes me see things from a cash-flow angle. Can RESCUE survive this kind of financial blow?"

"I certainly hope so." He looked at her and sighed. "I don't mean to insult you, Rae, but you seem to be taking this awfully well. If I had just started work and someone told me I might have been accidentally subjected to even a mild dose of radiation, I'd probably be screaming and running the other way. Yet it's almost as if this mess makes you more comfortable."

Rae smiled. "The other day when I ran into the forest was really not like me. It's just, sometimes since my husband's death, certain things seem overwhelming."

Ashe pulled her into his arms. "We're all overwhelmed at one time or another."

Her fingers grazed his cheek before she rested her face on his chest and relaxed. "Maybe the smart thing to do would be to run away screaming, but I doubt it. RESCUE gave me a chance to do what I love when no one else would. There's so much to discover here, and especially now, it'll be unique. Besides, I'm learning to accept that life is full of danger. If it wasn't radiation, it would be something else—maybe not this second, but sooner or later." She shivered and added, "If it wasn't so damn cold, I'd probably be happy as a clam."

"If you'll tell me where to find them, I'll go to your tent and get you a change of clothes and some shoes."

"No way! I don't want you running around in this lightning. I won't freeze to death."

Reluctantly, he pulled away to search the trailer. In a back closet was a clean, dry pair of overalls. Tossing them to her, he said, "Here, change into these."

Rae slipped into the narrow bathroom and emerged a few minutes later looking slightly less disheveled. "Thanks. I feel much better."

"I found these, too." He dangled several pocket hand warmers and grinned. Once he snapped them, the chemical reaction instantly began to generate heat. Leading her to the tattered sofa, Ashe waited for her to sit, then placed a warmer under each of her feet. "Mind if we share body heat?"

Grinning, Rae shook her head.

Sitting at her side, Ashe wrapped an arm around her and pulled her close. Wrestling with his conscience, he wondered again how wise it was to get involved with an employee. He was afraid it was too late. Softly stroking her hair, he said, "I'm sorry."

"You shouldn't be. That is, unless you're the one who sabotaged the well."

"That's not what I was talking about." With one finger he tilted her head so their eyes met. "I meant for this." Pulling her closer, he kissed her tenderly. He reveled in the softness of her mouth, the willing acceptance he felt in her response.

Moments later, she opened her eyes to breathlessly ask, "What was it you were sorry for?"

Still tasting her, wanting her, he sighed. "For making things even more complicated than they already are . . ."

Chuck Kelmar leaned back in his leather chair, propped his feet next to his overflowing in-box, then grabbed the phone. "How'd the grand jury investigation go?" he asked.

"Better than we'd hoped. As we suspected, the girl didn't give RESCUE any proof, so we're off the hook."

"What about the professor?"

"Our scholarly friend wasn't even called to testify."

"Any idea when the grand jury will make its decision?"

"It won't be long. They don't have shit to work with, so I'm betting there won't be any indictments handed down."

"Good. Thanks for the prompt report."

Kelmar cradled the phone and swung his feet around. Standing, he stretched. Pretty soon RESCUE would be history, brought to its knees just as they'd been planning for years, thanks to the invaluable help from one of RESCUE's own trusted employees.

The phone buzzed again. Kelmar picked up the receiver. "Yes."

"It's Karl. I just got a call from Elk City from our man on the RESCUE crew."

"Really? So soon?"

"Rig 114 was shut down again a few hours ago."

"What's the reason this time?"

"That's what's so interesting. There really wasn't a reason, at least not a mechanical one."

Kelmar chuckled, his voice laced with sarcasm as he said, "You know, Karl, they aren't ever going to get those holes drilled if they don't stop shutting down every other day. They might as well be standing out there throwing handfuls of hundred-dollar bills down the hole every hour."

"It's a real shame, isn't it Chuck?" Karl Ross snickered.

"It sure is."


Although physically exhausted from traveling for two days, he was too excited about planning his next job to rest. The very idea was tantalizing. Getting Greenwall out of the picture for a while, but not permanently, certainly presented a challenge. After all, the job would have to be skillfully arranged since, for once, he and the target were on the same side. Revenge against PetroCo came in many forms—some short-term, while others didn't reap benefits for years. Manipulating both sides was becoming quite a rush. Using PetroCo's own funds to slowly destroy them was half the fun.

Glancing at his reflection in the rearview mirror, he noted his hair was still perfectly slicked back and his tie was impeccably knotted. This time everything would be perfect. With two to three weeks to plan, he had plenty of time to devise something clever, which was the only choice in this situation.

The parking lot of RESCUE, Inc., was different from any he'd ever seen. Near the building were bike racks, and even though it was almost six p.m. on a business day, they were actually full of bicycles. Beside them were about twenty spaces for mopeds and motorcycles, and most of those were occupied, too. The few cars scattered about the lot were fuel-efficient models, and a couple even appeared to be some sort of solar-powered prototypes.

Smiling, he proudly realized these people actually practiced what they preached, and they were willing to work long hours to prove it. *Environmental activists like myself,* he thought. It occurred to him how angry his RESCUE contact would be, though, if she knew he handled special jobs for PetroCo, charging them millions of dollars to do their dirty deeds. But she'd understand when she saw the proof. Every call, every job, had been recorded to use against them when the time finally came. *Someday she'll realize how much I've done to help her accomplish our goals. Someday PetroCo will be history, thanks to the undeniable evidence I've accumulated. Then they'll all understand. I'll be worshiped like a god.*

Releasing the trunk from inside, he stepped out and watched it slowly open. Glancing around once again, he realized he might need a different car to pull off this job, one that wouldn't command so much attention if he ever found the need to follow Greenwall.

He thought about the days ahead. This would undoubtedly be one of the most interesting jobs, a work of art that would go down in history. For the first time he didn't need any false ID's or cover stories. He actually had a valid business reason for being at RESCUE, a solid alibi that would hold up under even the closest scrutiny. Even so, he rubbed the clearly sheathed tips of his fingers together and was glad he had still taken a few precautions.

Peering into the trunk, he wondered if he could find a way to use the lethal ice molds again. It was always dangerous to repeat a tactic, but these were so special, so truly symbolic of everything he stood for—pure, sharp, accurate, even environmentally sound—that he had to use them again. Although he'd left the larger pieces of surveillance equipment at the hotel, the crossbow was by far his favorite. It excited him to know the weapon was tucked in the hidden compartment just inches from his fingertips.

After he grabbed his briefcase, he softly shut the trunk, pushed the button to arm the car alarm, and walked briskly to the building. The sun was beginning to set, bathing the windows in breathtaking slashes of reds and golds. Most people would have stopped and stared, but he totally ignored the sight.

Little else eluded his attention, even though his step was quick. He noticed the relatively simple security system, the lack of guards, the types of glass used on the windows, the after-hours magnetic identification setup.

Once inside the lobby, he was only momentarily taken back by the transformation of the interior. The waterfall and foliage provided him a reason to slow down, to observe. Pretending to be fascinated, he appeared to study the plants and the strange walls, although he was actually noting the exact locations of several key items. As soon as he was back in his hotel, he would carefully diagram the position of everything in the lobby—the stairway, the elevators, the doors. He realized this job might be easier than he thought. There didn't appear to be much security at all. No cameras, no guards. He was dealing with trustworthy souls.

After a few minutes he glanced at his watch and went to the company marquis. Nathan Greenwall was listed as President and CEO, and his office was shown as Suite 500. He walked to the stairs and effortlessly climbed five flights. Being in top physical shape was one of the many things he demanded of himself.

When he reached the end of the hallway, he stopped at Dinell Blanchard's desk to announce his arrival, even though it was obvious. He knew Greenwall was already in his office, since he could see him through the interior glass walls, and the familiar sound of the secretary's voice confirmed he was right where he should be. Extending his arm to shake her hand firmly, he said, "Good evening. My name is Harvey Walters. I'm here to see Mr. Greenwall."

Dinell cocked her head and smiled at him the way old friends do when they cross paths. "It's been a long time, Mr. Walters. I don't suppose you remember me."

His eyes narrowed as he returned her smile. "I'm sorry. I'm afraid I really don't have a very good memory for names. In fact, I'm much better at recognizing voices."

Nodding, she said, "As busy as you are, I'm not surprised. I'll bet you do most of your business on the phone. I've heard your company is doing quite well. Congratulations."

"Thank you."

Dinell stood to escort him inside. "Mr. Greenwall's expecting you. Can I get you something to drink?"

"No, thank you," he replied. Following her into the office, he watched the walls become opaque as she excused herself. Nodding in approval, he asked, "Liquid crystals?"

"Exactly." Nathan crossed the room to greet him warmly. "After all these years, it's finally good to be able to put a face with your name."

"I feel the same way." *So far, so good,* he thought as he pulled his hand away from Nathan's. *He didn't notice the polymer sheath on my fingertips.*

"Sit down. Can I get you anything? We make a mean raspberry sparkling water here. Plus there's a cafeteria in the building if you're hungry."

"It's very kind of you to offer, but no, thank you. I really don't want to take up much of your time. I know you're a busy man. Basically, I'm just here to tell you how much all of us at Pure Air Systems appreciate your business."

"You have a good line of products. We're happy to be able to use them."

"The new entrance to your building is even more impressive than I'd heard. It's no wonder your electrostatic orders have been down this year."

"The NatureAir system does work wonders, but we still use your company's filters in all our Solar and Wind products. They keep the engines free of dirt and dust. Our engineers estimate they more than triple the life of the mechanical parts."

"I'm glad we could work with you. By the way, don't get me wrong, even with the decrease in RESCUE's orders, you're still one of our best clients. In fact, that's why I'm here." He opened his briefcase and slid out several small devices. "We'd like you to personally have our latest products to test."

He set them on Nathan's desk. One was the size of a pack of chewing gum, the others about the size of packs of cigarettes. Picking up the smallest one, Walters said, "This is for your car. Simply plug it into the cigarette lighter, and it will constantly filter the air inside the vehicle. You'll be amazed how much air pollution it will eliminate, not to mention allergens and carbon monoxide."

Walters picked up one of the larger devices and continued, "These babies plug into any outlet in your house. Each one will keep a forty-by-forty room totally free of air impurities for over a year. I've slept with one in my bedroom for the last six months, and I haven't woken up with a headache since I installed it. I brought five for you to try, but if you need more, I'll be happy to send them."

"Five is plenty. I'm still a bachelor, so I don't have a very big place."

"I know how that goes. I'm hardly ever in my own apartment."

"I spend too much time on the road. I'm sure you know how it goes. . . ." His voice trailed off, and he quickly changed the subject by adding, "I must be more tired from the drive down than I thought. I almost forgot to take care of your office." Walters removed one more of the larger devices from his briefcase and slid it into a wall socket in the corner of the room. "Considering the quality of air in this building, it's probably a waste of time, but it can't hurt."

"Thanks again," Nathan said.

Walters stood and walked toward Nathan's desk, extending his hand. "I'd best be going now. If RESCUE needs anything, just give me or one of my assistants a call. Our engineers would love to help in any phase of your designs that we can." He slid his briefcase off Nathan's desk, dangling it at his side as he started to leave.

"I'll let my people know," Nathan said.

As they shook hands, the briefcase Walters held popped open and its contents spilled onto the carpet. Both men squatted, rounding up the stray items. Walters apologized, "I'm so sorry. The latches on this thing are getting to be pretty unreliable."

"No harm done," Nathan said as he helpfully laid the last item, a leather-bound calendar, back in the briefcase.

"Thanks. I'll be in touch. And let me know how the new filter prototypes work. We're hoping to have a line tooled to manufacture them within the next six months."

"I'm looking forward to trying them. Are you flying out this afternoon?" Nathan asked as they walked toward the door.

"No. I have six different customers to meet, plus I decided to take a few days off while I'm here, so I drove."

Nathan nodded. "California is certainly the right place to vacation. Enjoy your trip."

Walters smiled. "I will. In fact, I expect it to be quite an experience." As he crossed the office, the smile never left his face. Everything had gone perfectly. On the calendar inside his briefcase were Nathan's fingerprints; implanted in the car filter was a homing device; nestled inside the other filters were sophisticated listening devices; and between the thumb and forefinger of his left hand were several carpet fibers from RESCUE's plush executive suite. He wasn't sure which devices he might need, but now he had every base covered.

Nathan opened the door, and the two men walked through. Dinell was still sitting at her desk, typing on the computer. "Doesn't anyone who works here ever go home on time?" Walters asked.

Chuckling, Nathan replied, "Dinell is one of our best employees. She arrives before everyone else, and she usually won't leave until I do. Right?"

Dinell smiled and shrugged. "I wouldn't want to miss anything important, now would I?"

Walters slipped her one of his business cards, winking playfully as he crossed the room. "If you ever decide to leave, I know a great place you could work."

She nodded politely, and their eyes held for a few moments before he slipped into the hall.

Walters' step was light as he walked slowly through the building's entryway. It truly was magnificent. Studying it again, he was fascinated by the marriage of nature and architecture. When he was finally satisfied he could diagram the basic design, he opened the door and stepped into the growing darkness. The sun was already well below the horizon, causing the lights in the parking lot to spark to life.

Without pulling the small plastic bag out of his pocket, he flicked the carpet fibers inside, then sealed it. The thin coat of polymer on his fingertips was beginning to irritate him, so he roughly rubbed his fingers together, effectively shredding the thin substance. Layers of the clear coating fell imperceptibly to the ground as he walked. He was confident he hadn't left any fingerprints behind.

Walters was deep in thought as he crossed the parking lot. So deep that when he reached the place where he'd left the Lincoln a short time ago, he was certain he had merely forgotten where it was parked. The lot wasn't very large, so he walked down each row. With every step his heart pounded a little harder.

By the time he slowly circled the entire lot twice, he was a nervous wreck. His entire body was moist with a thin layer of sweat. Running his palm across his brow, he could not have cared less that the Lincoln was gone, but he cared greatly about the item tucked inside the hidden compartment of its trunk—the only thing in the universe that directly tied him to the murder of two U.S. senators.

# Chapter 5

The early morning tranquility made Rae painfully aware that she and Ashe were the only people left in the camp. A misty shroud of chilly fog seemed to taunt their isolation, making her shiver and pull her jacket firmly around her neck to protect against both the elements and her overactive imagination. Glancing out the window of the old trailer, she was anxious to see Ashe again.

For the tenth time that morning she fought the urge to go to his tent and wake him in ways she'd only dreamed of since she lost her husband. Confusing thoughts of death added to the emotional upheaval she experienced every time she laid eyes on Ashe. Each time she let her guard slip, a promise made on a cold, damp morning much like this one would taunt her. A promise from her soul to her heart that she'd never allow herself to be hurt like that again. Never.

Watching the sun give birth to what she was certain would be another fascinating day made Rae almost forget there could be an invisible, silent killer in the ground just a few feet away. She was so lost in her thoughts, the sound of the door swinging open and Ashe's voice startled her.

"Well, hello! When did you get back?" he asked with a broad smile.

Quickly regaining her composure, Rae replied, "About an hour ago. Did you sleep well?"

"You should've come to wake me up," he teased.

"Believe me, I thought about it. But I was too anxious to use the new equipment."

His eyes locked on hers. "And?"

"The new Geiger counter confirmed that parts of the site actually are radioactive."

"Then I'd better call the crew at the motel. Looks like we're out of business for a while."

"Here, put this on." She handed him a small badge with a clip on the end, then continued, "The badges will tell us if our exposure level reaches a dangerous zone. Keep it on at all times you're in the area, even when you're asleep. Okay?"

"Whatever you say. Will you be able to tell if someone sabotaged the well?"

"Probably. Nathan faxed me the results of the tests performed by Mark Olender. Not surprisingly, he did test for radioactivity two years ago, before RESCUE bid on the land and mineral rights for the HDR project. His work seems to be very thorough. All the tests were negative, well within the acceptable normal range."

Ashe asked, "Is it possible to develop naturally occurring problems, let's say, within the last two years?"

"Anything is possible, but in this case it'd be highly improbable. With plutonium's half-life being over twenty thousand years, the chances of a high-speed molecular breakdown suddenly beginning in the last two years would be phenomenal. Especially considering the original dry hole was drilled almost twenty-five years ago."

Ashe laughed. "You're beginning to sound more like a nuclear physicist than a geologist."

Wrapping her arms around his neck, she kissed him lightly. "I learn fast."

"I'll say," he said, pulling her closer.

Twisting away, Rae smiled to hide the sudden surge of uneasiness that washed over her. Part of her wanted to melt into his arms, while another part screamed at her to run away. Stammering, she explained, "As much as I hate to say this, I'm afraid I have a ton of work to do."

"I'll help," he offered.

"No!" Realizing she sounded a bit overbearing, she softened. "Right now I'm afraid I won't be able to concentrate if you're too close."

Pushing open the door, Ashe cocked his head and grinned. "I believe I'll take that as a compliment."

"As you should!" The blast of cold air felt good on Rae's flushed cheeks as she rushed outside and crossed the camp. Another, more powerful flash of anxiety struck her, twisting her stomach into a knot. *What if it happens again? What if he dies? How can I live through that kind of agony?*

After taking a taxi to his hotel, Walters settled in for a long night. Hour after hour he paced as he listened to the police scanner for any report on a stolen Lincoln. Twenty-twenty hindsight tortured him as he listened to the endless chatter. *Why didn't I rig the damned car with a tracking device? My secretary told them it was stolen from Colorado yesterday, but can they prove it was actually stolen here? How did the son of a bitch get around the alarm system? What will happen if the police recover it and find the hidden compartment?*

Suddenly Walters stopped, the answer clear. The only option was to cut his losses and get out of town. He would have to take care of Greenwall, and he'd have to do it right now. Forty-eight hours was as long as he dared to risk. The luxury of waiting a few weeks was no longer an option, but then again, lately he'd done some of his best work under pressure. It forced him to be more creative, more adaptable.

Looking out the window, he smiled at the thought of getting Greenwall out of the way, even if it was only temporary. In fact, he was confident everything would work out perfectly.

The police scanner crackled to life at five a.m. Every nerve in his body tingled as he listened to the discussion of the newly discovered crash site. The description matched his Lincoln perfectly, right down to the out-of-state tags. A boy was dead at the scene, impaled on a small tree trunk after being thrown clear of the car as it hurdled down an embankment. Inside the car they had found empty beer bottles and a half-empty whiskey bottle. When the lieutenant arrived on the scene, Walters switched to his frequency so he could follow the conversation of the officers working the wreck.

On the edge of his seat, he waited to hear the words he dreaded. Waited to hear they had found the weapon, the secret compartment in the trunk. An hour passed and no one ever mentioned it. But some of what they said chilled him to the bone: The coroner said the dead kid was a twelve-year-old named Cory Williams, and they were pretty sure he wasn't the driver.

*Whoever drove that car has my crossbow. But not for long!*

Across the road from the crashed Lincoln, a lanky sixteen-year-old was crouched behind the bushes, his entire body trembling. The bump on his forehead no longer pounded so hard he couldn't see or hear. Instead, the ache had become dull, somehow numbing most of his face. He couldn't move his left arm without fiery pain shooting through his entire being, so he sat motionlessly and listened, even though what he heard made him nauseous.

Beside him was the dented silver metallic case that held the fancy weapon his brother had thought was so cool. After running a gloved finger across the shiny lid, he wiped away a tear and prayed it was all just a bad dream. The worst dream ever. He glanced at his hand. It seemed foreign—so foreign he stared at it. *Gloves. We wore gloves to steal the car. To make sure we didn't leave fingerprints. This isn't a nightmare!*

Jace Williams was old enough to know that stealing a car could only mean trouble. He still couldn't believe he'd done it. And why? To impress his baby brother! *Stupid! Stupid! Stupid!* His mother was going to kill him!

Voices carried on the morning breeze as the officers talked among themselves and on their radios. He heard his brother's name mentioned, and wondered how they knew it. Even though he'd known in his heart his brother was dead when he saw that thing poking through the middle of him in the dark, the horrible reality didn't sink in until he heard the coroner callously say he wouldn't be eating shish kabob for a few days.

The shock and pain was too much for Jace to bear. He slumped sideways onto the brush-covered ground, tears streaking his dark skin as he silently sobbed. *Her good boys,* Mama always called them. *She raised good boys who didn't get in trouble like those stupid kids who ran in gangs.*

"Jesus," Jace cried. "Why him? Why didn't you just take me?"

Walters was unrecognizable in the rented van parked down the street from Nathan's house. His hair and eyes were now almost black, thanks to a quick stop at a local drugstore and colored contact lenses. The shopping spree yesterday ensured his entire look was different, his imposing suit and tie replaced by a breezy casual outfit, complete with sunglasses and a baseball cap.

Thanks to the listening devices, he already knew his target's plans for the day. Walters expertly tailed Greenwall as he left his house, drove straight to RESCUE, and went inside. When he was sure it was safe, he pulled into RESCUE's parking lot and chose a space a few rows behind Greenwall's car. He shut off the motor and crawled through the empty gap behind the front seats, leaving the police scanner on so he could monitor it. The rented mini-van was merely a shell, but it suited his needs perfectly. It was light blue, a shade that blended easily into traffic and provided excellent cover.

Walters perched near the small window in the back of the passenger side and withdrew his binoculars. From a distance his van appeared to be empty, but from inside he could easily watch both the main entrance to the building and Greenwall's car. After tinkering with the receiver to find the right frequency, he slid on the headphones and waited. It was only a couple of minutes before he heard Nathan's voice through the static. Walters listened as Greenwall greeted Dinell and she informed him of his agenda for the day.

For several hours he watched and listened. Greenwall's conversations were, for the most part, unbelievably boring. Fatigue from the sleepless night was rapidly catching up with Walters, and he mentally fought to stay awake by concentrating on clever ways to only *temporarily* dispose of Greenwall.

Just as he was about to lose the battle with fatigue and nod off, a large white bus lumbered into the parking lot. It pulled slowly around to the front entry and stopped.

Walters immediately perked up. His view of the front door was now blocked, forcing him to reevaluate his observation point. Even more intriguing, the vehicle blocking his view was an American Red Cross Bloodmobile, and two volunteers were unfurling a banner that read GIVE THE GIFT OF LIFE—BLOOD DRIVE TODAY. At the same time, the conversation in Greenwall's office had suddenly become downright interesting. Pushing the Record button, he thought the folks at PetroCo might be willing to pay to hear it.

A smile creased Walters' weary face. If he was lucky, the solution to his problem had just fallen in his lap. His ingenious idea would keep Greenwall out of the way for quite some time and advance his own cause, while sucking money out of PetroCo for worthless information.

*God, I'm good!*

"Can you believe this crap?" Dinell tossed the *Wall Street Journal* onto Nathan's desk. With trembling hands she paced across his office, her anger growing with each step. It took

all her strength to remain silent as Nathan read the short
article out loud.

> "PetroCo announced late yesterday that Charles 'Chuck'
> Kelmar has been appointed President and Chief Executive
> Officer of the corporation.
>
> "Mr. Kelmar has held various positions in the oil and
> gas industry for over ten years, including his last position
> as Vice President of Marketing for PetroCo. He holds a de-
> gree in petroleum engineering, and has been with the cor-
> poration for eight years.
>
> "Mr. Kelmar was in Las Vegas attending the National
> Conference of Petroleum Leaders when the announcement
> was made. In a telephone interview he said, 'I intend to
> follow in the footsteps of my predecessor, who has led this
> corporation to greatness with a firm but gentle hand. My
> hope is to guide with the strength I find in God, and to ap-
> ply His standards to our business each and every day.' "

When Nathan finished reading, he leaned back in his
chair. "Don't tell me Kelmar's promotion caught you by
surprise, Dinell."

She scowled. "With someone like Kelmar at the helm,
God only knows what PetroCo will try to get away with."

Nathan shook his head and slowly tore the article out of
the newspaper. He held it in the palm of his hand, then
crumpled it into a tiny ball. "I can't believe he'd stoop to
using bible belt tactics. Most of the stockholders of PetroCo
are God-fearing Midwesterners and Southern Baptists. He's
really kissing up to his public." His voice dropped to a whisper as he added, "A bullet between the eyes would solve
the problem."

She slumped onto the sofa. "What?"

"Nothing," Nathan snapped. "Just wishful thinking."

Dinell sat up a little straighter. "I certainly hope the public figures out what kind of asshole he really is before he
manages to screw up the world even more than he already
has."

Nathan stood, shaking his head as he looked out the window. "I honestly believe people get what they deserve in the long run. Kelmar's screwed so many people, sooner or later it will catch up to him." He turned and tossed the wadded article toward the trash can. "Just wait and see. He'll get his."

"We can always hope," Dinell said.

"Sherrie Rosen called me at home last night. Looks like it's almost time for me to head to D.C. to try to defeat the Evans-Giles bill. Book me a flight for day after tomorrow."

"Okay."

Nathan glanced out his window. "You'll have to excuse me. The Bloodmobile is here."

"I'm amazed that you still donate every sixty days."

He nodded. "I'd donate every week if they'd let me. It's the least I can do."

She stood and walked to him, wringing her moist hands. "You still miss her, don't you?"

"Every day. My mother was quite a lady."

Dinell shifted nervously, unable to return his steady gaze. "That's true. Have you ever heard any more about the clean-up of the toxic waste that made her sick?"

"The city bought the entire chunk of land, then just fenced it off. I'm sure that was cheaper than trying to remove all the chemicals. The problem is, rainwater still carries the same pollutants downstream. Who knows how many more people will have to die of leukemia before they figure out a better solution?"

"You've done all you can."

As he walked out of his office, he wondered, "Have I?"

Rae peeled off the protective suit before she stepped inside the motor home. She was grinning, stepping as lightly as a teenager. "I've got good news," she said.

Ashe jumped up and excitedly asked, "The site isn't as contaminated as you first thought? We can keep drilling?"

She frowned at him and shook her head. "Sorry. I said it was good news, not a miracle."

Rae walked over and stood next to him, his face reflecting utter frustration. "See this?" She held up her safety badge. It showed a small color change, but most of it was still black. "I wore it on the outside of the protective suit the entire time I tested the area." She glanced at her watch. "I spent over an hour on or around the rig. The other half hour was spent testing random points from the rest of the camp area."

She sighed at his blank expression. "Don't you see? This badge didn't register a lethal dose of radiation, or even a particularly dangerous level. We can relax now. Since I was handling only a small amount of the material from the mud pit for around fifteen minutes, neither of us should have any long-term exposure problems." At his gloomy expression, she added, "Gee, I'm glad I didn't have really bad news. If you get any more excited, you might accidentally regain consciousness."

Ashe said, "Sorry. I was just on the phone with Nathan discussing whether this problem could be fixed, or if it would be the end of the HDR project."

"I hate to be the bearer of bad news, but so far all my tests indicate that the source of radioactivity is deep inside the hole. In fact, one of the preliminary tests shows that at the top of the well the reading is over 3,500 mBq. That's more than four times the regulated rate for Naturally Occurring Radioactive Material. I have a feeling that if we could get a reading from the bottom of the hole, it would be much, much worse."

Ashe stiffened, his eyes suddenly alert. "So what you're saying is the well *was* sabotaged."

She nodded. "I'd bet my life on it."

"But isn't there some way to fix this? Couldn't we extract the radioactive material from down the hole and then dispose of it like hazardous waste?"

She shook her head sadly. "I've been wondering the same thing. There are several problems. First of all, it would be dangerous for anyone to work the equipment. Not only would RESCUE be opening the door for a string of lawsuits, you'd never get government approval.

"Then there's the problem of spreading the contamination. We don't know what kind of material we're dealing with, there's no easy way to find out, and it would be very expensive to try. The source is twenty to twenty-five thousand feet down, so it would be virtually impossible to deal with it in any economically feasible way. If the contaminant is at the bottom of the hole, each time anything is brought out, it would spread more of the hazardous material upward. The cost of disposing of whatever comes out of there would be astronomical."

Ashe fumed, "Those bastards! Worthless, no-good bastards." He leaned against the wall and stared at the ceiling, his hands clenched as though every ounce of his anger abruptly demanded an outlet.

Suddenly slamming a fist through the thin inner wall of the mobile home's makeshift bedroom, he seethed, "Nathan was right. PetroCo paid someone to come that night. Andy got in the way, so one of their son of a bitch hired hands killed him." Ashe turned, his face dark with rage. "They won't get away with this!"

Rae watched in stunned silence as he paced back and forth. After a few moments she hesitantly asked, "Is the old Ashe back yet?"

Stopping in his tracks, he nodded. "I suppose so. Who was that other guy?"

"I don't know, but I wouldn't want to tangle with him."

Painfully stretching his bruised fingers, he laughed and said, "Neither would I."

It was just after sunset when the Bloodmobile finally pulled into the parking lot of the Red Cross regional headquarters building. With great care it was backed into its parking slot under a protective awning. The two volunteer nurses were exhausted, but pleased with the day's excellent turnout as they opened the doors. Each crawled slowly out of the vehicle, ready to wrap up a long day of work.

An instant after the first woman stepped onto the pavement, she felt a sharp sting in the back of her neck. She barely had enough time to swat at the source of her pain before she lost consciousness and slumped onto the concrete. Less than a minute later, the driver came around from behind the Bloodmobile, spotting her friend lying on the ground. Before she could make a sound, she, too, felt a burning sting, then crumpled limply onto the pavement.

Walters watched for a few moments, making certain no one was going to come to their aid. After tucking the sophisticated blowgun into his belt, he rushed to where the two women lay motionless. The darts were only an inch long, and he carefully pulled one out of the back of the second victim's neck. The first woman had managed to knock out the dart that hit her, and he searched frantically for it for several seconds. He couldn't leave without both of them. When he finally rolled her over, the silver needle gleamed on the pavement beneath her shoulder. After sticking both darts firmly into the cork on the side of the blowgun, he pulled the women behind the vehicle, where they would be out of sight while he worked.

In less than five minutes, he quietly trashed the inside of the Bloodmobile. Purposely leaving the impression he was searching for drugs, he carefully chose a few of the day's generously donated blood supply to take with him making certain Greenwall's was one of them. Grabbing an odd selection of needles and medical supplies, he zipped the loot inside his jacket, then nonchalantly walked into the quiet night.

It was dark by the time he reached the rented van parked several blocks away. He glanced at his watch. If everything went as planned, the second part of the job would be finished in less than twenty-four hours. Hopefully, by then he'd have some idea exactly what the finishing touch would be that could tie this reckless plan together.

Business came first, of course. Only when it was finished could he set his sights on finding the police department's prime suspect in the car theft. Jace Williams didn't know it yet, but he'd stolen the wrong person's car, and it was going to cost him more than just his brother's life.

# Chapter 6

Chuck Kelmar kicked off his shoes and flopped onto the oversize bed, never taking his eyes off the voluptuous woman at his side. He had no idea what her name was, and didn't really give a damn if he ever found out. The only thing he did care about was whether she had a condom with her. He was horny, not stupid.

"Well, do you have one or not?"

The tall redhead looked at him as if he were crazy. "One what?"

Kelmar knew when he'd met her downstairs in the casino she wasn't exactly brilliant, but her tantalizing figure and obvious willingness more than made up for her lack of brains. "A rubber, sweetheart. We need a rubber. Ever heard of safe sex?"

She abruptly stopped her clumsy yet still provocative striptease. "You mean *you* don't have one?"

He consciously shifted into his persuasive routine, hiding his irritation as he convincingly repeated his standard lie. "Remember what I told you downstairs, sweetie? I'm married. Not only am I married, but I'm married to a woman who hates sex. She thinks doing it once a month, straight missionary style, is too demanding. I haven't bought a condom in years. I just need someone to help me celebrate my big promotion. Couldn't you at least give me a blow job? I'll pay you."

"You poor baby." She walked to him and bent over, her ample cleavage just inches from his face. "I know you think I do this kinda thing all the time, but I don't!" Standing, she angrily started to button her blouse. "I'm outta here."

Kelmar grabbed her by the wrist and pulled her onto the bed next to him. It took all his willpower to control his rising temper. "We can still have fun, even without a rubber."

She tried to pull away, but he held her down with one hand, while ripping away her blouse and bra with his other until her breasts were free. He rolled easily on top of her, his weight keeping her in place while he licked and bit her neck and nipples. She struggled at first, then began to respond beneath him. A moan escaped her lips, and he relaxed his hold on her arms.

"Let me help you out of those," she said breathlessly, her fingers nimbly unzipping his slacks when he freed her hands. He anxiously stood, but when the slacks fell around his ankles, she swiftly landed three solid, totally unexpected kicks. The first one caught Kelmar off guard, sending him flying backward to the floor. He was not only shocked, his ankles were hopelessly tangled in his pants, leaving him vulnerable. By the time he saw the second kick coming, it was too late for him to defend himself.

The redhead's heel smashed his testicles like overripe tomatoes, shooting waves of nausea through him. Even as he recoiled from the second kick, she followed with another, this one catching him under the chin and snapping his head backward. Reaching down, she dug her long scarlet fingernails across his face, leaving thin trails of blood. While he lay semiconscious and gagging on the carpet she said, "If you call the police, I'll scream rape all the way to the courthouse." She waved her hand back and forth. "I've even got your precious skin buried under my nails as evidence."

He was in the fetal position, so she grabbed his slacks and yanked them. Digging out his wallet, she stuffed all his money into her purse, then went to the closet. Her blouse was ripped, so she dropped it on the floor and put on one

of his freshly starched, designer dress shirts. Keeping an
eye on his unmoving form, she rolled up the sleeves, knotted it at her slender waist, and gathered the rest of her things
in her arms.

A knock at the door made her freeze in her tracks. Peering through the peephole, she was relieved to see it was
only a hotel employee. When she threw open the door, he
started to speak, but stopped when he saw the man on the
floor. His eyes locked on hers as he asked, "Are you all
right?"

Even though his eyes were distorted by thick horn-rimmed
glasses, a primordial shiver still ran down her spine as her
instincts reacted to his nearness. She gingerly nodded to
answer his question.

"Looks like today's your lucky day. I'll make sure he
never bothers you again."

Although his words weren't threatening, those eyes made
her certain she was in more danger than she'd ever been in
her whole life. Clutching her purse to her chest, she squeezed
past him to run to the elevator. Furiously slapping the Lobby button until the doors finally slid closed, she swallowed
hard. *God, two creeps in one night. I gotta get out of this
town!*

Unfortunately, less than ten minutes later she realized
that was not meant to be—tonight or ever.

The next thing Kelmar knew, the phone was ringing. He
must have passed out, he couldn't really tell. Grabbing the
receiver, he mumbled, "This better be good."

"Chuck, how's it going? Are you believing this shit?
You're actually the president! God, I'm jealous. Listen, I
know it's getting late there, but I figured you'd be partying hard tonight."

Rolling painfully onto his butt, Kelmar fought down the
urge to moan as he asked, "Who the hell is this?"

"It's Karl. Karl Ross. Are you okay? Your voice sounds
just like it did a few years back when you tried to ride that

mechanical bull down at Gilley's. If I remember right, the bull won."

"That pretty much describes how I feel. Except that night at least I was smart enough to get stinking drunk first."

"What happened?"

Kelmar was beginning to think his balls might not explode if he moved, so he carefully shifted his weight. "Don't worry about it. What did you want?"

"I got a report today on the RESCUE site that I knew you'd be interested in. I've been trying to reach you all day. It really isn't anything I care to leave in a message, if you get my drift."

"Well? What is it?"

"They've shut it down! The last RESCUE people packed up and left. And get this—the entire site is blocked off with black and gold warning signs that say, EXTREME DANGER— HAZARDOUS MATERIALS—DO NOT ENTER. Our inside man says they're calling it quits. What the hell do you think is going on?"

A smile crawled through the pain as he lied, "I haven't got a clue, but it sounds like they just bought themselves a friggin' drilling rig. Have our legal department look into it." There was a strange sound behind him, a kind of dull thud. Realizing he wasn't alone, he quickly said, "I'll call you tomorrow."

Without even attempting to stand upright, Kelmar staggered toward the bathroom, where he was sure he would find the bitch that did this to him. Instead, it was a man in a crisp black suit.

Kelmar was too shocked to think fast. The man didn't seem dangerous. In fact, he was average-looking, wearing thick horn-rimmed glasses. But his hands were sheathed in surgical gloves, and he was holding a vial of a dark red liquid—*Blood!* "What the hell—?" Kelmar started to ask, but the expertly placed blow to his neck instantly severed his words.

* * *

Brada's eyes were wide when she walked into Nathan's office the next morning. He was asleep on his couch, and as she came in, he stretched and yawned. The *L.A. Times* was folded in her arms and held firmly against her chest.

Quietly she asked, "Did you read the newspaper or watch the morning news yet?"

Nathan was haggard-looking, still wearing the same clothes he had worn the day before. Running stiff fingers through his hair, he asked, "Do I look like I have?"

She shook her head. "Rough night?"

He slowly stood and walked to the window as he rubbed his eyes. "Couldn't sleep, so I came back here. I must have dozed off reading the latest information on the HDR site. It doesn't look good, you know."

When he turned toward her, Brada gasped. "Nathan! What happened to your arm?"

Nathan looked down, as shocked as she was to see a blood stain on the forearm of his shirt. "What the hell?" he muttered. As he pulled the shirt away from his skin, the crusty wound started to bleed again. The shirt and the first few layers of skin appeared to have a three-inch cut. The wound wasn't deep, it was clean and straight, as though it had been inflicted by a razor-sharp object.

Brada grabbed some tissues and handed them to Nathan. "How did this happen?"

A nervous laugh escaped his throat. "I know this sounds crazy, but I thought it was just a bad dream."

"Looks like a damned realistic dream to me."

He yawned and mumbled, "I'll say."

"Tell me about it," she said, folding several tissues together to form a makeshift bandage.

"I was asleep on the sofa last night when I thought I heard someone coming through my office door."

Brada stopped and looked at him. "What did you do?"

"Nothing. I laid absolutely still. I figured they'd leave when they saw me. When I barely opened my eyes, I thought

I saw something white—a rag or piece of cloth coming toward my face."

"And?"

"And nothing. That's all I remember."

"So how'd you cut your arm?" she asked.

He shook his head and shrugged. "Beats the hell out of me."

Brada laughed. "Nathan, old pal, I think you need to take that vacation you've been putting off. Right away. If someone had broken in here, the security alarm would've been going crazy. I must admit, though, you have quite an imagination." She walked to his desk and picked up an empty bottle of Dominus wine from the corner. "Since when do you drink?"

"I had a headache last night. I thought it would take the edge off. I would've sworn I only had one glass, though. There's no way I finished off the whole thing, even though my head does feel like it's going to implode."

Turning the bottle upside down, she skeptically raised her eyebrows when not even a drop fell onto the desk. "Dominus, no less. At least you have exquisite taste. A bad memory maybe, but good taste."

"Not me. That was delivered here yesterday." He rubbed his temples as he added, "And no, I don't know who sent it. Dinell's been working way too hard, so I insisted she take the afternoon off. When I got back here last night, it was on my desk with a note that said, 'Relax and enjoy.' Okay?"

Brada put the bottle in his trash can. "Okay, I'm not trying to pry. It's just, well . . ."

Nathan snapped, "Well, what?" After a few moments of awkward silence he walked to her, placing his hands on her shoulders. "Stop worrying about me, Brada."

Grazing a finger over the prickly stubble of his beard, she said, "Easier said than done. I've been worrying about you since we were kids."

"Then it's high time you stopped. The trip to D.C. will

be like a vacation, I promise. Besides, what could be easier than convincing a bunch of bureaucrats not to pass the Evans-Giles bill?"

Brada shrugged and headed for the door. "If you say so. I'll run down to the employee lounge and get you some real bandages from the first-aid kit."

Nathan said, "Wait, Brada. What did you want to tell me that was so important?"

She stopped, then walked back to him. "First, I need to ask you something. Will you be honest with me?"

He cocked his head, looking irritated as he grumbled, "Why wouldn't I be honest with you?"

She narrowed her eyes and asked, "What were you doing last night? Really. You can tell me."

Impatiently he muttered, "What I just told you. I couldn't sleep, so I came back here and caught up on my reading. Why the inquisition?"

Brada didn't answer; instead she just handed him the morning newspaper.


"Have you ever noticed that bad things come in streaks?" Rae asked as she stared out the window of the jet at the patchwork fields far below.

Ashe was seated next to her with his head tilted to one side. Without opening his eyes he replied, "Well, it all started with Andy's murder. The well was sabotaged. We've been trying to get back to California for, let's see . . ." He narrowly opened one eye to glance at his watch, then said, "Fourteen hours, eleven of which were spent sitting in an airport terminal. We look like death warmed over, and I don't know about you, but I'd kill for a shower right now. Is that enough to qualify as a streak of bad luck?"

"I certainly hope so, but . . ." She shrugged.

Opening both eyes, he sat up to glare at her. "Oh, God. But what?" He leaned across her to look out the window. "It doesn't look like any of the engines are on fire."

She laughed. "Shhh . . . You'll create mass hysteria. Nothing else is wrong. I was just thinking of a friend of mine who swears streaks of bad luck last for a whole year. My last one certainly did."

"Was that the year your husband died?"

She nodded. "It just seemed like every time I turned around, something else went wrong."

He reached over and took her hand in his. "I know this doesn't mean much, but I'm sorry. I've been working for RESCUE for years, and this is the first time things have been like this. I wouldn't have hired you if I thought it wasn't a great place to work. I swear."

With one look at his tired eyes she knew he was sincere. "I know you wouldn't have. I feel like I'm the one who should be apologizing."

"For what?"

She shrugged, turning her face to the small window.

Ashe leaned toward her. "If you're somehow implying that you leave a trail of destruction wherever you go, I'm not going to buy it. We had problems on the HDR site long before you even interviewed with RESCUE. In fact, six years ago when we first discussed it at a board meeting, Brada wanted to fund solar projects instead. She thought HDR was too risky."

Rae turned back to face him. "Why?"

"She wouldn't say. Women call it intuition, men call it gut instinct. Looks like whatever people choose to call it, she was right."

"I take it you don't believe in such things?"

"I believe we all make our own destiny. Unfortunately, the destinies other people are carving for themselves frequently screw up our own plans, but we all have a chance to react. It's how you react to adversity that shows your true character. You're a perfect example."

"How's that?"

"You could have withdrawn after you lost your husband, crawled into a shell and lived the rest of your life dwelling on the past. Instead, you built yourself a new career, a new life. You took control of your destiny." His eyes searched hers as he said, "I respect and admire you for it."

She closed her eyes and quietly sighed. "I'm not nearly as brave as you think. In fact, you should know that I decided a long time ago not to ever get involved with anyone again."

"Really?"

"Really."

"And you think that I'll just back away because of some silly decision you made at a crappy time in your life?"

"But it would be the wise thing to do. Trust me, I've thought about it a lot."

Ashe grinned. "Do you really think I'm the type that would just stand by and watch someone who needs help?"

Rae blushed, then defensively snapped, "What makes you think I need help?"

His smile widened. "Do you know you're cute when you're really pissed off?"

Rae tried to find fuel for her anger, but his lighthearted gaze kept disarming it. Finally she smiled with him. "Okay. Assuming I could use a little help, what makes you think you're qualified to provide it?"

"Because I believe in you."

His warm fingers wrapped around her hand, and she stared at them for a few seconds before she said, "I'm glad I'm here. Even if the HDR project has to be abandoned, at least I had the chance. Thank you."

With his free hand he caressed her cheek, then gently kissed her. As he slowly pulled away he said, "I know part of your problem. You think work and romance don't mix." He grinned and added, "But I've been trying not to fall for you ever since we met."

She pulled him back toward her, and this time she kissed him. Sighing, she said, "Besides, we may as well admit it, working together may not be a problem for long."

His eyes widened. "What gave you that crazy idea?"

"If the HDR project is dead, I'm out of a job. Remember?"

"Bullshit."

"Bullshit?"

"Rae, RESCUE doesn't hire people unless we need them. And that's Need with a capital N. Our people are our only truly valuable asset, or to be even more specific, their time, devotion, and energy are. First, you'll be in charge of re-evaluating the alternate sites we've already found. If my memory serves me, several were quite promising. Then, if none of them are still feasible, you can find one that is. We both know HDR can work. . . ."

She finished his sentence, ". . . *if* there weren't the economic constraints."

Ashe leaned against his head rest and pulled her close. "Someday, maybe people will understand that oil prices don't include the true price of burning hydrocarbons. Think how much money is spent every single day cleaning up our environment and coping with medical problems that are directly related to pollution. If people considered all the true expenses of relying on oil for energy, maybe they'd see oil is uneconomical now, instead of thirty or forty years from now when the supply starts to dwindle. But people like you and I will change all that. We'll do what's right." Softly kissing the top of her head, he added, "And you're going to have a hard time convincing me that *this* isn't right."

Rae was intrigued, as always, by his enthusiasm. It was easy to relax in his arms. Easy to feel the beat of his heart beneath her hand. Easy to leave behind years of frustration and loneliness.

Brada handed Nathan the *L.A. Times* and backed slowly toward the door. Sinking into his chair, he read the story on the front page of the business section:

NEWLY APPOINTED PETROCO CEO MURDERED
Charles "Chuck" Kelmar, who only two days ago was appointed President and Chief Executive Officer of PetroCo,

was viciously murdered in his hotel room in Las Vegas last night. Mr. Kelmar had been attending the National Conference of Petroleum Leaders when he was apparently killed in an attempted burglary.

Police have not released any information at this time, but did confirm that Mr. Kelmar struggled with his assailant or assailants, and that the apparent cause of death was multiple stab wounds.

PetroCo is listed on the New York Stock Exchange. A representative from the company stated that the news of Mr. Kelmar's death is a shock not only to his co-workers, but to everyone in the industry.

Nathan looked at Brada, his eyes wide. "You don't think that I . . ."

She hesitated as though she was going to say something but thought better of it, then said, "Of course not. It's just I know how you feel about him and, well . . . when I came in . . . there was blood on your shirt and the empty bottle of wine. You have to admit it looked a little suspicious."

Nathan slumped into his chair and stared at her. Grabbing the paper, he reread the article. "Thank God he was killed in Vegas. There's no way I could have done it."

"Actually, if you flew each way, there was plenty of time."

"Brada! You know I'm not a murderer!"

"I know, but does everyone else?" she asked.

"Listen to you! We both know Chuck Kelmar was a lowlife bastard who finally got what he deserved! What's wrong with you?"

"No! Can't you see? We'll lose everything we've worked for!" Shaking, Brada stormed out of his office. Stopping at Dinell's desk, she snapped, "You really should quit eavesdropping all the time."

Dinell blushed. "I—I was busy typing."

"Sure you were."

The plane jerked as the tires touched down. The massive engines roared for a moment, then purred as they taxied to the terminal. As they briskly walked to the baggage-claim area, Rae caught a glimpse of a local newscast. She grabbed Ashe by his shirtsleeve, and they watched together.

The story was brief. The police were not yet releasing any information about the murder of Charles Kelmar. As the reporter switched to the next story, Rae said, "Isn't that one of the guys RESCUE's been having trouble with?"

Ashe nodded, obviously deep in thought.

Rae said, "He looked really young. It's a shame."

Ashe's voice was laced with contempt as he said, "Actually, it couldn't have happened to a better guy. Chuck Kelmar was an asshole through and through. It sounds like someone finally got tired of his bullshit."

Rae turned to him, shocked. "Ashe, I'm surprised at you. Ever heard of respect for the dead?"

"People have to earn respect. Believe me, Kelmar never earned my respect while he was alive. Why should he have it just because he's dead?"

Karl Ross sauntered into his Midland office a little after nine in the morning. He'd stopped for his usual morning massage, and was relaxed as he mentally prepared for the day. His secretary was on the phone, grimly nodding. "What's wrong?" he asked as she hung up.

She was an older woman, biding her time until she could retire. Her voice cracked. "That was the chairman of the board's secretary. She said Mr. Kelmar was killed in Las Vegas early this morning."

"That's impossible. I talked to him on the phone last night. He didn't sound great, but he certainly wasn't dead."

"Really? You'd better call the police. I'm sure they'd want to hear about your conversation." She hesitated, then added, "She said an executive board meeting has been scheduled for one o'clock this afternoon, and you're expected to attend."

Ross leaned against the door frame of his office as his briefcase dropped to the floor. Thoughts were flashing through his mind so fast he couldn't sort them. Over the last few years only he and Kelmar had worked on what the two of them called the Protection Program. Even though a few key employees had been given occasional responsibilities, Kelmar was the only one who knew the entire scheme. Ross wasn't even sure if the members of the executive board knew of the activities Kelmar had undertaken to try to secure the future of the petroleum industry.

Kelmar had always been the one who attended board meetings and manipulated the budget to fund the program. Ross had accepted him as the mastermind from the beginning, never thinking about the future of the program if something should happen to him. Now, suddenly, he was gone.

The thought of additional power intrigued him more than he had imagined, yet at the same time it made his stomach tighten. He picked up his briefcase and practically stumbled into his office. Closing the door, he slid into the nearest chair. *What if the board appoints me president? Chuck's death may be the biggest chance I'll ever get!* A smile slowly spread across his face. The opportunity of a lifetime had just landed in his lap, and he had no intention of letting it pass him by.

Sunlight pierced the clouds hanging over the cemetery as the brief graveside service concluded. Cory Williams had been laid to rest just three days short of his thirteenth birthday amidst loud sobs from his mother and little sisters. His older brother said nothing. In fact, he had barely uttered a word since the night of the wreck, even though the police had grilled him for more than four hours.

Walters watched the austere service from far across the rolling hill, pretending to pay his last respects to another recently departed soul. His eyes never left the tall black boy who stood behind his mother—the one whose left arm was in a sling, rendered useless by a full cast, while his right hand rested on his mother's shoulder.

Had Walters not known what scum the kid actually was,

he might have been moved. Besides stealing his car, the kid
had been kicked out of school twice in the last six months
for starting fights. Without binoculars Walters couldn't see
if the boy was crying, but he doubted it. The kid looked
tough, even from a distance. And he'd been smart enough
not to leave a single fingerprint at the scene of the crime.
The police didn't have enough evidence to arrest him, at
least not yet.

A murmured chorus of "Amens" signaled the conclu-
sion of the service, and the mourners began to stir. Walters
watched every step the teenager took, until the time he slid
into the backseat of the old Ford and they drove away. Casually, Walters began the trek back to his own vehicle, but
there was no hurry. He'd already been to the kid's house.
He even knew where he hung out most of the time, the name
of the doctor who had treated his injuries, and that the kid
claimed he had broken his arm and hit his head in a makeshift game of football that turned violent.

Walters had to get the crossbow back soon, just in case
the kid, maybe for the first time in his life, decided to tell
the truth.

"That arm hurting you, Jace?"

He shook his head, staring out the window of the car. He
couldn't bear to look at his mother, to see the pain in her
eyes. Even as she drove, he knew she was staring at him in
the rearview mirror, searing a hole through him so the truth
would ooze out.

Thankfully, his sisters started fighting just as they arrived home. With his mother occupied, he rushed inside,
hoping to hide in the tiny bathroom. Instead, he stopped,
his mouth gaping open.

They didn't have much, and what little they did have had
been ransacked. "Oh, God," he mumbled, then ran back
outside. Stopping the rest of the family before they stepped
onto the narrow porch, he said, "Mama, I forgot to tell you

Aunt Vivian called. We were supposed to go to her house right after the funeral."

"What? But she didn't say anything at the service—"

"Nobody said anything at the funeral. It ain't polite. Just go. You don't want her getting all upset, now, do you?"

Taking her by the shoulders, he twisted her around, then grabbed each of his sisters by their sleeves. Opening the car doors for them, he ushered them nervously inside.

"What's wrong, Jace?" his mother asked, her eyes brimming with a fresh batch of tears.

"Nothing. My arm's starting to hurt. Gonna lay down for a while. Tell Aunt Viv I'm sorry I couldn't come." Slamming the car door, he watched until they were driving away, then rushed inside.

It took several minutes to find the phone, since it had been jerked off the wall. With a screwdriver Jace quickly opened the wall plate, reconnected the wires, and fiddled until he got a dial tone. Calling his aunt as fast as he could, he nervously tapped the wall. "Aunt Vivian?"

"Yes."

"Mama and the girls are coming over. Someone wrecked our house and I didn't want her to see it this way. Can you keep 'em busy for a couple of hours while I clean this mess up?"

"But—"

"Please, Aunt Viv. Mama has enough to worry about now."

"Okay. Should I send over my boys to help?"

"No. I can handle it. Thanks."

Jace scanned the rooms, one by one, straightening furniture along the way. It was a small house, only a kitchen, a living area, a bathroom, and two tiny bedrooms. When he opened the door to the bedroom he shared with his sisters, he froze.

The center of his pillow was pinned into the mattress with an oversize butcher knife. Moving closer, he recognized the knife his mother used to cut up chicken. Between it and the pillow was a neatly typed note:

> I know who you are. I know what you did. If you want your mother and sisters to live, you'd better think twice about talking to the police.
> I'll be in touch. Soon.

# Chapter 7

The letter was marked CONFIDENTIAL in bold red letters. It was addressed to *Detective in Charge—Homicide Division—Las Vegas Police Department,* and it was printed on plain white paper, the kind sold in reams at any office-supply store. The type appeared to be as ordinary as the paper, probably from a common laser or ink-jet printer.

Yet unlike most correspondence, this letter bore no postage, no postmark that might have revealed even a scrap of information about its sender. In fact, it seemed to have miraculously appeared on the front desk out of nowhere.

The detective on duty in Homicide that day held the envelope to the light to inspect it before he sheared its top edge with his letter opener, ignoring the fact it was addressed to his superior officer. He blew it open with a quick whiff of air, then unfolded the plain white paper and read the contents:

> I know it isn't right, but I can't afford to get involved in this. I didn't do it, I only had drinks with him in the casino and went to his room for some fun. We had a fight, but I didn't kill Charles Kelmar, and I don't know for sure who did.
>
> He told me there was a guy out to get him, even pointed him out to me in the casino. He said the guy was from California, some kind of ultra-paranoid ecology freak, and his name was Greenwall or something. They've hated each other for years because they're in some sort of competition.
>
> Maybe he's the one who did it, because I didn't. Don't

bother to look for me. I've already left this sleazy town and I'm never, ever coming back.

He held the letter for several minutes, reading it again while he plotted his next move. It could have been sent by any crackpot, and at first glance appeared to be written by one. Greenwall was a pretty common name, and California was certainly a state chock full of ecology nuts. But they had found a woman's blouse at the scene, and scratches on the victim's face. He thought for several minutes, deciding it was definitely worth his effort to follow through, and that Los Angeles would probably be his best place to start.

With the letter still in one hand, he picked up the phone, dialed the LAPD, and asked for Homicide. It didn't take long to find out the basics: Greenwall's first name was Nathan; he was head of a multimillion-dollar alternative-energy company; the people of California loved him for creating jobs, his environmentally sound business principles, and his generosity to charities; his reputation was spotless, far from a criminal stereotype.

After ten minutes on the phone, he was confident he had solved the Kelmar murder investigation, and the killer was the type the media loved—stinking rich, with a long, hard fall ahead.

Logically, Walters knew better than to lurk around in the state he was in. It had been well over seventy-two hours since he'd slept for longer than an hour or two, yet the extreme fatigue made him feel more jumpy than tired. He was certain the nervous exhaustion gave him an edge, somehow sharpening his senses instead of dulling them. All he had to do was track down the kid, find out what he knew about the crossbow, then kill him. Easy. In no time at all he would be out of California, as he should have been right after his late-night visit to RESCUE to set up Greenwall for Kelmar's murder.

Finding Jace Williams turned out to be the easiest thing he had done in ages, in spite of the fact the kid hadn't been home since the day of the funeral. He was exactly where he had expected him to be, talking with a few friends outside the youth center on the edge of his neighborhood.

From a distance, Walters studied the scene. Blending in would definitely be impossible. Well-dressed, middle-aged white men didn't hang out on street corners at this hour of the night. He would have to settle in and wait. Several hundred yards from the center, he eased behind a garbage can to watch the boys with his starlight binoculars until it was time for the chase.

By the time the gathering finally broke up almost an hour later, Walters had almost nodded off. Caught off guard, he was shocked when his first attempt to stand gave him a vicious leg cramp that almost sent him tumbling onto the concrete. His foot banged the can as he rolled to one side, proclaiming his position with a resonating metallic clank. Holding perfectly still, he couldn't believe no one was alerted by his writhing agony. *Why should they? Jace Williams has no idea what's in store for him!*

With his right calf muscle on fire, he futilely rubbed it, trying to increase the circulation before he dared to stand again. There wasn't time for him to wait for the cramp to pass. In spite of the pain, he forced himself upright, expending an incredible amount of effort. The hunt was on.

Although some of his friends headed down the street the opposite way, Jace started walking directly toward him. Drawing his gun from the holster inside his jacket, Walters expertly screwed on a silencer without his eyes ever leaving the approaching boy. He knew he had to be careful. The kid had to drop but not die. This kid knew about the crossbow, probably even had it. He would make him spill his guts before he finished him off.

Although Walters was tempted to fire just to end his personal torture, years of practice made him hold back until exactly the right moment. Squeezing the trigger, he watched for a split second—but Williams didn't fall like all the others before him. At the precise instant Walters fired, the boy wheeled around to answer a question shouted from the door of the youth center.

The bullet whizzed within a quarter inch of his thigh, then thumped into the concrete curb on the far side of the street. Jace whirled around, his questioning, stunned eyes meeting his for an instant, and in that instant he knew what lay ahead. The boy's bloodcurdling scream alerted everyone in the youth center as he came to his senses and ran. Six or seven kids seemed to come out of nowhere, all shouting and running in a panicked frenzy.

Walters stared in shock for several seconds, frozen in surprise that he had actually missed. He glanced at the people running up and down the street, and knew he had blown his chance. With his right calf still cramped into a rockhard knot, he half limped, half ran as fast as he could toward the rented van.

The initial hysteria slowed his adversaries, but youth was in their favor. As he approached the van, a rock flew past his head, shattering the driver's window. He dropped, rolling onto his side as he began firing in the direction he had just come. Bodies dropped; screams filled the still night.

Walters wasn't used to his victims fighting back. In spite of his lack of aim, two bullets struck home. One boy screamed as he went down, the bullet shattering his kneecap, the second silently dropped when a bullet caught him just above his right eye. "Got ya!"

Watching their friends collapse made the others think twice about the wisdom of their chase. They scattered for cover, then froze like frightened quail. Two retreated, but the other three managed to find hiding places along the side of the deserted road.

In the blink of an eye Walters ran to where the wounded boy lay, shocked to see it wasn't Williams after all. The boy was rocking, his knee clutched to his chest as he wailed.

Walters didn't waste any time. He grabbed him by his hair and dragged his body in front of his own. Shoving the gun under the boy's chin, he shouted, "I'll kill him if any of you even think about trying to save his ass!"

Walters began to move backward, using the boy as a shield. No one moved. No one even breathed. When he felt the van against his back, he shoved the shaking, whining boy away from him, carefully keeping him in his line of fire. Climbing quickly into the van, he sped away.

It was several miles before reality sunk in—Jace Williams was still very much alive. Alive and scared.


Across town, the night was endless. Each minute seemed to click audibly away. Staring at the ceiling revealed nothing new, not even some trivial morsel of information that would help fit the pieces of the puzzle together. Sleeplessness was not unusual—in fact, it had been a part of a lonely existence for years. But tonight was different. For the first time in years, the plan seemed to be unraveling.

Something had gone wrong. Terribly wrong. Some people might believe Chuck Kelmar had been struck down by random violence in a town where such things happened all the time. But it wasn't true, it couldn't be. Somewhere out there was Chuck's killer, and his killer was tied to the plan. But how?

The ache deep inside was too fresh to allow logic to creep in. The window to the future had exploded into a million meaningless slivers with the news of the murder. Without Kelmar's help, RESCUE might survive, might actually thrive. So much work, such a complicated scheme, ruined by the senseless death of a close friend.

A silent vow was made sometime before that timeless night turned into morning—Chuck's death would be avenged, and somehow, some way, Nathan Greenwall would die a poor, miserable man.

* * *

Rushing to catch Rae as she walked down the hall, Ashe suddenly slowed his pace, falling in a few steps behind her to enjoy the view. As he watched the swing of her hair, the subtle but sexy motion of her hips, he wished he could sweep her into his arms, hold her, make love to her over and over again. When he tapped her shoulder, she greeted him with a smile so genuine it seemed to touch his heart.

That smile made him realize how different this relationship was from any he had experienced in the past. Before there had always been periods of strained silence, moments when each person wondered where they were headed, what their future together held. Yet with Rae the sizzling undercurrent of sexual tension could actually take his breath away. It was always there, barely covered by the fabric of their growing personal and professional relationships.

"Did you get your things unpacked?" he asked as he stirred his morning coffee and strolled at her side.

Rae rolled her eyes and sarcastically replied, "Oh, sure. The radiation gave me super powers, so I flew through all fifteen boxes my parents shipped in no time at all; then I rushed out to save the world from certain doom. It was a long, hard night, but very satisfying."

Ashe didn't playfully grab her as he would have liked, since they were walking down the central hall of RESCUE's headquarters. Instead, he merely stopped dead in his tracks. After several steps Rae realized he was no longer beside her and glanced back at him curiously. Ashe frowned and shook his head. "Life certainly isn't fair."

"You're forty-some odd years old and you just figured that out?" Rae snapped. "No wonder the people around here think you're some kind of genius. I'm impressed."

He jutted his lower lip into a quivering pout. "I'm jealous. You got super strength and can fly. All I got from the HDR site was a nasty case of poison ivy in a very embarrassing place."

Rae smiled and moved closer to him as she whispered sexily, "Poor baby. Want me to scratch it for you?"

Ashe was about to answer when they both heard Dinell right behind them. "Excuse me," she said.

Rae visibly jumped and blushed, while Ashe managed to politely say, "Good morning, Dinell. What can we do for you?"

"There's a woman in Mr. Greenwall's office who insists on seeing someone 'with authority' right away. She asked for Brada first, but Brada already left for the National Scientific Research Contest this morning. She won't be back for a few days."

Ashe asked, "How did you end up with her?"

"She was making a pretty big scene in the lobby, so someone brought her up to see Mr. Greenwall. Unfortunately, he won't be in until late this afternoon, if at all. He's attending a golf tournament to raise funds for leukemia research." Dinell caught her breath, adding, "I hate to beg, Ashe, but this woman will not leave. Could you please meet with her for just a few minutes?"

"Do you have any idea what she wants? Who she is?"

Dinell shook her head. "Not a clue. She won't even tell me her name."

Ashe looked at Rae, winked, and said, "Rae and I will both talk to her. Sounds like it might be educational."

Dinell sighed and said, "Thanks. Follow me, you can use Mr. Greenwall's office. She's already inside."

They followed Dinell to the executive suite, past her secretarial station, then into Nathan's office. Dinell quickly introduced Ashe and Rae, then slipped out the door, closing it silently behind her. Ashe leaned against Nathan's desk and asked, "What can RESCUE do for you, Mrs.—?"

"Prosser. Margaret Prosser."

Ashe nodded, immediately recognizing the last name. "Good morning," he said, extending his hand.

Margaret was in her mid-fifties, with short gray hair neatly combed away from her face. She looked skeptically at Ashe and asked, "Exactly what do you do here?"

He glanced at Rae, then replied, "I'm head of one of RESCUE's primary divisions. Vice President of Geothermal Exploitation is my exact title."

Her eyes narrowed. "How long have you worked here?"

"I've been with the company since it was founded eight years ago. I'm sure I can help you, if you'll tell me what the problem is."

She hesitated, asking, "So you know Brada Stevens personally?"

Ashe shrugged. "I've known and worked with her for years. Why?"

She turned her probing gaze to Rae. "What about you? How long have you worked here?"

Rae started to answer, but Ashe held up his hand. "Mrs. Prosser, Ms. Majors is a loyal RESCUE employee. We'd both like to help you in any way we can, but you'll have to trust us. Your daughter did."

The woman seemed to relax slightly. "I know I sound paranoid, but I think I have good cause to be. You see, it's only been a few days since Marilyn died, and I guess I . . . I just haven't . . . ." As she started to cry, Rae handed her a box of tissues.

Ashe quietly said, "Take your time, Mrs. Prosser."

After a few seconds, she regained enough composure to carry on. "You're right. Marilyn did trust you, so I should too."

Ashe was aware of everything that had happened, but for Rae's sake he explained. "Marilyn wrote an excellent thesis on a hypothetical new way to drill wells which she called TriPlate technology. She was in a car accident shortly after she met with Brada to discuss her work. Is that correct, Mrs. Prosser?"

The woman nodded. "I went to her apartment yesterday, you know, to pack her things." She snapped open the purse on her lap and after taking a deep breath added, "I found this." In her hand was a small journal. "It was hidden in the same place she's been hiding things since she was a little girl. When she was six, she hid my Mother's Day present inside a cereal box in the back of the pantry. She was so proud of herself. I can't believe she still does that, I mean, did . . ."

Rae asked, "Can I get you something to drink, Mrs. Prosser?"

She shook her head. "The police had already gone through all her things, both at my house and at her apartment, before the grand jury investigation. Of course, they didn't find this journal."

Ashe asked, "Didn't they ask you where your daughter might have hidden important items?"

"Yes, but I'd forgotten. Besides, the day of the accident she called and told me to be careful for a while—not to trust anyone and not to talk to a soul about her work. When I asked her why, all she said was that I shouldn't worry, I should just be careful. If only I'd known." She took a calming breath. "When I read these notes, I knew I had to do something. I didn't believe it at first, but now I'm certain she really was murdered."

Rae asked, "Have you talked to the police?"

She shook her head. "What she did . . . I . . . I was disappointed that Marilyn would even think of doing such a thing, of selling her brilliant idea to the highest bidder. But then I realized how desperate she must have been, how scared—especially in the end when she tried to do the right thing. She was only twenty-four years old. She and her father never got along, but if I'd known how badly she needed money, I'd have found a way to help her." She stopped talking and sat for several seconds, just staring at the book in her hands.

Ashe asked, "Would you mind telling us what the journal says, or letting us read it?"

She didn't say a word. She merely extended her hand to give him the book.

Walking over, he stood next to Rae and carefully began

flipping through the pages until he found the last entry. Just from casual observation it was obvious the book was a diary of sorts, where Marilyn had recorded both notes about her studies as well as her personal feelings.

Together Ashe and Rae read the last entry:

> I can't live with myself. Even though KT says these kinds of deals are done every day, all this secrecy just doesn't feel right. Even if it is expensive, I think I can patent the TriPlate design myself in a few years. It must be really good, or they wouldn't want it so much! Five thousand dollars a month seems like such a fortune right now—but I've made it this far without much. Somehow I can make it a little while longer.
>
> I called Brada Stevens at RESCUE and set up a time to meet her tonight. Maybe she can help get me out of this mess. She seems to be the only one I can trust. On the phone she said the oil company would be upset, but she promised RESCUE could help. I hope she's right.

Ashe glanced at Rae, then asked, "Did you read the entire journal, Mrs. Prosser?"

She nodded.

Ashe began pacing across the office, obviously in deep thought. After several moments he quietly asked, "Are there any names or places specifically mentioned?"

She nodded, then said, "Several people are mentioned a few times, but most of them are referred to by their initials. I think the person she refers to as 'KT' is one of her engineering professors. She refers to another person who was involved in this awful business with the oil company several different times, but never uses a name. Can you tell me something?"

"We can try," Ashe said.

"Is what Marilyn did illegal?"

He shook his head and said, "Not at all. It was Marilyn's right to do whatever she wanted with her idea."

"Then why couldn't she ever tell anyone? Why was it all such a big secret."

"Because some oil companies don't want the public to know there are alternatives to the current methods, at least not yet. They buy technological breakthroughs and bury them until they decide the time is right—from a profit standpoint, of course. By keeping these deals secret, it minimizes outside pressure from companies like RESCUE."

Mrs. Prosser sighed, apparently relieved her daughter hadn't died a criminal.

Rae asked, "Did Marilyn mention anything about where her research work was done, or where she kept the information?"

"No, but she didn't have to. I know where it is."

Ashe and Rae looked at her in disbelief as they simultaneously asked, "Really?"

"She doesn't have a computer of her own, and she didn't feel comfortable using the ones they provide at school. I've always typed her papers for her. I'm a medical transcriber at MedicData. I typed a thesis for her called 'TriPlate Penetration and Augmentation' a couple of weeks ago. It was very technical, so I typed exactly what she wrote, just as I do for the doctors. Of course, her terminology is different than what I'm used to, but in some ways it's the same." She beamed with pride. "She was very smart, you know."

Ashe said, "I've never seen her work, but I'm sure your daughter was brilliant, Mrs. Prosser. Do you have a copy of the TriPlate papers?"

"No, but the file would be stored on my computer. I have a personal subdirectory for that sort of thing. It has a password so no one else can look at the files. I may even have kept a copy of her sketches, too. They're very good. She almost majored in architecture, but she changed to engineering at the last minute."

"Would you mind if we come with you and get copies of the information? I promise you, RESCUE will handle your daughter's work with the dignity it deserves. We won't exploit it."

She seemed nervous again. "You can't come to where I work. We're not supposed to use company time to do personal things." Sitting a little straighter, she added, "I didn't. I always went in early and typed her papers on my own time, but I still wouldn't want anyone to know."

"Could we meet you somewhere after work? You could copy the file onto a diskette. We'll put it in a safe deposit box and convince the police to reopen her case."

"I can do that. Why don't you come by my office after work tonight? Since I'm going to be late getting to work this morning, I probably won't be finished until about six. I'll meet you in the parking lot."

Rae handed her a note pad, and she jotted down the address. They thanked her profusely. Just before she left, she turned to say, "I knew as soon as I came into this building and saw all those beautiful plants and the waterfall that you were good people. Marilyn will be at peace knowing her hard work won't be ignored. Thank you for helping me."

"No, thank you. It took a lot of courage to come here, and we appreciate it," Ashe said.

As Ashe and Rae watched the woman disappear into the hallway, the phone rang. Dinell answered it and handed it to Ashe. "It's Brada."

"Ashe? Are you there?" Brada shouted.

"Yep. Where are you?"

"St. Louis. They're getting ready to unveil the entries. Supposedly there are several energy ideas worth our time."

"Sounds fascinating. You aren't going to believe what just happened here, Brada. Marilyn Prosser's mother stopped by."

There was a brief pause where Ashe could only hear loud whoops and yells, then Brada said, "Sorry about that. This place is a zoo. What did you say about Marilyn?"

"Her mother has the TriPlate designs. We're going to meet her tonight to get a copy."

"You're kidding!"

"You haven't heard the best part. Marilyn kept a journal.

We may be able to nail those bastards at PetroCo yet. It may not have specific names, but it does have initials, which should be enough to get the police involved again. I'm especially excited about discovering which one of her professors was involved."

"I think I'd better catch a plane back there. This sounds too good to be true."

"No need. We're going to put all the information in a safe deposit box where PetroCo can't get their hands on it. Then we'll present copies to the police. We'll handle it. I promise. Besides, with the HDR problems we're having, this will be a good distraction for Rae and me for the next few days."

There was another loud commotion on Brada's end of the conversation. She finally said, "I'd better head back."

"Don't worry. We've got it under control."

Ashe could hear her reluctance as she replied, "Okay. I'll see you in a couple of days."

She hung up, and Ashe turned to Rae, who was walking back into Nathan's office. He followed her inside and closed the door.

"I'm really getting paranoid," Rae said, shaking her head.

"Why?"

"The whole time you were talking, I was worried who would hear. Dinell was so busy listening she didn't even pretend to work."

"Dinell wouldn't hurt a soul."

"Let's hope not. This whole thing just doesn't feel right." Rae turned to sit down, when she saw something out of the corner of her eye. Walking to the far end of Nathan's office, she pointed at a black plastic box plugged into the lower part of the wall. "What is that thing, anyway?"

Ashe crouched to study it. "I haven't got a clue." He pulled it out of the electric socket and examined it more closely. "I'll ask Nathan when he gets in, but it looks like some sort of filter."

"I was just curious. It wasn't there the day I was interviewed."

Ashe cocked his head and looked at her. "How can you be so sure?"

"I noticed everything about this office that day. How the liquid crystal walls were constructed, the furniture, everything. I remember seeing that electrical outlet and thinking how ingenious it was that they encased the wiring in mirrors so it wouldn't be as noticeable when the crystals were clear."

"You never cease to amaze me. What do you think about Marilyn's mysterious death?"

Rae was quiet for a few seconds. She turned to stare out the window. "I'm really worried about her mother."

"Just because people heard about our meeting?"

Rae nodded. "I think she's in deep trouble. Emotionally, and physically."

Ashe said, "Emotionally, I'm afraid we can't help her much, except possibly by making certain her daughter's work is put to good use. I'm not sure why you're worried about her physical well-being. Only a couple of RESCUE people know about the information she has, so I don't think there's anything to be concerned about, at least not yet. Once the police get involved and the people implicated start getting nervous, then she'll need protection."

"I'm sure you're right," Rae answered unenthusiastically.

"You don't sound very excited about Mrs. Prosser coming forward." When his eyes met hers, he shook his head and sighed. "Oh, no. I've seen that look before. What could possibly be wrong?"

Rae attempted a smile and shrugged. "I just have a gut feeling that we've made a mistake. It's probably nothing. Forget it."

"What's probably nothing?" Ashe asked.

"Marilyn's diary," Rae said. "We should have kept the diary."

\* \* \*

Power corrupts quickly, or at least it did in the case of Karl Ross. Although he had been appointed acting president of PetroCo only until the board could call a formal meeting, for the last forty-eight hours he had lived like a king.

When the cell phone in his shirt pocket rang, he expected it to be his new secretary for the fourth time that morning. He finished merging into traffic on the crowded expressway, then answered the phone with a curt "Yes. What now?" He was shocked when he heard an unfamiliar woman's voice ask if he was Karl Ross. "Who is this?" he asked without answering the question.

"That's not important. I've always worked with Kelmar, but now that he's dead, I suppose I'll have to deal with you."

Ross didn't like the demanding tone of voice, but he knew better than to irritate the type of people Kelmar had on contract. "This is Ross. What kind of work did you do for Kelmar?"

"Let's say that I'm well aware of the secret Protection Program and that I've been an integral part of it since its inception."

He tightly gripped the soft leather steering wheel as sweat began to trickle down his brow. Over the knot in his throat he said, "I understand."

"I was hoping you would."

"Why are you calling on this line?" he asked nervously, then added, "Cell phones aren't secure."

"I didn't have a choice. We have a problem that requires immediate attention."

Ross attempted to sound professional by second-guessing the reason for the call. "I see. So you need permission to handle this 'problem' according to a certain plan of action? Or do you just need authorization to spend money?" The silence at the other end of the line went on for so long, Ross finally said, "Hello? Are you still there?"

The reply was cold, every word enunciated precisely as though immeasurable willpower was required merely to speak. "Listen, Mr. Ross. I realize that you have only attained your position of authority quite recently. Kelmar and I had an understanding. Do you wish to continue the relationship or not?"

"First, tell me what you perceive to be such a major problem, then I'll decide."

"Are you familiar with the Marilyn Prosser incident?"

"Extremely." He began sweating profusely. Glancing over his shoulder, he promptly swerved his new Mercedes convertible across four lanes of traffic, pulled off the expressway, and cut the engine.

"There's been a complication."

The woman finally had his full attention, but all Ross heard was silence. "So tell me," he said impatiently.

"Tell you, my ass. Either you're going to commit to continue the deal Kelmar and I had, or I'm not going to feed you any information. Ever."

"What was your deal?"

"Twenty-five thousand a month. Cash."

"What?"

"You heard me. It was actually much more complicated than that, but that's what I'll settle for now."

"No shit! I wouldn't think for that price you'd have to settle for anything!"

Moments ticked away in silence before the irritated voice continued, "You're wasting valuable time, Mr. Ross. The Prosser deal is about to blow PetroCo out of the water, and you're dangling on an unsecured phone line haggling over a few measly bucks."

"Okay. You win. Whatever you want."

"Wise choice. Prosser's mother has copies of the Tri-Plate files, plus some sort of diary her daughter kept that may name names. She's going to turn them over to RESCUE tonight, along with a copy of her designs. I'm sure you realize why that meeting cannot take place. Margaret Prosser must be eliminated immediately, and I believe Professor Tolmin has become a liability as well. He's the only true connection, the only way they can trace the murder directly back to PetroCo."

Ross merely leaned his head on the steering wheel and mumbled, "Oh, shit!"

# Chapter 8

Jace Williams' body quivered as streaks of white-hot agony radiated up his arm. He hadn't slept all night, his stomach was screaming for food, and his broken arm felt like it was going to burst through its cast. His house was only eight blocks from where he was hiding, yet it might as well have been halfway across the universe. For the second time in only a few days, he was stranded, afraid to go—yet equally afraid to stay.

Scanning the street from his hiding place in the weeds beside a bridge abutment, he continued to watch for the van from last night while he tried to think. What else could go wrong? The police were looking for him again. Two of his friends had been taken away in ambulances. His baby brother was dead. And for some crazy reason a gun-toting white goon was trying to kill him!

Closing his eyes, he rested his chin on his knee and lost himself in whimpering self-pity. Had he not been so absorbed in his own misery, he might have seen the same van drive under the bridge twice in only five minutes, once in each direction. It was not the van from last night. Although it was a similar style, this one was a rich shade of champagne beige, and all its windows were not only still intact, they were so darkly tinted the interior was practically undetectable.

Minutes passed while Jace simply rested. Soon the tears subsided, giving way to a weariness that ached to his bones. An innocent noise brought him back to reality—the faint crunch of brush slightly up and behind where he was crouched. Although he didn't want to move, he was compelled to look, to see what could be making the hair on the back of his neck stand on end.

When Jace turned his head, the chill of a gun barrel dragged against the flesh of his neck. Without moving, he merely closed his eyes and waited. *Jesus, help me!*

Instead of quietly accepting his fate, Jace dropped his face on his knees and cried, "Just tell me why you want to kill me. What did I ever do to you?"

For several seconds neither of them spoke. Jace was too tired and hungry to fight, but he still wanted to know. He took a deep breath and again pleaded, "Why, man? I didn't do nothing to you."

Walters pulled the gun away from the boy's head and sat down next to him where he was partially hidden by tall clumps of weeds. Keeping the barrel pointed directly at him, he managed to hide the gun behind his free arm so that passersby would not be alerted. Walters, too, appeared to be haggard, far more so than the boy. With a smile he simply said, "You stole my car."

Jace half laughed, half whined, "So you're going to kill me? Nobody kills somebody just for taking their frigging car. So what if I did wreck it? Don't you have any freaking insurance?"

"There was something inside the trunk that wasn't insured. Something I know you have. You picked the wrong car to steal. You made a mistake. A very big, fatal mistake. Unless, of course, you show me where it is."

Jace was trembling again, tears streaming down his face as he sputtered, "I don't know what you're talking about. Really."

Walters was too tired to laugh, but he managed a smile. "Let's not play games. You've been smart enough not to take my little toy to the police, which means you're a pretty shrewd kid. Just give it to me and I won't kill you. You have to live with knowing you killed your own brother. That seems like enough punishment all by itself."

Jace hung his head and shrugged. He knew the man was right. Raising his head, he watched the cars whoosh past just a hundred feet below, and he wished he were already dead. After several seconds he finally asked, "How do I know you aren't going to pop me after I show you where it is?"

Walters chuckled. "Guess you'll have to trust me." Forcing Jace to stand, he added, "You're going to walk nicely down this little hill and get in my van. I parked right on the other side of the abutment where you couldn't see me. I'm going to tie you up, then we'll go for a ride. I have some urgent business to take care of, but as soon as it gets dark, we'll find that nice silver briefcase together, won't we?"

Jace shrugged. "Like I have a choice? What kinda business do you do? Kill people?"

"Among other things. And I'm quite good at it."

"That's a relief. I wouldn't want to be killed by someone who was bad at it! Who are you gonna kill today besides me?"

"A sense of humor. I like that. Today I'm taking out two people—one loyal to the cause, one not."

"Why kill someone who's loyal?"

Shaking his head, Walters sighed. "You have no idea how complicated life can be. Sometimes sacrifice is part of getting where you want to be. For now, you can sit tight in the van. We'll have lots of time to talk later."

"I don't think we have much to talk about."

"Sure, we do. We can talk about never being able to walk, or even crawl again. I'll bet a lot of things would be pretty damned hard to do without any kneecaps, and if you decide to be stubborn and keep your little secret, that's where we'll start. I suppose your buddy could tell you how painful it is. Now get off your butt and slowly, very slowly start down the hill. I'm sure you're smart enough to figure out where my gun will be aimed. By the way, if you think you can get some kindhearted driver to help you, they'll end up just as dead as your other friend did. Understand?"

Jace nodded. A few minutes ago he would have welcomed death, but now adrenaline surged through his veins, making him momentarily forget the pain. All he could think of was his mother. How could he let her bury two sons in less than a week? The answer was simple. He couldn't.

The first few strides were easy enough, but Jace knew one of his next steps would either kill him or save him. A slight break in the oncoming traffic signaled his opening. He closed his eyes, then pretended to trip over a stone. As his body impacted the ground, he tucked into a ball, purposely accelerating like a rock, falling recklessly toward the road below. A scream ripped painfully out of his throat as he rolled atop his broken arm over and over again, half wondering whether it would be a bullet or the impact of a car that would end his miserable existence.

His excruciating trip down the steep incline landed him exactly where he knew it would—sprawled in the center of the closest lane of traffic. Chaos followed. Jace drew himself even tighter into a ball and listened to the horrifying sound of squealing brakes and crunching metal for what seemed like an eternity.

When he finally had the nerve to open his eyes, he was surrounded by a mass of wrecked cars. Somehow, the cars had managed to dodge him, but not each other. Before he had time to wonder what happened to the man with the gun, he tried to move and a new flash of pain ripped through him. Somewhere deep in his mind, he knew he should run, but instead he relaxed, and welcomed the growing darkness that enveloped him.

Ashe glanced over Rae's shoulder after he quietly walked into her office. She was so absorbed in whatever she was working on that she didn't notice he was behind her. His lips grazed her ear as he whispered, "Are you nervous?"

Rae practically jumped out of her chair. She tried to act

as though he hadn't startled her, shaking her head. "No. Why do you ask?"

He pointed at the pad of paper in front of her. It was covered with hundreds of doodles—some words, some drawings—but none of it made any sense. "I thought you were going to spend the morning outlining the steps needed to continue the HDR work." Ashe picked up her paper and pretended to try to read it, adding, "I don't mean to be critical, but I find this a little hard to understand. Maybe you can decipher it for me."

She tossed down her pencil in frustration. "Okay, so I'm having a little trouble concentrating. I told you already, I have a really bad feeling about Mrs. Prosser. I can't explain it, I just *know* we shouldn't have let her leave."

"And how could we have made her stay? She didn't exactly invite us along."

Rae scowled. "Good point."

Ashe perked up. "I just spoke with Brada again. She's very excited about one of the projects presented at this year's contest. It may be the solution to the avian mortality problem our Wind division has been having."

"Avian mortality?" Rae asked with raised eyebrows.

"Birds inadvertently committing hara-kiri by flying into high-speed wind turbines. I know it sounds crazy, but in some areas it's a major concern. Even though electric lines kill far more birds than wind generators, any energy system we market needs to be as environmentally friendly as possible. Obviously, RESCUE would rather not become a contributor to the mortality rate of any species."

Each day since she'd started work Rae had learned some new, intriguing bit of information. Her curiosity was obvious by the tone of her voice. "Are certain types of birds more prone to having accidental run-ins with the blades?"

"Surprisingly enough, yes. Raptors, birds of prey like eagles and hawks, have the highest risk of being killed by the turbines. Part of the problem is they like to perch on top of the structures, where they can watch for quarry."

Rae's face lit up, and she smiled slyly. "How interesting, and what a great idea!"

"Excuse me?"

"Maybe the turbine problem could be used to solve our HDR predicament."

Ashe pulled up a chair and sat down next to her. "This I gotta hear."

She shook her head. "Not the turbines themselves. The way I see it, whoever sabotaged the HDR well is like a raptor. Somehow they have managed, figuratively speaking, to perch on top of our equipment and wait to attack when we're least expecting it."

She had piqued Ashe's curiosity. "And . . ." he urged.

"And . . . maybe we need to toss out some more bait and see if anything swoops down to take it. Except this time we'll be watching and waiting to see which vulture strikes."

Smiling from ear to ear, he said, "Lady, I truly like your style."

With shaking hands Margaret Prosser copied her daughter's thesis file onto two different diskettes. She tucked one in her purse, the other in the envelope she had already addressed, then pulled out her bottom desk drawer as far as it would go. She removed a file marked LOW PRIORITY from the very back, and stood so she could glance around the office. On her tiptoes, she could barely see over the tops of all the cubicles. Everyone seemed to be busy working, so she sat down and discreetly opened the file.

The last papers in the back of the folder were Marilyn's original sketches. Tears welled in her eyes as she held them in her hands. One by one she folded them, making certain they were perfectly creased before tucking them in her purse beside the diskette.

Margaret took a deep breath, trying her best to focus on the work waiting at her fingertips. Still too nervous to begin, she carried the envelope past the ladies' room to the U.S. Mail chute in the hallway. Once she dropped it inside, she felt an overwhelming sense of relief. As quickly as she could, she hurried back to her desk, inserted the tape in her transcription machine, put on her headphones, and began to work. Years of blocking out everything made hours pass quickly as Margaret concentrated on doing her job.

At 5:55 that afternoon, she was still so absorbed in her work she didn't think twice about the repairman who stopped just outside her cubicle. After setting up a stepladder, he crawled atop it to work on the overhead fluorescent lights. He was dressed in the standard maintenance uniform, drab gray overalls with his name embroidered on the pocket, and he nodded politely at Margaret when she hesitantly glanced his way. Most of her co-workers were busily wrapping up their day's work, eager to leave as soon as possible. It didn't strike her as odd that none of the light bulbs he replaced were burned out, since she looked away from her work only once, then focused back on the doctor's voice stammering through her headphones.

Fifteen minutes later, a sharp pain in her side made her freeze, her fingers poised in midair above her keyboard. There was no time to scream because her mouth was simultaneously covered by a cloth that reeked of chemicals. For a fleeting moment before she passed out, she could see the repairman's image reflected in her computer screen.

Instinctively she knew it was the same bastard who'd killed Marilyn, even before he leaned close to whisper, "I'm sorry it had to be this way. I know you meant no harm. But I had to agree to kill you, so I could kill that deceitful professor who got Marilyn involved in all this in the first place. That's the way is has to be."

"She's late," Ashe said, his fingers rhythmically tapping the steering wheel as they waited in the parking lot outside Margaret Prosser's office building.

Rae placed her hand on his, effectively stopping his incessant drumming. "She didn't say she'd be here at exactly six tonight. Calm down. Worrying isn't going to make things better."

He scowled playfully at her. "I thought you were nervous about all this."

"I am."

"You don't act like it." He suddenly remembered how calm she had been at the HDR site after they were exposed. "But then again, you seem to work pretty well under pressure."

"Sometimes."

"Sometimes?"

"Okay, most of the time, as long it's not an explosive situation—" Catching herself, she quickly added, "Like the one at the HDR site the other day. But this is different. She's not coming. I just know it."

"I hate this intuition nonsense," he sighed, running his fingers through his hair. "It doesn't fit your analytical, rational personality."

She smiled. "Typical male logic. If you can't see it, touch it, smell it, or eat it, it isn't real?"

"Something like that." Ashe stared into her eyes for a few seconds, then meekly asked, "Are you usually right?"

Rae nodded.

"Shit!" he muttered.

Facing him, Rae smiled. "Maybe we should check inside. She should've been here by now."

He glanced at his watch. "Do you think we can still get in the building?"

She shrugged. "It's better than sitting here waiting."

Ashe grinned as she opened the car door. "Worried that gut feeling might be a little off base, aren't you?" he taunted.

She cocked her head, defiantly answering, "Not in the least. It's just the logical way to handle the situation."

As they climbed the stairs to the building, a maintenance man came rushing outside. 'Excuse me," Ashe called. "Could you tell us how to get to MedicData?"

Shrugging, the man mumbled, "No." Keeping his gaze on the ground, he practically ran down the stairs.

After exchanging a puzzled glance, Ashe and Rae entered the building. There was no security guard on duty, so they simply found the name MedicData on the marquis and took the elevator upstairs. Just as they stepped into the hallway, they caught a glimpse of a woman entering the stairwell.

"Was that Dinell?" Rae asked, then shook her head in response to the doubtful look Ashe cast her. "I really am getting paranoid, aren't I?"

Ashe shrugged. "Maybe a little . . ."

A young man was just leaving MedicData as they approached the entrance. "Can I help you?" he asked.

"We were supposed to meet with Margaret Prosser."

"I'll buzz her for you."

Following him into the reception area, they waited while he dialed her extension. "She doesn't answer. I could go check to see if she's already left."

"We would really appreciate it," Ashe replied.

The man disappeared for several minutes, then came rushing back, all the color drained from his face. "She's . . . I think she's dead!"

Rae grabbed the phone and dialed 911 as Ashe took the man by the shoulders and demanded, "Show me where she is!"

It didn't take long for Ashe to realize the man was right. Margaret was slumped in front of her computer. He touched her neck. It was still warm but carried no pulse. Even so, Ashe eased her onto the floor so he and Rae could administer CPR. Minutes later, a team of paramedics took over.

Stepping aside, he put his arm around Rae, and together they watched the paramedics' valiant efforts. When the blanket was gently pulled over Margaret's head, Rae buried her face in Ashe's chest. "We should've come sooner. They actually killed her! We should never have let her out of our sight."

Stroking her hair, Ashe was grim. "You're right. I can't believe this is happening. How could this happen?"

They were both quiet, each lost in shock and dismay until Ashe overheard one of the paramedics comment, "Never seen that before!" His eyes followed the man's hand as it pointed to streaks of soot left by a small fire inside the computer. Chuckling, the man said, "Probably scared the old gal so bad it gave her a heart attack."

Ashe suddenly grabbed Rae's shoulders. "Oh, my God! That maintenance man was in an awfully big hurry to get out of here, wasn't he?"

"So was that woman I thought was Dinell!"


Jace knew he was in a hospital long before he opened his eyes. Without moving a muscle, he concentrated on the antiseptic odor and muted whispers that filled the room. Grogginess quickly was replaced by terror as memories flooded back. *He'll kill me next time! I know it!*

Barely opening his eyelids, Jace evaluated his situation. He was in some sort of ward. There were four other beds to his right. A nurse was near the end of the room, reading to a boy whose leg dangled from wires over his bed. Behind them was a large window, and he could see it was almost dark outside.

Imperceptibly shifting his line of sight to the left, he found his bed was the one nearest the door. He knew his arm was still in a cast, and his head pounded with each heartbeat. Flexing first his feet, then screaming leg muscles, he knew he could probably walk, but it would hurt like hell.

*As soon as the nurse leaves, I'll sneak out of here . . . he knows I'm here . . . knows I'm alive . . .* Jace was so tired he could hardly think. As he drifted back to sleep, his last thoughts were, *Got to get up . . . Run . . . Hide . . .*


Ashe and Rae drove toward RESCUE in silence, both deep in thought. Rae quietly asked, "Are you as worried as I am?"

He nodded. "It's so unreal. Twice in the last few days I've touched the warm neck of a body and found no pulse. I actually feel like RESCUE is being swallowed by some horrible monster and there's nothing I can do to stop it. I keep wondering how this could be happening. And why . . ."

"I wish I knew."

"Be sure and let me know right away if you get any more of those bad feelings. Okay?"

Rae resisted the urge to say, *I told you so.* Instead, she curled her hand around his and squeezed. "I promise you'll be the first to know."

"Have you come up with any grand schemes to trap these bastards?"

"I've been thinking about it all day. For obvious reasons, I don't believe we should use the current site. But it might be very interesting to spread word that we've selected our new HDR location. We could choose an abandoned well that's currently up for sale, one we have no intention of actually buying, and see if anyone tries to beat us to it."

"What good would that do?"

"We might be able to find out if the problem is at home."

"Sorry, Rae, it's been a long week. What in the world are you talking about?"

"For starters, what just happened to Margaret. Besides the two of us, only Brada and Dinell knew she was giving us the information. What if that *was* Dinell I saw?"

Ashe shook his head, as if doing so could keep such ideas from being true. "But we don't know how many people Margaret told. It's even possible someone has been following her."

"Wouldn't it be better to be safe than sorry? Eliminating the possibility that it's someone within RESCUE wouldn't hurt."

Ashe sighed. "You just don't understand because you haven't been around these people as long as I have. RESCUE is a way of life, not just a job."

"I know! But I also know that two women who trusted RESCUE to help them are dead! Whoever's doing this shit is trying to cover their ass while at the same time cost RESCUE as much money as possible. Run us out of business. Right? So, if someone at RESCUE is leaking confidential information, our little trick might just pay off. If we pretend we're actually going to start drilling again, we might be able to flush them out."

"True. How do you plan to spread the rumor?"

"Maybe you could send a memo to the other departments. You know, one that says even though there were problems with the first Oklahoma site, HDR is still very much alive. . . . We plan to begin our next project in a few days at a new location, which has just as much, if not more, potential than the last. . . ."

"Nathan will go into shock. I'd better run this scheme by him first."

"Just keep in mind his office might not be the best place to have a private conversation."

When Jace finally woke again, the ward was dimly lit and the nurse was gone. He edged his feet off the bed and slowly sat up. The room seemed to float around him, the walls drifting back and forth until they settled into their proper places. Jace took a deep breath, pushing himself to think clearly.

He needed clothes to leave, and there was an IV in the back of his hand. But most of all he was afraid he would faint when he tried to stand. For a long time he just sat on the edge of the bed, paralyzed with fear.

"Whatcha doing?"

Jace almost jumped out of his skin at the sound of the whispered voice behind him. He slowly turned, certain it was the beady-eyed crazy man ready to finish his work. Instead, he saw a six- or seven-year-old boy in the bed next to his—a frail kid with one bandaged eye and skin so pale his face matched the bleached white pillow case it rested on. Jace caught his breath and whispered, "Gotta go to the head."

"I heard 'em talking about you. You got something called a concussion. You aren't supposed to get out of bed by yourself. There's a red button on the side rail if you need the nurse."

Jace stood slowly, wobbling to and fro. "I don't need no nurse to help me pee. Besides, I can't stay here."

The other boy sat up in his bed, wide-eyed. "You gonna leave?"

"Ssshhh . . . I got to. Someone's trying to off me, man."

The timid little boy thought for a second, then slowly whispered, "Someone is trying to hurt you with bug spray?"

Jace glared at him. " 'Off' means kill. Now, go back to sleep."

The boy was too excited to rest. "I know where your clothes are."

"Really?"

"Yeah. They're in that closet over there."

"Thanks." Jace moved along the edge of his bed, grasping it for support until his IV line was stretched to its limit. In one swift motion he pulled the needle out, grimacing but never making a sound.

"Did that hurt?"

Jace nodded.

"You scared?"

He nodded again as he tried to stand without the help of the bed. Swaying, he made his way to the closet, grabbed his clothes, and barely managed to get back to his bed before he collapsed.

Shaking his head, the boy said, "You don't look so good. Where you gonna go?"

"Don't know."

"Maybe you could stay at my house."

Jace stared at him in wonder. "Thanks, but it'd be too dangerous."

"When I get out, I could help you get the bad guy. I'm meaner than I look."

Jace almost smiled. When he was dressed, he worked his way over to the boy's bed. Bending close to him, he said, "Thanks for the help. You just worry about getting well. I can take care of myself."

He nodded, leaning back against his pillow.

Jace made his way to the door. He peeked through a crack and watched until he was certain no one was coming. Slipping into the hall, he grasped the wall for support as he inched his way toward a bank of elevators at the far end of the floor. When he was almost there, he heard the ding of one arriving. *Yes!*

A nurse walked briskly out of the elevator, heading away from him with her head buried in paperwork. Just as the doors started to slide closed, Jace rushed inside. He collapsed against the back wall and sighed, only to suck in his breath when he saw someone racing toward the elevator.

In spite of the green surgical scrubs, he instantly recognized the deranged man. His eyes burned through to his soul, practically screaming his intention to finish his work without ever uttering a word.


Walters had finished checking the juvenile wing of the hospital and was plotting his next move when he saw Jace creeping down the hall. Although he ran as fast as he could, his fists slammed futilely against the elevator doors as they slid closed. He was too late. Again.

There wasn't time to wait for another elevator, so Walters ran to the stairwell. Three flights down, he emerged. Besides the guarded underground parking area, the hospital had two main ground-floor exits, one directly in front of him, the other near the emergency room on the opposite side of the building. Since the kid was on foot, Walters had a fifty-fifty chance of catching the bastard.

Like dominoes falling, botching the Prosser girl's murder the first time had set off a chain reaction of outrageous proportions. Even now he knew he could've had Williams in the palm of his hand if he hadn't had to take care of the professor and the girl's mother first. And if he didn't know better, he would've sworn that damned kid had more lives than Wile E. Coyote.

*He'd better enjoy his last few minutes,* Walters thought. *Because I'm really going to enjoy putting a bullet right between his eyes, with or without the damned crossbow! It's time for this nightmare to end.*

# Chapter 9

Jace rushed off the elevator on the second floor, charging down the hall past a waiting room packed with people. Weaving through the confusing maze, he flew around a corner and ran straight into an elderly black man, sending them both sprawling to the floor.

The impact made Jace cry out. He was shaking so hard his feet kept slipping on the slick floor when he tried to get up, but he knew he had to keep going. When the old man grabbed him by his shirt, he was too weak to get away. "Let go of me!" he cried.

Calmly, the man shook his head, his eyes stern yet tolerant as he stared at Jace. The expression on the man's face seemed to be one of confusion and bewilderment, as if he didn't know what to say. Finally Jace asked, "What're you staring at? Did I grow an extra nose or something?"

As if a trance had been broken, the man shook his head. "Sorry. It's just you look so much like someone I know."

"That's real nice, but I gotta get out of here."

"Not until you tell me what your problem is."

Jace's eyes darted nervously back and forth, trying to figure a way out. Nurses were rushing toward them. His heart was pounding a million times a minute.

Seeing the unwanted attention they were drawing, the man looked Jace right in the eye. "It's all right, son. If you promise not to run, I'll help you. Just calm down."

Knowing there was no other way out, Jace simply nodded.

As an orderly and a nurse slid to a stop, the old man said, "It's okay, Mildred. We just didn't see each other."

"You know this kid?" the nurse asked skeptically.

"Sure. He lives in my neighborhood. Came up to see how Alice was doing."

Jace merely stared at the floor and nodded, but the nurse and orderly seemed convinced. Once they were out of sight, he asked, "You crazy or what?"

The old man smiled, answering, "Maybe. My name's George. What's yours?"

He considered lying but muttered, "Jace."

"Who are you running from, Jace?"

"Nobody."

"Could've fooled me. You know, I've seen lots of sick folks in my time, and you're looking pretty puny. How'd you end up here?"

"The question is, how do I get outta here?"

"Seems easy enough to me. There's the elevator."

Jace shook his head. "Won't work."

"Police after you?"

"No. Some crazy white dude thinks he's gonna kill me for stealing his car."

George thought for a moment. "Did you steal his car?"

Jace nodded.

"You planning on ruining your whole life pulling stunts like that?"

He shrugged.

"I'll help you, because you remind me of my own son, and because you look like you could use my help. But stealing isn't the way to live. You're only gonna be in this world a little while. It's time you figure out if you want to trash your life or do things right. A man who knows he's done good can always hold his head high, no matter who he is."

"I've heard it all before. . . . What makes you so sure you could help me, anyway?"

George smiled. "I was a janitor in this place for thirty years. I know every inch of this building."

Jace looked around. "What're you doin' here now?"

Worry creased George's brow. "My wife got real sick this afternoon. But she's out of surgery, and the doctors say she's going to be just fine. God answered my prayers tonight. When God smiles on a man, he should show he's thankful by helping someone else."

"That's great, but I really gotta get outta here. Fast."

George cocked his head. "Then come with me."

Jace followed him, surprised how painful it was to start walking again. They went through a maze of hallways and service elevators until they emerged somewhere deep inside the employees' underground parking garage. George led him through several rows of cars, stopping at an old Dodge van. He pulled out his car keys and opened the side door. "I can't leave just yet, but if you'll stay awhile, soon as I get a chance I'll get you some food and a place to rest."

"Thanks, George. Hope your wife is okay."

George rolled down each of the front windows a couple of inches, then said as he slid the side door closed, "Think about what I said. You're the only one responsible for your life. Not your parents. Not some guy who wants to hurt you. Just you." He started to leave, then turned back. "Does your mother know you're okay?"

Jace shook his head.

"I could call her for you. Tell her you're going to stay with me for a while."

Jace nodded, mumbling his phone number. He watched George walk back toward the building and disappear into the stairwell, wondering why anyone would want to help him. Leaning against the seat, he was tempted to lie down and sleep until this nightmare ended. Instead, he knew what he had to do.

Enough light came through the windows to show him there were no tools in the back of the van. Jace gasped when he knocked his broken arm while wedging himself through the narrow space between the back and front seat, then moaned when his head bumped the roof. Opening the glove box, he rummaged through years of trash until he found an old screwdriver and a rusty pocketknife.

Easing himself onto the front floorboard, he bent to look under the steering column. His head pounded as blood rushed to it, launching a wave of nausea that made him crumple to the floor. Jace lay motionless for several minutes, waiting for the pain to pass before he tried to start again. Each movement seemed to take hours, every stage a different battle.

Hot-wiring a car was hard enough with two good hands. It was next to impossible with only one. Sparks flew as the third wire made contact. The van's motor turned over in a matter of seconds, and Jace finally exhaled. His head fell painfully to the dirty floor mat as he listened to the miraculous sound of the engine idling.

He wondered what time it was, then moved his head so he could see the digital clock on the dashboard. If it was right, what should have been accomplished in just a few minutes actually took over an hour. With great effort he managed to sit up, then move into the driver's seat.

His good hand gripped the gear shift as he slipped the van into reverse. The transmission groaned and the van lurched backward when he gave it some gas. Halfway out of the parking space he put his foot on the brake and shifted into drive. The van eased back into the exact same spot it had been in all along. He slammed it into park and laid his head on the steering wheel.

Jace couldn't do it. When he closed his eyes, his mother's tears poured through his soul until he thought he would drown. His shame was intensified by George's kindness, and his searing words: *It's time you figure out if you want to trash your life, or do things right. . . .*

Crawling back on the floorboard, Jace disconnected the wires and the engine died. In less than a minute, he was sound asleep.

\* \* \*

Ashe and Rae were solemn when they arrived at RES-CUE's headquarters. When they went through the front door to the lobby, Rae gently touched his arm. "Why don't we sit here and talk for a while? It's such a beautiful place."

He shrugged and followed her to a wooden bench.

"We need to call the police, don't we?" she asked.

"I've been thinking about that. What in the world are we going to tell them?"

"Exactly what Margaret told us."

"Do you realize how fanatical we're going to sound?" he asked.

Rae leaned against the bench and thought for a few seconds. "You're worried because the grand jury didn't hand down any indictments when Marilyn Prosser died, aren't you?"

"I know you haven't been here long, Rae, but one thing we try very hard to do is keep our reputation clean. We try not to make huge waves—that's Greenpeace's strategy, not ours. In order to survive, we've got to play the corporate game, and we've got to play it well. That means making sure we don't become so controversial that potential investors are scared away. Right now we're surviving on Nathan's funds, but our future depends on outside capital. Without it we're dead."

"Appropriate choice of words, considering everything."

"Sorry."

Rae stood, pacing to and from the water's edge. "Then, what are we going to do?" she asked.

"First, we're going to call Brada. She may have a contact at the police department who will look into Margaret's death without spreading the word around that RESCUE was involved in another murder."

"We'd better do it fast," Rae said.

"Why?"

"I didn't see anyone treating that cubicle like a crime scene. Plus, Margaret's body should be autopsied. If she's cremated like Marilyn was, any forensic evidence will be gone forever."

"You scare me sometimes. How in the world did you know Marilyn's body was cremated?"

Rae cocked her head. "I don't suppose you'd believe it was intuition?"

"No."

"Okay, you're right. Brada told me about Marilyn's memorial service when we were at the HDR site. She said it was heartbreaking to see someone so young and innocent killed because they wanted to do the right thing."

"Maybe Brada will have an idea how we can get our hands on the information Margaret was planning to give us, too. She has a reputation as being very resourceful."

"That's right, a true zero-tolerance woman."

Wrapping his arm around her, Ashe managed a weak but worried smile. "I seem to be surrounded by them."

The next morning in Midland, Texas, Karl Ross arrived at work before the sun peeked over the horizon, even though it was Saturday. He was too excited, too anxious to sleep. For years he had known only some of the intricate details of the Protection Program, and now that it was all in his hands, the feeling of power was almost overwhelming. When news of the Prosser girl's death had come, it had had no more effect on him than watching an evening news report of any other stranger's demise.

But yesterday's confirmation of the deaths of Margaret Prosser and Professor Tolmin had been different. He was directly responsible for them. No one else. What would have nauseated most people only made him more aware of the incredible potential his future held. The amount of money at his disposal was almost unfathomable. It could buy anything. Anyone.

Staring at the phone, he knew it would ring in the next ten minutes. The people Kelmar had dealt with were extremely punctual, very professional in their attention to detail, and quietly lethal. He was grateful for those traits, even though that nagging voice in the back of his mind warned that the same abilities could easily be turned against him.

The phone rang. He picked it up, simply saying, "Yes."

"Now that everything is under control again, we need to talk."

His hand was shaking from the edge of nervous excitement. "That's why I'm here."

"Do you plan to continue Kelmar's activities?"

Ross drew a deep breath, then said, "Of course."

"Good. Do you feel you can handle all future issues alone?"

After several seconds Ross replied, "I don't feel I'm in a position to make that decision at this time. Kelmar could've had arrangements with outside parties that I'm not yet aware of. Until I have time to sort through everything I've inherited, so to speak, I won't know what kind of expertise I may need."

"I need a commitment. Do you want to continue at my offered price or not?"

"I'll need to know exactly what services I'm paying for."

"You're paying for observation and damage control. Yesterday's timely deaths were proof of the efficiency of the information I can provide. Both Margaret Prosser and the good professor could have destroyed your precious empire."

"True. Define observation."

"Let's just say I have ways of protecting your interests. I warned you in time, didn't I? Yet you haven't forwarded the money. I thought we already had a deal."

"Okay, okay. I'll need a few days to get you the money." Silence.

"A few hours?" Ross asked.

"I don't have time to play games, nor do I wish to be involved with anyone who can't handle responsibility. Wire it in the next three hours, or not at all."

"It will be there." Ross cradled the phone, controlling the urge to stop the plan before it spiraled out of control. A sense of impending doom wrapped around him, threatening to steal the thrill of his newfound power.

Standing, he shook off the dread, knowing he couldn't let his panic stop what had worked for years. Besides, with that cold-hearted bitch on PetroCo's side, they could do anything they ever dreamed, and more.

The lobby of RESCUE was quiet on Saturday morning. Too quiet. Every falling droplet echoed in the entryway as Rae sluggishly walked past the waterfall, then up the stairs with the morning newspaper tucked under her arm. Although she planned to read the rest of the paper, the sound of raised voices coming from Ashe's office was too much for her to ignore.

Ashe and Brada were in the middle of a heated discussion when she quietly knocked. They both stopped talking to glare at her. "Should I come back later?" she timidly asked.

Ashe walked toward Rae, relaxing slightly. "Of course not. Come in. When we left last night, things were in limbo since we couldn't get through to either Brada or Nathan. I'll bring you up to speed, and you can join in the discussion."

Rae raised her eyebrows. "If that was a discussion, I'd hate to hear you two having a full-blown argument."

Brada laughed. "We don't pussyfoot around. It's much healthier and faster to say what's on your mind. Get straight to the point."

Rae nodded. "If you say so."

Ashe explained, "Nathan called me at home around midnight, and I finally got through to Brada at one o'clock this morning. We all agreed Brada was needed here, so she flew back. Believe it or not, we've only been here about ten minutes."

Brada said, "Ashe told me what happened to Margaret on the trip from the airport. We were just in the middle of discussing how to report it. I'm afraid, as usual, he disagrees with my tactics."

Ashe chimed in, "Her tactics are a little on the illegal side. Brada thinks we should get proof before we contact the authorities with our suspicions—"

Brada interrupted, "Because the police didn't take us seriously, and the killer is still out there! The diary Margaret found had incriminating evidence, but it was never disclosed to the grand jury. I think we have to find a way to thoroughly check all of Marilyn's things, so this time nothing falls through the cracks. Who knows, maybe Margaret wouldn't be dead if they'd uncovered the truth earlier."

Ashe said, "And, of course, Brada doesn't want to wait for the police to handle things. She thinks we should mosey over to MedicData and check the place out for ourselves, which I think is ludicrous."

Brada snapped, "We don't all have to go. Just one of us. Even though I've been up most of the night, I'd prefer to do it myself. They said her computer blew, which gives us a perfect cover. I'd make a convincing delivery person. I could take in a new machine and bring the old one out in a matter of minutes. Jim, down in Technical Assistance, could have a field day trying to find anything salvageable on her hard drive."

"No way," Ashe countered.

Rae agreed, "I don't think it's a great idea, either. We'd be stealing confidential MedicData information, not to mention their equipment. Besides, if we did find something still on the machine, how could the police use it as evidence?"

Brada said, "And if they don't investigate her death as if it was a murder, they won't find anything anyway. Right?"

"If we're dealing with professionals, what makes either of you think anything was left behind?" Ashe asked. "Suppose they killed her because they knew she was going to turn over the evidence. What kind of murderer would leave without destroying all the files?"

Brada said, "A pro wouldn't. That's why her computer was ruined. Somehow they knew everything she had was on her hard drive, and since unlocking her password to erase only certain files would take valuable time, they eliminated the problem, then eliminated her."

"And next they eliminate us?" Rae asked. "Like Andy and the HDR site?" No one spoke for several seconds. Finally Rae asked, "Ashe, what were the initials of that U.C. professor Marilyn referred to in her diary?"

"KT, I think."

"That's what I thought." Rae opened the newspaper and pulled out the city/state section. She pointed at a small article inside:

UC ENGINEERING PROFESSOR DIES AT 53

Kelsey Tolmin, a professor with the University of California, collapsed and died of an apparent heart attack on his way to class yesterday.

Mr. Tolmin was a native Californian, born and raised in Stockton. He held degrees in both engineering and physics, and has been a faculty member with the university for over fifteen years.

In lieu of flowers, the family wishes donations be made to a scholarship fund established in Professor Tolmin's memory. A memorial service will be held at the University Chapel at noon Sunday.

Rae asked, "Do you think he was the 'KT' in Marilyn's journal?"

Brada and Ashe exchanged a knowing glance as he said, "Probably. They're tying up all their loose ends. Something spooked them."

Rae started to pace. "Am I the only one who's getting really scared? First Marilyn dies in a suspicious car wreck; then her mother *and* one of her professors die on the same day. There's no way this is all a coincidence!"

"I couldn't agree with you more!" Ashe replied. "We just have to figure out a way to catch the people responsible for this."

"You sound as if you know exactly who's behind all this."

Brada said, "We do. It has PetroCo written all over it."

Shaking her head, Rae said, "But PetroCo is in a crisis of its own right now. Its CEO was murdered the other night. Right?"

Ashe thought for a moment. "Maybe we are barking up the wrong tree. The problem is, who else would want Marilyn, Margaret, and this Tolmin guy dead?"

Nathan stuck his head in the door. "No one. Brada's right. This is PetroCo's work, just like the problems at the HDR site. And for the icing on the cake, you won't believe what just came by certified mail." Nathan held up a thick legal document. "PetroCo is suing us for the full replacement cost of rig 114. They claim the EPA received reports of 'unmanageable' levels of radioactivity in and on their equipment. Explain to me how they got their hands on that tidbit of information."

Ashe shrugged. "Last I heard, we were going to leave the EPA out of this until a specialist could test the site in more depth to determine exactly what we're up against."

Nathan nodded. "The only person I told was my lawyer and friend, Sherrie Rosen. She hasn't said a word about the HDR site to anyone. She was as shocked as we were that information had leaked, and even more surprised the EPA would confirm or issue any kind of report at this stage. As you'd expect, they have a reputation for being slow to respond."

Brada ran her hands through her hair and headed out the door. "I need some caffeine. Anyone else?"

They all shook their heads as Rae said, "Frankly, I'm not surprised at all by the lawsuit." Even though she felt comfortable with these people, the probing look Nathan shot her instantly reminded her exactly where she fit in the corporate chain. She looked down, took a deep breath, then said, "What I meant was, if PetroCo was responsible for sabotaging the well, then they would know exactly how it was contaminated. They could file an anonymous report with the EPA, then proceed with their lawsuit. It was probably part of their plan all along."

Nathan smiled. "You think like I do."

"Ashe and I have been discussing the possibility of luring PetroCo, or whoever is doing this, into a trap."

With a gleam in his eye Nathan asked, "What did you have in mind?"

Rae apprehensively shot Ashe a look to gain his approval, then continued, "So far, nothing spectacular. We could spread a rumor that we're transferring all our HDR funds to a different drilling site. I know it isn't any of my business, Nathan, but are you planning on selling any RESCUE stock anytime soon?"

"No. I'm hoping we can make it at least another year without outside investors. Once they get hold of you, things are never the same."

"Since you own the majority of the stock, all RESCUE's financial records are confidential. Right?" she asked.

Nathan nodded. "Only our controller and a few of our suppliers have copies. Plus the bank, of course."

"Then a rumor that the next HDR investment will either make or break the company could help bring in the vultures. If someone is trying to guarantee our failure, they may not be able to resist such an easy way to finish us off. Maybe they'll swoop in for the kill a little prematurely."

Ashe laughed. "And get caught in our turbines." Answering Nathan's inquisitive glance, he added, "It's a long story. Let's just say Rae has a brilliant idea. I guess it's pretty hard to shake off that accounting background of yours, isn't it, Rae?"

Rae blushed. "I suppose so."

Nathan agreed excitedly, "I think it's a great idea. But how do we do it?"

Rae answered, "I took home the files on several sites last night. There's another abandoned deep-gas well in the Anadarko Basin, about five miles north of our previous location. It wouldn't be prime property if we were really drilling, but for this it may be perfect since it's covered in the surface lease we already have. Some equipment could even be moved from the first site since it's so close. That'll make things look really convincing without costing an arm and a leg."

"Considering PetroCo is suing us, I doubt if we'd be able to get our hands on a rig," Ashe said.

Rae nodded. "And a rig would be too expensive to set up anyway. We shouldn't need one to be convincing for a few weeks. Just having some of our people milling around may be enough."

Nathan said, "Sounds like you planned for everything."

Rae raised her eyebrows. "Not quite. I have no idea what to do if we catch them."

It was past noon when Nathan walked out the front door of RESCUE. He was immediately approached by two men who emerged from a forest green Suburban parked near the curb. The taller man gruffly asked, "Are you Nathan Greenwall?"

"Yes. Can I help you?"

They both flashed badges as one said, "We're homicide detectives. If you don't mind coming downtown, we'd like to ask you a few questions. Of course, you don't have to answer anything without your lawyer present."

Stunned, Nathan asked, "Questions about what?"

"The murder of Charles Kelmar."

# Chapter 10

Monday mornings were normally quiet at RESCUE, as employees recovered from their busy weekends. Most had an extra cup of coffee at their desk while they slowly eased back into their daily business routines. But this Monday was different. The crowd that gathered in the employee break area almost vibrated with restless anticipation and tension.

Ashe carefully listened to tidbits of various overlapping conversations until it was apparent how twisted the story had become. He stood in the doorway disappointedly shaking his head for several seconds before he shouted, "Excuse me! Excuse me! All of you, listen up!"

Discussions slowly dwindled until all eyes turned his way.

Raising his voice, he said, "I'm not sure how things like this spread, but I know you've all heard the rumors about several RESCUE employees, including Nathan Greenwall, being questioned by the police this weekend. First, let me assure you that neither he, nor anyone else, has been arrested.

"As a matter of fact, right now I'm on my way to his office to meet with him. From what I understand, people are saying he's a suspect in last week's killing of the head of PetroCo, Chuck Kelmar. Each of you who has worked with Nathan could end such a vicious lie. He is one of the most generous, giving men I've ever had the honor of working with, and I am shocked and irritated his employees would believe such utter nonsense."

Suddenly, people began shifting back and forth, their eyes downcast in shame.

Ashe continued, "Nathan has devoted his life to making the world a better place, and to providing all of us the opportunity to get paid for doing what we love. I, for one, plan to stand behind him and support him in any way I can."

Heads nodded.

"Now, I think we all have work to do. If anything happens to Nathan or to RESCUE, rest assured you will be notified. In the meantime, we need to show Nathan we're backing both the company, and him, one hundred percent." Ashe watched the crowd disperse, then turned and briskly walked down the hall and up the stairs to Nathan's office.

Dinell smiled sheepishly from behind her desk. "How'd it go?" she asked.

"I didn't knock any heads together, if that's what you're asking. Although it would've been a pleasure. Apparently, loyalty is tougher to find than I thought."

She shifted nervously, turning to stare at her computer.

Ashe motioned to the closed door of Nathan's office as he impatiently paced, asking, "Is he in yet?"

She shook her head. "He called from his house and said he'd overslept and he'd be here a little late. I'm glad you broke up the mob scene before he arrived."

"Me, too."

Dinell was unusually fidgety, her fingers tapping on her desk. "Ashe, did they question you?"

He stopped pacing. "No. Did the police call you?"

She nodded. "A detective came by my house early yesterday morning, just as I was leaving for church. He said they only wanted to ask a few routine questions. I know he had Brada on his list to contact, and he asked me if I knew which security guard would've been on duty the night Chuck Kelmar was killed. When I told him we didn't use security guards, he looked at me like I was crazy. They asked a lot of rather pointed questions, Ashe."

"If they talked to that many people, it explains the rumors that have popped up. I wonder who else they called."

"From what I've heard, you and Rae are about the only ones who spend much time around Nathan that they didn't call yet. The detective is probably holding off since I told him you were both at the HDR site in Oklahoma the night of the murder."

"Exactly what kind of questions did he ask?"

"At first just background things. How long have I worked here? What kind of place is RESCUE to work? Do I think the people who work here are happy? How do people feel about the oil industry, about PetroCo, in particular? You know, general information. But then the questions started targeting Mr. Greenwall. Does he have a bad temper? Does he drink a lot? Have I have heard him threaten anyone? Has he had any recent meetings with Mr. Kelmar? Did they argue?"

Dinell took a deep breath, then continued, "I feel just terrible about all this. I told them the truth, Ashe. Everything happened so fast, and I wasn't expecting them. I didn't have time to think about how it would look—especially how he crumpled up the newspaper article about Chuck Kelmar and threw it across the room. And, even worse, what happened the day before the murder. It just didn't dawn on me to lie!"

"Calm down," Ashe said. "No one here expects you to lie about anything. What in the world are you talking about?"

"Mr. Greenwall ordered me to take the afternoon before the murder off. He said I'd been working way too hard, and that he didn't want to see me back here until noon the next day."

"So?"

"So . . . I don't know! The detective really snagged on that for some reason. He kept asking why I needed the time off, and when I told him Mr. Greenwall was just being generous, he acted like he didn't believe me."

"Is that all you're worried about?"

"No. I'm worried about other things I told them, too."

"Which are?"

"That two weeks ago when Mr. Kelmar and Mr. Ross were here, I could hear them arguing. I heard Mr. Greenwall accuse them of trying to make sure our geothermal test well was a financial disaster. And, worse still, that not too long after that meeting you discovered the HDR well had been contaminated with radiation and the site was ruined."

Ashe paled. He should have realized Dinell would know everything about the HDR problems, but it never dawned on him how incriminating the situation would appear to be. "Is that all?"

She shook her head. "It gets worse."

Ashe tried to make her feel better by smiling and saying, "So far all you've described is a typical adversarial business relationship. Last time I checked, that wasn't a crime."

"But I told them what Mr. Greenwall said when I gave him the newspaper article describing Chuck Kelmar's promotion to CEO of PetroCo." She was shaking, extremely upset.

"It couldn't have been that bad, Dinell."

"We were talking about what a hypocrite Mr. Kelmar was, about how he professed to be a Christian when he was the least Christian person we knew."

Ashe stared at her until she finished.

A tear ran down her cheek as she muttered, "Ashe, I told them I heard him say how the Kelmar problem could be solved!"

"So?"

"He said something like, 'I'd enjoy putting a bullet right between his eyes!' "

"Wake up, boy. You need to eat."

Jace forced himself to open his eyes, even though the morning light streaming in the window stung them. He groggily scanned the tiny bedroom before hoarsely asking, "Where am I?"

George chuckled. "I wondered if you'd remember. You've been out for a whole day. I figured you could use the rest, so I let you be. But you need to drink some water, or you'll get even sicker. I've got a can of chicken noodle soup heating on the stove to warm you up. Bet a growing boy like you eats quite a bit. Your head still hurt? Yesterday you said it was pounding pretty hard."

Jace slowly remembered George helping him, taking him in, telling him to rest, and . . . the white guy who wanted to kill him! He bolted upright in bed and instantly regretted it. Holding his head with his good hand, he mumbled, "What day is it?"

George gently pushed him back down. "Monday. But you listen to me, son. Don't go being stupid again. You need to rest. Promise me you won't do nothing crazy like try to leave."

Jace didn't respond; he merely stared wide-eyed at George, as if he were trying to decide which of them was crazier.

After several seconds George said, "Either you promise, or you can leave right now—without eating any of that chicken soup that's smelling so good. I'm not gonna feed you just so you can get your strength back, then go out and get yourself killed. Understand?"

"Yeah."

"Promise?"

Jace hesitated, then asked, "Yeah. How's your wife?"

George smiled. "So you do remember. She's doing real fine, may be back home in a few days. Now, try to sit up, and I'll go get you some food. You willing to tell me your real name yet?"

"It really is Jace."

As he walked away, George shook his head and mumbled to himself, "Jace? Whatever happened to names like Bill, Joe, and Bob?"

\* \* \*

Rae hung up the phone and turned to face Ashe. "It's all set. I've arranged for the site to be cleared and the mobile home to be moved next week."

Ashe unenthusiastically replied, "Good job. Now it's my turn to get busy. I'll have tents set up after the land is cleared. We'll reactivate our accounts in Elk City, and put out the word we may be looking for contract help. At least it will look like a lot's going on, even if it isn't. Probably wouldn't hurt for the two of us to schedule a trip out there."

Rae's eyes searched his. "I know we haven't known each other for long, but you seem really down today. Anything I can do to help?"

Brada barged into the room and interrupted by saying, "Probably not. He's got a good reason to be down. Dinell said Nathan just called from the police station. They formally arrested him before he left his house this morning."

Rae was shocked. "For what?" she asked.

Ashe answered, "First-degree murder. But it isn't as bad as it sounds."

"How can being charged with first-degree murder not be as bad as it sounds?" Brada asked sarcastically.

"He's innocent. All we have to do is keep calm and find him a good lawyer," Ashe replied.

Rae agreed. "Nathan doesn't seem to be the type to do such a thing."

"Still, it looks really bad." Brada hesitated as she reacted to the stunned glares cast her way by Ashe and Rae, then continued, "It's just . . . I was there the morning after the murder. Nathan was not himself, but I didn't tell the police."

Ashe defensively crossed his arms. "What's that supposed to mean?"

Brada reciprocated his irritated tone of voice with an equally defensive one of her own. "Listen, I care as much, if not more, for Nathan than you do, Ashe Freeman, and I'm not saying he did it. What I am saying is that it looks pretty bad. Apparently the Las Vegas police wanted him arrested days ago. They waited this long only because the D.A. wanted to be damn sure they were right before they brought in such a high-profile person. Supposedly they've built a hell of a case against him."

"Such as?" Ashe asked.

"I wish I knew. Our best bet at this stage would be to find the most aggressive lawyer in town. But before we do anything, we need to talk to Nathan. He has probably already contacted someone. From what I heard, they not only questioned him this weekend, they took blood samples. Surely he didn't go through all that without calling an attorney."

Ashe said, "I'll bet he did. After all, from his viewpoint he's just being cooperative. He probably assumed if he answered their questions, they'd realize it couldn't have been him and leave him alone. Brada, what did you tell the police about the morning after the murder?"

"Nothing. I didn't tell them Nathan had been drinking that night. All I said was that I woke him in his office about seven the next morning."

"How do you know he'd been drinking?"

"There was an empty bottle of Dominus on his desk."

"But Nathan doesn't drink," Ashe said.

"That's why I asked him about it that morning. He said he had a headache the night before, so he had a drink."

"Where would he have come up with a bottle of Dominus?"

"He said someone sent it to him."

Rae asked, "How could he have made it to Vegas and back in time?"

Brada answered, "The police say he paid cash for a round-trip flight. Quit staring at me like that! Unlike some of the people who work here, I didn't tell the police a damn thing!"

Ashe nodded. "Actually, it sounds like you were pretty uncooperative."

"Of course I was. We have to stick by him. That's why I purposely left out the most incriminating piece of information!" she shouted.

"Which was?"

"That Nathan had a fresh cut on his forearm. Right through his shirt, and he said he didn't even remember how he got it."

Ashe's eyes clouded as he contemplated the ramifications of what he had heard. "No shit."

"Yes, shit!" Brada stood. "We can plot how to help him later. Right now I promised to meet Dinell. She's pretty distraught about the whole mess, maybe a little too much so. You know, we'd better be careful around her."

"What's that supposed to mean?"

"It means, she's being awfully cooperative with the police. Maybe a little too cooperative. Doesn't it strike you as odd that the one day she decides to take off, the shit hits the fan?"

"Why are you meeting with her?"

"Apparently there's a pile of reports that have to be reviewed and some sales agreements that need signatures. I figured the least I could do was volunteer to help organize things so we can go over them with Nathan. Besides, someone will have to run things while he's gone."

Brada started to leave, then popped her head back in the door to say, "By the way, Ashe, would you mind being the one to issue an employee memo about all this?"

He sighed. "I'll get right on it." When Ashe was certain Brada was gone, he slumped into a chair next to Rae. "This doesn't make sense. In fact, it's giving me an overwhelming sense of déjà flu."

"Déjà flu?" Rae asked with raised eyebrows.

"It's sort of like déjà vu, but déjà flu is when something revolting flashes through your mind and makes you sick to your stomach."

Shaking her head, she said, "At least you haven't lost your sense of humor."

"What's that old saying, something about it being better to laugh in the face of adversity than cry . . ."

Rae leaned toward him, her gaze holding his. "I meant what I said. Nathan didn't kill anyone. I just know it. He's not a violent man, and he's very intelligent. What would he have to gain from killing Kelmar? I interviewed with Petro-Co a month ago. It's a huge corporation. Places like that don't change because one person is gone. Someone else just slides into their place like a shark replaces a lost tooth. I think the real question here is, Who's trying to frame Nathan, and why?"

Ashe smiled. "As usual, you're right, and sitting here isn't helping him one bit. For starters, I think I'll run downstairs and put some pressure on the lab. I know they're swamped, but now we really need to understand what that black box you noticed in Nathan's office is for."

"Are we going ahead with the plans on the fake HDR site?"

"Unfortunately, I think it's more important now than ever."

Walters yawned for the thousandth time Tuesday morning as he listened to his secretary cover everything he had missed in the last few days. She was accustomed to handling everything during his prolonged absences after all these years.

Having spent an unsuccessful Saturday night at the hospital and all day Sunday chasing phantoms, he'd given up Monday and flown back to Denver. He needed to rest and regroup, develop a foolproof scheme to stop Jace Williams once and for all.

That was the problem with the last few days. There had been no time to plan. He suddenly realized his secretary was asking him a question. "I'm sorry, what did you say?" he asked.

"I asked if you were feeling all right. You don't look

very well at all, Mr. Walters. Can I get you something to drink? An aspirin?"

"A whole bottle of aspirin might be enough to help, but don't bother. I think I'm going to have to go home and hit the sack. This bug I picked up in California is a real killer."

"I was shocked to hear about that nice man from RES-CUE being arrested. Who would have guessed?"

Walters acted nonchalant, even though he was inwardly pleased with the fruits of his labor. Maybe things were finally going to go his way. "What are you talking about?" he asked innocently.

"Nathan Greenwall was arrested for murder. I still have this morning's paper if you want it."

Nodding, he said, "I *have* to read about it. It could directly impact our sales to RESCUE. You'd better notify our controller to immediately put a flag on their credit line, possibly even demand a letter of credit be in place before we ship any more filters."

"Yes, sir." She left, then returned with the newspaper. The article was buried on the second page of the business section:

### RESCUE, INC., PRESIDENT ARRESTED

Nathan Greenwall, the president and founder of RES-CUE, Inc., a California-based corporation specializing in the development of renewable energy sources, was arrested on murder charges in the case of Charles Kelmar, the newly appointed CEO of PetroCo.

Sources say Greenwall has been despondent over the failure of RESCUE's latest undertaking, conversion of an abandoned oil and gas well in the Anadarko Basin of Oklahoma to an alternative-energy source commonly known as Hot Dry Rock. The company reportedly lost millions of dollars when they were forced to abandon the project after the site was apparently sabotaged. RESCUE was leasing PetroCo drilling equipment at the site.

Charles Kelmar was killed in his Las Vegas hotel room three days ago. Sources indicate Greenwall and Kelmar were openly hostile toward each other. Las Vegas police confirmed Greenwall is the only suspect in the murder at this time, and that they will seek to extradite him to Nevada as soon as possible.

Walters' heart was pounding in his ears as he read the sentence again. *The company reportedly lost millions of dollars when they were forced to abandon the project after the site was apparently sabotaged.*

He was certain he had defiled a PetroCo oil well in the Anadarko Basin, not an HDR site. Their damned sign declaring it to be PetroCo #114 had even been lit with spotlights bright enough for the whole world to see. His fight was against PetroCo, and everything it stood for, not RESCUE!

Closing his eyes, he remembered each recent job. The senators, the college girl, the oil well, the professor, the girl's mother, and finally, framing Nathan Greenwall. He had managed to suck money out of PetroCo while punishing the traitors, but his RESCUE source must have lied to him about the oil well . . . and about Greenwall. Walters tasted bile when the pieces of the puzzle finally started to come together.

The bitch must have been using him all along!

"Are you cross-eyed yet?" Ashe asked.

"Almost," Rae answered.

"I'll bet you never expected your degree in geology to land you in a basement looking at security photos."

"True. But I didn't exactly expect it to land me in the middle of nowhere covered with radioactive mud, either. At least this is a little safer."

"Let's hope so."

"I'd have never guessed there were cameras in the lobby. Even after I knew where to look, I had a really hard time spotting them. Mother Nature provides great camouflage."

He nodded. "Has anyone told you why we added the hidden surveillance cameras a few years ago?"

"Nope. I assumed it was same reason every other business does, to protect its assets and employees."

"Yes and no. We were pretty trusting until we were hit."

"Were the cameras installed because RESCUE got robbed?"

He laughed as he shook his head. "Actually, it was because of a prank. Someone added a bottle of kid's bubbles to the NatureAir waterfall one night. You can imagine what happened by the next morning."

"I'll bet that was quite an experience," she said. "And I can imagine the manhunt it took to capture the culprit. What'd they book him on?"

"First-degree murder."

"You're kidding!"

"Actually, I am. We never caught anyone. Until then we didn't have much of a security system at all. But, unfortunately, that little prank cost a shitload of money. The bubbles killed most of the fish, algae, even some of the plants. So we became a little more cautious. Now an outside security firm maintains the cameras just in case anything happens again."

"Do they monitor them?"

"I don't think so. The magnetic locks on the front door supposedly will keep just anyone from wandering in after hours."

"I know." She nodded toward the monitor. "I've been watching various employees and the cleaning people come and go all night. Sometimes caution is a good thing," she said.

"Have you found anything yet?" he asked.

"I've only covered the day before the murder so far. No one came into the building that day carrying a bottle of wine. At least not openly."

"Meaning?"

"Meaning four people came in carrying bags large enough for a bottle of wine to fit completely inside."

"All employees?"

She shrugged and said, "At least two of them are. Quite frankly, after watching this for three hours, everyone is starting to look alike."

"Which employees did you recognize?"

"Dinell and Brada. These are the others." She moved the arrow backward, freeze-framing two images.

Ashe nodded. "The first guy is Greg Burns. He's head of our Solar/Wind division. Doesn't surprise me he'd have a gym bag. He works out religiously in RESCUE's fitness center. The other man is vaguely familiar. I think he's one of our suppliers, but I'm not sure. Can we print a copy of this frame somehow?"

"These digital cameras are awesome, especially the way the two units alternate pictures. I think we can get a print, but I don't know how. I'd be happy to track down the company we lease them from and find out."

"That'd be great." He started to leave, then stopped and added, "Thanks, Rae. Your attitude really means a lot to me. In fact, I'm beginning to wonder how we survived around here before you came along."

"I'm sure you did just fine."

"I don't want to upset you, but the lab finished with that black box from Nathan's office. It's quite a complicated contraption. At first glance they thought it was just a miniature air filter that worked like the larger, electrostatic ones. But when they dismantled it, they found a sophisticated electronic listening device inside as well."

Puzzled, Rae asked, "Why listen to what you're filtering? Are they sure that's what it is?"

"Positive. They even found the frequency and tested it. Apparently it has a range of almost half a mile. This could be the break we're looking for. Brada's going to talk to Nathan about it tonight."

With wide eyes Rae said, "So someone could've heard our conversation with Margaret Prosser! That's how the bastards knew she was going to turn over Marilyn's information that night!"

Ashe smiled and nodded. "Exactly."

Nathan was shocked to see Sherrie Rosen waiting for him in the small room used for prisoners to consult their attorneys. "What in the world are you doing here?" he asked. "I thought you were swamped handling the late senators' estates."

Before uttering a word, she embraced him. It was a long, warm greeting. Stepping back, she took his hands in hers and said, "You'd expect me to stay in New York when one of my best friends is in trouble?"

He hugged her again. "I'm honored."

She smiled. "You gave me a good excuse to delegate for once, and I brought work with me, so I'm not totally playing hooky. With fax machines and overnight mail, they won't even know I'm gone."

He loved the way her words flowed through him, warming every part of his body. "Thanks for coming, Sherrie. It really means a lot to me."

She stepped back, her brown eyes probing his. "I must admit, I *am* pretty hurt."

"Why?"

"I thought we were good friends, Nathan. You could've called. I know I spend all my time working, and that I really should watch the news or read the paper, but still . . . Do you know how I found out you'd been arrested?"

He shook his head and meekly asked, "From one of the other lawyers?"

"I should be so lucky. I saw it at the grocery store, for God's sake! You're on the cover of this week's *Nation's Inquirer*!" She pulled out a copy of the paper and handed it to him. "I must have no shame. I actually bought the damned thing. Hopefully, no one I know saw me, or my reputation will be ruined forever."

He laughed, then scanned the article and dejectedly said,

"Is this true? Do they really have enough evidence to convict me?"

"That's why I'm here. I know I'm not up on criminal law, but I couldn't rest until I was sure whoever is representing you is the best. Who are you using?"

Smiling, he said, "I'm thinking of using a public defender."

Sherrie stared at him wide-eyed.

Nathan tousled her wavy brown hair. "I'm joking. Lighten up, will you?" He pulled her to him and suggestively asked, "Why don't you defend me?"

She slipped away, shaking her head. "Impossible. I'm just here to help, and besides, I'm too close to you. If you need me to call a few of my lawyer friends who have been transplanted to Earthquakeland, I can help you find the best."

"No need. Jill Burkhart is representing me."

"Great." She winked and added, "At least you had the sense to choose a woman. I'll check her out."

He shrugged. "If it'll make you feel better, go ahead. She's brilliant, though. I dated her most of last year. I don't think she loses very often."

"Why'd you break up?" she asked, a little too nonchalantly.

"You know I've got my sights set on you. When are you going to give in and marry me?"

"When you move back to New York."

He pulled her into his arms. "You'd love the West Coast."

She backed away again. "We really don't have time to go into all this again, Nathan. If I'm going to help at all, I need to know a few things."

He sighed. "Such as . . ."

"Under normal circumstances I'd never ask this, but we both know things are far from normal. Did you do it?"

"Do you think I did it?"

"What I think is irrelevant." Looking him straight in

the eye, she asked again, "Nathan, did you kill Charles Kelmar?"

"No."

She smiled. "That's all I needed to hear."

With a concerned look he added, "Sherrie, do you think I could have done it? I know this sounds crazy, but I can't help but wonder. I don't clearly remember anything that happened that night; it's all a haze. God, I hate this!"

"You definitely didn't kill anyone, Nathan. Someone wants you to take the fall for this, and they've gone to a lot of trouble to make sure you do. So, who would want to frame you for his murder?"

Nathan began pacing. "The only obvious answer is Chuck Kelmar, but somehow I don't think he'd have himself killed just to see me locked away."

"Then we've got to dig deeper. There has to be someone who wants you to suffer. Any bitter girlfriends lurking around?"

"If I didn't know better, I'd think you were jealous."

"Even if I am, it's still a relevant question. You're a handsome, very wealthy man. Losing you might be enough to push someone over the edge."

"I'm flattered. But, really, I don't date that much, especially not seriously."

"What you perceive as a casual relationship might be serious as hell to someone else. Just think about it, okay? Who else?"

"Maybe Karl Ross, Kelmar's right-hand man. I've been considering his potential motives, and he'd win both ways. He takes over Kelmar's shiny new position as president, and gets RESCUE out of the picture once and for all."

She'd pulled a pad from her briefcase and was scribbling furiously. "He's at PetroCo in Midland, Texas?"

"Right."

"I'll hire someone to check him out," Sherrie said.

Nathan took her hand. "Some of my friends are working

on leads here. I'd like you to work with them, if you have time."

"I'll make time."

"You can stay at my place, and work at RESCUE."

Sherrie shook her head. "I don't think that would look very good."

Winking, he asked, "Worried someone in California will recognize you?"

She laughed. "No. I just think it casts the wrong impression. It implies we're, you know . . ."

"Friends?"

She shrugged. "Okay. It would be easier to stay at your place."

"Stop by RESCUE in the morning. Ask my secretary, Dinell, to introduce you to Ashe and Brada. They're looking after RESCUE while I'm gone, and doing a little investigating on the side. Right now we're not sure who we can trust, so we're not taking any chances."

"Isn't Brada the one you used to talk about in college?"

"In the flesh."

"Is she still brilliant?" she asked.

"Are you still jealous?" he mocked.

"Maybe a little, but right now we have bigger things to worry about. I'll get hold of your lawyer and see what's taking so long to get you out of here."

"Sherrie, bail has already been denied. We're busy fighting extradition to Nevada right now."

"Why the hell was bail denied? You're an upstanding member of the community. A frigging model citizen! You've probably never even gotten a parking ticket before!"

"Whoever we're up against is very good, and money is no object. They not only covered their tracks, they somehow managed to put my tracks in their place. It seems day before yesterday they paid cash to book me on a flight to Australia, which, of course, makes me appear to be a flight risk to the court. And it gets worse."

"That's not the worst news?" she asked, obviously disheartened.

"The DNA tests aren't all back yet, but apparently there's an even bigger problem." He slumped into his chair as he said, "My blood matched what was found at the murder scene."

# Chapter 11

Twelve hours after reading the article on Greenwall's arrest, Walters was still furious. Logic was beyond his grasp, pushed aside by his primal hunger for revenge. His life had been devoted to destroying PetroCo, using schemes against them that were as clever and deceptive as those they used to fool the public.

He tried to convince himself there must be a bigger picture, one he didn't yet understand. He knew that college kid's design would make drilling for oil much less expensive, but she had sold out. How could contaminating RESCUE's HDR well hurt PetroCo? And what was the real reason Nathan Greenwall needed to be out of pocket for a while?

Mentally chastising himself, he was plagued by negative thoughts. *Since when do I trust anyone? How could I have been so damned stupid? What the hell is really going on here?*

The answer was clear. He had let his guard down, broken his own stringent rules. Again. Sloppiness was unforgivable, and now it was time to pay the price.

The real cost was to his spirit. His entire life he had backed away from relationships. So few people ever met his standards and expectations that he had become a loner by choice. After years of brilliantly designed jobs, he finally deemed his contact at RESCUE trustworthy, a kindred spirit in the fight against PetroCo and its related concerns. He had stopped questioning every move, instead relying on the judgment of the person he had grown to respect. Trusting one person might just have cost him everything.

Pacing across his living room, he tried to calm down. His next move would be critical. Jace Williams loomed over him like a hurricane hovering a mile offshore. Dealing with him would require assistance at this point, since Walters couldn't risk being seen in California again.

A boyish grin crossed his face at the thought of his double-crossing friend. Two could play her game. With a little special attention, he had a feeling that, in this case, vengeance would truly be a pleasure.

When the ingenious idea struck him, Walters knew he couldn't wait. He placed the call in spite of subconscious warning signals that were screaming, *Slow down. Plan each step thoroughly. This is how you blew it last time.* But his need to hear that deceptive voice was overwhelming, not only to refocus his hatred, but to prove to himself he was back in control.

On the second ring, the phone was answered with a clouded, hoarse "Yes?"

He quietly, very calmly, said, "I know this call hasn't been cleared, but I need to discuss something with you. Is it safe? Are you awake?"

". . . Yes."

"After the, um, let's call it the liquid incident, you mentioned you might want to participate in a more direct way. I indicated you were more valuable where you were. There's a way you can do both in the near future. Are you still interested?"

"That depends on what you have in mind. Things are hectic since Greenwall's arrest."

From the tone of voice, he could tell grogginess was quickly being replaced by the level-headed temperament he was used to. Bragging, Walters said, "I do good work, don't I?"

"What are you talking about?"

"Who do you think framed him? You said you needed

him out of the way but not dead. I'm quite proud of the way it is going. It was a difficult, complicated plan to carry out, but obviously worth the extra effort. He'll be locked away for quite some time. Unless, of course, Nevada has the death penalty, in which case we might have a tiny problem."

"But . . . so . . . you killed Chuck?"

Walters laughed. "I can't believe you didn't realize it right away. Who else could carry out such an elaborate scheme? Wasn't his blood at the scene a nice touch? And what about booking the flight to Australia? A stroke of pure brilliance, if I do say so myself."

"But . . . it wasn't time! We didn't agree . . ."

Walters was ecstatic as he listened to the agitated voice. He continued by explaining, "There were extenuating circumstances that made the original time frame impossible. The plan had to be changed, and you know flexibility has always been my forte. Unfortunately, there's been a small snag. That's why I contacted you. I need some assistance."

"What kind of assistance?"

"There's a person I need taken out, and soon. It shouldn't be too difficult. The hard part will be locating him."

"What concern is he of mine?"

"Let's just say he could be the thread that unravels all we've done together. And I do mean all. Understand?"

"Yes."

"Are you willing to help?"

"Do I have a choice?"

"Not really. After all, I've been coming to your rescue for years. Maybe it's time you came to mine. I'll get back to you with details in the next two days." Walters hung up without waiting for a response.

He finally started to relax, knowing that this time *he* had the upper hand.

Several hundred miles away, the night held as many questions as it did answers. *That stupid son of a bitch killed Chuck just to frame Nathan! Oh, my God, what have I done? Who does Walters want me to handle, and why after all these years, does he suddenly need my help? Could I actually kill someone? If he ever finds out I tricked him, will he hunt me down and kill me, too?*

*Of course he will!*

Jace moved slowly across the small living room of George's house, thankful pain no longer cursed his every move. When the glow of headlights splashed against the dingy wall, then disappeared, he realized George was finally home. Very carefully Jace eased himself into the old recliner and waited.

When George shuffled in, Jace asked, "How's your wife doing?"

It was late, and George was obviously exhausted. "Little better every day. Kinda like you. It's harder on her, though. Old bodies don't heal like young ones. I waited till I knew she'd sleep through the night, then I came on home. What're you doing up at this hour? You still gotta get lots of rest to get well."

"I needed to ask you a favor. I know you've already done plenty for me, so I'll understand if you say no."

George wearily dropped onto the sagging sofa, propping his feet on the coffee table. "It's good to know you trust me that much. I have a feeling a couple days ago you'd have just taken whatever it is you wanted without bothering to ask first."

Jace hesitated, then said, "I probably would've. But you've been really good to me. Better than anybody ever, except maybe my own mama."

"Everybody deserves a break now and then. What kinda favor did ya have in mind?"

"Your van. I just need to borrow it for a couple of hours tomorrow afternoon. I could take you to the hospital and then come back and pick you up whenever you want me to. It's real important."

George looked at him skeptically, then asked, "Will you tell me what you've got planned?"

Jace scowled, then stood, steadying himself by leaning against the wall. "I need to watch for somebody. That's all I'm going to do. Watch. I promise."

"Does this have anything to do with the white guy who was following you?"

Jace nodded.

"Sounds dangerous."

"No way. Your van's safe. Besides, he'd never expect me to show up where he works."

"Why would you want to do a fool thing like that anyway?"

"One way or another, I've got to stop him. He's not the type to give up. He's a pro."

"How's watching for him going to stop him from coming after you again?"

"Thanks to you, I've had a lot of time to think about things the last couple of days. First, I need to make sure he actually works at that place where I stole the car. Then I can turn him over to the cops."

"Why not call them from here?"

"And tell 'em what? 'Hey, I stole a car, killed my own brother, and now I need you to protect my sorry, thievin' ass'?"

George shook his head. "I see your point, but it still might be the safest thing to do."

"No way! We both know they ain't gonna believe me if I just tell 'em some white creep's been chasing me all over the place. But I figure if I can show them who it is, exactly where to find the guy, they might cut me some kinda deal since I've got the goods on him. You know, let me off on the car-stealing thing in exchange for arresting a hit man."

George nodded. After several moments he stood and walked into the kitchen. Jace followed, asking, "Well?"

"You can use the van." He reached into his pocket and

tossed him the keys. "Start it with these this time. It's a little easier than hot wiring. By the way, where did you learn that?"

"At school."

"Really? Some new kinda class?"

Jace defensively turned away. "Not exactly. I paid attention in shop class, learned a lot about computers, too. It comes easy. I'm just good with wiring and things like that."

"My son was, too."

Turning slowly around, Jace scrutinized George's face. "That's his picture in the den, isn't it?"

"Sure is."

"I look a lot like him, don't I?"

George glanced away, nodding.

"What happened to him?"

"Got killed in the Gulf War."

"And that's why you're helping me. 'Cause I look like the son you lost?"

"That may have been why I started, but now I'm doing it because I like you. I can tell you need a friend, and that someday you're going to be a fine young man, just like he was."

Jace simply nodded, the knot in his throat choking back his words.

No one would have guessed Nathan wasn't in his office on Wednesday morning. The glass walls were opaque, as though they could deter the invasion of any further problems. The room was buzzing with activity as Dinell, Brada, Ashe, and Rae did their best to brainstorm ways to help him.

Brada asked, "Have you guys heard the latest piece of incriminating garbage they turned up?"

Everyone shook their heads. It was early in the morning, and they all looked as though sleep had eluded them for days.

"They found out about his mother," Brada divulged.

Dinell and Ashe nodded as though they understood perfectly, but Rae shrugged. "What did they find out about her?"

Ashe explained, "Nathan's father died when he was only six. He was very close to his mother, Elizabeth. She was a wonderful woman. She grew up sixty years ago when kids and adults didn't think twice about where they played, or what the consequences of pollution were. It wasn't until thirty years later, after Nathan was born with a mild birth defect, she discovered the truth.

"Unfortunately, her childhood home was downstream from a processing plant that dumped waste products into the river. She was one of about fifty people who all grew up in the same neighborhood and went to the same grade school. Of those who could have kids, several had children with deformities. Others were like Nathan, who had a cleft palate. He's led a normal life after having a couple of corrective surgeries when he was a kid. Most of Elizabeth's friends died of mysterious diseases before they were fifty years old. Last I heard, only one was still alive."

Rae shook her head. "That's horrible. What did his mother die from?"

"A rare form of leukemia," Dinell said.

"And that's why Nathan is so involved in ecology?"

Ashe answered, "Yes. Right after she died, he blamed the worst offenders, some of which, I'm sure you guessed, are in the petroleum industry."

Brada chimed in, "And he was openly hostile to Chuck Kelmar. Kelmar's personal quest to lobby against every bill designed to control pollution caused by the oil industry particularly offended him. But lately they seemed to have been getting along a little better."

Dinell said, "I don't think so. During their last meeting they had a pretty heated argument. Even with the door closed, I could hear every word they said."

Rae asked Dinell, "So do you believe Nathan truly wanted Kelmar dead?"

Dinell blushed and shrugged.

Ashe quickly answered, "Nathan accepted his mother's death and went on. I don't think it would ever cross his mind to solve problems illegally. He truly believes the future can be changed by hard work, and that includes using legislation to make it happen."

Brada said, "Which is exactly what we need to be doing—working hard. The prosecution is making it sound like Nathan's been lurking in the shadows all these years waiting to catch Kelmar off guard so he could avenge his mother's death. What a crock of shit. We need to find ways to prove Nathan wasn't carrying a grudge. But how?"

Ashe answered. "I don't know. So many people know why he started RESCUE; plus it's common knowledge in the industry that one of our biggest problems is PetroCo. Unfortunately, the story of his wanting revenge for his mother's death is like another nail in Nathan's coffin. It sounds terrible and will be impossible to disprove."

Brada said, "We've got to figure out how Nathan's blood could be at the scene without him being there. Then we need to prove it."

Rae offered, "It seems pretty obvious to me. Nathan may have actually been there. After all, he doesn't remember anything that makes much sense. Maybe he was drugged and taken to Las Vegas, and someone cut his forearm so he would bleed at the scene. Nathan's innocent, but whoever killed Kelmar was smart enough to take him along. A perfect setup."

Ashe said, "But the security photos don't show Nathan leaving the building. Besides, I've never heard of a drug that totally wipes out a person's memory but leaves them conscious enough to travel from here to Las Vegas and back without people remembering him acting oddly."

Dinell said, "But he had to be in Las Vegas. O.J.'s jurors are the only people on the face of the earth who don't grasp the accuracy of DNA blood tests."

Rae shook her head. "The police are sure he was there,

but it doesn't add up, Brada, the cut on Nathan's arm wasn't very deep, right?"

Brada nodded.

Rae continued, "It's only been a few days, and the cut is already healed. According to his lawyer, there were drops of blood in the hotel room and leading down the hall to the elevator. But Nathan's slacks didn't have any spots, or his shoes, or his car, for that matter. Only his shirt, and just around where the cut actually was—like his arm hadn't moved much. When you add that to the fact someone had his office bugged, it makes the prosecution's case a lot more suspicious."

Brada stood and stretched. "I'm going to see Nathan in an hour. I'll ask him about the blood."

"What did he say about that black box?" Rae asked.

Grimacing, Brada snapped, "Shit! I completely forgot to ask where he got that thing! I'll talk to his lawyer about it when we discuss how to turn over the surveillance photos."

Ashe added, "Make sure she finds out if the police checked his house and car for bugs, too. And you'd better bring her up to speed on the murders of Marilyn, Margaret, and Andy. There's a good possibility all this is connected."

Rae replied, "Poor Margaret, I feel terrible about what happened to her. Do we know if the autopsy showed signs of foul play?"

Ashe shook his head. "Ever since Nathan's arrest, the police are treating everyone at RESCUE as though we're a bunch of homicidal maniacs. I doubt if they'd tell us the time of day right now."

Dinell said, "Can you blame them? First, Marilyn dies under questionable circumstances. Then we're some of the last people to see her mother alive. Throw Mr. Greenwall's problems in, and you've got a certified bunch of troublemakers."

Rae asked, "Has anyone besides me wondered how Nathan suddenly became a suspect? I mean, Kelmar was murdered in Las Vegas, and the first news stories said the police there thought it was a hotel robbery gone bad. Then, out of the blue, they start questioning Nathan. Quite a leap, don't you think?"

Sherrie Rosen poked her head in the door and answered, "Not if you consider the Las Vegas police received an anonymous tip." The four of them all stared with wide eyes at the perky brunette. She continued, "I'm Sherrie Rosen, a friend of Nathan's from New York. I don't mean to intrude. It's just no one was in the reception area, and I could hear your conversation. Nathan's lucky to have so much support."

Dinell hopped up and practically ran to Sherrie's side. "I'm sorry. I completely forgot Mr. Greenwall told me you'd be coming by. This is Brada, Ashe, Rae, and I'm Dinell." As she introduced them, each one smiled and nodded.

"Nathan's told me a lot about all of you. In fact, I probably know as much about Brada's college antics as she does."

Brada muttered, "Oh, no . . ."

Sherrie said, "Don't worry, even back then Nathan always spoke very highly of you. I flew in from New York to try to help get him out of this mess."

Dinell added, "She's his personal attorney, so she'll be using his office for a while."

"Of course, if any of you would prefer I didn't, I can always work out of Nathan's apartment." Seeing the look Brada shot Ashe, Sherrie quickly added, "He insisted I stay there."

Ashe said, "Any friend of Nathan's is welcome here. If you need anything at all, just ask."

Sherrie smiled warmly. "Thanks, I will. If you've all got a minute, I'd like to fill you in on what Nathan and I covered yesterday." She set her briefcase on his desk and flipped it open, pulling out a legal pad filled with notes. "First, he's worried RESCUE will get off track once he's extradited to Nevada. As usual, he's more concerned about the company's future than his own. He asked me to have Ashe handle the financial end of RESCUE while he's out of pocket."

Brada interrupted, "But I've already begun working with Dinell on the financial reports."

"He said you were doing a fine job, but that your,"—she flipped through her notes—". . . I believe he called them 'killer instincts' would be better utilized to help find who did this to him. He asked me to see if you would go to Midland to speak to Karl Ross."

"I'd be glad to, but what good will it do?"

"He thinks he has a motive for killing Kelmar, and that you might be able to rattle his cage a little."

Brada smiled widely. "No, I'll rattle his cage a lot!"

Nathan paced the cell like a caged animal, unable to believe his world was crumbling around him. That afternoon, the look of pity on Sherrie's face had told him more than he ever wanted to know. He was in real trouble.

Sitting on the hard cot, he cradled his face in his hands. There had to be an explanation. Someone had gone to a hell of a lot of trouble to frame him, to be certain he rotted in jail for the rest of his life. But who? Who would want him out of the way? Wouldn't it have been easier just to kill him? The thought made him shiver.

Pacing again, he thought, *Money*. Greed is always a motivating factor. Yet, even from prison he would still control his mother's money. It had to be something deeper, a longstanding grudge. Someone who hated him with all their soul.

There was only one person he knew who felt that way, who had told him to his face that she hoped he rotted in hell. But that was years ago. The thought of telling Sherrie to have her checked crossed his mind, then just as quickly disappeared because he knew she had so many problems to deal with right now. Surely, after all this time her hatred had waned.

Besides, she wasn't capable of pulling off a complex scheme like this. At least, he hoped she wasn't.

\* \* \*

That evening Ashe and Rae shared dinner atop a cozy blanket spread on the outer edge of RESCUE's grounds. As the last blush of a spectacular sunset eclipsed the building, Rae sighed. "Isn't this a beautiful place? Everything seems so peaceful here. Like there couldn't possibly be anything wrong in the entire world. But we both know how far that is from the truth."

"I suppose that's a matter of perspective."

The fine, sheer dress Rae wore offered little warmth, and she shivered as the chill of night began to settle in. Turning to face him, she asked, "So you don't think things are going badly?"

He grabbed another carrot stick and munched on it. "Things can always get worse."

"Let's see, since I started, the HDR well has been sabotaged, we've been exposed to God knows how much radiation, four people have been murdered, and the head of the company is in jail. How much worse can it get?"

"At least Nathan is still alive, and so are we. We could've worked on the HDR site for years before discovering it was slowly killing us, but we didn't. Losing Andy and the others is truly horrible, but all in all, I think we still have a lot to be thankful for."

Moving closer to him, Rae ran her finger along the middle knuckle of his right hand. "I don't remember you being so optimistic at the HDR site. In fact, I seem to recall you knocking a hole in the wall. Still a little swollen, isn't it?"

"Maybe. But I've learned a few things since then." He leaned to gently kiss her.

"Like what?" she whispered, her lips brushing his.

"Like life's too short to take for granted the good things that are waiting right at your fingertips." He kissed her again as the first stars welcomed the awakening night.

Rae shook her head, trying to clear her senses. "If you don't stop that, we won't notice when the cleaning crew arrives. Remember, that's why we stayed late—so we could interview the cleaning people. Especially the janitor in the security photos the night of Kelmar's murder."

"And I thought you agreed to share a romantic, starlit dinner with me for other reasons."

She kissed him, long and sensuously, then said, "I did . . . but, Ashe . . . someone just pulled up in front of the building."

He rolled away from her and sat up. There were only four cars left in the parking lot. His, hers, an old van, and a white utility truck that had CUSTOM CLEANING painted along the side. "Okay, you win." Ashe held out a hand and pulled her up. "But don't forget where we were."

She laughed. "How could I forget any of this?"

Together, they folded the blanket and stuffed the remnants of dinner back in its basket. As they started to walk toward the building, Ashe asked, "What'd you think of Sherrie?"

"She seems very nice. She must care a lot for Nathan to come this far to try to help him."

"In a way, it's really sad. Nathan's never gotten over her. They dated most of the time they were in college. When Nathan's mother became so ill, he moved her here to be near a specialist who was researching innovative bone-marrow transplants. Nathan proposed, even begged her to come with them, but Sherrie didn't want to leave New York."

"I take it the transplants they tried didn't work."

"Quite the contrary. She was given less than six months to live before the treatment. Afterward, she went into remission for almost five years. She got to see Nathan's plan to build RESCUE, but the second onset of the disease was faster than anyone expected."

Ashe pulled his key card from his pocket and slid it through the security lock on the front door so they could follow the two women who had just disappeared inside. Rushing to catch them near the elevator bank, he extended his hand as he said, "Excuse me, I'm Ashe Freeman, one of

RESCUE's directors. Would you mind answering a couple of questions?"

One woman nervously asked, "Is there a problem with our work?"

"Oh, no. We just need to talk to the people who clean on Friday nights. Could you tell us how to contact them?"

The other woman asked, "Was something stolen?"

Ashe shook his head as he explained, "No! Nothing is wrong. We just need to ask some questions. That's all. Really."

Both women relaxed but only slightly. The first one said, "We clean this building every night."

"Every night?" Rae asked.

"Monday through Friday."

"The two of you do the whole thing?" Ashe asked.

They both nodded. "It takes us a little over an hour to do each floor. We work from the top down—dusting, vacuuming, and emptying the trash. The bathrooms are handled by a different crew who comes during the day. We start each night at eight and finish around two in the morning."

"Are you familiar with the large glass office in the northwest corner of the fifth floor?" Rae asked.

They nodded.

"What time do you usually clean that office?"

"Between eight-thirty and nine."

"Has anyone ever been asleep on the sofa when you arrived to clean?" Rae asked.

They looked at each other, then shook their heads and said, "No."

Ashe and Rae exchanged a glance. "What about the man? Does he join you later?" Rae asked.

"What man?"

"Don't you have a man who helps you clean?" Rae asked.

They both shook their heads.

"Are you sure?" Ashe asked.

"Positive. We work alone. Always have."

Ashe handed each of them a twenty-dollar bill and said, "Thank you, ladies. You've been very helpful."

"Thank *you*, sir!" They hurried into the elevator and disappeared.

Rae walked over to the far side of the NatureAir entry and sat on a marble bench. She laid the blanket beside her. Ashe leaned against the closest window, and they watched the waterfall for several minutes. Finally Ashe asked, "Did you find out how to get prints off the tape?"

"I gave the security company the frame numbers of everyone who came in or out that night. They're sending over pictures. Sounds like we need to order copies of the frames where the mysterious janitor goes in and out as well."

Ashe stared at the front door and asked, "How could someone get in without a key card to release the magnetic locks?"

Rae shrugged. "Somehow, I don't think those locks would slow down a very sophisticated criminal. After all, whoever framed Nathan was pretty clever."

"True."

Admiring the lobby, Rae said, "It's hard to believe one man's dream could build all this."

"That's why we have to stop whoever's doing this. Nathan is a rare soul—a person who cares more about other people than himself."

With a smile she replied, "RESCUE has several of those running around."

Ashe began to pace. "I feel like we're missing something. Like the answer is here somewhere, and we just can't see it."

As he walked back toward Rae, he suddenly stopped. "What the hell is that?" he asked.

Rae followed the line of his sight, almost jumping off the bench toward him when she saw what was just outside the glass wall behind her. "Oh, my God! Not another one!"

Resting his hands on her shoulders, he said, "Stay calm. It can't be what it looks like."

Even though they were alone, Rae whispered. "It looks like an old tennis shoe, and with the way our luck's been going, it's probably still attached to the dead body someone hid behind those shrubs."

"I'll go check."

She grabbed him, holding on a bit too tightly. "No, you won't!"

"Why not? If it's what it looks like, it certainly isn't going to hurt anyone."

"We should call the police. What if whoever dumped it there is still lurking around? What if they jump out and grab you?"

Ashe stared at her as though to say, *I can handle it.*

Rae took a deep breath, then dug to the bottom of her purse and pulled out her "bodyguard. " Forcing the gun into his palm, she said, "All right, all right. But at least have enough sense to take this with you."

"Rae! I can't believe you're carrying a handgun in your purse in California! Are you *trying* to get thrown in jail, or do you just have a death wish?"

She shrugged. "I forgot I had it. I usually leave it locked in my glove box, but the other night I needed to run some errands after dark, so I moved it to my purse. I read this book once where the robber hid under a car and slit the woman's Achilles' tendon. It scared the hell out of me."

"Your imagination is in overdrive, Rae. All I'm going to do is see if whoever's lying out there has a pulse. They may need help, you know."

"Right. Most people dive in the bushes when they feel chest pains coming on. Or maybe the poor guy had a heart attack while he was window peeking."

"Good point. Maybe he was just window peeking."

"Could it be a homeless person?"

"I doubt it. Surely no one would choose to sleep in a spot right under the sprinkler system, where they're sure to get soaked at the crack of dawn," he replied as he started toward the door.

"I still think we should go upstairs and call the police."

"And tell them what? Excuse me, officer, but there's a shoe in our bushes and we're terrified of it?" He smiled at her and added, "Let me go see what we're dealing with. Then we'll know who to call—police, the coroner . . ."

"Okay. But I have a bad feeling about this. I'll hold the front door open so you can run back inside if you need to."

He rolled his eyes. "If it'll make you feel better, then by all means hold the door." Ashe walked briskly out toward the shrubs, the gun in his hand. Before he checked the bushes, he glanced over his shoulder at Rae, who was glaring at him from the open front door.

Carefully spreading the dense leaves of the bush aside, he leaned closer, now certain it was a body. His right hand instinctively tightened around the trigger as he reached forward with his left hand.

Although the grassy area was dimly lit by both the lights inside the building and across the parking lot, the shrub effectively blocked most of Ashe's view. Slowly, he extended his fingers to check for a pulse, gingerly touching the neck of the teenager lying before him. The flesh was warm, sweaty. Relaxing, he realized whoever it was, he was still very much alive.

Before Ashe could react, fingers viciously dug into his left arm, jerking him hard and fast against the thick glass wall.

# Chapter 12

When Jace awoke, the first thing he saw was a white man leaning over him with a gun. *The bastard found me again!* As his eyes focused, he was confused by his surroundings, hoping he was in the grips of another nightmare. Then he remembered . . . There was a man inside the building late that afternoon who looked like *the* man, walked like him, even dressed like him.

Earlier, from the parking lot, Jace couldn't be certain if it really was the homicidal maniac who'd been stalking him, or just a figment of his exhausted imagination. He was positive about one thing—he had to get a closer look, had to know for certain.

Gripping the van's keys in his hand, he had made his way carefully across the parking lot. After sneaking to where he could peek inside the glass walls without being seen, he quickly realized it wasn't him. Jace had disappointedly slumped against the wall to rest. For a long time he waited, but he was trapped in his hiding place by the constant stream of people hurrying in and out at quitting time.

When he saw the gun in the darkness overhead, he quickly realized he must have fallen asleep. He knew he couldn't afford to waste any time. With all his might he used his good hand to grab the man's forearm, hoping to catch him off guard. When he heard a dull thud against the glass wall of the building, then a loud groan, he knew he'd accomplished his goal.

Before the man could regain his senses, Jace crawled up

to steady himself. But he instantly fell back down, screaming in agony from an unexpected kick that landed directly on his broken arm. The bastard was even stronger than he remembered.

Jace reacted instantaneously, wildly swinging his fist to catch the man in his left eye. He kicked everything in range, doing more harm to the nearby landscaping than anything else. By the time he stopped flailing, he was in front of the row of bushes, standing on the sidewalk. His adversary was still tangled in branches, trying to find his footing and free himself from the prickly grip of the broken shrubs.

Jace started to run toward the van, then realized his keys were no longer in his hand. They were in the bushes—somewhere—and he knew he wouldn't have enough time to hot-wire the van and escape. Out of the corner of his eye, he saw a woman near the front door of the building. He ran toward her, his aching free hand groping for the switchblade buried somewhere in his jacket. When his fingers finally grasped it, a quick push sent the gleaming blade flying out.

He smashed into the lady blocking the door at full speed, knocking the shocked look right off her face.

As Rae watched Ashe wrestle in the bushes, she was torn between going for help and going to help. She didn't have her key card, and she knew if she let go of the door, it would automatically lock them out. Searching the landscape, she saw a rock the size of a cantaloupe nearby. Praying the door would close slowly, she ran to the rock, grabbed it, then wedged her fingers in the door just before it latched.

After propping the door open with the rock, she whirled around and frantically tried to find Ashe again. Finally, she spotted him stumbling out of the bushes. She stepped toward him, intent on helping, but was promptly thrown against the door by the impact of a teenager's body striking hers.

Grabbing a fist full of her hair, he threw her in front of him as he yelled, "Tell him we're all going inside. Now!

Him first. And that I got a knife ready to slice you!" He poked her rib cage with the point, wanting to make sure his message was understood.

Rae did as he said, barely raising her voice as she called to Ashe, "He's got a knife. He wants you to go inside the building first."

Ashe held up his hands and stepped slowly toward them. As he walked past, he muttered, "That damned intuition of yours was right again." Grabbing the door, he kicked the rock in first, then followed it inside.

Rae stumbled as the teen roughly shoved her through the entryway. Catching her balance, she cried, "Hey! I'm doing what you asked me to do. You don't need to be rude!"

He shoved her again, plainly setting the ground rules.

Watching Ashe, Rae knew he was searching the Nature-Air lobby for anything he could use as a weapon. Unfortunately, as far as she could tell, the most lethal thing in the room was a poisonous plant. She fleetingly wondered what had become of her "bodyguard," whether Ashe had hidden it in his clothing or dropped it in the fight.

Rae's eyes met Ashe's again, and she sensed his defiance, his unwillingness for either of them to be a victim. She followed his glance to the rock and back, knowing he was trying to tell her it could be a way to stop him. Her mind raced as she weighed each of their options. *There are two of us and only one of him. He's already hurt. How much harm can one knife do? If Ashe has the gun, he can make his move if I distract the bastard. How am I going to get to that damned rock?*

Remembering the self-defense class her father had insisted she take, Rae decided to act first and worry about the consequences later. With a blood-curdling scream she wheeled around, her well-placed kick catching the boy's knees. He wailed as he crumpled to the ground, his knife sliding in circles across the marble floor before coming to rest in the gently waving pool of water.

Rae scrambled toward the rock, while Ashe defensively

positioned himself between the two of them. Two seconds after her attack, all three were staring intently at one another, waiting for someone to make the next move.

She could hardly believe her eyes when she watched the battered teen crawl back to his feet and lurch at Ashe. Even though the kid was obviously in great pain, he would not give up.

Ashe kept his distance, carefully jumping away from the boy's attack, then warily guarding him again. When he saw the boy's eyes dart toward the knife glimmering beneath the shallow water, he knew what the kid was foolishly thinking. In an instant they were both bounding toward the water, each intent on reaching the blade first.

As Ashe's body struck the boy's light frame, the impact threw them both into the water. They slid away from the knife on the slippery marble, struggling through lily pads and slimy weeds. Rae dropped the rock, then rushed toward the knife, losing her balance and plunging headfirst into the shallow water. While still sliding, she grabbed the weapon. Whirling to face them, she thought about tossing it to Ashe, but quickly decided to hurl it into the deepest part of the man-made pond instead.

Ashe overpowered the teenager, easily pinning him down with one knee against the slick marble. Holding the boy's good arm in one hand and his soggy cast in the other, Ashe tightened his grip. Through clenched teeth he muttered, "What the hell do you think you're doing?"

"Going for a little swim. Let go of me!" he spat.

"What were you doing in the bushes?" Ashe demanded.

"Sleeping. You're hurting me!"

Ashe smiled, shaking his head and showering the boy with water. "Good. Maybe you'll tell the truth."

"I'm telling the truth. Look at me, man, I'm soaked. So I *am* swimming. And I *was* sleeping. Don't you believe me?"

Keeping the boy pinned, Ashe settled into a more comfortable position. "Listen, we've got all night. You can keep up the smart-ass answers, or we can figure out why you just tried to kill us."

"What? I wasn't trying to kill nobody! You scared the hell out of me!"

Soaked from head to toe, Rae waded out of the water, her dress clinging provocatively to every curve. She moved near the men, coughing as she said, "This isn't getting us anywhere. We don't want to hurt you. We just want to know what you were doing, and we aren't going to let you leave unless you tell us."

The boy leered at her. "Listen, lady, I really need to get outta here. If someone sees me, it could mean big trouble for all of us, and I didn't come here to get nobody hurt."

Ashe said, "If I help you up, are you going to run?"

"Who, me?" he mocked.

Shaking his head, Ashe said, "If I didn't know better, I'd think that was another one of those smart-ass answers." He looked at Rae. "Why don't you go call the police? I'll just wait here with our friend until they show up." As she started to walk off, Ashe added, "You might want to wrap up in that blanket over there first."

Rae glanced down, blushing as she realized how little was left to the imagination from her clinging, wet clothes. She ran to the blanket they'd used for their picnic, covered herself, then rushed toward the stairs.

She stopped when the boy yelled, "No! You can't call the police!"

Ashe nodded to her to go on, but she stopped again when the boy screamed even louder, "Please! Don't call the police. I'll tell you what you want to know."

Rae walked back toward them as Ashe literally lifted the kid out of the water and stood him upright. She asked, "Why are the police looking for you?"

"They're not. Well, not directly. It's someone else."

"Who?" Ashe asked.

"Some white guy who works in this building. He's trying to kill me."

"Why?"

"I stole his frigging car."

Rae said, "I thought you said the police weren't looking for you."

"They don't know for sure I stole it. They think I did, but they can't prove it."

"But he's sure?"

He nodded.

"What's your name?"

When he hesitated, Rae spun around, briskly heading toward the stairs. "Jace," he replied.

"Jace what?" she asked.

"Jace Williams. Now can I go?"

Ashe smiled as he shook his head. "First, we're going upstairs where we can talk. Then we'll see."

"But—"

Ashe said impatiently, "But nothing. Why'd you jump me outside?"

"You white guys all look alike in the dark."

"Very funny."

"I ain't trying to be funny. I thought you were *him*. Besides, you're the one who had a gun pointed at my head."

"The gun was in my hand. It was not pointed at your head."

"Whatever. When someone's got a gun on me, I try not to hang around and figure out which piece of me is gonna be Swiss cheese first."

Rae asked, "Do you frequently have guns pointed at you?"

"Just lately."

She shook her head. "That's too bad. Maybe we can help change that."

"Yeah, right," he muttered.

They rounded the top of the staircase as Ashe said, "She's right. We will try to help. How do you know the person works at RESCUE?"

"Do what?"

Rae explained, "This building belongs to RESCUE, Inc."

"Oh, I get it. You folks get off by coming to the rescue of poor people like me. No way. I don't need no help. I just need to find out who that guy is so I can stop him. He's dangerous."

"And you're not?" Rae asked.

"Nothing like him. This guy's lethal. And he doesn't give up. He's like that pink rabbit on TV; he keeps coming and coming and coming. . . ."

Whether it was because they were all soaking wet, or just because their tautly wound nerves finally snapped, they all started to laugh. By the time they were in Ashe's office, they were practically hysterical. Except for the dark, wet weeds clinging to them, they looked like the end result of a wet T-shirt contest.

Rae said, "I'd better get some bags of ice. Ashe, your eye's starting to swell, and Jace, those knuckles look pretty mangled."

Ashe said, "Speak for yourself, lady. You've got quite a knot on your temple."

Rae gingerly touched the spot Ashe described. "Then I guess I'll get three bags." She disappeared into the hallway.

Ashe motioned for Jace to sit down. "What did this dangerous man look like?"

"He's white."

"That much I already figured out."

"The first time his hair was black, then the next time it was light brown. It was short both times. But it was his eyes that made him easy to recognize." Jace shivered. "His eyes and his voice. Even when he was screaming at my friends, he said every word perfect."

"Did he have an accent?"

"No. He just talks real careful. Like he has to think about every word before it crawls outta his mouth, or like he has lots of money."

Ashe walked to his bookshelf and took down a framed eight-by-ten color picture. As he handed it to Jace, he said,

"These are the employees of RESCUE. And by the way, we don't rescue people. We're trying to rescue the environment. We design and market products that don't pollute the air or water."

"I noticed those pictures in the hall. Pretty gross stuff, especially that bird covered in oil."

"We'd like to stop all that, but we can only do so much."

Jace looked carefully at the picture, pulling it close to his face so he could see the tiny facial images clearly. "This ain't everybody who works here."

"How do you know?" Ashe asked.

"That wet lady isn't in here, and there's another woman I saw come and go twice today, always carrying a black briefcase. She's kinda short, with wavy dark brown hair. Real classy-looking, has a New York accent. She was the only one I saw all afternoon who was dressed up, even had on high heels."

Ashe was truly amazed. "You are observant, aren't you?"

Jace cockily answered, "Gotta be if you're gonna survive the streets."

"You're right. The woman you met wasn't working here when this photo was taken, and that other woman is only temporarily using an office at RESCUE while she's in town."

"So the white guy I'm looking for doesn't work here?"

"RESCUE hasn't hired any men in over six months, at least not to work in this office. When did you steal this guy's car? What kind of car was it?"

"Seems like years, but it was only about a week and a half ago. It was a new Lincoln."

"No one who works here drives a Lincoln, much less a new one. We don't exactly pay top wages. In fact, most of our employees could work somewhere else for substantially more money."

"Then why do they stay here?"

"We're a dream magnet. People who work at RESCUE are all drawn together to meet a common goal. They feed off each other's enthusiasm while they get the chance to fulfill their visions. Hopefully, we pool our talents to make the world a better place."

"Must be nice," Jace sneered.

"What?"

"Being able to worry about the world. Where I come from, you worry about food, whether someone's gonna pop you in the head if you cross the wrong street with the wrong color on."

"No one's forcing you to stay there," Ashe said.

Jace muttered, "And no one's offering me a million bucks to leave, either."

"Did it ever dawn on you that you could work your way out? Why does someone have to give you the money?"

Jace's temper was rising. "How would you know what it's like? Any place you go, they'd give you a job."

"How many places have you applied for work?" Ashe asked.

"Gotta have wheels to get back and forth. Besides, one look is all they need. I'm out the door before I ever get in."

"You didn't answer my question. How many times have you applied for a job?"

Jace stared at him defiantly. "Twice."

"And did you have that chip on your shoulder?"

He scowled.

"Ever think that might be your problem?"

"Right now I have lots of problems. Mainly with the police."

"What a coincidence. Lately a lot of detectives have been hanging around here, too."

With a puzzled expression on his face Jace asked, "Why are cops hanging around? 'Cause I took that car?"

He shrugged.

"What time is it?" Jace frantically asked.

"Around nine forty-five," Ashe answered.

Jace jumped to his feet. "Shit! I gotta go."

Ashe cut him off before he could get to the door, grabbing his shoulder and spinning him around. "Hold on. What's the big hurry?"

"I promised someone I'd pick him up at ten. I'm not gonna let him down."

"How can we contact you?"

"You can't. The last thing I need is that maniac finding out where I'm staying."

"We have security tapes showing every person going in and out of RESCUE for the last month. Will you come back tomorrow? Maybe you can spot him for us."

"And maybe you'll have the police waiting here for me."

Rae walked in, tossing each of them a small plastic bag of ice. She said, "If we were going to call the police, they'd have been here by now. I had ample opportunity to contact them while I was gone."

Jace thought about it, then asked, "Tomorrow night at seven?"

Ashe smiled and held out his hand. "Tomorrow night."

With each step Ashe took, Thursday morning's bruises reminded him of the events of the night before. He walked slowly up the stairs, giving in to his aching muscles. Not one part of his body was immune to the soreness. For the first time he could remember, he felt old.

Just moments after he eased himself into the chair behind his desk, Rae rushed in. Bursting with excitement, she said, "You aren't going to believe it, Ashe!"

Rubbing his head, he asked, "Believe what?"

"I was in Brada's office this morning when—"

Ashe interrupted, "I thought she left for Midland already."

"She was supposed to leave at six this morning, but her flight's been canceled. She's booked another one at ten."

"And?"

"Dinell came rushing in with an envelope from Medic-Data addressed to Brada."

Ashe immediately perked up. "You're kidding!"

"No! It had a diskette inside and a note from Margaret.

The note said she was just making certain we got the information we needed, and thanked us again for being nice to her daughter."

"What did the diskette have on it?"

"I don't know. Dinell and Brada are checking it now. They asked me to come get you so we could all—"

He was out of his chair and halfway to the door before she finished her sentence.


Sherrie paced across Nathan's office, occasionally stopping to gaze out the window at the horizon. In New York the leaves had already fallen, autumn's crisp air a sign of colder days ahead. But a few stories below where she stood, the lush Southern California landscape seemed to deny the passage of time, of seasons.

She glanced at her watch. Nathan was already well on his way to Nevada, extradited for a crime she was certain he didn't commit. On his desk was a pile of notes she had read backward and forward a hundred times.

To her relief, Nathan's criminal lawyer had been impressive—efficient, knowledgeable, and cool under pressure. Her performance at the extradition hearing had been outstanding, but the case against Nathan appeared to be airtight. A little too airtight to be believable.

Sherrie grabbed the phone and dialed the number of the private investigation agency they had hired in Las Vegas. "This is Sherrie Rosen. Could I speak to someone working on the Greenwall case?"

After several seconds a woman's voice answered, "Kate Spears."

"Ms. Spears, my name is Sherrie Rosen. I hired your firm to look into the arrest of Nathan Greenwall. I had an idea that might turn up a lead."

"We'd appreciate any help we can get. So far we've confirmed the rumor that the police received an anonymous tip leading them to your client. Apparently it was unusual."

"In what way?"

"It was in writing, typed or printed on a computer. Most people make a quick phone call, or the greedier people call the police hot line, where they might eventually get a reward for their information. This tip was clean as a whistle. No fingerprints, no stamp, run-of-the-mill paper stock. Very unusual."

"Interesting. It dawned on me that the hotel might have surveillance videotapes. The tapes of RESCUE's lobby don't show Nathan leaving and returning in the middle of the night."

"We already checked. The entrances and casino are both monitored, but the tapes are rotated every week. If the police got them before the rotation, then there's hope. Otherwise, they've been erased."

Sherrie jotted a note to herself to ask Nathan's lawyer if the police had seized the tapes in time. "Anything else?" she asked as she tossed down her pen, then nervously grabbed a small gold and red lapel pin from the desk and began turning it around and around as she listened.

"Possibly another problem. There was a guy in the casino that night introducing himself as Nathan Greenwall. The description isn't quite right, but it still doesn't look good. Most of the people who remember him were rather intoxicated."

"Great," she said sarcastically. "Call me if you find out anything encouraging, okay?"

"Sure."

Sherrie hung up and examined the piece of jewelry in her hand. Excitement rose as she recognized its significance— the Red Cross awarded such pins to people who donated gallons of blood. "Anything's possible," she mumbled as she grabbed her purse and ran out the door.

Ashe and Rae rushed down RESCUE's hallways, practically falling into Brada's office.

"I can't find anything on this damned diskette!" Brada moaned. She was so upset her hands were shaking.

Rae said, "Maybe it wasn't made using standard word-processing software. MedicData probably uses specialized programs for deciphering medical dictation."

Ashe added, "Why don't we take it downstairs to Jim in Technical Assistance? The last thing we need is for anything to happen to it."

"Good idea!" Brada popped the diskette out of her machine. She started to stand, then slumped back into her seat. "Except that Jim is on vacation this week, and both his technicians are at the Solar/Wind test facility reprogramming. That lightning strike did plenty of damage, and they're trying to find out why the system's surge protectors didn't work."

Rae asked, "So the HDR site isn't the only RESCUE site where strange things are happening?"

Ashe said, "I hadn't connected the two, but I suppose you could be right—if someone unplugged the surge protectors."

Brada stood again. "You two are nuts! Do these mysterious saboteurs manufacture their own lightning? Are they little green aliens who secretly want us to fail so that in a couple hundred years we'll all be dead from pollution and they can have our planet without worrying about us? Wake up! We're just having a frigging streak of bad luck."

Ashe smiled at Rae and winked. "Brada, I wish you had shared this tidbit of information with us a little sooner. The radiation at the HDR site was probably from their spaceship. If only we'd known . . ."

Brada grabbed a book and hurled it at Ashe. He ducked, easily avoiding its path. "A little short-tempered, aren't we?"

Dinell rushed into the office, anxiously asking, "Well?"

"Well, nothing!" Brada shouted. "There's nothing on the damned thing!"

The two women's eyes met in silent challenge. "What's your problem?" Dinell asked.

"That depends. What did you do to the diskette?" Brada seethed.

"How dare you—" Dinell stepped forward, but Ashe blocked her path.

"Okay. That's it!" he sternly commanded. "We're here to solve problems together, not make them. Brada, give me that diskette. Everybody else, get back to work. Now!"

Walters hung up the phone, his last call finally made. Except for his stock in the air-filter business he'd founded, all his interests had been liquidated. After converting some of his funds to gold, the remainder of his assets had been wired to accounts in Switzerland and the Cayman Islands. In all, he had a little over two million dollars to begin his new life, as soon as he decided where to go.

Every fiber of his being warned him to leave the country now. But he had to finish the business he started. There were three loose ends to tie up, things that would haunt him forever without some degree of closure.

First, PetroCo had to be stopped once and for all. Years of nibbling away at them had obviously been unsuccessful. It was time they went down, and hard.

Second, Jace Williams had to die. At this point he didn't care how or if he ever saw his precious crossbow again, but that kid would pay.

And last, he would personally make sure that bitch at RESCUE never double-crossed anyone again.

# Chapter 13

By four o'clock Thursday afternoon, Sherrie's patience was running thin. After three hours of being shuffled from one person at the Red Cross to another, she knew little more than when she arrived. Nathan's well-deserved reputation for his personal and corporate donations to one of his favorite causes was apparent. Almost every person Sherrie met not only knew Nathan but respected and admired him.

Ironically, the very people who wanted to help him the most were prohibited from telling her anything without a court order. They danced around her questions with vague generalities, implying the answers Sherrie needed but purposely skipping the details necessary to present to the police. Finally, one encouraging tidbit of information was tucked in her hand by a particularly zealous volunteer who regularly worked RESCUE's on-site blood drives.

After a harrowing taxi ride across town, Sherrie was glad to be back at RESCUE. As she walked up the stairs, she looked at the clipping in her hand for the hundredth time in the last hour. It was a one-paragraph article from the local paper describing the recent vandalism of one of the Red Cross Bloodmobiles. Little information was given, only that two volunteers had been treated and released from a local hospital, and that damage to the vehicle had been minimal.

Dinell was at her desk when Sherrie came into the room. "Do you happen to know if Nathan gave blood recently?"

Dinell seemed distant, thoughtful as she replied, "It's been so hectic lately, but he does believe in giving. The

Bloodmobile regularly comes here every two months. Now that I think about it, I guess it wasn't very long ago they were here."

"Does he give every time they come?"

"I think so. Why?"

"Is there any way to find out the exact date they were last here?"

Dinell flipped through her desktop calendar and shook her head. "I'm afraid I didn't write it down. They're here so often that it's become pretty routine. If it's important, I'm sure I can find out."

Sherrie walked back into Nathan's office as she said, "Maybe later. Thanks anyway." Closing the door behind her, she picked up the phone. After several calls to various people at her New York law firm, she finally got through to a partner specializing in criminal litigation. "I'm sorry to bother you at home," she said. "The time difference between coasts can be hard to work around."

"Don't worry about it. What can I do for you?"

"I heard through the grapevine that you took a special interest in the Simpson trial a while back."

He laughed, then said, "You mean you didn't?"

"I'm afraid I actually had a life at the time. How closely did you follow it?"

"Closer than I care to admit. What do you need to know?"

"I'm interested in the blood evidence in particular. Didn't his attorneys claim blood was planted at the scene?"

"Among other things. They claimed there was EDTA in some of the collected samples their people tested. If I remember right, the prosecution's testing didn't show any EDTA."

Sherrie was scribbling frantically. "EDTA?" she asked.

"EDTA is a chemical preservative used to protect blood samples taken from victims and suspects. It's already in the vial when they draw blood, so it mixes readily with it. EDTA prevents blood samples from coagulating in the test tubes, so the serology and DNA tests can be performed."

"Do you think blood donated to the Red Cross would have some sort of identifiable chemical in it as well?" she asked.

"I know it does. The last time I donated blood, I asked. I don't remember the exact name of the chemical, but the nurse showed it to me before she drew my blood. The bag the blood flows into has the compound already in it. My curiosity is killing me, Sherrie. Why does an estate attorney care about blood evidence?"

"Because it may save a man's life. A very good man."

Brada came back from the airport for the second time that afternoon, angrier than Ashe had ever seen her. "I can't believe the frigging flight was canceled twice in one day!" she barked.

Ashe said, "Calm down. Ross didn't even know you were coming to see him, did he?"

"Hell, no. I want to catch him off guard."

"Then another day won't make any difference, will it?"

"Another year wouldn't make any difference. I've thought of every question I could ask him, and I really don't see why Nathan wants me to go. What's Ross going to say, 'Why, yes, Ms. Stevens, now that you ask, I did frame your boss, and knocked off my own at the same time. And by the way, we arranged to have Marilyn Prosser and her mother killed, and we dropped some plutonium down your HDR well.' Hell, no, he's going to feed me more of the same garbage. He'll have an airtight alibi. Going there is a total waste of time and money."

Ashe thought for a moment. "You know, you're probably right."

She whirled around to look at him. "You've got to be kidding. You're agreeing with me?"

"As a matter of fact, yes. Ross appears to be irrelevant at this point, either way. Sherrie said the police verified his call from Midland to Kelmar's room in Las Vegas the night of the murder."

"That proves a call was made from his house, but not who made it."

"True."

Brada said, "I think I'll hang around here instead of booking another flight. Besides, if they cancel my flight again, it'll be *me* you're trying to get off the hook for murder."

"I don't doubt that a bit. Anyway, Rae and I are planning a trip to the new HDR site in western Oklahoma early next week. We could easily swing down to Midland if Nathan still thinks it's important someone check out Ross."

"That makes a lot more sense to me," she said. Ashe turned to leave but Brada added, "Before you go, I have a couple of things I'd like to run by you."

He stopped, facing her again. "Fire away."

"Rae told Dinell and me what happened in the lobby the other night. Have you considered that this Jace kid may just be another PetroCo spy?"

He laughed. "A spy? Isn't that taking all this a bit too far?"

"Ashe, you have to admit his story is a little far-fetched. I just think we need to watch him. Closely."

"We are watching him."

"Really? According to Rae, you two let him walk out of here the other night without a care in the world. And that was after he pulled a knife on you. Pretty darn generous of you."

"Maybe we shouldn't have let him go, but the only alternative was to send him to jail. Deep down, he seemed like a nice young man who deserved a break."

"Andy was a nice man, too. He certainly didn't deserve what he got."

Ashe's face hardened. "I agree, but it's too late to change how we handled it now. What else did you want to discuss?"

Brada walked to the door to be certain she couldn't be overheard before she lowered her voice and asked, "Do you think Dinell's been acting a little odd lately?"

Ashe hesitated, then said, "Not odd, just tired."

"Why would she be so tired? As far as I can see, the rest of us are putting in just as many hours, if not more."

"True, but I think Nathan's absence impacts her directly. She has to sit there looking at his empty office all day, and you know how close they are. Half the time it seems like she's reading his mind."

"If you say so. It's just odd that, oh, never mind."

"Come on, Brada, say it."

"I've been giving all this 'bad luck' we've been having a lot of thought. Dinell has access to all the confidential information and everyone's schedules, including things like when HDR would be drilling and when testing would be done at our Solar/Wind facility. She even knew about my meeting with Marilyn, and you told me yourself she knew why her mother came here the day she was killed. And that diskette Margaret sent, she had access to it before anyone else ever even knew it existed. She could've erased it to be sure her secret was safe. It just seems like too many coincidences to ignore, especially when you consider everything."

"Everything?"

"Don't you know? Dinell's IQ is up in the clouds somewhere. She's a member of Mensa, and yet she's a secretary. I've always thought it was strange. She could do anything, anywhere, yet she works here in a job where she has no control, no authority, no people to supervise, no chance for advancement. Does that make sense to you?"

"Maybe she likes what she's doing," Ashe said.

"And maybe she's doing what she likes."

Clearly frustrated, Ashe said, "Speak English, Brada."

"What if someone from outside wanted to hurt RESCUE? Can you think of a better way than having an informant in the executive office?"

Ashe paced, deep in thought for several seconds, then said, "This whole conversation disgusts me. If we turn on each other now, we'll never pull through."

Brada held up her hands. "Okay, I didn't mean to start a war. I'm just trying to help Nathan."

He turned to leave. "We all are. Even Dinell."

"That's him!" Jace shouted.

Rae froze the frame of the security tape. It showed a rather average-looking white man in a business suit carrying an oversize attaché case. "You know, he looks a lot like that janitor." Fast forwarding, Rae stopped on the second image. One glance at Jace confirmed her suspicions.

Ashe asked, "Are you sure? Both are pretty fuzzy images."

Jace was visibly shaking. "I'll never forget him as long as I live. No matter what disguise he wears, he can't hide those eyes."

Rae touched his shoulder and calmly told him, "At least he can't hurt you now."

Pulling away from her, Jace sputtered, "Bullshit! No wonder you want to protect the ozone layer, lady. That must be where you've been living. 'Cause of him, I'll probably never see my mama again, or my baby sisters."

Ashe said, "But, Jace, we'll help you. With this information we can contact the police. I guarantee you they'll listen."

"Yeah, right. Look at him. Once the police have me, he'll have me. Which one of us you think they're gonna believe?"

Rae replied, "Then we'll just have to handle this matter a little differently then we'd planned. Ashe and I will meet with the police. We don't have to mention how we found out about the car theft, or the man who's trying to kill you. We'll come up with a way to—"

"To get me killed!" Jace shouted.

Ashe said, "Calm down. She's right. We can work around you for a while. No one has to know your name, or who you are. You feed us the details, like how you stole the car, where you left it, what you took. Basically, we need to have something concrete to work with so the police will know there really is a problem."

Jace laughed. "Stealing it was easy. I got the recipe for a grabber off the Internet."

"A grabber?" Rae asked.

Jace proudly said, "It's a thing that intercepts the signals people send when they remotely set their car alarms and lock their doors. We waited in the bushes and watched for an easy target. Once he was inside the building, all we did was use the grabber to send the same signal to unlock the car. It was awesome! The door locks popped up and we were in!"

"You built one of these all by yourself?" Rae asked.

"Sure. I'm really good with electronics. I can fix almost anything."

Ashe said, "Good. Where'd you leave the car?"

Jace's jaw clamped tightly closed as he walked toward the basement's narrow door. Just as he reached it, Ashe said, "Walk out now, and he'll be after you for the rest of your life, which may not be very long."

Jace's hand froze on the doorknob for several seconds before he turned back to face them. "What difference does it make? I can't go near my own family! I got no friends left. Anything I do in this town, he'll know."

"Who'll know?"

He stomped back, thrusting his finger at the picture on the surveillance screen. "If I was ready to die, I would've rolled over and let him kill me the first time."

"Because of that car you stole? If he's so lethal, how'd you manage to get away?"

Jace hung his head and shrugged. "Luck?"

Ashe's eyes narrowed. "You've got something he needs, don't you?"

Jace's eyes darted around the room.

"Where is it?"

"Someplace nobody but me knows. It's safe there."

Rae couldn't contain her anger. "Jace! You've got to go to the police!"

"No!" Looking her right in the eye, he added, "If you don't quit pushing the police, I'm leaving!"

"Why?"

"Because he'll hurt my mama and my sisters! He already ransacked our house when we were at Cory's funeral. I won't risk them!"

"Who's Cory?"

Jace ignored Ashe's question for a moment, then softly said, "My baby brother. The one I killed when I wrecked the damned stolen car!"

Absolute silence fell around them. Finally Rae said, "I'm sorry, Jace."

"Me, too," Ashe said.

"Yeah. Me, too," Jace sighed.

"If you trust us, we can help," Rae said.

"How?"

Ashe leaned close. "Tell me where the evidence you have against him is. I'll take it to the police. They can finger-print it and put a warrant out for his arrest."

Jace eyed them suspiciously, then asked, "And what if they don't have them on file? Then what?"

"We'll print this picture and find out. I'm sure someone who works here will recognize him. We don't have many strangers coming through RESCUE, especially disguised as janitors."

"And you'd leave me out of it? You won't turn me in?"

"For as long as possible. But sooner or later, Jace, you're going to have to make this right."

He shook his head. "I can't make it right. I can't hurt my mama like that. It's bad enough Cory's dead. It would kill her if she knew her other son killed him."

Ashe and Rae exchanged a look of concern, but before they could argue with him, he said, "If I tell you where to find the thing, will you get off my back?"

"Sounds like we don't have a choice," Ashe muttered.

Jace grabbed a piece of paper and quickly sketched a map. "It's under this bridge not far from where we went off the road. If you crawl up the grass and reach around the steel girder, you'll feel the handle. It's a silver briefcase, and inside is a crossbow like you've never seen before. Laser sights. The works."

"Are your fingerprints on it?"

"I'm not stupid. I had on gloves. We weren't going to keep the car. Cory just wanted to ride around for a while. You know, pretend he was somebody."

Rae walked over to Jace and hugged him. "You've certainly been through a lot lately."

Stiffening, he said, "I ain't coming back here. They'll be watching for me."

"Fine. You name the place we meet again."

"I'll call."

Ashe jotted down the phone number and handed it to him. "Leave a message on my voice mail if I'm not at my desk."

"Okay. I'll call tomorrow to tell you where to meet me. Just the two of you will know, right?"

"Right."

They walked silently up the stairs to the lobby. Ashe and Rae followed Jace to the van, then watched as he pulled out of the parking lot. Just after he turned the corner at the far end of the street, a car slid into the lane behind him, its headlights dark. They could barely see Jace's taillights as he turned left a block away. The other car turned left, too, it's brake lights never glowing as it rolled through the intersection.

Ashe muttered, "Oh, shit." He exchanged a quick glance with Rae and grabbed her hand. Together, they ran across the parking lot to his car. The tires screeched as they fishtailed into the street.

Ashe and Rae ran three red lights, praying they were going the right way. Luckily, traffic was light, and after about a mile they could see both cars ahead. "Are you buckled?" Ashe asked.

"Yep," Rae answered nervously. "What are you going to do?"

"I think the best thing would be to stay back and follow them."

"Do you have your cell phone?" she asked.

Ashe pulled it out of his pocket and handed it to her. "The problem is, by the time we call for help, whatever they have in mind will probably be over. We need a way to make sure Jace gets away."

"Why don't you pull in front of the car that's following him and slam on your brakes? That should at least slow down whoever it is."

"Good idea." Ashe floored the accelerator, easily passing the late-model blue sedan with darkly tinted windows. "Hold on," he said. His car squealed to an immediate stop, catching the other driver off guard. They both watched as the car behind them expertly veered around them, then slid sideways. Its front tire bounced over the curb as it came to a sudden, screeching stop.

Rae grabbed Ashe's arm as she twisted to watch. "We'd better get out of here!"

"I'd rather see who it is first. But don't worry. We'll be outta here before you can blink if whoever's in there comes out with a gun."

"Thanks. I feel a lot better now," she said sarcastically. It didn't take long for someone to step out of the car, and the two of them shared a confused look when they immediately recognized the woman.

Brada was storming toward them!

Ashe jumped out of his car, meeting her halfway.

"What the hell are you doing?" Brada screamed.

His voice matched hers in both volume and intensity as he answered, "We thought we were trying to help Jace! Why in the world were you following him?"

"Because we both know he could be part of our problem! I was just going to find out where he's staying, so we can get some background information on him. You're too damn trusting! We don't even know if he's really who he says he is!"

"Damn it, yes, we do! He doesn't know it, but I already contacted the police. Even though I gave them only sketchy details, apparently at least part of his story is true."

"Really?" she asked incredulously.

He was starting to calm down. "Really."

Brada wrinkled her nose. "Then I just screwed up, didn't I?"

Ashe looked down the road they'd been traveling. "Let's hope not. I think he was far enough in front of you that he wouldn't have noticed. Besides, I doubt if he would think the little traffic stunt I just pulled had anything to do with him."

"God, I hope I haven't blown all your hard work! I'm really sorry, Ashe. I should've trusted your judgment."

"It's okay. Is your car all right?"

"Probably needs a front-end alignment, but I think it'll be fine."

"Then let's all go home. It's been a long day."

As they drove away, Rae kept her eyes on the road behind them for a few moments, then asked, "We're not really going home, are we?"

"Of course not."

Thirty minutes later, they found the bridge. Ashe drove past it, then pulled onto a dirt road and parked.

"Are you making sure no one's following us?"

"Absolutely. There's no use taking any chances."

"What if someone stops?"

Curling his fingers around the back of her neck, he pulled her gently to him. After a long, sensual kiss he whispered, "They'll think we had other reasons for parking here."

While romantically sprinkling light kisses over his face,

Rae said, "Life with you . . . gets more exciting every minute. Murders . . . hidden treasure . . . what next?"

"Hopefully, a big climax!"

"Ashe!" Rae laughed, blushing as she pulled away. "We have a lot to learn about each other before we take that step."

"I was talking about retrieving the crossbow, but your interpretation is much more intriguing. What exactly do you want to learn about me?"

Rae was obviously embarrassed. "I . . . didn't mean that quite so . . . so literally."

With a mischievous twinkle in his eye, Ashe tickled her. "Oh, come on. Let's see. My favorite color is blue. I've never been married, and I think you have the prettiest smile in the entire world."

She couldn't help but laugh. "Thanks."

"Now it's your turn. Favorite color?"

"Purple."

"How long were you married?"

Rae was instantly serious. "Oh, Ashe, let's not go there."

"We have to sooner or later. As far as I can tell, it's the only thing standing between us."

Rae was quiet. Gazing out the window at the stars, she said, "I'll always love him. Always."

"That doesn't mean you can't love someone else, too."

"How can you be so sure?"

"I can see it in your eyes, in that smile. He'd want you to be happy, wouldn't he?"

"Of course. It's just . . . you don't understand!"

"Then make me understand. Tell me why you can't let go."

Rae was silent for a long time. Finally, she sighed as tears welled up. "I lost my husband in the Oklahoma City bombing. He left to run an errand, to deliver some copies, and I never saw him again."

Ashe pulled her into his arms relieved to finally know the truth. "I know how horrible it must have been, and I know the pain will never leave. But it was years ago, and you deserve to move on." As if a light had just snapped on, Ashe tilted her face so he could see her eyes. "Is that why you ran off at the HDR site the night of Andy's murder? Because you thought there might be a bomb?"

She nodded. "That brought it all back. Then I was so embarrassed, and I didn't want you to feel sorry for me. The people killed in the bombing weren't the only victims."

"I'm sure that's true. But keeping it a secret isn't necessary."

"Don't you see? That's why I wanted this job! I needed to get away from Oklahoma. Everyone here has been wonderful, very supportive of me, and I don't have to wonder if it's because they think I need their help. It's just, after a while, you get worn out seeing that 'poor thing' look in people's eyes when they pass you on the street. It's a constant reminder of something horrible that happened in the past."

"Rae, I'd like you to feel free to talk to me about anything, at any time. I respected you before you told me because you've earned it. All that's changed now is that I know I was right. You're a very special woman. A woman I've fallen hopelessly in love with."

After wiping away her tears, Rae kissed him, and for the first time in years her heart and soul became one.

At noon the next day, Rae was absentmindedly staring out the window of Ashe's office, waiting for him to return. She was fascinated by the heat waves shimmering from the parking lot, as if they were crawling back to their home in the huge California sky. Hearing him behind her, she whirled around. "So, how'd it go at the police station? Is one of our suppliers really a cold-blooded killer?"

"Looks that way. Harvey Walters certainly has some explaining to do."

"You don't sound very enthusiastic."

Tossing aside his briefcase, Ashe plopped into the desk

chair. "That's because I just spent three hours trying to say things without *saying* anything. Helping Jace is next to impossible without his cooperation!"

Rae rubbed his shoulders. "I know it's frustrating, but I have to admit, I can see his point. I don't think I'd be in a hurry to turn myself in under these circumstances. I know it's wrong for him not to be punished, but I think he's learned his lesson."

Ashe sighed. "I'm not sure if they were just trying to scare the hell out of me, or if it was the truth, but Jace was right about that crossbow we recovered last night. The police weapons expert said it was something only a pro would use. Remember those odd blue molds? He thinks that it's the crossbow that was used to murder Senators Evans and Giles. By the time I left, there were FBI agents crawling all over the place. I'm afraid we may be in way over our heads!"

"Oh, my God! Now what are we going to do?"

"Before the FBI gets to him, I want to see if Harvey Walters is safe and sound in Denver where he can't hurt Jace. Why don't you listen on the extension?"

Rae nodded and grabbed the other phone when Ashe signaled the long-distance call had gone through. "This is Ashe Freeman with RESCUE, Inc. Could I please speak to Harvey Walters?"

"I'm afraid he isn't in right now," the receptionist replied.

"When do you expect him to return?"

"I'm afraid Mr. Walters will be out of the country indefinitely due to a family emergency."

"Oh."

"Would you like me to transfer you to your account rep?"

"No. Actually, I thought I just saw him here in town. Do you happen to know if Mr. Walters drives a late-model Lincoln?"

"He did until a couple of weeks ago, when it was stolen."

"I see. Well, thank you for your help."

Silence filled the room until Ashe finally said, "Walters could be anywhere."

"So what do we do now?" Rae asked.

"We have to get Jace to turn himself in, or lie to him and take him to the police ourselves."

"Or . . ." Rae smiled. "What if we put him someplace where no one can find him? That way he's safe, and we don't break our word."

Ashe nodded, pulling her close. "Great minds really do think alike."


Jace watched the hands move slowly around the face of the old clock hanging on the kitchen wall. George was bringing his wife home from the hospital today, and they would be there any minute. Time was running out. He dialed the phone number and waited.

"Ashe Freeman."

"I want to do it right away."

"Fine, but we need to talk first. The police verified your story. You're in grave danger. Do you trust me?"

Jace sucked in a deep breath. "Like I got a choice?"

"Rae thought of a way to keep you safe, and I think it's our best bet. We'll leave the police out of the picture for a while, but you have to trust us."

Jace heard the van pull into the driveway, then the sound of George talking softly to his wife. His stomach clenched as he realized he was risking the life of the only man who had ever treated him with respect. "Okay. Tell me what you want to do."

"We can pick you up, or meet you at the airport."

"Airport," Jace said.

"Gate twenty-two?" Ashe asked.

"Okay. Leave now?"

"Now's great. Everything's going to be all right, Jace. And, remember, no weapons at the airport."

"Whatever." He hung up just as George helped his wife in the door. Jace took her hand and said, "I've heard lots of nice things about you. George really missed you. I'm glad you're feeling better."

She smiled. Tears welled in her eyes as she studied Jace's familiar face. After casting a glance at George, she warmly said to Jace, "Thanks for keeping him company while I was gone."

Jace beamed at George. "I kept him in line for you." Turning serious, he added, "He's been real good to me. I hate to ask, but can I borrow the van one last time?"

George threw him the keys. "It runs better now than it ever has. You're quite a mechanic."

"Thanks for everything," Jace said as he stared at him, wishing he could hide with these people forever. "I can't tell you how much you helped me."

The finality in Jace's eyes was apparent. "What goes around comes around, son. I'll sure miss you. Remember, do what's right and the rest will work itself out."

"I'm trying to."

George hugged him, carefully avoiding his broken arm as he whispered in his ear, "Just call and tell me where you leave the old rattletrap. Put the keys under the driver's-side mat. I'll come get it later."

Tears were in Jace's eyes as he ran out the door.

# Chapter 14

"What do you mean, right now?"

"I mean, we have to leave for the airport. Immediately."

Rae's eyes widened. "But . . . I haven't packed . . ."

Ashe grabbed her hand. "Neither have I. We'll have to pick up a few things when we get there. I'm sure Jace will need some warm clothes, too. We both know how cold that HDR site can be."

Rae stopped in her tracks. "Wait!" She rushed back in her office, opened the bottom drawer, and grabbed a Geiger counter and the radiation badges they'd worn at the site. As she stuffed them inside her briefcase, she said, "We might need these."

"Good thinking."

They dashed down the hall, practically running over Dinell as she came out of the executive suite. "Where are you two off to in such a hurry?" she asked.

Ashe answered, "We're meeting Jace at the airport. I'll check in every day."

"Where will you be?" she asked.

He quickly looked up and down the hall, then whispered, "You know Jace can identify Harvey Walters as a professional killer. We're taking him to the fake HDR site, where he'll be safe. Have you told Sherrie and Nathan?"

"First thing. She was on her way to visit him, so I'm sure by now they're thinking of ways to stop Walters."

"Good. We'll see you in a few days." They hurried down the hall, then ran down the stairs.

When they were in Ashe's car, Rae asked, "Why'd you tell Dinell we were going to the fake HDR site? I thought we agreed to pitch a tent at the old site where no one would expect anyone to be, just in case our trap worked and someone from PetroCo shows up to cause trouble."

"That *is* where we're going, but this way we may find out who we can trust and who we can't. Maybe Brada was right about Dinell. I don't want anyone to know where we are really staying besides you, me, and Jace. You wouldn't happen to have your "bodyguard" in your purse, would you?"

Rae smiled shyly and shrugged. "Well, yes."

Ashe reached over the seat, grabbed a duffel bag, and dropped it in her lap. "Unload it, then put it and the Geiger counter in here. We'll check it as baggage, so you don't get thrown in jail."

"Good plan. Wait a minute, no lecture this time?"

"I can't exactly blame you for not feeling safe lately. But after all this is through, you'll have to promise not to—"

Holding up her hands, she said, "Okay, okay." She winked at him as she leaned close and wound her arm around his. "Besides, I'd rather have a real live bodyguard around to protect me."

"I'm sure that can be arranged," he said.

Walters shut off the engine of the Land Cruiser he had bought with cash the day he left Denver and stared at the headquarters of PetroCo. During the drive across New Mexico and the Texas panhandle, he'd had plenty of time to think of ways to make them pay. The answer came to him at the end of a long day on the road. It was time to start the wheels turning that he'd set in motion years ago.

Stopping at the first motel he saw, he paid cash for a room and carried his bags inside. Two briefcases held all the documentation he had accumulated over the last twelve years with the help of his contact at RESCUE. Unzipping the carrying case, he gently lifted out his laptop computer and set it on the table. After connecting his modem, he was ready to begin.

In a matter of minutes, he drafted an outline. Changing files, he scanned his personal phone directory until he found the numbers he needed. He dialed the first phone number and waited.

"Corbin White," the woman snapped, her voice gravelly, tired.

Walters spoke through a device that rendered his voice unrecognizable. "You are the youngest journalist ever to land a Pulitzer prize, aren't you?"

"Yes. Listen, I'm sorry to be rude, but I was on my way out. What can I do for you?"

"Would you be interested in a story that could bring down one of the largest oil companies in the world? Are you willing to expose them as the greedy bastards that they are?"

There was a pause, then, "Of course. What have you got?"

"Do you have a fax machine you can personally monitor?"

"Yes."

"Give me the number. Wait by the machine, then read what I have. I'll call you back in ten minutes." He jotted down her fax number, then hung up, switched on the modem, and faxed her the outline. Precisely ten minutes later, he called again.

"Corbin White." This time she was alert, eager to talk.

"Did you get it?"

"You bet. Where did you get this information?"

"That's irrelevant, but I assure you I have documentation to support every claim. The important question is, are you willing to set up PetroCo's current president, Karl Ross, to prove the allegations are true?"

"Anything illegal involved?" she asked.

"Slightly."

"What did you have in mind?"

"I can arrange for him to meet with you. He will believe

you have designed a revolutionary lightweight battery, capable of efficiently running automobiles and small vans utilizing a combination of electric and solar power. Your invention supposedly allows the economical production of electric cars in the very near future. Of course, you would have to arrange for the meeting to be secretly filmed, et cetera, and be convincing. I want the public to see what kind of people are running America."

"What am I supposed to do if he wants the plans for this wonder battery?"

"If my guess is right, you should be able to get the evidence you need without bringing the actual product to the table. I've already planted enough hype about it that any area checks will verify the product exists. The point is to show PetroCo's desire to hinder the progress of pollution-free transportation—that their arrangements to purchase brilliant ideas, although perfectly legal, are somewhat less than ethical."

"And you'll provide actual documentation of the other items you listed?"

"PetroCo has effectively buried most of the technology I mentioned in my fax. I can, however, give you the write-ups the inventions received before the inventors suddenly withdrew their ideas from the public. Of course, my identity will remain unknown, for obvious reasons. Are you interested?"

"That depends on the price."

"Ah, a woman to be reckoned with. My payment will be watching you nail them to the wall. But there is one catch."

"There always is."

"You'll have to meet with him tomorrow."

"Tomorrow! How do you expect me to set everything up so soon?"

"That's why you have a Pulitzer and I don't. You're resourceful." Walters hung up and smiled. He checked his watch, then dialed the second number on his list.

"Hello."

"Find out anything?"

"Ashe and Rae know everything. Who you are, what you look like, everything."

Walters was quiet for a while. "Where are they?"

"An HDR site in Oklahoma."

"What the hell are they doing there?"

"Apparently, they believe you're trying to kill Jace Williams."

"With good cause," he muttered.

"Being the good little Samaritans that they are, Ashe and Rae are hiding him until you're locked up."

"Not a wise decision."

"If there isn't a warrant out for your arrest already, there will be soon. Not only from the information Williams gave them, but from Chuck's murder. Apparently, the evidence against Nathan is unraveling quickly."

"Shit. I expected it to take them months. Where, exactly, are they hiding Jace?"

"About five miles due north of the site you sabotaged. There's another abandoned well there. I'll fax you an aerial map." She laughed, adding, "Rae had this harebrained idea that PetroCo would try to sabotage that site as well!"

Inwardly he seethed. She didn't even bother to pretend that it wasn't a PetroCo well she had asked him to contaminate with radiation. He took a deep breath to calm himself before asking, "How long will they be there?"

"Your guess is as good as mine. When will you take care of them?"

"Sunday morning. I can wrap up what I'm doing here anytime, for that matter, from anywhere. Don't worry, I'll make sure no one is available for future comment." Covering his irritation with her, he sweetly said, "As always, your information has been extremely helpful."

Gently cradling the receiver, he made certain the line was disconnected, then added, "And when I'm finished with them, it will be your turn to pay. No one is going to make a fool out of me. Not you, not that stupid black kid, no one!"

Sherrie walked out of Nathan's office just as Dinell hung up her phone. "Everything okay?" she asked.

Dinell nodded nervously, then took a deep breath. "I'm just having a hard time right now."

Sherrie smiled and waited, encouraging her to continue by being silent.

"That was my . . . sister on the phone. She found out a couple of weeks ago she's very ill. They want to know if I'm a possible kidney donor. This is the third time she's called this week."

"Are you worried about the procedure?"

Dinell's eyes darted about the room. "Yes and no. My sister and I have never been close. Even when we were kids we fought all the time. In fact, we haven't spoken in more than ten years. It's almost like having a total stranger come up to you and ask you to undergo a serious operation. Then, on top of everything else, they need help paying for it because they don't have medical insurance. I want to help, I really do, but my husband thinks I'm crazy. He wants me to refuse to even be tested—"

"Why?"

"Because he doesn't think it's fair for her to even ask. He doesn't care that I may be her last chance. He thinks that because she always treated me so badly, she should find someone else. I told him I could sell some of my RESCUE stock to pay for it, and he went nuts. That stock has always been for our retirement."

"So you're damned if you do, and damned if you don't. Nothing like loading on the guilt, right?"

"Right." Dinell dabbed her moist eyes with a tissue.

After an awkward silence, Sherrie asked, "It seems awfully quiet around here. Where is everybody?"

"Ashe and Rae went to an HDR site in western Oklahoma, and Brada's been out all day chasing down some lead she says will help Mr. Greenwall. The rest of the employees are either keeping their noses to the grindstone or out looking for jobs."

"Is it that bad?" Sherrie asked bleakly, for the first time realizing that clearing Nathan's name might not be enough to save RESCUE.

"The articles the newspapers keep running are really getting to everyone. They make it sound like an open-and-shut case, like the prosecution has enough evidence to . . . you know. I guess some people who work here think he's guilty; others are just afraid they won't have a job tomorrow. Dreams are nice, but they don't put food on the table and pay the rent. Are you making any progress at all on the case?"

"Definitely." Sherrie excitedly added, "You've heard about the carpet fibers the police found near the body?"

Dinell nodded. "They were mentioned in the paper."

"But what the paper didn't say was that even though the fibers match the carpet in Nathan's office, they're unusual."

"Really? Why?"

"First, they've been stretched, like they've been pulled out. Plus, they have microscopic pieces of latex on them that can't be explained. Both support our framing theory."

"That's great. I really don't mean to eavesdrop, but I can hear most of what is said in Mr. Greenwall's office. You've been talking an awful lot about blood samples lately."

Sherrie nodded. "The final lab work won't be back for several days, but the preliminary reports show there is some kind of chemical in the blood found at the scene."

"What kind of chemical? Alcohol?"

"No. Preservatives. If they're present in the samples at the scene, it might prove someone stole Nathan's blood from the Bloodmobile the last time he donated, then used it to frame him."

Dinell shook her head. "Who would think of such a thing?"

"Obviously, someone very clever, but not quite clever enough. The forensic expert we hired said the blood-splatter patterns leaving the hotel room aren't typical of the minor injury sustained by Nathan. The drops of Nathan's blood the police photographed and collected are large and round."

"So?"

"So Nathan didn't have any wounds serious enough for blood to be pouring out. The flesh wound on his arm wasn't deep at all. In fact, it was practically healed before they even arrested him. Besides, for the drops to be perfectly round, Nathan would have to have been holding still, literally dripping blood, not struggling in a fight to the death with Kelmar. If the lab verifies our suspicions, Nathan's problems are over."

Dinell cocked her head and flatly stated, "Not necessarily."

"Excuse me?" Sherrie asked, amazed at how quickly Dinell had not only regained her composure, but assumed an aggressive attitude.

She shrugged as she stood up. "Obviously, he's been set up by someone who wants to hurt him, or get him out of the way for quite a while, if not forever. When they release him from jail, that problem will still be there. And this time, whoever is trying to harm him and RESCUE may not take such an indirect route."

Rae jumped out of the pickup, holding the Geiger counter in front of her as she walked along. Ashe and Jace unloaded three camouflage pup tents, plus the six boxes of supplies they had just purchased in town. They had stopped at an Emergency Medical Center long enough to get a new cast on Jace's arm. It gave him a little more flexibility since it only went from his wrist to his elbow, and was wrapped in camouflage to fashionably match the brown, green, and gray pup tents.

"Are you sure the two of you will be all right here?" Ashe asked.

Rae winked. "Positive, after all, I've got my 'bodyguard.'"

Jace perked up, puffing out his chest and lowering his voice to mimic Ashe: "That's right, I'll take care of the little woman."

After rolling her eyes at Jace, Rae turned her attention back to Ashe. "You'll be back before dark, right?"

"I certainly hope so." Ashe hopped back in the pickup. "All I'm going to do is pitch the other two tents at the new site."

Rae and Jace watched the truck bump away along the dirt road. Tugging on the chest of his brand-new insulated coveralls, Jace asked, "How long do I have to wear these things? They itch, and they're hot."

Rae laughed. "If you want people to believe you're working on a well site, you have to dress the part. Believe me, you won't be hot once the sun goes down." He shook his head and started to walk off. "Stay by me, Jace," she warned. "I need to check for radiation before you go anywhere."

"Yeah, right. Radiation. I thought you were trying to protect me. Seems to me you're trying to kill me!"

"We wouldn't have brought you here if there was any real danger. Walters couldn't possibly know where you are, and the only people who might show up at the new HDR site are some of PetroCo's spies. The chances of either happening are slim since we haven't even cleared the site."

"Why would PetroCo send spies?"

"To keep us from succeeding." Pointing to the west, she quickly changed the subject. "Our tents need to be under that grove of scrub oaks over there, so they won't be easy to spot from the air, or at night, for that matter. If you don't mind helping me carry these things—"

"Whoa! You're expecting them to look for us with airplanes and helicopters?"

"I'm not expecting them to look for us at all! It's just since we don't know what to expect, we're going to prepare for the absolute worst. After all, we promised you'd be safe."

"Why can't we stay in that mobile home over there?"

"It might be contaminated. Besides, camping out is more fun. Right?"

"How would I know?"

"Haven't you ever communed with nature before?"

"I ain't sure what that means, but if it means not having hot water and a place to . . . sit in the morning, I don't think I'm gonna like it much." Jace grabbed a load of supplies, including the gadgets they'd picked up at various electronic stores. "When do I get to rig up those things we talked about on the plane?"

"After we get everything ready for tonight. We need to pitch the tents and get the supplies squared away so raccoons or other critters don't run off with them."

He stopped in his tracks. "Raccoons?"

"Jace, we *are* in the middle of nowhere, you know."

He searched the area. "What other kinda animals haven't you bothered to tell me about? Bears? Lions? Tigers?"

"More like deer, elk, wild pigs, and stray dogs. Nothing that won't be as afraid of you as you are of it."

"What about snakes? I don't like snakes. Or spiders."

"Too cold for snakes. Now, if it was warmer . . ."

They reached the trees and put down the first load of supplies. Jace immediately started rummaging through the boxes. Rae asked, "What are you looking for?"

"That hunting knife we bought. I think I'll keep it with me. I feel kinda naked without my blade."

Rae laughed, but in reality she thought it was an excellent idea.

The site of the abandoned well was much rougher than when RESCUE first tested it and had pictures taken years ago. In fact, the area was so overgrown, Ashe wasn't certain whether he was still on the road or not, especially since there were so many potholes and washed-out places. Finally, after inching and bumping along for several minutes, he decided it would be faster to walk.

With the aerial photo of the site in hand, he searched the

area until he finally found a pile of gravel he recognized. Pulling back some dead weeds, he located the old well site, which obviously hadn't been touched in years. Kicking through the crunchy overgrowth, he located the rest of the equipment nature had disguised so well.

Glancing at the sun falling low in the sky, he knew he had a problem. It was already late afternoon, and there were no clear places to pitch one tent, much less two. Black-jacks and scrub oaks had covered the land, most of them three to four feet tall. Even though a 'dozer could clear the area in a matter of minutes, Ashe knew that it would take him hours using a machete. Even the hand-held torch they had brought along to burn brush couldn't be used.

Hiking to the pickup, he decided to go back to the real campsite. They could return in the morning to pitch the tents, and at the same time rig the booby traps they'd de-vised. When he reached the driver's side, he realized the truck was listing at an odd angle. Walking around the bed, he saw the back passenger-side tire was flat.

Kicking the dirt, he muttered, "Shit!" Stomping back to the cab, he cursed the entire way. Digging under the seat, he found the pouch of tools he needed to fix the tire. As he wedged the jack under the frame, the soft ground crumbled with every move. After thirty minutes of dragging rocks over, he finally had the tire far enough off the ground to take it off.

It hadn't dawned on him that there might not be a spare.

"You worried?" Jace asked.

"Of course not. Ashe can take care of himself, and so can we." She stirred the chili cooking over the camp stove, ladling some into a bowl before she turned off the stove and put a lid on the pot. "I don't think he'd care if we ate without him. It's getting pretty late."

The night was quiet except for the wind rustling the few stubborn brown leaves still clinging to the branches. Jace took the bowl of chili and immediately started eating as though he hadn't been fed in years. Halfway through, he slowed down long enough to ask, "Aren't you gonna have any?"

"I'm not hungry."

"You sound mad," Jace mumbled as saltine cracker crumbs fell from his lips.

"Only at myself. This was not a good plan. We should've all stayed together, or at least kept the cell phone so we could call for help. I can't believe I agreed to it."

"I'm having a hard time believing I'm even here." He set down the empty bowl and pointed at the evening sky. "Look how clear it is up there. You can see every star."

Rae turned off the lantern, leaving them in darkness. Relaxing, she sat next to Jace and stared at the constellations with him. "They're pretty awesome without any city lights to fade them."

Jace was quiet, then asked, "Did someone die here?"

Startled, Rae answered, "Yes, but how'd you find out?"

"There's a little wooden cross over by that drilling rig. It says, 'Daddy, We miss you.' "

The first thing that crossed Rae's mind was concern for Andy's family, but exasperation at Jace for ignoring the warning signs quickly took over. She unleashed her anger by shouting, "Jace! I told you not to go anywhere near there without me! We're not kidding about there being radiation problems here. When did you go? How long did you stay? Do you understand how dangerous radiation poisoning can be?"

"Jeez. I just walked over while you were pitching the tents to see what it said. I wasn't there but a second, and I didn't touch anything."

"You don't have to touch anything. Just being near the source exposes you, and we know the well is contaminated. It can kill you, Jace. Not necessarily that instant, like a bullet, but over a period of years—cancers, horrible things. Don't do it again. Please?"

He stared at her, then nodded.

"Promise?"

Jace didn't answer. He was too busy jumping up and struggling with the hunting knife at his side.

They had both heard the rustling noise a few yards from camp. Rae hurried into the pup tent where her things were stowed, pulling the gun from under the pillow of her sleeping bag. "Jace, get in here!" she whispered.

Jace had succeeded in removing the knife from its leather sheath, and it was the first thing Rae saw as he crawled into the small tent. Rae pulled him close, breathing, "Shhhhh . . ."

Twigs snapped outside as leaves blew against the side of the tent. Whatever it was, it was approaching fast.

# Chapter 15

Rae clutched Jace's arm as the rustling noise moved closer. "It's probably just a raccoon," she whispered.

"Must be a damn big one," Jace muttered. "Sounds more like a bear."

"I told you, there aren't any bears around here."

Glaring at her, he asked, "A mountain lion?"

"How many mountains did you see on our drive out here?"

"Maybe it's just Ashe."

"I didn't hear the pickup."

Jace shrugged. "Could've broke down. That would explain why he's so late."

"Ashe wouldn't sneak up on us. He knows I have a gun."

"I think we should run. This flimsy tent is a death trap."

Rae looked around the small enclosure, instantly realizing Jace was right. The pup tent's material was too thin to stop anything that really wanted to harm them, and the narrow exit made a quick escape impossible. She shifted to her knees. "I'll peek out and see what's out there. The problem is, where do we run?"

"That mobile home?" Jace asked.

"It's locked."

"The rig?"

She glared at him. "Do you remember where the road is?"

"Of course. I keep telling you, I ain't stupid."

"Then get to it and head north. I'll be behind you. Maybe

we'll run into Ashe. When I give you the signal, you go for it. Remember to stay low, and that most animals are more afraid of you than you are of them."

"What if it ain't an animal? What if it's a person? What if it's *him*?"

Trying to sound calm, Rae said, "How could it be? No one knows where we are. No one except Ashe, and he wouldn't do anything like this."

"What if he has a sick sense of humor?"

"Under the circumstances, that wouldn't be very wise, now would it?"

"Maybe it's that dead guy's ghost from the oil rig. Maybe he don't like people running around here bothering him."

She rolled her eyes, then leaned forward, poking her head out the zippered opening that served as the tent's door. "I don't see anything."

"I don't hear nothing." But the second he stopped talking, they both heard a low, guttural bawl. With wide eyes Jace asked, "What the hell was that?"

"I don't know, but it's pretty close. I've got the gun. You make a run for it, and I'll cover you." Rae rolled out of the tent and landed in a crouch, the gun ready to fire in her extended hand. Jace followed, lurching forward, then running at top speed toward the road.

From the brush a huge animal emerged, aggressively charging Jace at an impressive pace. In the moonlight Rae could tell it was only a bull, complete with long, lethal-looking horns. Jace, no doubt, was certain he was being attacked by a beast straight from hell.

Rae dropped the gun to her side, watching as Jace climbed the first tree he came to, the new cast on his left forearm not slowing him down a bit. Unable to control herself, she started snickering as soon as she knew he was safe. In a matter of seconds she was laughing so hard she could barely see past the tears in her eyes.

Jace was busy trying to climb higher in the gnarly tree, the limbs beneath him bending each time he pulled his legs away from the bull's horns. When he finally found a branch strong enough to hold him, he glanced down at the bull, which seemed intent on standing guard directly below until he surrendered.

Just as Jace was about to call for help, he caught a glimpse of someone emerging from the shadows behind Rae. She heard Jace's warning at the exact moment a hand touched her shoulder from behind. Screaming at the top of her lungs, Rae whirled around, bringing the gun to shoulder level, ready to fire.

Ashe instinctively ducked sideways as he shouted, "It's me! Don't shoot!"

"What the hell are you doing here?" she howled.

"Looking for you! Don't the lanterns we bought work?"

She lowered the gun and took a deep breath. "They work fine. We were watching the stars when we heard *him*." She pointed toward the bull.

"Oh, I know all about him. I've crossed his path a couple of times in the last hour. I think he lost his girlfriend. A little testy, isn't he?"

"I'll say. He scared the hell out of us," Rae muttered. "As a matter of fact, you both did."

"Where's Jace?" Ashe asked.

Jace answered by calling, "I'm up here. Would you two shut up and make him go away!"

At the sound of Jace's anxious voice, Rae started snickering again.

Ashe walked a little closer. "Exactly how do you propose I make him leave you alone?"

A long silence was followed by Jace shouting, "Use the rest of the chili as bait. Maybe he smelled it cooking, and that's why he came."

"Hey, Jace!" Ashe hollered back. "What do you suppose is in that chili?"

More silence. Ashe and Jace had caught Rae's contagious laughter, and Jace answered from high in the tree, "I suppose it's some of his frigging relatives. Maybe he came to avenge their deaths."

"Probably," Ashe called.

Rae wiped more tears from her eyes. "Where's the pickup? Maybe you could convince Mr. Bull to move with a friendly little push."

"Flat tire. No spare. That's why I'm late, and on foot."

"Maybe this place really is possessed!" The bull snorted, turned completely around twice, then took several steps toward Ashe and Rae. She glanced down, picking up the ladle and the lid to the pot. Banging them together, she started to walk toward the bull, who backed up a few steps, then stopped to stare at her.

"What are you doing?" Ashe hissed. "He charged me twice on the way. I don't think he's in any mood to be taunted."

"I'm just scaring him a little. Letting him know we aren't going to put up with his nonsense. Trust me, my grandpa John had a farm, and I spent a lot of time there as a kid. But just in case, if I were you I'd pick which tree you want to sleep in tonight."

Jace yelled, "Oh, yeah, he looks absolutely terrified of that racket you're making."

In response to a distant, similar bawl, the bull grunted again. He whirled back around, lumbering slowly down the road with his tail swishing. When he was almost out of sight, Jace shouted, "I can't get down!"

Ashe winked at Rae and yelled, "What was that?"

"I'm stuck up here!"

"And?" Ashe shouted.

Exasperated, Jace screamed, "And I can't get down!"

"So?" Ashe asked, smiling from ear to ear.

"So, you goin' to get me outta this frigging tree or not?"

"Are you asking for help, Jace? Because I haven't heard you ask for help yet, and I know you don't like us helping you all the time. You said so yourself on the plane yesterday. At least, that's what I assumed all those silent glares were implying. One of these days you're going to realize we aren't doing all this for ourselves."

Thirty seconds later, they barely heard him mumble, "I'm never getting on a plane again. Besides, I was tired yesterday. And my arm hurt."

"And Rae and I weren't tired?"

"I'm sorry!" Jace bellowed.

Rae winked at Ashe. "Apology accepted!"

"I still can't get down!" he yelled.

Ashe took Rae's arm, turning her around with him. They both started to walk back to the tents, ignoring Jace's incredulous screams from high in the tree.

"Any chili left?" Ashe asked as he moved toward the camp stove.

"Sure. So, you had to walk all the way back from the other site?" she asked.

He nodded. "It took awhile, since I didn't have a flashlight and Mr. Bull kept harassing me. I wish I'd had a chance to charge my cell phone before we left. It was pretty weak when I used it to call someone to bring out a new tire. Naturally, they couldn't be here with a spare until morning. While I was at it, I lined up a 'dozer, too."

"A 'dozer? I thought we were minimizing costs."

"This plan isn't going to work if we can't make it look like we're staying at that site. Right now it's covered with such thick brush, it's hard to walk, much less pitch a tent. We only need to clear a small area."

"It's just as well. I was worried about burning brush when the grass is so dry. We'd need a good rain first, and we don't have time to wait for one." Ignoring Jace's cussing in the background, Rae asked, "Isn't this getting out of hand?"

"Jace? No, he'll figure out how to say 'please' sooner or later."

"I wasn't talking about him. I meant this whole plan. Maybe we should just find a motel for him to stay in where we know he'll be safe."

Ashe shrugged. "What? And miss all this?"

She laughed. "It is entertaining, but I have to admit, I was pretty damned scared when you didn't come back on time."

"We can't afford to baby-sit Jace while RESCUE falls apart. At least this way, while we're watching him, there's a slim chance we might catch whoever's trying to run us out of business."

"Do you think it's the same people who framed Nathan?" she asked as she handed him a bowl of chili.

Sitting down, Ashe said, "I honestly don't know. Hopefully, when I check in with Sherrie tomorrow, she'll have some good news. You know, I still don't really understand why she came, much less why she hasn't gone back to New York yet, especially now that Nathan's been extradited to Nevada."

Rae walked behind him and rubbed his shoulders. "Sometimes people don't realize how much they care about someone until it dawns on them they might never see them again. I think she finally realized her priorities were a little screwed up."

"More intuition?"

"Nope. Common sense. Plus, I have firsthand experience with that damned biological clock ticking away, not to mention regrets about not saying things before it's too late." She paused, then added, "It certainly got quiet, didn't it?"

They both listened. Finally, they barely heard Jace say, "Would you *please* help me out of this tree?"

Ashe sat his chili down and jumped up, grinning from ear to ear. He pulled Rae into his arms. Taking his time, he kissed her, holding her tightly against him in spite of Jace's groans floating past them on the wind. Finally he whispered, "Come on, we've got to rescue him from himself. Again."


Walters awoke Saturday morning refreshed and invigorated. It had been a long time since he had slept so deeply.

He felt certain his restful night was a sign his times of trouble were finally a thing of the past. After a quick shower and a light breakfast, he loaded the Land Cruiser and headed north, intent on making it to Oklahoma well before sunset. It saddened him to think that it would probably be the last time he used his lethal toys, but the thought of watching Jace Williams die revived his spirits.

Along the way, he used his cell phone to call Corbin White on the private number she had given him. "Did Ross take the bait?" he asked, not bothering to identify himself or disguise his voice.

"I'm meeting with him this afternoon. When I mentioned I had discussed my options with a certain professor at the University of California before his untimely death, he was all ears."

"Where are you meeting?"

"I insisted on a neutral place. We're setting it up at a bar in Stillwater, Oklahoma, called Eskimo Joe's."

"And you're certain he's personally coming?"

"He said he would. I'm working on finding a picture of him so I'll know if he's the real thing when he shows up."

"Does he understand you won't have the plans with you?"

"I told him they were in safekeeping until I decided what options I cared to pursue."

"Good. You'll be safer that way."

"Two of our cameramen will be discreetly watching. If he tries anything funny, they'll be all over him."

"Then I'll get back to you on Monday. If you have the videotape, I'll provide the rest of the documentation."

"Wait! Don't hang up."

"Why?"

"I want you to know how much I appreciate this. It could be the story of the year. I'd like to meet you someday."

He hung up, laughing out loud at the irony. No woman had given him a second look in years, and now one of the top reporters in the nation was coming on to him just days before he had to leave the country for the rest of his life.

* * *

In New York, Corbin hung up the phone and turned around. One of the FBI agents sitting behind her listened intently to his partner on his headset, then smiled. He patted her shoulder and said, "I know you were having second thoughts about contacting us, but you did the right thing. If it makes you feel any better, this is the lead we've been searching for. It's the same man who was tied to the car theft in California, where the murder weapon was found."

"Right," she grumbled as visions of another award-winning story faded before her eyes. Glancing at the outline of PetroCo's purportedly devious undertakings the mystery man had faxed her, her stomach knotted as tightly as it had the first time she read the sixth entry:

> PetroCo made extensive cash payments to Sen. Evans and Sen. Giles to induce them to sponsor the controversial bill currently before Congress. The corporation is, therefore, indirectly accountable for their untimely deaths.

Corbin glanced at her watch and laid down the fax. Standing up, she said, "If I'm going to be in Stillwater by this afternoon, I've got to catch a plane."

"We'd prefer you let one of our people handle this."

Smirking, Corbin said, "No way! We had a deal, remember?"

Shaking his head, he said, "We'll still have agents there to meet you."

Corbin was becoming agitated. "I don't think that's a great idea. You might blow my cover, and then I won't have anything to show for all this. After all, what the head of PetroCo is doing isn't illegal. Is it?"

"No, but the person you just talked to might be nearby. We don't want to miss our chance to nail him."

"Fine, but stay outside. Deal?"

"You still don't understand what caliber of person you're dealing with, Ms. White. Let's suppose he is watching, and he doesn't care for the way your little meeting is going. He's more than capable of killing everyone in the place without batting an eye. Is that the kind of risk you're willing to take?"

Corbin glared at him, then finally said. "One. One agent inside the bar. But that's all, okay?"

"Okay."

She tossed her oversize handbag over her shoulder and walked briskly out of the room.

As soon as they were certain she was gone, the two men burst into laughter. They both knew Eskimo Joe's would be crawling with so many FBI agents by five o'clock that afternoon, there wouldn't be room for any of its regular customers.

Neither of them had any intention of telling Corbin White. After all, it was for her own good.

"I thought I was the only one crazy enough to work on a Saturday morning," Sherrie said.

Brada smiled. "A few weeks ago you'd have run into half the office. Now it looks like I'm the only one here. It's pathetic."

"What are you working on?"

"The real question is, what aren't I working on?"

Sherrie walked around Brada's desk, leaning over the papers. "You're reviewing a financing agreement?"

Brada nodded. "We've got a Solar project ready to go. It'll run ten to twelve million. Dinell asked me to look over the paperwork."

"Does Nathan know about this?"

"Of course he does. It's been in the planning stages for almost four years."

Sherrie nodded, then picked up an airline ticket from the corner of Brada's desk. "Are you leaving town, too?"

"Nathan asked me to go to Midland to talk to Karl Ross. I canceled the first trip I had scheduled, but I decided Nathan was probably right. It wouldn't hurt to lean on Ross a little. He has more motive than anyone else on the face of the earth."

Sherrie started to open the ticket. "When are you leaving?"

Brada snatched it, stuffing it in her purse as she curtly answered, "In a couple of hours."

Skeptically, Sherrie asked, "You've arranged to meet him on the weekend?"

She nodded. "It was the only time he would agree to see me. Believe it or not, RESCUE employees don't exactly have the red carpet rolled out for them at PetroCo."

"That's not surprising."

Brada closed the file she had been studying. Standing, she said, "If you'll excuse me, I need to see if I can find the files that list which assets we can post as collateral."

Sherrie nodded as she backed out of Brada's office. "Well, have a good trip." When Sherrie was out of Brada's sight, she practically ran back to the executive suite. Flying through the door to the reception area, she was shocked to see Dinell coming out of Nathan's office.

"My goodness, you almost scared me half to death. Why are you in such a hurry?" Dinell asked nervously.

"I've just . . . got a lot to do. What are you doing here?"

Dinell sat at her desk. "I'm wrapping up a few things before I leave. I decided to be tested to see if my tissue type matches my sister. My flight leaves at noon."

"I think you made the right choice. Where are you going to have the tests run?"

"Oklahoma City."

"Really? I didn't know they had high-tech medical facilities there. Usually you hear of people going to the Mayo or to Houston. Can't they test you here?"

Dinell shrugged. "I guess not. Besides, my sister wants to see me."

Sherrie started to back into Nathan's office, physically withdrawing from the strain of continuing the tense conversation. "When will you be back?"

Dinell grimaced. "Whenever it's finished. I'm afraid this could get complicated." She grabbed her purse and headed out the door. "I'll call you when it's over."

"Good luck," Sherrie replied. Once she was certain Dinell was gone, she rushed inside Nathan's office and locked the door. She pushed the button on his desk, turning the walls opaque, and she sighed. Her anxiety was apparent as she tried to dial the phone, her hand visibly shaking. All she heard was the roar of equipment. "Ashe? Can you hear me?" she yelled.

"Not very well. The 'dozer's making a lot of noise. Let me walk to the top of the hill." After a couple of seconds he asked, "Is this any better?"

"Much."

"Sorry, but you'll have to speak up."

Loudly, Sherrie said, "I did what you asked, and things are more confusing now than ever."

"Are either one of them leaving town?"

"That's the problem. They both are."

"Interesting. Did you find out where they were going?"

"Brada says she's leaving for Midland to see Ross. Dinell says she's headed for Oklahoma City for medical tests."

"Shit! Both of those are close enough to here to be trouble."

Sherrie sighed. "How could I find out more about the new Solar project?"

"There isn't a new Solar project."

"Are you sure? It's supposedly going to cost ten to twelve million dollars."

"What?" he screamed.

"Brada was working on the financing for what she called 'the new Solar project.' She said Dinell asked her to review the paperwork."

"Are you sure? We haven't used outside financing since Nathan's mother died. Last I heard, Nathan still had several million left."

Sherrie said, "I know. That's why it struck me as odd."

"Can you get your hands on the papers Brada was working with?"

"I can try, but last time I saw the files, she had them with her."

Ashe warned, "Don't take any risks, just in case."

"Is there anything else I can do?" Sherrie asked.

"Nothing I can think of right now."

Sherrie paused, then asked, "Ashe, does all this look as bad as I think it does?"

"No," he said. "It looks worse."

Sherrie hung up the phone and laid her head on the desk, momentarily surrendering to her fierce headache. If the walls to Nathan's office had been transparent, she might have caught a glimpse of the woman who had listened to her conversation and was quietly slipping out the door.

"What's going on?" Rae asked, thankful the 'dozer was finally gone and the countryside was once again peaceful.

Ashe shook his head and answered, "More than I expected. We need to hurry. The tents and traps have to be set before this evening."

"Why the rush? I thought we'd at least have a few days."

He hesitated, then said, "I'm beginning to think you were right. Our problem probably is someone at RESCUE. Someone knowledgeable enough to feed Harvey Walters information."

Rae was quiet, then said softly, "So do I."

He touched her chin, turning her face toward his. "Next time you have doubts, feel free to hit me over the head to get my attention. I should have listened to you before."

She shrugged, her eyes cast down. "I didn't want to press the issue. Besides, I wanted to watch what was going on without anyone knowing."

"And what conclusions did you come to?"

"Brada and Dinell both had access to the information about Marilyn, her mother, when we would resume drilling at the HDR site again, the diskette that was erased. . . .

They were both filmed carrying large bags into RESCUE the day before Kelmar's murder. . . . Both are very bright, quite capable of devising a way to get Nathan out of the way for a while if they wanted to. . . ."

"So they can bankrupt RESCUE? Do you think they're working together?" he asked.

"Maybe, but why? Why would they want to hurt RESCUE? What could either of them possibly have to gain?"

Ashe was quiet, then said, "Could be money. PetroCo would probably pay a small fortune to make sure we disappeared." He shook his head, "But I don't believe either of them would stoop to murdering people just to make money."

Rae watched Jace working diligently in the bed of the pickup at the foot of the small hill where they stood. "Thank God you didn't tell anyone where we're really staying," she said.

"No kidding. I'm beginning to regret pulling Jace into all this. He had enough problems without getting sucked into RESCUE's mess."

"Look at him, though. He's really quite talented. Those traps he's working on are ingenious, very clever. I'm amazed at his knowledge of electronics."

"He's probably had his share of exposure," Ashe said.

"He told me he learned most of it in school."

"You're so naive about some things, Rae. He's street wise. Hot-wiring cars, drug deals . . ."

"What do drug deals have to do with electronics?"

"I doubt if Jace came up with the booby-trap idea by himself. More than likely he found out on the Internet how drug dealers protect their marijuana fields. But their traps are a lot more lethal than the ones we're going to use."

"Lethal?"

He looked up, then to the side. Finally, his eyes met hers as he explained, "I don't want to upset you, but they usually wire them with explosives. Protecting their crop, so to speak."

Rae didn't respond; she merely shook her head in disbelief.

Ashe continued, "I do agree with you, Jace has a lot of potential. He's mechanically inclined, and sharp enough to do anything he wants to in life. The problem is convincing him of that."

"He politely asked if he could have more cereal for breakfast this morning. And he didn't complain once about coming with us to help. I think we may actually be getting through to him."

"I hope so. Speaking of helping, we have a lot of work to do. We'd better get busy, so we can wrap this up in time to go into town and rent another truck."

"What do you want me to do?" she asked.

He tossed her a roll of garbage sacks. "Fill these with leaves and sticks. I'll need you to help set up the tents in a few minutes."

Rae headed into the woods, then turned back around. "Ashe, be careful," she called, her brow furrowed.

Stopping, he saw the unmistakable look of warning in her eyes. Shaking his head, he muttered, "Oh, no. Here we go again."


Sherrie waited inside Nathan's office for over an hour, then dialed Brada's extension. When there was no answer, she slipped out, feeling like a criminal as she crept silently through the empty halls. The door to Brada's office was locked, so she used Nathan's magnetic key card to open it.

After she slid inside the office, the door closed behind her and she felt the lock engage again. She wasn't surprised to find the top of the desk cleared, all the papers and files that usually cluttered the surface removed.

Sherrie sat in Brada's chair, rolling out each drawer to check for the Solar project file she had seen. It wasn't in the desk, so she tried the file cabinet. With her nerves on edge, she quickly checked all the hiding places she could think of, then left.

Back in Nathan's office, she gathered her things and locked his door as she prepared to leave. After peeking out of the reception area to be certain she was alone, she conducted a similar search of Dinell's desk and file cabinets. When nothing unusual turned up, relief washed over her. Toting her briefcase and purse, she walked down the hall, her step much lighter than it had been only minutes ago.

Bounding down the first flight of stairs, she held the banister as she rounded the corner. Sherrie never saw the ultra-thin metal wire stretched four inches above the second step of the next flight. She did, however, feel it catch the toe of her shoe.

As she painfully crashed head over heels down the marble staircase, Sherrie would have sworn she heard footsteps and laughter echoing all around her. The instant before she lost consciousness, she looked up to see a woman peering down at her from the rail upstairs.

"Why?" Sherrie whispered just before she drifted into a silent, black void.

Ross chose to drive from Midland to Stillwater, hoping the long hours alone in the car would help him decide how to handle things. He knew Kelmar had never actually participated in the purchases, yet he had not had enough time yet to develop the underground contacts necessary to find trustworthy outside parties to perform the services.

Since the phone call yesterday, his stomach had been on fire. Reaching for the bottle of antacid beside him, he chugged another dose. Taking a deep breath, he convinced himself that he was capable of handling any situation.

He wanted to believe today's meeting would be the beginning of a new reign—his. It had to be. With the professor dead, Ross knew that a new network would have to be established, and this was his chance to start the ball rolling in the right direction.

But one thing would change. Unlike Kelmar, as soon as

this woman's battery design was in his hands, she would immediately become an unnecessary liability. In the long run, killing such people would be much cheaper than paying them off.

# Chapter 16

Even though it was mid-autumn, by early afternoon both Ashe and Jace had shed their shirts. The wind had died, and the sun was warm on their backs as they worked, first wiring the area, then raking the leaves and sticks Rae had collected into a convincing pattern over the freshly cleared dirt.

When they heard Rae calling from over the hill to the north, they both dropped their rakes and ran. "What is it?" Ashe called as they reached the crest of the small incline.

"Come see!" she shouted.

Jace rolled his eyes, plodding apathetically toward her. Ashe followed. After hiking several hundred yards, they came to a small clearing next to a pond. Rae was sitting on a blanket, a picnic spread before her. "Anyone hungry?" she asked.

For the first time that day they ate, stuffing themselves with peanut butter and jelly sandwiches, chips, and Oreos. Relaxing, Jace lay back on the sun-warmed blanket and said, "This ain't half bad."

Rae asked, "What isn't bad?"

"Working outside. Fresh air. I never knew it could be so quiet anywhere."

"Have you ever thought about what you want to do with your life?" Ashe asked.

Jace shook his head. "I never thought past tomorrow. You learn that real young when every day is a disappointment."

"Maybe it's time to think about it. RESCUE is always looking for bright young minds."

Jace glared at Ashe as though he were crazy. "So?"

Rae said, "You can do whatever you want, Jace. It just takes hard work."

"Maybe I don't like hard work."

Ashe laughed. "You weren't complaining a minute ago. In fact, I think you've had a very productive morning."

"Maybe, but I wasn't learning things outta books."

"There are lots of ways to learn, Jace. The key is, you have to be willing to try."

Back at the freshly cleared site, a few hundred yards to the south, the cell phone in Ashe's shirt pocket rang, and rang, until finally the last of the battery's power was gone.

Ross walked into Eskimo Joe's and glanced around. He ordered a beer at the bar, then scrutinized his surroundings. It was obvious some of the people in the bar were college kids, ready to get a head start on their Saturday night partying. An equal number of people inside the bar were older men, possibly local professors or businessmen.

The woman he was meeting had told him she would find him, so he wandered awhile, then chose a table away from the late-afternoon crowd. It wasn't long before a blonde with thick glasses and a ponytail approached him. "Mr. Ross?" she asked.

He stood and shook her hand. "You must be a friend of the late professor. It was truly a tragedy, his heart attack at such a young age."

Shaking her head slowly, she agreed. "It really was a shock."

"I'm sorry. I don't mean to be rude. It's nice to meet you, Ms. . . . ?"

"Black."

"Can I get you a beer, Ms. Black?"

"No, thanks. I'd prefer we get this over with as soon as possible. I need to catch another flight this afternoon."

Glancing around, he said, "Why did you choose this

place? Wouldn't somewhere in California have been more convenient for you?"

"No. I'm not attending school there anymore. Besides, I thought a college town bar would be an inconspicuous place for us to make our arrangement. I'm sure they're used to professors meeting students here."

Looking around, he nodded in agreement.

Wringing her hands, she asked, "Listen, this whole thing makes me nervous, so can we just get down to business?"

Ross nodded again. "What exactly did the professor tell you?"

"He said your organization was interested in purchasing the rights to cutting-edge technological advancements, especially those that reduce the consumption of our world's natural resources. He also said you would be willing to pay handsomely for them."

"That's true."

"I was wondering, since my design is for a lightweight, rechargeable battery, what interest would a petroleum company have with it?"

"What makes you think I represent a petroleum company?"

"Mr. Ross, I'm neither stupid nor blind. I know you are president of PetroCo, one of the biggest oil companies in the world. And I know what kind of—let's call them—'ideas' you've purchased in the past."

Ross tried to appear calm. "Really?"

Rolling her eyes, Corbin said, "Does TriPlate ring a bell?"

Ross froze. After several seconds he stared at her and said, "The professor was not at liberty to discuss such transactions with anyone. I'd like you to forget you ever heard such a thing."

She held up her hands. "Okay. He was just trying to convince me to talk to you. When will you start marketing my battery if we come to a mutually beneficial understanding?"

"Although we try to incorporate the technology we purchase into our current products and systems, it isn't always immediately feasible. Plus, many of the designs we purchase are utilized behind the scenes to reduce consumer costs. The general public benefits but indirectly. Even if we can't currently put your battery design to use, rest assured, we are still very interested in purchasing your work."

Corbin hesitated, then asked, "Let me get this straight. You're not going to use the battery I designed right now, but you still want it?" She acted puzzled. "I guess I'm kind of naive, but could you tell me why?"

"Our main interest is to have control of the product, for sometime in the future."

Corbin nodded. "I see. Like a kid who wants to hoard all the newest toys for himself?"

Ross shook his head. "Not at all. We want to test and develop the product so that when the proper time comes to market it, it will be ready."

"How much are you willing to pay?"

"That depends. Our rates are negotiable, depending on the report our engineers give your work."

"Let's talk ballpark here. Two thousand? Ten thousand? Ten million?"

Ross laughed. "Somewhere between the last two figures. We'll guarantee ten thousand, just for your time and trouble to this point. Then, based on what our estimate of your invention's prospects are, we'll arrange for a generous monthly stipend. Of course, everything we do is strictly confidential."

"Why?"

Glaring at her as though she were a moron, he explained, "Because it has to be. If word were to get out that we pay so much for 'ideas,' as you call them, we would be swamped with inventions from every nut around the world. We work through a very exclusive network of professors, only on recommendation, thus minimizing our exposure."

"And what happens if I change my mind after we come to an agreement?"

"Our deals are final. We commit our resources, and we expect you to commit yours."

She laughed. "No refunds, no exchanges?"

Ross was not amused. He stood and said, "I believe this conversation is over."

"No! Please sit down. I was just kidding. My friends tell me I have a weird sense of humor. I'm sorry."

He hesitated, then sat back down. "Did you bring your work?"

"No. I wanted to be sure you were legitimate before I risked losing it."

Ross acted insulted. "Why would our meeting risk you losing your work?"

"For all I know, you could grab my research, then knock me off as soon as I walked out the door. Like I told you, I'm not careless."

Ross took several deep breaths, trying to think. From his aching head to his knotted stomach, he sensed this girl was trouble. "So what exactly do you want from me? Surely you don't expect to be paid before we test your designs? What if they're worthless?"

"No, I don't expect money at this point. I just want some sort of proof of your good faith."

"Such as?"

"Such as the name of someone else you've dealt with. Someone I can contact and find out if you really came through on your end of the bargain. Like maybe the person who designed TriPlate?"

Ross stood, then angrily said, "That is not possible! In fact, this whole arrangement will not work. We're obviously wasting each other's time."

Without looking at her again, he stormed out of the bar.

Corbin pulled off her glasses and smiled directly at the camera.

\* \* \*

Rae sat in the trees on the side of the road, well outside
the newly cleared site. She held the two-way radio in her
hand, listening for the signal. Even though she was expecting it, she still jumped when she heard Ashe's voice, indi-
cating he and Jace were ready for her to test what they had
painstakingly worked on all day.

Rae stood, brushing moist soil from the seat of her blue
jeans as she stepped forward. Although she knew exactly
where to look for the clear fishing line that would trigger
the perimeter alarm, she had a hard time seeing it in the
waning light of day. Almost imperceptibly, it caught her
foot as she crossed it, and she was certain it wouldn't alert
an unsuspecting intruder, or even a large animal.

A few seconds later, she heard Ashe's voice on the walkie-
talkie again, and she walked into the campground. Outside
the entrance to each tent were pressure-sensitive pads, the
kind commonly used under carpets in burglar alarms. They
had carefully covered the pads with thin layers of dirt, then
scattered leaves and twigs across the rest of the freshly
turned soil to hide their tracks.

"Everything's working," Ashe said. "We'll be there to
get you in a couple of minutes."

Pressing the button, she responded, "Okay, but hurry.
This place gives me the creeps."

Laughing, Ashe asked, "What happened to that logical,
mature woman I hired a few weeks ago?"

"She glows in the dark from radiation exposure and has
a sick feeling in the pit of her stomach. Just hurry, okay?"

"Be right there."

One last time, Rae fluffed the sleeping bags stuffed with
leaves to make them look occupied, then ran from the tent
to the extra pickup they had rented that afternoon. The temperature was falling as fast as the sun, and she shivered as
she hopped inside the cab. After locking the doors, she took
a deep, calming breath, mentally scolding herself for al-
lowing her gnawing fear to overwhelm her logic.

By the time Ashe arrived, she had calmed down. They

were leaving the spare pickup at the new site, under the assumption that no one would believe anyone was actually staying there without transportation. "Where's Jace?" she asked as she hopped out and locked the door.

"He wanted to lie down. I figured he deserved a rest after the day he put in."

"Intense, wasn't he?" Rae said.

"It's been a long time since I saw anyone as proud as he was when you triggered those alarms a few minutes ago."

"With good cause. He worked hard, and I think he earned something very important."

"What's that?"

"Self-respect. Maybe now he'll decide he does have a chance to make something of his life."

"Let's hope so."

They climbed into the other pickup, and Ashe started down the bumpy road. Rae shivered, the fear grabbing her again, this time with a vengeance.

Ashe pulled her close. "Are you okay?"

She snuggled against him. "Physically, I'm fine. Mentally, I just can't shake this feeling that something terrible is going to happen. Soon."

On the crest of a hill a quarter mile north of the new site, Walters dropped his night-vision binoculars to his side and smiled. Although lightly disappointed that Williams apparently wasn't staying with them at the site, he knew he was getting close. Very close.

Dinell's flight landed in Amarillo, Texas, a little after three o'clock that afternoon. With a Texas map in one hand and an Oklahoma map in the other, she pointed the rented Jeep Cherokee due east and drove like a madwoman until it was too dark to read the maps any longer. Pulling into the first gas station she saw in Elk City, Oklahoma, she filled the gas tank and ran inside.

"Excuse me, but I'd like to know how to get to this location." She showed the cashier the aerial photograph, complete with the legal description of the acreage.

He was an older man, with a huge pot belly and a stubbly beard, which he scratched as he studied the picture. "If this ain't the darnedest thing. No one's cared a flip about that hunk of land for years, and now twice in one day someone's asked about it."

Her stomach turned, but she managed to ask calmly, "Is it hard to find?"

Glancing out the window, he replied, "Not really. But the roads out that way are a mess, especially if you're going in from the south. Those are mostly oil-lease roads, and since that land's full of dry holes, they ain't been used much lately." Nodding at her Cherokee, he asked, "That thing got four-wheel drive?"

Dinell shrugged. "I guess so. It's a rental."

His yellow teeth showed as he snidely said, "Really. I'd have never guessed."

She was getting impatient. "Would you mind telling me how to get there?"

"Just head north on Route 34. When you pass the red barn on the east side of the road, turn west. Follow that about three-quarters of a mile until the road dead-ends. You can get in either way, but it's easiest to follow the road around and come in from the north. I'll warn you, all the gates on that property are supposed to be locked."

"Then how do I get in?" she asked, exhausted.

"Depends on where you're going. It's a big hunk of land, mostly overgrown. I used to coon hunt out there, back when they kept the place up. Guess you could hike, if you don't have too far to go. But if I were you, I'd wait until tomorrow. There's a storm blowing in from the north. Might get some sleet before the night's over. Could be pretty nasty."

She was wringing her hands, her eyes nervously darting around. After grabbing a sandwich and two bags of Sugar Babies, she paid for everything and rushed out.

He called after her, "If you don't mind my asking, what're you planning to do out there?"

Over her shoulder she yelled, "Meet someone." But under her breath she added, " 'Kill someone' would probably be more accurate."

When Ashe and Rae arrived at the campsite, Jace was sound asleep in his pup tent, still wearing his coveralls and boots.

"Should we wake him for supper?" Rae asked.

"I don't think he'll starve. Besides, missing our gourmet hot dogs and canned pork and beans is probably better for him than eating them."

"We'll be more creative with our menu when we go into town in the morning. Can we make a camp fire, or do you think that would draw too much attention to us?"

"Sorry, I don't think it would be a good idea. The wind's really starting to come up, and the fields are still pretty dry. Hopefully, we'll be able to make it to town in the morning like we planned."

Rae's eyes narrowed. "What's that supposed to mean?"

"It means I heard on the radio that the weather service has issued a winter weather advisory for tonight. The roads may be pretty hazardous by morning. I wish my cell phone wasn't dead."

Rae smiled and snuggled into his embrace.

He kissed her, then rested his head atop hers. "I'll never figure you out. You like the idea of being stranded out here?"

"No. But I like the idea of everyone else being stranded somewhere besides here."

Once Walters was sure they were gone, he circled wide to the road Ashe and Rae had driven out on. In a matter of seconds he had disabled the pickup they left behind, then scurried back into hiding, since he was uncertain how long they would be gone. Fighting the frigid wind, he backtracked in his own footsteps until he reached the north gate of the land. From there he stayed on the dirt road, hiking back to the Land Cruiser. The black ATV blended so well into the trees where he had backed it off the road, he walked past it the first time.

Working without light, he shifted part of his gear into the two front seats, clearing a narrow place behind the seats to sleep. After unrolling his sleeping bag, he took off his boots and climbed into the warmth of the snug, down-filled fabric. He wasn't sure how long he stared at the dark ceiling, plotting ways to find out what hole Williams had managed to crawl into this time.

Jace's absence certainly complicated his plans simply to kill Ashe Freeman and the unlucky woman who was with him, since they were probably the only people who knew where the little bastard was hiding. Finally, he developed several alternative solutions, and fell asleep looking forward to the challenge of tomorrow.

The sound of gravel crunching under tires abruptly aroused him from a dead sleep. Resisting the urge to bolt upright, he rolled to one side, then crawled to look over the top of the front passenger seat. Sometime in the last few hours a light mist had begun to fall, and the temperatures had plummeted. The windshield was covered with a thin sheet of ice, and his breath fogged as it escaped through clenched teeth.

Although his view was blurred, he could tell it was a red Jeep Cherokee crawling along the bumpy road. When it was out of sight, he pulled on his boots, then climbed out of the truck. Tiny ice pellets were pinging off the car, stirring the leaves, blanketing the land. Rummaging through his bags, he finally found his winter gear and several of his deadly toys.

Once he was completely outfitted, he began his hike. The gate to the land where he had briefly seen the RESCUE workers was only a quarter mile ahead. Following the Cherokee's tire tracks made his job easy, in spite of the weather.

In fact, he enjoyed the challenge. Fighting the elements made his tasks more interesting, adding a degree of unpredictability that he frequently used to his advantage.

Trudging along, he knew his luck had definitely changed. This time the odds were all in his favor.

When Dinell reached the gate described by the disgusting man at the gas station, she was so tired she knew she couldn't hike far. What should have taken minutes to find had actually taken hours, since she got lost several times and the weather had turned bad.

In her hand she held one of the good things her round-about way of finding the place had provided—a pair of wire cutters she purchased at a hardware store in a little town called Clinton. She'd also purchased gloves, a knit ski mask, coveralls, insulated hiking boots, an ice scraper, and the most lethal things she could find—a lightweight hatchet and a hunting knife.

Awkwardly, Dinell pulled the warmer clothing over the things she already wore. Although she'd been driving in the freezing rain for over an hour, she was still shocked by the blast of cold air and the tiny ice pellets striking her face when she opened the car door. She was immediately grateful for the extra layer of clothing as she pulled the ski mask to cover her chilled face. Climbing out, she ran to the gate, quickly scanning the area illuminated by the halo of the Cherokee's headlights.

A culvert ran along the entrance, leaving two-foot-deep channels in the dirt in front of the fence line. Choosing the flatter of the two sides, Dinell hurried toward the barbed wire. The brand-new boots didn't grip the slick grass as well as she expected, and she slid precariously down the slight incline, her face stopping inches from the dangerous fence line.

Sitting up, she caught her breath, trying to relax. Using wire cutters for the first time in her life, she barely managed to snip the taut bottom wire. When the wire suddenly popped, each end instantly curled toward a fence post, shocking Dinell so much she lost her balance and tumbled back into the ditch. She stayed there for a few seconds, regaining her strength, her nerve. Working quickly in the cold, she snapped the other two wires and climbed back into the Cherokee.

After warming herself on the car's heater vents, she backed up and drove slowly through the brand-new opening. Once inside, she maneuvered back to the dirt road and stopped again, using the aerial photograph to locate exactly where she thought she was. Besides the problems darkness brought, the picture was several years old, taken when RESCUE had initially evaluated the site. What little she could see looked totally different than what she expected.

According to the map, she needed to drive south for a half mile. The oil well itself was only a few acres south of a small pond. The road built by the oil company to access the actual site came in from the other side of the pond and ended at the wellhead. She knew she could drive most of the way, but she would have to hike around the pond to get to the actual site.

Looking at the grim, rough country awaiting her, she wondered if she had lost her mind. But deep down she knew she had no choice.

Walters watched the woman struggle with the wire cutters, almost laughing aloud when she tumbled backward the second time. He was too far away to see who it was, but he had a feeling it was his friend from RESCUE. Maybe she was having second thoughts about telling him to kill two of her co-workers, or maybe she wanted to help carry out the plan. Either way, coming here was a fatal mistake on her part.

Even though she drove most of the way to the pond, he had no trouble keeping up with her on foot. He had the advantage of knowing where she was going, so he took a shorter route, cutting through the woods. Ironically, she had faxed him the aerial map of the site, making his job infinitely easier. When he neared the edge of the treeline, he could see the pond in the clearing. He wasn't surprised to find the Cherokee parked beside it. Pulling out his night-vision binoculars, he was shocked to see she had already made it halfway around the pond. *Maybe she's more competent than I thought.*

Stepping up his pace, he maneuvered as silently as he could through the crunching, frozen brush underfoot. He was torn between stopping her before she had a chance to warn them, and watching to see if, instead, she was there to make sure they never told anyone what they knew. Even though she appeared to have planned her attack, he doubted if she was capable of handling both of them. Unless, of course, she was well equipped.

The thought of her being armed unexpectedly disturbed him. Over the years he had grown to respect her shrewd tactics, sometimes even relying upon them. He suddenly realized that in many ways they were alike. If she was here to kill them, she probably intended to kill him as well. The bitch wouldn't be happy until every link to her was severed. Forever.

# Chapter 17

At the real campsite, Ashe, Rae, and Jace were burrowed into their sleeping bags, resting peacefully. Even though it was sleeting, the inside of each small pup tent was dry and comfortable. To prepare for the storm, they had moved the tents into a circle, the openings turned inside. The camp stove and some of their supplies were covered with a blue tarp in the center of their makeshift wind block. Everything else had been packed into the toolbox attached to the bed of the pickup.

When the alarm sounded, for several seconds no one moved. Each thought they were imagining the sound, that they could bury their heads even deeper in the warm covers and it would fade away like a bad dream. But it didn't.

Jace was the first to react. "It worked!" Several seconds later, as reality sunk in, he said, "Shit! Now what do we do?"

Ashe groggily answered, "Maybe it's the weather." He poked his head out of his tent and added, "Everything's covered with ice. Could the extra weight trigger either one of the alarms?"

Jace replied, "No way. The fishing line has to have at least a ten-pound pull, and those pads require twenty-five pounds of pressure."

Rae stuck her head out of her tent, tiredly muttering, "Then we'd better get dressed."

Jace snapped, "It's probably that damned bull."

"You know . . . it could be," Rae said as she pulled on her boots.

Ashe was busy dressing. "I don't think we can take that chance, do you?"

No one answered.

"That's what I thought. I'll go and check. You two stay here."

Rae stopped and stuck her head out. "But, Ashe, what if it's . . . It could be, you know . . . You'll need someone to back you up."

"First of all, the chances of this being who we thought it might be are slim to none. Why would anyone at PetroCo give a damn at this point? Second, I don't think we should risk exposing Jace to anyone—"

Jace shouted, "Do you two think I'm deaf? Quit talking 'bout me like I ain't here. If it is him, I don't wanna be anywhere near that place. I'm staying here!"

Ashe snapped, "Fine!"

Rae came out of her tent. "Then you'll have to stay here alone, Jace. I'm going with Ashe."

"Good. Go. Get the hell out of here. I'm going back to sleep."

Rae snickered. "What are you going to do if that bull comes back?"

Jace didn't answer; he only grunted and zipped the door to his tent closed.

Rae walked over, unzipping an opening big enough to stuff in one of the walkie-talkies. "Keep this by you just in case," she said.

"Right," he mumbled.

Ashe said, "It'll probably take us awhile in this ice. Do you want us to check in with you?"

"Can't hear you, I'm already sleeping," Jace shouted.

Rae said, "Fine. We'll try not to disturb you when we get back."

After Ashe and Rae climbed into the pickup, she said, "I see Jace is back to his old self."

"Makes you wonder why we bothered, doesn't it?"

"Yep. I don't suppose we have an ice scraper?"

Ashe dug through the glove compartment and said, "Of course not. No spare tire, no ice scraper. That rental agency is going to hear about this." He started the engine and turned on the defroster. "At this rate, by the time we get there, whoever or whatever triggered the alarm will be long gone."

"Let's hope so."

Dinell didn't feel the fishing line tug against the toe of her hiking boot as she crept through the woods surrounding the well site. She was too busy trying not to make a sound. Everyone at RESCUE had heard the stories of the night of Andy's murder, complete with details of the gun Rae carried.

She knew the reason they were camping in the middle of nowhere was to hide Jace. It was only logical that they would be prepared for trouble. Dinell slumped against a tree, too tired to think clearly. They might shoot her if she just walked unexpectedly into their camp in the middle of the night.

Laying her head on her knees, she wished it were daylight. At least she could announce her presence and gain their trust, if they could see her. It was awfully cold, but maybe it would be best to wait till daybreak.

The hair on the back of her neck stood on end as she heard two noises. One was behind her in the woods, the faint snap of a twig. The other was the sound of a vehicle cautiously approaching. As its headlights illuminated the two tents, Dinell shifted behind the tree where she couldn't be seen.

The deep holes in the dirt road were hard to navigate when they were dry, and even harder when covered with a thin layer of ice. By the time they made it to the well site, both Ashe and Rae were worried they wouldn't be able to make it back out.

"You see anything?" Rae asked.

"Nope," Ashe answered. "I'll go check the line."

Rae pulled the gun out of her pocket and handed it to him. "Take this with you. And please . . . be careful!"

He hesitated, then answered, "I'll leave the truck running. Lock the doors. If there's any trouble, you get the hell out of here. Understand?"

Touching his cheek, she hugged him. "Be careful, just in case."

He hopped out, adding, "I'll be right back."

Rae pushed the automatic door locks and sat in the truck, nervously clutching the walkie-talkie. She watched as Ashe found the tree alongside the road where they had rigged the alarm. He disappeared into the brush, creeping along with his hand cupped around the line.

If she strained her eyes, the truck's headlights allowed Rae to spot Ashe, crouched above the alarm line, and she relaxed a little. Seconds later, sheer terror ignited every nerve in her body when she heard a gunshot.

Ashe's thighs were beginning to ache as he inched along, his right hand on the gun, his left cupped around the clear fishing line. In the light from the pickup, he watched for any sign of an animal recently crossing, even though he had already decided they were on a wild-goose chase.

When he saw the figure of a person dart from behind a tree directly in front of him, he jumped so violently the gun fired into the dirt. "Shit!" he muttered. He climbed awkwardly to his feet. Making his way through the woods, he plowed over small trees and around large ones, his only goal to catch whoever was running away from him.

The person dressed from head to toe in coveralls emerged from the woods, running at top speed toward the opposite side of the site. As Ashe crashed out of the bushes in chase, he heard Rae slam the pickup into drive. The entire time he ran, he knew she was following.

By the time they reached the top of the incline, his legs

were burning. Below, the glow of the headlights allowed him to see the figure cutting in and out of the brush.

The added light was all he need to finally catch the person he'd been chasing. From behind he tackled the darkly clad figure. The two of them rolled down the pond dam before crashing into the icy water below.

Walters was several hundred yards away, watching as much as he could with his night-vision binoculars. Although he lost sight of them when they crested the hill by the pond, he quickly slipped back through the woods until he found a spot where he could see them again.

He found the entire scene absolutely entertaining. Sliding his gun out of its shoulder holster, he checked the clip to be certain it was loaded, and started screwing on the silencer.

Ashe gasped when they hit the cold water, but he had no intention of letting go. Struggling, he managed to grab hold of the stocking cap at the nape of the person's neck. Wrestling under the water, he finally wrenched one of the person's arms behind their back. A pained cry as they came up to gulp for air told him he had successfully overpowered his adversary.

Literally picking the person up, Ashe waded out of the water and slammed them down on the ground. With one knee in the middle of their back and still twisting their wrist in his hand, he struggled to catch his breath.

Looking up, he saw Rae sliding down the embankment toward them.

"Are you all right?" she called.

"I guess. Just once I'd like to catch someone without having to get wet."

Rae skidded to a stop next to him. "Where's the gun?"

He jerked his head toward the water.

Rae muttered, "Great."

Ashe pushed the person's arm farther up their back as he asked, "Who the hell are you?"

Weakly she answered, "Dinell. Will you let go of me now? You're hurting my arm."

Rae leaned over, peeling back the soggy knit stocking cap from her head. "It *is* Dinell," she gasped.

Ashe looked inquisitively at Rae, then used his free hand to check Dinell for weapons. Roughly rolling her over, he pulled a hatchet, still in its leather case, out of her belt. "Rae, get whatever's inside her boots."

Rae did as she was told, pulling a sheathed hunting knife out of Dinell's right sock. After Rae tucked it into her overalls, she removed a pair of wire cutters from the left boot and handed them to Ashe.

"What the hell are you doing here?" Ashe demanded.

Dinell's teeth were chattering as she answered, "I came to warn you. I think Brada . . . is coming here to . . . to kill all of you."

Rae asked, "Why didn't you just call us on the phone?"

"I did! I probably called . . . a hundred times. No one ever answered the stupid thing!"

Ashe glanced at Rae. "That could explain why my cell phone battery went dead." He hesitated, adding, "If you're here to help, why didn't you just tell me who you were instead of running?"

"You sh—shot at me!"

"What about the police? Aren't they answering their phones either?"

"I thought about calling them, but I don't have any real proof. Besides, RESCUE doesn't need any more bad publicity."

Ashe helped Dinell to her feet, but was obviously still wary of her. "What about the hatchet and knife?"

"Br—Brada's dangerous. I didn't know if I could make it here before she did. Needed to . . . protect myself."

"Why do you think she's so dangerous?" Rae asked.

Dinell started crying, obviously distraught. "I saw what

she did to Sherrie! It was horrible. I'd never have believed anyone could be so devious, so cruel. . . ."

Ashe said, "Wait. What did she do to Sherrie?"

"She rigged the staircase so she'd trip and fall." Dinell was sobbing. "The poor thing . . . lying there . . . a pool of blood under her head . . ."

"Is she all right?" Rae asked.

"I don't know. I went back upstairs . . . called an ambulance, but I knew if Brada saw me she'd kill me, too. I locked the door and watched from a window until she drove away. By then I knew the ambulance would be there any minute, so I tried to warn you. When you didn't answer, I knew coming here was the only way to stop her. . . . I have proof in the car. The diskette Margaret Prosser sent wasn't blank. Brada erased it. Could we go in the tent now? I'm . . . freezing to death!"

Ashe shook his head, not sure who or what to believe anymore. "Okay. Lead the way."

When Dinell was several yards in front of them, Rae rushed to Ashe's side, tugging on his jacket until he stopped. She whispered, "We can't trust her! She could be making all of this up so we'll let our guard down."

"I know. In the morning we'll call and find out if her story about Sherrie is true," Ashe said.

"Even if it's true, Dinell could be the one responsible. I don't think we should take our eyes off her, much less let her know where Jace is, just to be safe."

"Good idea. Once we get to the top of the hill, I'll watch Dinell while you get Jace on the walkie-talkie. Tell him to ignore the alarms we're going to set off outside the tents, and that you'll be back in a few minutes. First thing in the morning when this storm lets up, you can take him into town. Obviously, anywhere near here isn't a safe place for him to be."

"What will you do the rest of the night?"

"Make sure Dinell doesn't have any more tricks for us. There's a sleeping bag inside each tent. I'll stay here with her until morning, then take her into town. Hopefully, we can figure out a way to get to the bottom of this."

"What if Brada really is coming to kill us? She'd come to these tents, too."

Ashe thought for a second, then said, "Leave your walkie-talkie with me. Once you're back at the campsite, I'll tell you when we're inside the tents for the night. Jace can re-set the alarms. If one goes off, you can warn me with the walkie-talkie he has."

"By then they'll be too close, and now you don't have a gun. How are you going to protect yourself?"

He pulled out Dinell's hatchet. "I guess I'll have to use this. Besides, what are the chances of anyone else being crazy enough to come out in this kind of weather?"

They had reached the top of the hill, and Rae slid into the truck, which was still running. She closed the door so Dinell wouldn't be able to overhear her as she grabbed the walkie-talkie. "Jace . . . Wake up, Jace! Now!"

After several seconds of static, he finally replied. "What?"

"We have a problem at this site, but it's under control. Stay where you are. Ignore the alarms in front of the tents until Ashe calls you back. Ashe is going to stay here, and I'll be back there to stay with you in a few minutes. We'll go into town in the morning when the roads are better and find you a place to stay."

Jace was obviously wide awake, his voice sharp as he asked, "What the hell's going on? Is it him?"

"No, it isn't him, it's a woman we work with at RES-CUE. I'll explain everything as soon as I get back." She got out of the truck and went to Ashe's side, whispering, "Jace has been taken care of."

"Do you have another pair of coveralls back at camp?" he asked.

"Yes."

"You'd better let Dinell have those, so she doesn't freeze to death."

"What about you?" she asked.

"I'll survive," Ashe said.

Shaking her head, Rae said, "I'll bring back some dry clothes for you from the other camp."

"No. You're going to have your hands full just making it back to camp once on that sorry excuse for a road. Besides, we don't want her to know how close Jace really is, just in case."

Rae knew he was right, and she was already dreading the short drive alone.

When they were near the tents, which were considerably larger than the pup tents they had at the other site, Ashe said, "I'll stay out here while you two change."

Rae went inside the tent, peeled off her coveralls, and tossed them to Dinell, who was shaking from head to toe. She took the hunting knife and stuck it into her own boot. Emerging in clinging long underwear and hiking boots, she held up her hands and said to Ashe, "Don't say a word. I know how ridiculous I look."

Admiring every curve of her figure, he shook his head. "Actually, I think you look damn sexy."

She leaned toward him, trying not to get wet, and kissed him lightly. Rummaging through some of the boxes in the bed of the truck, she found the shirt he had worn yesterday, a blanket, and a flashlight. "Maybe these will help warm you up," she said as she handed them to him.

"You've already managed that, but I suppose anything's better than these wet clothes. Thanks."

Climbing into the pickup, Rae gave him the walkie-talkie. "See you in the morning?"

He kissed her one last time and said, "Count on it. Be careful."

"Don't forget to call Jace on the walkie-talkie so he'll know to reset the alarms."

Ashe was beginning to shiver again. "I won't," he said.

She started to roll up the window but instead reached out and touched his cheek. "I love you, Ashe."

"I love you, too."

\* \* \*

Jace was wide awake, waiting for Ashe to signal him to reset the alarms. His muscles involuntarily tensed when he heard the distant crunching of gravel down the road. Nervously, he burrowed into the sleeping bag, using his flashlight to look at his watch again. It had been only three minutes since Rae called. Even in broad daylight with good road conditions, he knew dodging the potholes made it take at least eight to ten minutes to get back from the other well site.

He turned off the flashlight and crawled out of his sleeping bag. After slithering into his insulated coveralls, he pulled his boots back on and felt in the darkness for his gloves, hat, and overcoat. Stuffing the walkie-talkie into his pocket, he took out his hunting knife, unzipped the tent, and slipped into the darkness.

Working his way into the woods, Jace stayed low. Hiding behind a tangled mass of fallen dead limbs, he watched the headlights of a vehicle approaching from the south. Totally unnerved, he pulled out the walkie-talkie with shaking hands. "Ashe? Ashe!" he whispered, terrified no one would answer.

"What's wrong, Jace?"

"Someone's coming down the road, and it ain't Rae."

"Calm down. How do you know it isn't Rae?"

"They're coming into camp from the south, and she'd be coming from the north! It must be him. I gotta get outta here!"

Ashe thought for several seconds. "Jace, do you think you can hike to the road and head this way without being seen?"

"Yes."

"Do it fast, but be sure to stay out of sight in the woods alongside the road. When whoever just pulled up there realizes no one is at that site, they might move north on that road to try to find us. You need to stop Rae before she gets close enough for them to see her headlights. Are you still in the tent?"

"No. I'm deeper in the woods, by that big pile of dead brush."

Ashe realized it was too late to worry about getting more warm clothes from camp for either Rae or himself, so he said, "Then start hiking, and go as fast as you can without getting hurt. Okay?"

"Right."

"And, Jace, keep telling me what's going on and where you are, every ten minutes or so. I'm going to get in the pickup we rented this morning and head your way. We need to stick together."

"Yeah. That way he won't have to go to the trouble of picking us off one by one."

Ashe ignored Jace's comment and paced inside the tent, glaring at Dinell. "You need to come with me," he finally said.

She had been quietly listening and waiting with a sleeping bag wrapped around her shoulders. Though she was still shivering, her lips weren't quite as blue as they had been earlier. "What's going on?"

"I wish I knew."

Wide-eyed, she said, "It's Brada, isn't it? She's close, isn't she?"

"Right now I wouldn't be surprised to see an entire circus, complete with clowns riding elephants, marching through these woods. Let's get going . . ."

Dinell started to walk out, then abruptly stopped when Ashe yelled, "Wait! Don't step outside! It'll set off the alarms, and whoever's at the other campsite might hear them!"

"What alarms? What other campsite?" Dinell asked excitedly.

"It's a long story. Trust me, we can't go out that way." He pulled the hatchet out of his wet coveralls and cut a slit along the bottom of the back wall of the tent. They squeezed through, then Ashe led her carefully around the booby traps to the pickup.

When they were inside the truck, Ashe turned the key, but the engine didn't start. After four more attempts he slammed his fist against the steering wheel and seethed, "Shit!" Sliding out the driver's-side door, he lifted the hood and immediately saw the problem, even in the darkness. Virtually every wire in sight had been cut.

His eyes full of hatred, he marched back to the door of the pickup. Glaring at Dinell, he shouted, "Did you tamper with this truck?"

"No! Really! I came here to help, Ashe."

"Then why did you have wire cutters, and what were you doing traipsing around the woods in the middle of the night? I want the truth this time!"

"I told you! I was trying to decide how to safely get your attention, when I stumbled, and you shot at me. I used the wire cutters to get inside the barbed-wire fence. The man in Elk City warned me that the gate would probably be locked, so I stopped and bought some warm clothes and the wire cutters so I could drive around the gate. I'm telling you the truth!"

"So you cut the fence and drove in? Where's your car?"

"Off the road, on the other side of that ice-cold pond you tried to drown me in."

"Stay here!" He slammed the door to the pickup and walked away. After taking a few deep breaths, he used the walkie-talkie. "Jace? Jace?"

"Yeah."

"Are you all right?"

Jace was obviously breathing hard as he said, "I can see Rae's headlights up ahead!"

Rae was concentrating, inching the pickup along the road at a snail's pace for the first mile to build her confidence. It had been years since she had driven anything larger than her compact car. With virtually no clothes on, and no two-way radio, the last thing she needed was to end up stuck in a ditch.

After the second mile passed without a problem, she gained enough confidence to pick up her speed a little. She was anxious to get back to camp, and even more anxious to have the chance to talk to Ashe again, even if it was only on a radio.

She was only a little over a mile from the original HDR site when Jace darted out of the bushes directly in front of her. Screaming, Rae automatically slammed on the brakes. The pickup's rear end slid sideways, the back tires dropping into a muddy ditch alongside the road while the front tires stayed where they belonged.

Jace ran to the door and jerked it open. "Turn off the headlights!" he whispered breathlessly. "Hurry!"

Flipping them off, she shouted, "You scared me half to death! What are you doing out here in the middle of the night?"

"Shhhh! There's someone at our camp. They just drove up."

"Who?" Rae whispered, trying to regain her composure. "Did they spot the tents?"

"I don't think so, but I didn't exactly hang around to chat. Where are your clothes?"

Rae glanced down, immediately blushing. "Get in, it's a long story."

Stepping back, Jace looked at the odd angle of the truck. "I don't think we're going anywhere in this."

Holding the door slightly ajar, she lightly stepped on the gas, leaning out to watch the back end. The rear tires threw mud and slid sideways, but the truck didn't budge.

Jace held up his hands and shook his head. When she opened the door, he said, "It's no use, it's high-centered."

"Can we push it out?" she asked.

"Ashe can probably pull it out with the other pickup if

we can find a rope." Smiling slyly, he said, "There's plenty on the rig."

"A lot of good that does us."

Jace grabbed the walkie-talkie and quietly asked, "Ashe, where are you?"

After several seconds of static, Ashe answered. "Still at the other camp. Are you with Rae?"

"Yeah."

"Let me talk to her."

"Right." Jace glared at Rae and warily handed her the radio. "I guess he doesn't trust me."

Shaking her head, she said to Jace, "You know that isn't true. He's really worried about you. Besides, you have to earn people's trust." Speaking into the walkie-talkie, she said, "Ashe, the pickup's stuck on the side of the road about a mile from the old HDR site. Do you think you can come pull it out?"

"We've got more problems than we thought, Rae. Some-one cut the wires in the pickup we left here. It'll have to be towed out of here."

Rae's own emotions mirrored Jace's as the expression on his face turned from fear to desperation. Almost whispering, Rae asked, "Was it Dinell? She had wire cutters on her when we found her."

"She swears she didn't have anything to do with it."

For a few seconds Rae and Jace stared at each other. Finally Rae asked, "What do you think we should do, Ashe? Is there any other way to get out of here?"

"Dinell left her car on the other side of the pond. We're hiking there now. The road doesn't go through to where you are, so we would have to leave from the north and circle around to the south entrance to come get you. That would take too long, and since we don't know who's there, we don't want to have to pass the other camp."

"Should Jace and I start hiking your way?"

"Won't you freeze?"

Jace peeled off his overcoat and handed it to Rae. "No. I think we'll be all right," she said as she slipped it on.

"Then that's our best bet right now. I'll call you when we get to her car."

"Be careful, Ashe. Please."


Brada remembered the way to the old HDR site from her last trip there with Ashe and Rae. Keeping her eyes only on the slick road, she maneuvered into the clearing and parked near the mobile home. The icy yellow DANGER - HAZARDOUS MATERIALS ribbon that surrounded the area around the rig gleamed eerily in her headlights.

She sat there for several seconds, staring at the black tower and thinking how much things had changed in the last few weeks. No spotlights lit the rig, and she squinted to see the PetroCo sign at the top. There was no one to trust anymore, no hope for the future she had been certain would come to pass.

Turning off the engine, she climbed out and stretched. The cold air refreshed her dull senses, and she was glad she was almost at the end of her long journey. From the back of the rented Jeep CJ5, she pulled out a sleeping bag and her suitcase. As an afterthought she reached under the driver's seat, removed the loaded .44 she'd brought with her and the extra boxes of ammunition she'd picked up along the way.

Using the duplicate key she'd kept from her first trip to the site, she unlocked the mobile home and climbed inside. It was almost two o'clock in the morning, and she was exhausted. Dropping her things on the floor, she kicked out the sleeping bag and crawled inside.

Brada knew she needed rest, even if it was just a couple of hours. If her plan was going to succeed, she had to be at the site where Ashe, Rae, and Jace were sleeping well before dawn.

# Chapter 18

Walters practically wore a path in the woods between the pond and the well site. With amused curiosity he watched the entire scene unfold before him, almost laughing aloud when he recognized the woman Ashe had so easily defeated.

Regretfully, he wished he had thought to bring along one of his sound-amplification devices so he could listen to what they were saying to each other. Instead, he had to rely on what he could see of their body language, which was quite a challenge when everyone was freezing.

When he watched the pretty brunette emerge from the tent in her long johns, he was tempted to follow her instead of keeping an eye on the other two. But without a car he doubted if he could keep up with her. As soon as she left, he regretted his decision. What if she was on her way to town for help? But if that was the case, why didn't they all go?

Then he observed the most puzzling thing of all. Ashe and Dinell crawled out a hole in the back of the tent instead of using the zippered door in front. Walters smiled when he realized they had somehow set a trap. But for who? And why? They couldn't possibly know he was coming, unless she had come to warn them.

Their attempt to leave in the pickup was, of course, futile. Walters momentarily panicked when they started to hike back toward the pond, realizing they were probably heading toward the Cherokee. He couldn't believe he had passed so close without disabling it. It was definitely time for him to get out of the business. One careless mistake could cost him his life, and he was making far too many.

Moving as fast and quietly as he could, he darted through the woods. When he reached the edge of the road, he stopped and searched the area with his night-vision binoculars. Ashe and Dinell were halfway around the pond, headed directly toward him. Opening the pouch on his belt, he stuffed the binoculars back in and took out a small, razor-sharp knife.

Crawling on his stomach, he edged his way to the back of the Cherokee, then around to the driver's side. After putting his gun back in its shoulder holster, he slid under the car and started to work.

It was difficult in the tight space and with gloves on, but Walters managed to reach around the motor and slice several wires. As he disappeared back into the woods, he hoped they were important ones.

Ashe grabbed Dinell's arm and stopped her, his hand motioning for her to be quiet. Leaning close, he said, "I thought I just saw something move behind the Jeep."

She didn't answer, but stared into the darkness before them. "It was probably the shadow of a tree, or something blowing in the wind. I don't see anything," she whispered. "It's pretty misty, though."

"At least it stopped sleeting. Let's slow down just to be sure," Ashe said. They moved on, walking softly toward the car. Using the walkie-talkie, he said, "Rae, I've got one of those feelings like you usually get."

"Then turn around and come back! With all four of us pushing, we can probably get the other pickup out of the ditch."

He hesitated, then said, "We'll be careful. Where are you now?"

"Near that tree that was split by lightning."

"Good, you've made it halfway already. See anything unusual?"

"No. But then again, I'm not sure what would be normal for sometime after three o'clock in the morning in the middle of nowhere, and I'm too cold to care. I'll call when we get closer."

He stuck the radio back in his pocket and pulled Dinell toward him. "We're going to swing wide and come in from the back."

"Better safe than sorry, right?" she whispered.

Ashe shook his head, almost certain now that Dinell was not their leak. "More like better alive than dead. If we're up against who I think we are, he's got a lot of high-tech weapons on his side."

"You mean you don't think it's Brada?"

He squatted, trying to look under the car from the edge of the trees. Pulling her down beside him, he said, "I wish it was. Give me your keys."

She patted her pockets, then said weakly, "They're either in my wet clothes back at the tent, or they fell out of my jacket when you knocked me in the water." The furious look he shot her made her wish she could crawl off and die. "I'm sorry, really. I'm just so tired, and cold."

He stood, shoving his hands in his pockets to block them from the wind. "Did you lock it when you left?"

"No. It never dawned on me anyone would try to steal a car out here, especially on a night like this."

"Either way it'll be all right. Even without keys Jace will probably be able to start it. We'll just have to wait for them to get here, and hope that whoever disabled the pickup didn't do the same thing to the Cherokee."

From the woods behind them, Walters said, "Actually, I just took care of it a few minutes ago. I'm glad to hear Jace Williams is lurking around here somewhere. . . . Both of you put your hands up, very, very slowly. I'm sure you've guessed that I have a gun. You wouldn't want me to use it, would you?"

Before pulling his hands out of his pocket, Ashe pushed

the button on the walkie-talkie and loudly asked, "What do you want with us, Walters?"

"I don't know whether to be insulted or flattered that you know my name. To answer your question, it's Williams I'm after, among other things. Now get those hands up!"

Lifting his hands above his head, Ashe said, "I don't suppose you'd believe we don't know where he is."

Walters laughed. "You're right. I don't believe it. Besides, I just heard you say they were coming here, and that Jace's hot-wiring abilities might come in handy. Did you know that's how this all started?"

Ashe nodded.

Walters laughed. "I can't wait to see who shows up with him this time. This is getting to be quite an interesting little party."

Jace stopped dead in his tracks. "Did you hear that!"

"Of course I did. Be quiet!" Rae shoved him behind a tree to block the wind while they talked. She squatted so the jacket covered her ice-cold legs, and pulled Jace next to her. After several seconds she whispered, "We're not moving another inch until we have a plan."

"A plan? Are you kidding me? How about running like hell? Sounds like a plan to me!"

"No! Ashe's and Dinell's lives are in our hands."

"Wrong, lady. Their lives are in his hands, not ours. He wants me dead, and he don't care who else he has to kill along the way. They're probably already dead by now anyway."

"No, they aren't! You listen to me, Jace Williams. We are all going to get out of this alive! Understand?"

He nodded sheepishly.

Rae took a deep breath and said, "Okay. He won't kill Ashe and Dinell, because he'll try to use them as bait to get you. That is his style, isn't it?"

Jace was quiet, then said, "He'll probably wait for us at

the camp, but if we don't show, he'll come hunt us down like dogs."

She rubbed her aching legs. "Do you think you can make it to the highway alone? I know it's four miles, but you could probably flag down a semi and get a lift into town."

"Right. Like anybody's gonna stop to pick me up on a dark, deserted highway. Are you nuts?"

"You need to get away from here. It's you he wants, not the rest of us."

"He'll kill all of you either way. You know too much. He didn't bat an eye when he was shooting at me."

"We'll have to take our chances, Jace. Head for the road, but stay in the brush. Try not to leave a trail he can follow, just in case."

Jace stared at her for a long time, then began shaking his head. "No. I'm staying with you. I been out there alone before, twice, and he found me both times. It's like he can smell my fear and go right to where I am."

"It's very noble of you to offer to stay, but I can take care of myself. Really."

"I ain't leaving. He'd find me—sooner or later."

"Jace . . ."

He shook his head.

She took a deep breath. "Okay. We've got our work cut out for us. Any brilliant ideas?"

Jace said, "We could sneak back to the other camp for some supplies."

"What! There's somebody back there!" Rae said.

"But now we know it isn't Walters. He's the main one we should worry about."

"But we don't know who it is!"

Jace anxiously said, "Maybe it was the police. Maybe someone saw everyone coming and going tonight and thought we were trespassing or something."

"And maybe your fairy godmother is going to turn

Walters into a mouse at dawn. What do you want to get from back there, anyway?"

"There must be something on that rig we could use. I saw lots of pipe, chain cutters . . ."

"I told you, that rig is radioactive."

"Maybe it is . . . but where else can we find something to stop him with?"

Rae's frown slowly turned into a smile. "We'll have to move fast. It may not work, but I have an idea. . . ."

Walters shoved Ashe as he said, "Lean against the car and spread 'em." Pushing Dinell, he added, "You, too, lady."

They did as he said, and he frisked each one. Pulling the hatchet out of Ashe's coveralls, he tucked it in his pants. Running his hands along Ashe's jacket, Walters stopped when he felt the walkie-talkie. "What's this?" he asked.

"My ticket to Jace's funeral?"

Ashe stared silently ahead.

Walters grabbed Ashe's shoulder, turned him around, and shoved the gun under his chin. "You do realize, I'll find them with or without your help." Grabbing Dinell by the hair, he added, "However, Greenwall's little secretary probably wouldn't care for the slow death she'd have to endure all because of your uncooperative attitude."

Through clenched teeth Ashe replied, "Leave her alone. I'll do what you ask."

Walters released her, and she fell against the Cherokee in tears. Turning to Ashe, he said, "I'm going to tell you exactly what to say over that radio. If you warn them in any way, there'll be a bullet hole between her pretty brown eyes. Understand?"

"I understand perfectly, you bastard."

Rae and Jace ran as fast as they could back toward the stranded pickup, staying in the woods alongside the dirt road. Breathlessly Jace said, "I'm tired of getting kicked in the face by the branches you hit. Why can't we use the frigging road?"

"Footprints. Besides, the road is even slicker than these leaves. We don't want them to know we got this far and turned back."

"Why are we going back to the truck anyway?"

"Have you ever siphoned gas?"

Jace nudged her from behind. "What'd you think I am, a juvenile delinquent?"

"Yes or no?" she asked, purposely letting go of a branch just before he reached it.

"Ow!" After a second he muttered, "Yeah, I know how to suck gas. We gonna make a bomb?"

Rae cringed. "No. What we'll do depends on what's in the back of the pickup for us to work with. I know there's a small torch, because we bought it to start fires to clear the new site. Hopefully, there'll be some hose, rags, maybe a jar or a container. The tire tool might come in handy, and the Geiger counter's in the front seat."

"Ashe didn't want any raccoons chowing down, so he had me put last night's trash in the toolbox."

"Good. There's got to be something flammable there; plus it should be dry," she said.

When they could see the truck, Rae made Jace stop. While they caught their breath, she said, "Look for fresh tracks, and listen before we go out in the open. We still don't know where that other car stopped, or who was in it."

He did as she said, and when they were confident they were still alone, he was the first to the truck. Climbing into the bed, he began rummaging through the supplies.

At the sound of Ashe's voice, Rae yelled, "Jace, be quiet!" Rae waited until Ashe called again before answering on the radio. Even though she could hear him loud and clear, she said, "Ashe, you're not coming in very well. You're breaking up."

Slowly Ashe asked, "Where are you?"

She hesitated, then answered, "In the pickup. I twisted my ankle and can't walk."

When Jace was sure he couldn't be heard over the radio, he snapped, "You told them exactly where we are! Are you crazy?"

Rae glared at him, signaling him to be quiet. After several seconds Ashe asked, "Where's Jace?"

Still glaring at Jace, Rae answered, "I sent him back to the original HDR site to get the first-aid kit and something to use as a splint."

Another hesitation, then Ashe asked, "How long ago did he leave?"

"Say again, Ashe. Your radio's really fading. I told you not to carry it around in those wet coveralls. It probably has a short. Or maybe it got jarred when you helped Jace chase off that bull. Actually, Jace is headed back up to where he hid from the bull as we speak."

"How long ago did Jace leave?" Ashe flatly repeated.

"Just a few minutes. He helped me back here so I wouldn't freeze to death out in the wind, then left. It'll probably take him an hour to hike back and forth. Did you get Dinell's car started?"

After an even longer silence Ashe said, "Yes. We're going to drive around and come back in from the south road. We should be there by the time Jace gets back."

"Great. I'll be watching for you." She laid the radio in the front seat.

Jace was still furious. "Why did you tell them where we were?"

"I told you, I have a plan," she growled.

"And I told you, he's gonna kill us!"

"We'll see. What time is it?"

Jace strained to see his watch, then answered, "Two thirty-five."

"California or Oklahoma time?"

"California."

"That means it's four thirty-five here. The sun will be coming up in about two hours. I hope they hurry. This plan won't work in daylight."

Jace shook his head. "Ashe won't just lead him to you, you know."

Rae was digging through the toolbox as she said, "Weren't you listening when I was talking to him on the radio?"

"Yeah. So?"

"He knows enough about what I have planned to bring Walters right here to us. It's better than the two of us walking into whatever clever trap Walters would devise."

"You really are crazy, aren't you? You didn't tell him nothing."

"Sure, I did," she said as she unscrewed the gas cap. "I told him you'd be up in a tree waiting for his help."

Jace dropped the box he was holding. "I'd be where? First of all, I ain't climbing no tree. Second, you didn't tell him anything like that."

"The story about the twisted ankle is our way of making them come to us. He knows there's nothing wrong with his radio, and that I never told him not to put it in his wet coveralls. That was his clue that we heard his warning and know exactly what is going on where he is. And the only way he helped you with the bull was by getting you out of the tree. Trust me. He'll figure it out."

"Well, I ain't climbing no tree again. You should have checked with me first."

Rae instantly regretted slamming down the lid of the toolbox as the noise vibrated around them. Through clenched teeth she said, "Sorry, Jace, I guess I should have cleared every single thing with you first! Forget my plan! Instead, we'll just politely ask Walters to let us all go! It's up to you, since I'm sure you'll be the one he kills first." She pointed at the large limb hanging directly above them. "Either you climb this damned tree, or you die. It's your choice!"

"Jeez. You don't have to be so hateful."

She took a deep breath. "We have to work together to survive. Okay?"

"Okay . . ."

"I don't believe they're driving anywhere in this weather. My bet is, they'll come on foot, so it'll take them awhile to get here. Are there any supplies left from the alarms you rigged?"

"Some wire and some fishing line," Jace answered.

"Can you fix something to make a little noise when they cross it? Preferably not too noticeable. Loud enough for us to hear but natural, so it won't arouse their suspicions too much."

Jace thought, then said, "I think I can, if everything isn't too wet."

"Just try. Make it as wide as you can on each side. I'd bet they'll stay close enough to see the road so they don't get lost, just like we did. You work on that while I figure out the rest."

"The rest of what?"

Pulling the hand-held propane torch out of one of the boxes, she said, "Just wait. You're gonna love it. Give me your flashlight."

He handed it to her, and she followed each step as she read the side of the twelve-inch-long tank out loud. "Danger. Propane Fuel. 2500°F. To operate: Screw tank into valve body tightly. Turn fuel button completely on, and press Ignite button."

Jace laughed when Rae jumped back from the nozzle's unexpected whoosh of bluish-white flame. Rae admired her lethal weapon, then turned the fuel knob counterclockwise, immediately extinguishing it. "Pretty impressive. That empty milk carton in the trash should hold enough to do the job. Now all we have to do is siphon the gas."

Shaking his head, Jace said, "That's gonna be pretty hard, considering we don't have any hose."

"We can use a vacuum hose off the motor. If not, there's a screwdriver and a hammer in the toolbox. For now, you worry about the alarm, I'll worry about the gas."

"Be careful. If this place stinks of gas, he won't come anywhere near it."

"Hopefully, we can get done soon, and the wind will blow any odor away. Besides, from the awkward angle of the truck, he'd probably assume the gas tank was leaking."

Jace looked right in her eye. "You really capable of this?"

Confidently glaring back at him, Rae snapped, "I'll fry his balls and serve them on a platter if he gives me half a chance. Now get busy."

Jace instinctively cringed, then smiled as he walked away. "I gotta see this. Good luck."

"Thanks. You, too. And, Jace . . ."

"What?"

"Hurry!"

Ashe's mind was racing as they trudged through the woods. Walters had tied his hands, then attached a three-foot piece of rope between him and Dinell. The rope attached to her hands, which were tied in front of her. As Ashe expected, he was forced to lead the way, with Dinell in the middle and Walters bringing up the rear.

Everyone silently endured the first mile. Then Dinell suddenly slipped, stumbling to the ground. The rope pulled Ashe backward, almost on top of her. He swung around, hoping Walters was close enough to kick, but he was at least six feet away.

Walters warned, "Try that again, and you won't live to see tomorrow."

"Will we anyway?" Ashe asked.

"Possibly. Contrary to what Williams has probably told you, I'm not a psychotic killer. As a matter of fact, we have similar goals. Saving the environment can be done in many ways. I prefer to systematically destroy PetroCo at the same time."

Ashe grumbled, "How does killing an innocent kid help save the environment or stop PetroCo?"

"If you're speaking of Jace Williams, he's far from being an innocent kid. Sometimes people do foolish things, and they have to pay the price."

Ashe wanted to keep him talking, hoping Jace and Rae might hear them coming. "Other than your air-filter company, how else have you helped the environment?"

Walters laughed. "Do you have a death wish?"

"No. But I'm curious. You've gone to an awful lot of trouble to track down Jace just because he stole your car. Either you really liked that car, or there's more to the story."

"There's more, but if I tell you too much I'll definitely have to kill you. How much farther is it?"

Ashe lied. "How should I know? She said the pickup slid off the road about halfway between the two camps. It's probably at least another mile, maybe two."

"Then pick up the pace. I need to be out of here before sunrise. And no more talking. If I decide to announce our arrival, I'll do it myself."

They walked the rest of the way in silence, the eerie quiet broken only by their footsteps and the sound of bits of ice blowing out of the barren trees.

"When they trip the line, I'll hear the twigs I rigged fall. I'll drop an acorn in the bed of the truck so you'll know," Jace whispered. He sensed the urgency in the air, fully aware their time to prepare was almost up.

Rae asked, "Are you sure you understand the plan? I'm going to pretend to be asleep in the truck. I disconnected the inside light, so he won't be able to see the torch in my hand when I open the door. When he gets directly under you, dump the gas on him, and I'll let him have it."

Jace shook his fist in the air. "And hopefully he'll fry even before he gets to hell!"

She gave him a little hug. "You'd better get up there now. I'll hand you the gas."

Jace let Rae give him a boost to the closest limb. Then he nervously watched the ground move farther away as he climbed higher. When he was positioned on a large limb directly over the truck, he took deep breaths. Until yesterday he had never realized how much he hated heights.

Rae climbed into the bed, then on top of the cab. She carefully rubbed mud all over the milk carton full of gas to keep it from standing out, then handed it to him. When she was safely back on the ground, Jace said, "I guess we should be glad it finally stopped sleeting."

"I'm not so sure. The sleet made it harder to see. I hope he doesn't spot you."

"I'm glad I picked the camouflage cast instead of the blaze orange one."

"Me, too." She looked up, throwing him a timid smile. "We'll celebrate when we get out of here. How about a nice, thick slice of prime rib for dinner tonight?"

Jace felt his stomach knot. "Forget dinner. Right now I'd settle for a big stack of pancakes for breakfast. Did you have to mention food? Now I'm really hungry."

Rae climbed inside the truck. "Then it's an official date. Pancakes, hash browns, sausage, orange juice, eggs, toast, muffins . . ."

Jace groaned, practically drowning in his own saliva. To take his mind off food, he began searching what little he could see of the horizon. With the clouds blocking the moonlight and the brisk wind blowing the tree limbs, it was impossible to tell if anyone was coming.

But within a few short minutes, he heard what he was sure was a pile of twigs falling. His alarm had worked.

Brada's head was resting on her hands when the alarm on her wristwatch sounded, practically scaring her to death.

She bolted upright, her legs hopelessly tangled in the sleeping bag as she groped for her gun. By the time she realized no one else was in the mobile home, she was wide awake, her heart pounding in her ears.

Unzipping the bag, she freed herself and stretched. She tried the light switch, but wasn't surprised to find there was no electricity in the mobile home. Using a flashlight, she reviewed the aerial photograph of the other site for the last time, then refolded it and stuffed it into her jeans. It confirmed the decision she had made yesterday. She would drive halfway, then hike the rest of the way to the other HDR site.

The element of surprise was essential. Brada needed to find a good hiding spot where she could watch Walters, literally, execute his plans. Then she could execute hers.

"Stop here!" Walters hissed.

Ashe and Dinell halted. Both of them had heard the sound of sticks falling just a few feet from where they were. It could have been from the build-up of ice, or it might have been a person.

"Stay right where you are. Don't even breathe." Keeping them in his sights, Walters moved cautiously toward the road. The truck was half off the road, only thirty yards ahead. In the darkness it appeared to be abandoned.

Easing his night-vision binoculars out of his utility belt, he concentrated on the cab as well as he could without losing sight of Ashe and Dinell. It looked as though a woman was asleep in the driver's seat, her head resting against the window. The rest of the pickup appeared to be empty.

Marching back to them, he shoved the walkie-talkie into Ashe's bound hands. "Ask her how she's doing."

Ashe simply stared at the ground, purposely antagonizing him. "Ask her yourself, you son of a bitch."

In a flash Walters kicked him in the jaw. Unable to defend himself with his hands tied, Ashe fell backward, pushing Dinell into the tree behind him. As he fell, he flung the walkie-talkie as hard as he could into the woods.

After helping Dinell up, Ashe wiped the blood from the corner of his mouth with the back of his hand. "I hope Rae is as far from here as she can get. Jace, too, for that matter."

Shaking his head, Walters said, "Well, then I'd better explain things to you. If she isn't in that truck, both of you are dead. Right now." He walked into the woods and emerged with the walkie-talkie. Shoving it into Ashe's hand again, he seethed, "Call her!"

Ashe hesitated, then spoke calmly into the walkie-talkie, "Rae. Are you okay?"

There was no answer, only static.

Even as Walters' second kick sent him reeling, inwardly Ashe was smiling.

Rae's heart almost stopped when she heard Ashe's voice so clearly, but she didn't move an inch. Although she had decided not to answer the radio again, she desperately wanted to talk to him. Instead, she very slowly reached into her pocket and switched her radio off, making certain to maintain her exact position. Walters needed to believe she was asleep.

Her hands held the propane tank against the door, one ready to open the fuel valve, the other ready to push the Ignite button. She closed her eyes and silently thanked God Ashe was still alive. Her second prayer was that they would all stay that way.

Walters deliberated for several minutes before deciding how to approach the pickup. His natural distrust of people made him evaluate every angle of his strategy. Using the piece of rope that bound Dinell and Ashe, he placed them on opposite sides of a sturdy tree, then tied them together once again.

He hiked well past the pickup, crossed the road, then approached it from the rear. Nothing appeared out of the ordinary. Moving only inches at a time, he stepped from the woods onto the road, waiting for movement. Walters was certain that if she had a gun, the temptation would be too great. She wouldn't wait much longer to use it. After several minutes of waiting in the open, he would have bet she was asleep and, more important, unarmed.

Years of experience had taught him two things: patience and the importance of being more prepared than your enemy.

He thought he had covered both.

Every muscle in Jace's body was screaming to move, but he remained frozen, concentrating on Walters' strange movements, or rather, the lack thereof. Even though Walters was covered from head to toe in camouflage, Jace could see each step he took. He wondered if it would hurt much, dying from a gunshot wound. In the darkness the gun that hung by Walters' side looked as though it were a natural extension of his right hand, a gleaming reflection of the evil deep inside.

When Walters reached the center of the road, near the bed of the truck, he suddenly dropped to the ground. Instantly rolling to the driver's door, he stopped. The unexpected maneuver surprised Jace, but he didn't flinch. Looking straight down, he saw Walters crouching by the driver's door, covered with a fresh layer of mud.

In the darkness Jace couldn't tell if Rae swung the door open, or if Walters reached up and yanked it open himself. All he knew was it was his turn to act, and fast.

Rae rolled out the driver's-side door when Walters jerked it open, igniting the torch as she hit the ground. Walters was screaming, no doubt from the unexpected shower of gasoline pouring over both of them. Rae felt it splash across her face and arms, but it was too late to stop.

The bluish-white flame touched Walters' pant legs first,

but the wet, muddy fabric didn't ignite. Rae tightly squinted her eyes, the horrible smell of gas assaulting her senses. She knew she was risking her own life as much as his by holding the torch so close, but it didn't matter—there was too much at stake.

Frantically holding the hissing cylinder at arm's length, she prayed the flames would engulf only him. The smell of singeing material mingled with the stench of fuel as sparks flickered on his pant leg. Then she heard the sickening whoosh of his gas-soaked face and hair flashing into flames.

As Walters screamed, his finger tightened on the trigger of the gun. Dropping to one knee, he fired blindly in every direction.

Inching northward without headlights, Brada was concentrating on the dark, wet road, wondering how long she would have to wait for Walters to arrive. When an arc of bright yellow flames suddenly appeared in the distance, followed by the flashes of a gun barrel, she instinctively slammed on the brakes.

At first Brada was certain she was imagining things. She knew otherwise when she watched the burning mass drop lower, then disappear.

Slamming the CJ5 into park, she grabbed her gun and filled her coat pockets with extra shells. Excitement pulsed through her as she jumped out of the truck and silently closed the door. Easing into the woods, Brada worked her way closer, confident her long struggle was finally at an end.

The second bullet caught Rae in the shoulder, hurling her against the front tire of the pickup, away from the flames. The torch flew out of her hand, coming to rest just outside her grasp.

Everything had happened so quickly, Jace barely had time to regain his senses. He cringed, instinctively freezing when the bullets started flying. Three sailed within inches of him; one struck the limb just above his head. When he finally pried his eyes open to look back down, Walters was rolling on the wet dirt road. The flames engulfing his head were quickly going out.

Jace could hear Ashe shouting at the top of his lungs. "Rae! The torch! Get the torch, he's coming back! Hurry!"

The torch was still lit, about a foot from her arm. Jace saw the dazed look in her eyes, then the dark spot growing on her right shoulder. He knew he had no choice. In spite of his fear, he wrapped his good arm around the branch and swung down, dropping onto the top of the pickup before falling painfully into the road.

Walters had struggled back to his feet and was heading toward Rae with the gun still dangling from his hand. As he slowly raised it, a sinister grin creased his burned face. He growled, "Finally! This time you won't get away, you little bastard!"

Just as Walters pulled the trigger, over and over again, Jace struggled to get up, then lunged for the torch. He cringed, anticipating pain, surprised when nothing ripped through his flesh. Walters must have run out of ammunition.

Jace's fingers reached for the torch, but it slid away from him. Mud was clogging the nozzle, extinguishing the flame he so desperately needed. Walters laughed, tossing his gun to the ground as he leaned down. Almost casually he started to remove something from his boot.

Grabbing the torch even though it wasn't lit, Jace turned the cylinder around and gripped it like a baseball bat. Leaning against the side of the pickup for only a second, he took a deep breath, then stepped toward Walters, swinging with all his might.

The smooth metal container slammed against the side of Walters' burnt face, sending him reeling sideways. Jace attacked with all his strength, alternating brutal kicks with vicious swipes of the butt end of the torch.

When he felt Rae's hand on his shoulder, Jace finally

stopped his attack and dropped to his knees. She was pulling him away, pleading with him not to kill Walters.

"Are you all right?" she asked as she sank to the ground beside him.

Jace's eyes burned with fury. "You should have let me kill him!"

Pulling at him, she shook her head. "He's not going anywhere. Help me find Ashe."

They stood, and Jace wrapped his arm around her waist to support her as they walked. Together they followed the sound of Ashe's voice into the woods. Jace helped Ashe free his hands, then did the same for Dinell.

"Are you hurt?" Ashe asked, gently touching her shoulder.

"Not too bad. Maybe a graze . . ."

Ashe swept her into his arms, carefully positioning her on the ground against the tree so he could check her wound. She flinched when he lifted Jace's jacket to look underneath. "I'm sorry, but it's a little more than a graze. At least it looks like the bullet went all the way through."

"I know it did," she said.

"Really?" Ashe asked.

Rae nodded, then weakly giggled. "It hit the tire behind me. I could hear the air hissing out of it . . ."

Ashe turned to Dinell. "See if you can find something clean in the truck to use as a bandage." Turning to Jace, he added, "I'm going to carry her to the pickup. She needs to be warm. Will it still run?"

"We pulled off a vacuum hose to siphon the gas. I'll try to find it and get it started again."

"Before you do that, would you take some of this rope and tie up Walters? Unless he's dead, he's still dangerous."

"Right. I'll check to see if he has any more surprises on him, too."

Ashe grabbed Jace, roughly hugging him. "Thanks, Jace. For everything."

Rae agreed, her voice growing weak. "You really came through when it counted, Jace. I'm proud of you."

Squatting beside her, Jace replied, "Don't you give out on me now, lady. We got a date for breakfast. Pancakes, remember?"

"I remember . . ."

As Ashe swept her gently into his arms and carried her, he playfully whispered, "Dating other men, are you? And I thought you only loved me."

"Wishful thinking."

"On his part or mine?" he asked as he lifted her into the front seat.

With her eyes closed, she mumbled, "Both."

When Sherrie Rosen finally awoke, her mother was at her side. She had no idea where she was, only that something was terribly wrong. Trying to sit up, she barely lifted her head. Her mother's voice soothed her. "Relax, Sherrie. Everything's going to be all right."

Looking around, she tried to ask where she was, but her throat ached so much she knew she couldn't talk. Raising her eyebrows, she silently pleaded with her mother.

"You've had a bad fall. You're in a hospital in California, but you're going to be fine. You need to rest."

Memories flooded back. The stairs, the fall, the wicked laughter . . . Nathan was innocent, and she knew how to prove it!

She tried to sit up again, but her mother held her gently. "Calm down, Sherrie. I know it's hard, but whatever it is, it will have to wait. You have a severe concussion and a broken leg. There's a tube in your throat to help you breathe. That's why you can't talk. Understand?"

A tear of frustration rolled down her cheek as she closed her eyes and nodded. She prayed Brada wouldn't succeed. Again.

Brada watched from the woods as Ashe, Jace, and Dinell frantically worked. Rae and Walters were both hurt, but she couldn't tell how badly, and she didn't want to risk getting any closer. There was no time to plan. She had to act now, before they managed to leave.

It was obvious Walters had wreaked havoc, but they had managed to win the first battle. Her fingers tightened around her gun as she thought, *But the last victory will be mine!*

# Chapter 19

Jace cautiously approached Walters' still body. Using a long branch, he prodded him several times before moving close enough to risk actually touching him. Since Walters was lying facedown, Jace used a piece of rope to bind his hands behind his back. When he finished the last knot, he sighed, relaxing slightly with the knowledge Walters could no longer attack.

Gripping Walters' shoulder, Jace rolled him over in the center of the muddy road. A gust of wind carried the sickening smell of seared flesh and gasoline, causing Jace to gag. The sight of Walters' burned, beaten face made his nausea even worse. Although Jace wanted to feel his neck for a pulse, just to be certain he wouldn't ever hurt anyone again, he couldn't bear to touch the grimy, blackened flesh.

A shiver ran through Jace's entire body when he realized how close they had all come to death. Jace shook himself, clearing his mind so he could finish searching Walters' body and get away from the horrible stench.

Walters moaned. Jace froze, first disappointed that Walters was still live, then immediately apprehensive. Was the bastard inhuman enough to spring up and strike again, even with his hands tied behind his back? Jace didn't care to hang around long enough to find out.

Working faster, Jace removed Walters' utility belt, quickly noting its pockets were filled with binoculars, a Swiss Army knife, brass knuckles, pepper gas, and an assortment of miniature high-tech gear. Jace couldn't begin to guess what some of the things were for, much less how to operate them. He strapped the belt around his waist and continued his search.

Nervously, Jace ran his hands down Walters' legs, not surprised to find a switchblade inside one boot and a larger knife inside the other. "Ashe! You gotta come see this stuff!" he shouted.

Ashe walked over. Jace handed him the weapons and showed him the utility belt. Walters moaned again. "Is he coming around?" Ashe asked.

"I think so. Maybe I'd better tie his feet."

"No time to worry about it right now. I need you to help me push the pickup. We need to get the hell out of here and get Rae to a hospital."

"What about the front tire? It's flat, you know."

"I'll drive on four rims if I have to. Dinell helped me bind Rae's wound tightly, so at least she's not losing as much blood. I'm still afraid she'll go into shock. Even if we could change that tire in this slop, there isn't time."

"I'll go gather some sticks. Putting them under the back tires should get us a little more traction. If we both lift up on the back end, it may crawl right outta there."

"Good idea." Ashe patted him on the shoulder and added, "And Jace . . ."

"I know . . . hurry!"

Dinell was inside the pickup with Rae, trying to keep her warm. Cracking the door open, she screamed, "Ashe! Jace! Look!" Pointing down the road, she added, "Someone's coming!"

Everyone temporarily froze, staring like frightened deer at the headlights bouncing toward them.

Brada stopped the CJ5 and hopped out. Running toward Ashe with her hands in her pockets, she yelled, "Thank God you're all okay. I've been worried sick about you."

Ashe said, "We're not all okay. Rae's been shot. We need to get her and Walters to a hospital. Fast!"

"You can take them in my Jeep. What's been going on here?" she asked innocently.

"It's a long story," he sighed.

"I need to talk to you for a minute first," Brada said, then pulled Ashe away from everyone else. She nervously looked around, then whispered, "Sherrie sent me. She said Dinell tried to kill her and that I needed to warn you. I went to the old HDR site first, because I didn't know how to get to the new one. When I heard the shots a few minutes ago, I knew something was terribly wrong. Since we can't all fit into my Jeep, we can tie up Dinell and I'll watch her while you take Rae to the hospital."

"Dinell isn't our problem." Ashe motioned toward Walters, who was quickly regaining his senses. "He is."

"You're wrong. If he's who I think he is, Dinell's been feeding him information for years. She's trying to run RESCUE out of business. I have proof."

Dinell climbed out of the pickup. Walking toward Ashe and Brada, she kept her distance while quietly stating, "Whatever she's telling you, don't believe it. I have proof she's the traitor at RESCUE, not me! Back in the Cherokee is a copy of the diskette Marilyn Prosser's mother mailed to us. I made copies before I gave one to Brada, and we all know what happened to the data on her diskette!"

Brada shook her head. "Surely you don't believe her, Ashe. Dinell paid Walters to sabotage your HDR well. She may as well have killed Andy herself! I have evidence back at headquarters. Besides, how do you know the diskette wasn't blank when she gave it to me? If she made copies, why didn't she tell anyone?"

Dinell fumed, "I gave copies to our computer division so they could prove you erased the information! I've been watching you for months, trying to find a way to stop your treachery!"

"Then why didn't you tell anyone?"

"I had to have proof!"

Ashe didn't like the fact he couldn't see Brada's hands. Holding up his own, he said, "We'll have plenty of time to decide who did what later. Right now I need to get Rae to a hospital."

The two women glared at each other, and Brada excitedly said, "Save Rae, Ashe! Dinell and I can stay here and guard Walters. When you get to town, you can send the police, and a wrecker."

Dinell was backing away. "I'd rather be thrown into a pit of vipers. At least they can't lie about what they are. She'll kill me if you leave me here, Ashe! After I'm dead, she'll blame all RESCUE's troubles on me."

Ashe mentally weighed his lousy options. "I'm not going anywhere until you give me the gun in your pocket, Brada."

Wide-eyed, she asked, "You mean you don't trust me?"

"No one should trust her."

Everyone turned to stare as Walters, a few yards away, futilely tried to get to his feet. He laughed, then groaned, his deep, gravelly voice carried by the cold wind stirring the leaves. Although he slurred his words, they all could understand everything he said. "She's your problem, not the other lady. Brada is a manipulative, sleazy bitch," he rasped. "I should know, she succeeded in making a fool out of me! Used me to do her dirty work for years, and I was stupid enough to trust her."

Brada stepped back, pulling the gun out of her pocket and pointing it at Ashe and Dinell. Ashe quickly evaluated the situation, realizing he would jeopardize Dinell's life if he attacked. Looking around, he was glad Rae was lying on the front seat of the pickup, out of the line of fire. It was Jace he was worried about. He was nowhere in sight. Raising his hands, Ashe sighed.

Walters stumbled, rolling back to the ground and coughing before he said, "She tricked me into sabotaging one of

RESCUE's wells by telling me it belonged to PetroCo. She even had me frame your buddy, Nathan Greenwall—"

Dinell interrupted, "So she could bankrupt RESCUE by sinking millions of dollars into a Solar project that hasn't got a chance in hell!"

Brada's eyes were wild as she squeezed the trigger and screamed, "Shut up!"

He laughed as the bullet flew harmlessly over his head. "You really think I'm going to make it through this? What have I got to lose? We've worked together a long time, Brada. If you don't kill me, I'll kill you, and you know it."

Ashe asked, "Are you saying you killed Chuck Kelmar just to frame Nathan?"

His voice was growing more hoarse each second. "That was the best part. Killed two birds with one stone—pinned it on Greenwall and made PetroCo bite one, too. Clever, wasn't I?"

Brada screamed, "Shut up!" She pulled the trigger again, firing three shots. Two struck Walters, one in the right chest, the other the lower abdomen. The third barely missed Dinell, who turned and ran.

"Stop where you are, Dinell, or I'll kill Ashe and Rae," Brada screamed.

Dinell slowed down near the bed of the pickup, but stopped so most of her body was blocked. "You'll kill us all anyway. We know too much!"

Turning the gun toward Ashe, she said, "That bastard deserved to die. He's murdered countless people. Senators, professors, even poor Marilyn Prosser. Now get over there by Dinell so I can think."

Out of the corner of his eye, Ashe caught a slight movement in the trees behind her. Purposely turning his back to Brada, he reached inside his coveralls and pulled out the knife Jace had taken off Walters.

Positioning himself behind Dinell where Brada couldn't see both his hands, he asked, "Why, Brada? Why would you want to hurt RESCUE? Nathan's been your friend since you were kids. He gave you the chance to do what you always dreamed of doing. Why betray him?"

"Saving the world from itself was never my dream, it was Nathan's. Chuck and I hit it off when I worked for him. It was our plan. He wanted RESCUE out of the way, and I wanted Nathan to pay for everything he did to me."

Ashe was bewildered, sickened by the hate that flowed so easily from Brada. "What could Nathan have done that would make you hate him so much?"

"You mean the poor little rich boy? Nathan Greenwall never had to work for a damned thing in his entire life. His mommy made sure he would never have to get his hands dirty, never have to grovel like the rest of us. Don't you know how they treated my mother? Don't you remember?"

Thinking back, Ashe barely remembered Brada's mother had worked for Mrs. Greenwall. But it had been only for a few short months. "You mean when she worked for them for a while?"

"I should've known he never told you. We needed money so bad, and they fired her! They said she stole something from them! Why the hell shouldn't she? Her kids had to wear clothes from Goodwill! Her kids lived for a month on the money she got from selling that stinking necklace she took! Her hatred for the Greenwalls has kept her drinking for years. I swore to her that Nathan would pay, and he will!"

"But, Brada, that happened so long ago. Nathan would never do anything to hurt you. Surely your mother wouldn't want you to do all this just to get revenge on him."

Brada was growing agitated. "Bullshit! I want him to lose hope just like she did. Nathan is a spoiled rich kid who'll do whatever it takes to get what he wants! Look at RESCUE!" Nodding toward Walters's body she screamed, "It was RESCUE, and that stupid bastard's fault! He killed my best friend. Chuck was the only person who ever really cared about me! He wasn't supposed to frame Nathan by killing Chuck. All he was supposed to do was get Nathan out of the way!"

Ashe seethed, "But why? Why sabotage his company for years instead of just ruining him once and for all?"

Brada was shaking. "Because he had to suffer! A long, agonizing life is what he deserves, just like the one my mother has had! I swore I'd give it to him, and I will!"

Ashe could see Jace slowly approaching Brada from behind. Loudly he said, "You were happy just screwing things up for a long time, weren't you? But everything started to fall apart when you told Walters to kill Marilyn."

"It was too late when I realized she was a lot like me. She just needed money. . . ."

Goading her, Ashe said, "And then her mother. She was just trying to help her little girl, like your mother did."

*"Shut up!"*

Pushing, Ashe shouted, "And you're still helping PetroCo, aren't you, Brada? Still selling our secrets to the highest bidder!"

She was screaming, "You bet I am!"

He yelled back, "And now you're going to murder all of us, too? You're insane! Stop now while you still have a chance!"

Brada must have caught a glimpse of Jace, because she whirled around. Ashe threw the knife just as she turned, but she still had time to fire two rounds before it struck her in the back of her thigh.

Screaming, she fell, the gun still in her hand. Jace ran toward her, but before he reached her, she turned the gun on herself. "One more step and I'm going to blow my brains out. Get back!"

Jace froze, staring first at her, then at Ashe, who was moving slowly toward her from behind.

"I mean it! Get away from me!" Brada reached back with her free hand and pulled the knife out of her thigh.

Ashe gently said, "Calm down, Brada. We'll get you help. There's no need to do anything rash."

With the gun still to her head, she stood and turned to look at Ashe. Shaking her head, she said, "Sorry . . ."

Just as she pulled the trigger, Jace lunged at her. He knocked her to the ground as the gun fired into the woods.

Ashe booted the gun away from Brada, then grabbed her arms, twisting them behind her.

"You filthy bastard!" Brada screamed. "Who do you think you are?"

Jace staggered to his feet. "A better person than you are, lady. You and Walters deserve each other."

Ashe turned to Dinell. "Can you bring me something to tie her with?"

Dinell nodded. "Gladly. Will duct tape do?"

Ashe said, "It'll do fine."

Jace added, "Put some on her mouth while you're at it."

Brada struggled again, her eyes wild with fury. "I'll get all of you. Just like Nathan. It may take me awhile, but you'll see. . . . I'll never give up. Not until I throw dirt on your graves . . . Never!"

Ashe slapped a piece of duct tape over her mouth, then bound her hands. After bandaging her leg as best he could, he looked at Jace. "Do you think you can watch her until I get back with the police?"

Jace realized the responsibility and trust Ashe was showing him, and he nodded. "You bet I can."

Rae watched the events unfold from inside the pickup, her eyes barely over the edge of the driver's window. When Ashe taped Brada's hands behind her back, Rae could hardly keep her eyes open. The numbing shock of the night's events had taken their toll.

Ashe and Jace moved Brada toward the truck while Dinell ran down the road to bring Brada's Jeep closer. Rae thanked God for the second time in just a few hours that everyone was going to be all right. Except Walters. Even though it was painful, she forced her eyes open and shifted her weight far enough up in the seat to cast one last glance his way.

But what she saw wasn't a dead body at all. In fact, his hands were free and he had curled into a fetal position, his torso facing her. Just as her eyes locked onto his, he struggled, then pulled a small handgun from under his clothes. The intensity of his eyes burned through her, and for a fleeting moment she froze. But she felt no threat from his compelling gaze; instead it held a plea for final justice. The instant he shifted his eyes away, the trance was broken.

Jerking the door handle, Rae screamed as she fell to the ground, "Look out, Ashe! He's got a gun!"

The echo of gunfire overpowered her voice as each of six shots rang through the still morning. Ashe raced toward Walters, but the gun was empty by the time he kicked it away.

Rae rolled over in time to see Jace crawling back up, apparently unharmed. As she turned over, a wave of pain ripped through her shoulder, but it was overpowered by the warm rush of relief that washed over her when she spotted Ashe, alive and well. Closing her eyes, she sighed.

Brada had fallen backward from the impact of Walters' shots, and now she was still, her eyes open but unseeing.

Ashe knelt beside Walters, feeling for a pulse. "He's dead," he said.

Jace squatted beside Brada. In a shaky voice he said, "She's dead, too. Man, he hit her all six times. He didn't miss once. Ashe, are you sure he's really dead? Absolutely, positively sure?"

Feeling the strength of Jace's fear even from a distance, Ashe checked for a pulse one last time. "He won't bother you again, Jace. I swear."

As Dinell helped Rae stand, she weakly said, "He wasn't trying to hurt any of us. She was his only target."

Jace asked, "How in the world do you know that?"

Rae leaned against the truck. "It was in his eyes. He did what he felt he had to do before he could leave."

Skeptically Jace asked, "Leave? Like go to heaven?"

Dinell countered, "More like hell. I guess you're lucky he decided to only take Brada with him."

Jace stared in disbelief, unable to absorb the grisly scene in which he stood. "But I tied his hands. How could he . . ."

Ashe held up a thin four-inch metal blade. "This was next to him. He probably had it taped to his wrist, or maybe it was in the cuff of his shirt. He had the gun in a soft pouch on his chest. The guy really was a professional killer." Looking up, he spotted Rae leaning against the truck with her eyes closed. Concern for her consumed everything else as he rushed to her side.

Jace was still staring blankly at the bodies. Almost to himself he asked, "Why do you suppose Walters said those things to Brada before she shot him? Why would he push her like that when she had a gun pointing at his head?"

Ashe's voice carried the urgency he felt as he answered, "I think he wanted to die. Even if he survived the burns, he knew he'd spend the rest of his life in prison." Cradling Rae in his arms, he hurried to Brada's car.

After he rested Rae in the passenger seat, Ashe said, "Come on, you two. I'll strap you on top if I have to, but no one is staying here. We'll send the coroner and the police when we get to town. After Andy's murder, and now this, I'll bet they'll pay us to drill somewhere else."

Neither Dinell nor Jace argued with Ashe when they crowded into the CJ5's warm, snug backseat. Ashe turned the Jeep around and drove away. Looking back in the rearview mirror, he saw the first rays of morning sun break through the trees, washing patches of the muddy road in soft light. Ashe shivered when he realized each body was cloaked in shadow, as though nature knew their souls didn't deserve to bask in the dawning light of day.

Jace leaned forward as they raced away. Touching Rae

softly, he whispered, "Don't forget those pancakes. We have a date, you know."

Her eyes were closed, but she mumbled, "Or the sausage, eggs, muffins . . . Oh, and waffles. Belgium waffles buried under tons of whipped cream . . . fresh strawberries . . ."

# Chapter 20

"I love you. Wake up so you can answer my question. Will you marry me? Come on, I know you're just pretending to be asleep."

Sherrie opened her eyes at the sound of his voice. For two days she had drifted in and out of the real world. Certain she was still dreaming, she closed her heavy eyelids again.

"Come on, Sherrie, fight for it. I don't think I can handle another rejection."

This time her eyes cracked open, and she tried to focus. Lifting her hand, she touched his face, which was only a few inches from her own. "It *is* you. But how?"

"They let me out of jail this morning. Ashe, Rae, and Dinell managed to convince the police that I was innocent, so here I am!"

A look of horror crossed Sherrie's face. "Oh, my God. Brada! I've got to warn Ashe and Rae!"

Nathan calmly said, "Brada's dead. And so is Harvey Walters. Apparently he was the one who actually killed Chuck Kelmar, then pinned it on me."

Sherrie pulled him to her and hugged him. "I knew it wasn't you who killed him . . . couldn't have been."

He smiled. "So you think I'm a wimp?"

"A wimp . . . no. I'd never agree to move to California . . . and marry a wimp."

"What?" Nathan asked skeptically.

"You have to promise to let me go back East whenever I want . . . to visit, shop, catch the shows . . ."

He kissed her, then said, "Okay, as long as I don't have to come every time. But when the kids start coming along, well, you know how hard traveling can be with babies."

Sherrie closed her eyes. As she drifted off, she contentedly asked, "What have I gotten myself into?"

Rae climbed into Ashe's car with a newspaper tucked under her arm. Excitedly she asked, "Did you see the story?"

"Not yet. Why don't you read it to me on the way?"

After buckling her seat belt, she opened the paper. "Do you mind if I just paraphrase?"

Running his hand provocatively up her thigh, he replied, "You can do whatever you like."

Rae smiled, shifting the paper so she wouldn't be distracted by the sexy grin on his face. "The byline is Corbin White, *New York Times*."

"I've heard of her. Didn't she win a Pulitzer?"

"A few years ago. The gist of the story is that an unknown informant, who we both know must have been Walters, tipped her that PetroCo was buying the rights to inventions that could minimize the world's dependency on oil. To find out if it was true, they set up hidden cameras and filmed a meeting with Karl Ross.

"It says the tape of their meeting will air tonight on *Dateline*. Corbin told Ross she was a graduate student, and that she'd designed a lightweight battery that could make solar-powered transportation much more feasible. Apparently, he tried to buy her silence as well as her invention."

Ashe said, "Not surprising, considering what happened to Marilyn."

"Corbin was working with the FBI, and they've agreed to release some of the evidence accumulated by the unknown informant in return for her cooperation."

"What did they do to Ross?"

"The police haven't done anything . . . yet. Ross's participation in the murders of Marilyn and her mother are being investigated, and his position with PetroCo seems to be rather shaky.

"PetroCo's board of directors called a press conference to be certain the public understood Ross was only the *temporary* president. They claim they never intended for him to have the position permanently, and they had always planned to announce his replacement next week." Rae crushed the paper and added, "Amazing how fast the board is backing away from him, isn't it? Really loyal to their employees, aren't they?"

"Doesn't surprise me a bit. They'll bounce back. PetroCo always does."

"At least Walters hurt them a little. Their stock fell over twenty dollars a share when this story broke."

"Did Nathan know how Brada might have gotten involved with Walters in the first place?"

"He and Sherrie are pretty sure it was right after college. Apparently, they met while she was working at PetroCo. You know, what amazed me the most was that neither of them ever seemed to give a damn. They'd cost countless lives, hurt hundreds of people, yet even when they knew they were going to die, they didn't stop hating."

"That was probably the hardest thing I had to come to grips with after the bombing. The senseless violence ate at me for a long time. Believe it or not, a letter left on the memorial fence was what finally made me let go of my hatred."

Ashe squeezed her hand, the love in his eyes urging her on.

"All it said was, 'Our lives honor those lost here.' "

"And yours has. He'd be proud of you, Rae."

She smiled, nodding as she brushed a tear from the corner of her eye.

Ashe pulled into the driveway of a small house in a well-kept older neighborhood. Looking at the address on a sheet of paper, he said, "I think this is the right place. Are you okay?"

"I'm fine," she replied, and he knew it was true.

As Ashe was helping Rae out of the car, Jace raced toward them from the front door. He carefully hugged Rae, then asked, "How's the shoulder?"

She cheerfully answered, "It'll be fine in a few weeks. Is your arm still itching?"

Jace rolled his eyes and said, "Yeah, but look what Mrs. Benton gave me." He rolled up his shirtsleeve and carefully pulled a knitting needle out of his cast. "It's loose enough for me to really scratch good with this thing. You gotta come in and meet Mr. and Mrs. Benton."

Ashe helped Rae up the concrete steps as he whispered, "Did you hear that? Mr. and Mrs. Benton! He's actually being polite!"

"Shhhh. They'll hear you!" Rae said as Jace led them into the living room of the Benton home.

Jace said, "This is Ashe and Rae."

George stood and shook their hands while his wife nodded politely. Laughing, he said, "I'm George and this is Alice. We've heard all the stories about you two . . . at least ten times!"

Rae replied, "It was nice of you to help Jace so much."

"He's always welcome here," George said.

Jace explained, "Mama wants me to come home, but she knows it's better if I stay in this neighborhood until I'm not on probation anymore. Besides, being home reminds me too much of Cory."

"I think the judge was a wise man to suspend your sentence," Ashe said. "Have you made up your mind about that RESCUE internship we talked over?"

Jace smiled and nodded. "Geothermal. I was tempted to do Solar/Wind, but I think Geothermal is more exciting. That TriPlate design you showed me is awesome!"

"Fantastic!" Rae said.

Ashe looked at him and asked skeptically, "So you're

willing to work days at RESCUE and go to school at night until you get your high school diploma?"

Jace frowned. "I've been thinking about that part a lot."

Shaking his head, Ashe said, "You know the offer is only good if you stay in school."

A wicked smile lit Jace's face. "Well, I was thinking maybe high school wasn't enough. Maybe I'd try some college, too."

Ashe and Rae both smiled and hugged him.

"When can I start?"

Rae grinned and said, "How about next week?"

"Great!"

"We've got to get you broken in before we drag you to New Mexico. But don't worry. In a few weeks we'll be finished lobbying against the Evans-Giles bill, and Dinell will be recovered from the surgery she had to help her sister. Then we're all going to the new HDR site to break ground."

"No shit?" Jace exclaimed.

George roughly said, "Jace! We don't use language like that in this house."

"Sorry, Mr. Benton." Jace stared at Ashe and Rae.

"What's wrong?" Rae asked.

"Nothing."

Ashe said, "Come on, Jace. We've seen that look before."

"Are you sure we're *all* going to go?"

"Why wouldn't we?"

"Since you two are, uh . . . involved . . ."

"What?" Rae impatiently asked, then suddenly realized the answer. "You don't think that our dating is going to keep me from working at RESCUE, do you?"

Jace looked at the carpet, then at George, then out the window. "When you were in the hospital, Ashe said it was too dangerous . . ."

"Jace Williams, I have no intention of quitting RESCUE, and even if I decided to leave, I'd still want to spend time with you! And what's this crap about it being too dangerous?" Reacting to the grimace on George's face, she immediately corrected herself, saying, "Excuse me. What's all this nonsense about it being too dangerous?"

Sheepishly Ashe explained, "Jace and I were talking while we waited for you outside the emergency room."

Glaring at Ashe, Rae snapped, "And you decided that women had no business being on a well site?"

Ashe answered, "Not exactly. Can't you understand, I was worried about you? Being shot isn't exactly something I'd like to put the woman I love through again."

Rae visibly softened, then said, "Okay. For now you're off the hook. But, Jace, surely after all we've been through, you've learned that anyone, male or female, black or white, can accomplish anything they really want to."

Jace nodded and smiled. "Only if they're willing to work hard, of course."